"Looks like we're gonna make it," Levi told his wife when they were halfway across the bridge. The Biters—nearly fifty of them in all—were rushing across the southern end of the bridge, but not nearly as fast as the three vehicles. Before long, they seemed small and insignificant in the Ram's side view mirror.

"I wouldn't count on it, Papa," Jem said from behind him. The boy reached across the seat and pointed directly through the windshield.

At the far end of the bridge, crowding through the northern entranceway was a multitude of Biters. It was impossible to tell how many, but it could have been as many as seventy or eighty.

"What are we gonna do, Levi?" Nell asked. "We can't go through them. It'll be like hitting a brick wall."

He knew she was right. He lowered his window and looked behind him. Others had joined the Biters at the rear of the bridge. Now there were as many behind them as in front. Within a matter minutes, the two groups of undead would meet at the center of the bridge and they would be hopelessly surrounded.

Levi parked the truck and grabbed his shotgun. He left the vehicle, followed by Nell and the boys. Soon, the others were also out of their vehicles, holding their weapons at the ready. They looked overhead. Beyond the steel girders of the bridge, the sky was obscured by a swirling black cloud of buzzards.

THE BUZZARD ZONE

BY RONALD KELLY

To the late George A. Romero
who showed me that zombies could be both frightening and fun
when I was 14 years old

&

Brian Keene
who reinforced (and reinvented) that dark, shambling apocalyptic
dream years afterward.

CHAPTER 1

The sky darkened, black and oily; swirling, turbulent, impregnated
with vigilance. It was not a bad turn of the weather promising rain or
storm or tornado. It was keenly alive.
Silent, yet ever moving, ever alert for what was commonplace in
those dark and dangerous days.
Always with its ravenous eye upon death.

Levi Hobbs stood on the front porch of the old house his grand-
daddy built on the western face of the Smoky Mountains in
1906, his eyes on the sky. The gray pall that had fallen across the
panes of the windows—ones that normally gleamed bright with
sunlight at that hour of the day—had brought him to the railing
and drawn his gaze upward.

Just looking at that sky—the constant swirling and swooping—caused a man to feel dizzy and disoriented, displaced on
the ground upon which he stood... or, in Levi's case, the weathered boards of the porch. It was nearly hypnotic to gaze upon.

He flinched when he felt a delicate hand rest upon the crook
of his right elbow. He relaxed, but not completely, for he recognized it as belonging to the woman he had been married to for
nearly thirty-five years.

"The nasty things are thicker than thieves today," she said.
Nell's voice, once cheerful and full of faith and optimism,
sounded weary and lackluster. "We'd best stay clear of town
today."

Levi turned and regarded her. Despite the lines on her face
and the gray in her strawberry-blonde hair, she was still as
pretty as the day they'd been wed. "We're going down," he told

her flatly and turned his attention back toward the sky.

Nell's skyward gaze matched her husband's. "You know what that means when they gather so close and drift so slowly. You know you can track those blasted zombies—and how many there are—by how many buzzards follow them overhead."

"I know that. But we no longer have a choice. We've put it off too long... two weeks too long. No beans or taters. Down to the last spoonful of flour and meal. There's no hunting to be done. Every living thing—deer, squirrel, rabbit, possum—have fled across the mountain in the wake of that horrible *stench.*" Levi swallowed dryly. "The children are growing leaner and so are we."

"It's too dangerous. You can't eat if you're dead," Nell told him.

Levi laughed. A sour smile peeked through the bristles of his black beard. "You know that ain't true."

The woman nodded. He was right.

"We'll be careful," he assured her. "Get in, get what we need, get out. Lickety-split. Besides, they move like molasses on a February morning."

"What they lose in speed, they make up for in numbers."

"Maybe. But we're faster and smarter than they are... and probably a mite hungrier, too."

Nell shook her head. "Nothing's hungrier. It's what drives them."

Levi turned around, irritated. "Well, I'm driven, too. By desperation... by the nagging in my belly and the sight of my children slowly starving." He looked away from her. "Gather the kids. We're going down."

Nell Hobbs nodded and turned to go in. She knew good and well not to push the subject when Levi got something set solid in his mind.

This time Levi did flinch, at the slapping of the screen door. He sighed and cast his eyes upon the lazy, counter-clockwise motion of the buzzards one last time. Then he set about preparing for the trip to the valley.

CHAPTER 2

They came down off Hobbs Ridge in the Smoky Mountains, along the old logging road to Highway 442, toward the cluttered jumble of buildings and hotels that made up Gatlinburg. The little mountain resort town was usually bumper-to-bumper with tourists out to see the fall colors at that time of year, or do some shopping and see a show. But now it was a ghost town. The four-lane street that stretched between gaudy museums, souvenir shops, and pancake restaurants was deserted. The traffic lights swung slowly in the breeze, their three vertical eyes blind and colorless. Only the carcasses of a dozen abandoned cars—as well as those of a few devoured humans—could be seen along the empty stretch of blacktop.

The Hobbs entered Gatlinburg slow and easy. Levi drove the big Ford flatbed logging truck, the vehicle of his chosen vocation... or so it had been before all hell had broken loose. Nell rode on the seat next to him, holding a shotgun—a Remington 870 twelve-gauge—tightly in her thin fingers. Levi had a big Ruger Blackhawk .44 in a holster on his right hip, a gift from his former son-in-law. He had thought the gun to be excessive and impractical... until just recently.

To either side of the logging truck were the twins, Jem and Avery, named after the boys in *To Kill a Mockingbird* and *Charlotte's Web*, two of their mother's favorite books. Jem straddled a big Honda four-wheeler, while the other drove a John Deere Gator. Both were tall, strapping, and cocky for going on sixteen, but then so had their father been at that age, and still was in his mid-fifties.

A yard or so behind the truck was a black GMC Yukon with

white-letter tires and tinted windows. It was driven by Levi and Nell's twenty-two-year-old daughter, Kate. She sat in the cab, hands on the wheel—pale, freckled, her hair as red as rust on a gate hinge. Kate had left Hobbs Ridge after high school, married a blowhard redneck by the name of Bill Franklin, and had lived in the town of Pigeon Forge—a stone's-throw from Gatlinburg, but a community that was equally smitten with the tourist dollar. Levi hadn't cottoned to Bill at all. He had always suspected that the man had treated Katie badly and had confronted him on the subject several times. His daughter's dream of going to college and becoming a nurse had dried up and died after their marriage and she had ended up making a meager wage selling tickets at Ripley's Believe it or Not. When everything had gone haywire and Katie had seen Bill taken down by a pack of Biters, she had loaded every gun and box of ammunition from her husband's three gun safes into the back of the Yukon and headed home to the Ridge to be with her kin.

They drove to the third traffic light from the state park entrance and stopped. The only movement they saw on the long, cluttered stretch of pavement was a couple of buzzards picking at a dead body lying on the center line in front of a shop that specialized in airbrushed t-shirts and license plates and cedar-hewn, hillbilly-themed knickknacks.

Their original intention was to roll into town, loot the various restaurants along the strip, and then head back for the hills. They had expected considerable opposition and had come armed to the teeth. They were no strangers to the damage that the Biters could inflict. Following the "end of civilization"—or so it had been called by the news media on radio, TV, and the Internet before the power had finally gone out for good—they had been visited by several of the flesh-eating zombies. Some of them had been neighbors and folks they had known all their lives, but whatever had infected them had changed them into something less than human. They had become things with only one goal… to sink their black teeth into you and eat until you were dead or disabled. And, if there was enough of you left, you would rise from the dead and do the same, mindlessly, without conscience or hesitation. Levi and the boys had killed a dozen or so, much to Nell's anguish. After she grew accustomed to their ways and what they were setting out to do, she had taken a hatchet to a couple of them herself.

But there, smack dab in the middle of one of the busiest tourist towns west of the Smoky Mountains, there was no one to fight. The place seemed utterly deserted. There were no Biters to be found.

"What's going on, Levi?" Nell asked him.

"I don't know." He laid his hand on the door handle of the truck.

His wife reached out and grabbed the sleeve of his shirt. "Be careful."

Levi grinned. "Who... me? I ain't ending up in no Biter's rotten belly."

He gently disengaged himself from his wife's grasp, then opened the door and stood on the bottom ledge of the doorframe, peering over the roof of the truck, from right to left. Nervously, he shucked the big Blackhawk from its holster and held it loosely in his hand, his thumb on the spur of the hammer.

"Keep sharp, boys," he warned his sons. "They're bound to be here somewheres."

Jem and Avery stepped off their vehicles, surveying the empty street. Jem disengaged a broad axe from two clamps mounted on the side of his four-wheeler, while Avery reached into the bed of the Gator and brought out a 4.7 horsepower Dolmar chainsaw.

"You know the sound of that confounded thing will bring 'em down on us like locusts on Egypt," Nell said through the open window.

"I won't crank 'er unless I have to, Ma," Avery promised. He grasped the chainsaw firmly in one hand, while the other held the rubber pull handle, ready to yank.

"What's the matter, Papa?"

Levi looked around to see Kate standing next to the Yukon.

"You get on back in there and shut the door, pumpkin. Let us menfolk handle this."

The red-haired girl rolled her eyes. "Give me a break." She continued to stand there, holding a Glock 9mm pistol in each freckled fist.

Levi wanted to argue the point, but decided not to. If they got swarmed by Biters, he could use every hand he could get. Besides, Kate was good with those guns. Damn good. And she could fire them both at once with deadly accuracy, if it came down to it. If her brief marriage to Blowhard Bill had reaped a single benefit, it was her familiarity with firearms, as well as her ability—and willingness—to use them.

"Are those buzzards still up there?" Nell asked.

Levi looked above him. The constant circling of large black birds, several dozen or so thick, continued directly overhead. "Yeah, we're still in the Zone." Puzzled, he looked at the two carnivorous birds picking at the naked arms of the corpse in the road. *So why is it just the pair? Why isn't the whole damn flock down here, fighting over that poor soul's carcass?*

Levi studied the pair carefully. They pecked and worried over the flayed arms of the dead body, but avoided its upper torso, neck, and head. He knew for a fact that scavengers like carrion crows and buzzards tended to work on the head of a dead animal first, especially the eyes. They regarded the tender orbs to be a sweet bonus, like eating dessert before the main course. But these two were keeping their distance from the dead man's head.

Levi lifted his eyes from the two birds and looked off down the street. He squinted and thought he saw movement at the far end where the Ripley's Aquarium was located. "Avery?"

"Yeah, Papa?"

"You got the binoculars?"

Avery shook his head. "Jem's got 'em."

"Here you go." Jem tossed the pair over the cab of the truck to his father.

Levi laid the .44 Magnum on top the truck and took the rubberized binoculars in both hands.

He was lifting them to his eyes, when a car horn began to blare.

CHAPTER 3

Levi peered through the lenses of the binoculars, bringing the far end of the street into focus.

He knew now why they had encountered no Biters upon entering the town limits. They had congregated three hundred yards away... perhaps forty of them in all. They surrounded a small car—a silver Volkswagen Bug from the looks of it—and were clawing and gnawing at the metal and glass of the vehicle. A couple had butted their heads against the windshield and side windows, causing the safety glass to fissure in cloudy cobweb patterns. A few more blows and the barriers would give way.

Levi worked the focus adjust with the ball of his thumb, bringing the ugly picture a bit closer. Through the windshield, he could see the face of an elderly man—bearded, spectacled, and as pale as a bed sheet. In the seat next to him was a gray-haired woman. Her head was lolled back and her eyes were closed. She was either unconscious or dead.

Lowering the binoculars, he hopped down out of the truck, the rubber soles of his work boots slapping against the pavement. He looked through the open door at his wife. "Scoot over here and drive behind us, slow and easy. There are folks down there who need help."

Nell said nothing, but the look in her eyes said the words that echoed in his own mind. *Leave them be. Loot the restaurants while the Biters are occupied and let's get back home.* It was a natural thought, born of self-preservation, but it was also a selfish one.

Levi reached out and took her hand as she positioned

herself behind the steering wheel. "We can't, Mama. It's not our way."

Nell nodded grimly. "I know." She handed him the twelve-gauge. "Here."

Levi took the shotgun and jacked a shell into the breech. "There's a .357 Magnum in the glove box, if you have need of it. Just hold it in both hands like I showed you. And, remember, it kicks like a mule with chiggers on its balls."

The woman reached over, opened the compartment, and laid the big, nickel-plated revolver on the seat beside her. "Let's get to it."

Levi turned and regarded his sons and daughter. "There's a man and woman down there with about thirty-five or forty of those sick bastards bearing down on them, looking for a free lunch. Spread out and be careful. And, no matter what, don't let 'em get hold of you and take a bite."

His children nodded. They waited until he took the first step and then followed.

They started down the street, six feet apart, their attention centered on the commotion at the traffic light of the fifth intersection coming into Gatlinburg from the west. As Levi approached the feeding birds, he waved a lanky arm. "Y'all git!" he hissed, loud enough for them to hear, but not enough that his voice would carry. "Head to the heavens with the rest of your scavenging bunch!"

The two buzzards—slick and black, except for their featherless, pink heads—eyed him balefully and then reluctantly took flight. Levi watched them ascend as he walked past the corpse… and nearly paid for his inattentiveness.

Before he knew what was happening, the dead man reached out and grabbed his ankle. Levi expected the attempt to be feeble, but it was anything but. There was some real strength in that decomposing muscle and sinew, fueled by the instinctive hunger that possessed their kind. The Biter—a middle-aged man with graying hair and a lower face ravaged with decay—sat up and craned his neck toward him, mouth open. His teeth were black and fuzzy and teaming with tiny motion, as if they were covered with gnats without wings.

Levi tried to pull away, but the thing's fingers—stiff and bony—refused to let go. With a grunt, Levi lowered the muzzle of the 870 toward the Biter's forehead.

Jem walked over to his father and lifted the shotgun's barrel with one hand. "You do that and that whole bunch will be off that car and on us quicker than a horny jackrabbit. I'll take care of it."

Levi nodded, lifted the Remington to his shoulder, and leaned back a bit. Jem's axe swung downward, cleaving the Biter's arm in half at the joint of his elbow. The blade struck pavement and threw sparks as it hit. Levi stumbled away. Disgusted, he reached down and wrestled with the forearm and hand that held him, careful not to touch the exposed flesh that the buzzards had been picking at. Finally, he pried it free and tossed it away. It rolled across the pavement, the fingers flexing and clawing, before finally growing still.

That seemed to anger the Biter to no end. He lurched, rocking back and forth, trying to get his legs and his good arm beneath him. Before he could get leverage and rise, Jem swung the axe again. The blade split the zombie's head open from scalp to neck bone. The two halves divided, revealing a half-devoured brain, purple-black and as moist and stringy as pumpkin guts. Amid it all swarmed a multitude of the tiny black things, spilling out onto the street, spreading like motor oil that should have been changed a long time ago.

"Avery," Levi called to his other son.

Avery laid his chainsaw down and grinned. He walked over and took a can of lighter fluid from side pocket of his overalls. Dousing the ruined head of the Biter liberally, he then took a box of sulfur matches and struck one. The boy stared at the guttering flame for a long second and then tossed it. The upper half of the dead man burst into flames, causing the spreading blackness to grow even blacker as it burnt to a crisp and then rose in the smoke in tiny pinpoints of cinder.

"Y'all steer clear and don't breathe it in," Levi instructed. "We don't know if that stuff is as dangerous dead as it is alive." He turned and regarded Avery, who bent to pick up his chainsaw, his eyes still glued to the flames. Avery was peculiar in that way; he loved fire and explosives. Levi used to frown on that flaw in his son's nature, but lately it had become downright handy.

Again, the four started down the street. They could hear the throaty rumble of the logging truck as Nell remained a steady twenty feet behind them. They were nearly upon the crowd of frantic Biters before they were noticed. A woman with matted blonde hair and a McDonald's uniform turned, spotted them, and then unleashed a shrill cry and shambled toward them. Two or three left the disabled Volkswagen and followed her.

Levi nodded to Avery. His son lowered the chainsaw again, took a bundle of three M-80 firecrackers from his pocket, and lit the short fuse. He tossed it, underhanded, and it rolled past the Biters' feet and under the front bumper of the car.

It went off almost immediately. The concussion knocked a dozen zombies to their knees and lifted the Bug clean off its front tires in the process. The little car slammed back down, shaking the other Biters off balance and startling the old man behind the steering wheel.

Levi and his children stepped in and went to work. Levi fired the shotgun as fast as he could pump it, decapitating the standing Biters with blasts of double-ought buckshot. Kate stood, lean arms outstretched, firing the twin Glocks in rapid succession. Within a span of fifteen seconds, eighteen had fallen.

Jem and Avery went to work on those who had been driven to their knees by the explosion. Jem welded the broad axe deftly, severing heads between the third and fourth cervical vertebrae. Avery cranked the string pull of the chainsaw, sending it into roaring, sputtering life. A cloud of blue gasoline fumes billowed from its engine as he stepped from one Biter to another, cleaving off heads and limbs, sawing torsos in half, crossways. Avery's siblings regarded him uneasily. Of the three, he had always been the wild card.

After all of the zombies were down, heads rolled on the pavement, snapping and snarling with angry red eyes and black-coated teeth. Kate calmly strolled among them, putting a 9mm slug above the bridges of their noses or directly through the crowns of their skulls. She was shucking a spent magazine from the butt of one pistol and replacing it with a fresh one, when she spotted movement behind the Bug. A tense smile crossed her freckled face, but her eyes grew as cold as stones.

Puzzled by the expression on his sister's face, Jem turned and watched as a large Biter rounded the back bumper of the VW and staggered toward them. "Well, look at who's come a-visiting."

"Bill," Kate said. Her eyes narrowed as he approached in a lurch.

It *was* Bill Franklin, Kate's husband, but a horribly altered version of the man. Part his face had been chewed away, revealing stark bone and a half-grin of exposed teeth, and one of his eyes lay flat and useless in its socket, the fluid having leaked out after hungry teeth had punctured it. Much of his shirt had been torn away, revealing pale muscle that was still toned, even after death had claimed him three months ago. A tattoo of a naked Bettie Page straddling a Harley Davidson shown on the tricep of his left arm, resembling a child's crayon doodle on stark, white paper.

As the man drew nearer, Kate turned to her brother and held out one of the Glocks. "Trade?"

Jem eyed her warily. "Sure, Kate." He took the pistol and handed her the axe.

"You boys stand back," Levi told them. He stared at his daughter as she stuck the second Glock in her jacket pocket and tightened her grip on the hickory handle. "Give your sister room to work."

Kate planted her feet and stood ready. "Come here, Bill. Come here, you sorry son of a bitch."

Although no recognition shown in his eyes, Bill shambled toward her, arms outstretched, grinning that skeletal half-grin of his.

When he was nearly upon her, she swung the axe, chopping his right arm off at the shoulder. Ink black blood spurted weakly from the severed artery, then slowed to a sluggish trickle. "Treat me like shit, will you? Put me down, humiliate me, call me a bitch?"

Her father and brothers watched as she swung the axe again and again, whittling Bill Franklin gradually down to size. Levi turned and looked toward the truck. Nell sat in the driver's seat with tears in her eyes.

"Beat me... burn me with your damn cigarettes... tear off my panties and rape me when I told you I wasn't in the mood?" Again the blade hit cold flesh, sinking, pulling loose with a loud suck. "Punch me in the stomach until I miscarried... until I sat on the commode, bleeding, with my baby hanging between my legs!" She swung low, taking his legs off at the knees, sending him crashing to the pavement.

Bill squirmed in the road, teeth gnashing, his single eye rolling like that of a mad dog.

"Kill our baby?" The axe came crashing down on his skull, crushing, mangling, time after time after time. "*My* baby... my poor... sweet... little... baby girl!"

By the time Levi reached her, she was crying, her narrow chest hitching with deep sobs. Gently, he took the blood-splattered axe from her hands. "My baby..." she muttered mournfully. "Oh God..."

Levi held her for a long moment and kissed her forehead, feeling his heart ache. Granddaughter? She had never told them... never breathed a word. When he released her, she turned and climbed into the truck. She snuggled closely to her mother and cried into her shoulder.

"Papa?" said Avery. "The folks."

Levi turned and walked to the Volkswagen. He stood at the side door, looking at the little bald and bearded man who stared back at him, his blue eyes magnified behind the lenses of his horn-rimmed glasses. "Sir? Are you alright?"

The man nodded and feebly reached for the door's handle. As it swung wide, he slipped off the seat and fell out. Levi was there to catch him before he could hit the pavement. He gently lowered him until he was lying flat on his back.

"I'm sorry," the man murmured in a thick foreign accent. "I haven't eaten in two days. I'm a little weak."

"That's okay," Levi told him. "We'll get some food and water in you soon enough." He looked over and saw that Jem and Avery were carefully lifting the woman from the passenger seat. "Your wife?"

"Yes," said the elderly man. "Agnes. She's diabetic. Her insulin was in the trunk, but we couldn't get to it." He craned his head and looked at the slaughtered forms around him. "*They* wouldn't let us."

"How did you end up here?"

"My name is Abraham Mendlebaum. I was a biological researcher in Oak Ridge... a scientist, if they still call us that these days. We left the facility there, intending to cross the mountains. Agnes has family in North Carolina... in a town called Hendersonville, near Asheville. We reached Gatlinburg and ran out of gas. I got frustrated and cranked the engine a few times. They heard us. We were trapped... couldn't get out."

Levi turned and called to Nell. "Bring some water."

A moment later, his wife appeared with a bottle of purified water in her hand. She unscrewed the cap and brought it to his lips.

Mendlebaum turned his head aside. "What is the lot number of that bottle?" he asked cautiously.

"Lot number?"

"Yes, it signifies the date and facility that it was processed at," he explained. "If it was bottled before June of this year, it is safe. If not, it is probably contaminated."

"We've been drinking from the same case," Levi told him. "So, I'd say that it's okay."

The old man nodded. Nell tipped the bottle and he drank. Mendlebaum took a couple of swallows and strangled. He coughed violently for a moment, then took some more.

When he finished, his eyes sharpened. "Where is Agnes?"

"On the far side of the car with my boys."

"Does anyone know how to give an injection?" he asked.

No one did.

"Bring her to me and I will do it," he said urgently. "There is a black duffel in the trunk. It has her medicine."

Soon, Agnes Mendlebaum and the black bag were within Abe's reach. He sat up weakly and began to work, drawing pale liquid from a vial and injecting it into one of the dark, protruding veins in his wife's left hand. "I only pray that it's not too late. I don't believe that she has lapsed into a diabetic coma, but she is close."

"You've got a helluva lot of food packed in that trunk, Mister," said Avery.

"We'll gladly share, if you'll shelter us until Agnes is back on her feet," the biologist told him, a ring of hopefulness in his voice.

Nell patted him on the shoulder. "Our home is yours, for as long as you have need."

Abe took her hand. "Thank you, dear lady."

While Levi and Jem looted a pancake house, a Mexican restaurant, a Starbucks, and a Burger King, Avery siphoned gas out of a Nissan Altima and filled the VW's tank to the quarter mark. "We've got more gas up at the house," he assured the old man. "Papa buys it by the tankload, for his logging business. You know, chainsaws, log splitters, generators and such." He took a plastic Ziploc bag full of dried meat from his side pocket and handed it to Abe Mendlebaum. "Deer jerky? Might perk you up some."

The elderly scientist eyed the offering skeptically.

"Weren't nothing wrong with the animal it came from," the boy assured him. "I'd say it was healthier than I was." As he replaced the Volkswagen's gas cap, he glanced into the rear of the car. "I see you've got an AR-15 in the back seat. Where'd you get it?"

"At the installation back in Oak Ridge," Abe replied. "I took it off the body of an MP... right before he turned."

"Got right ugly back there, did it?"

"Oh, yes." A shadow born of uneasy memory fell across the old man's angular face. "Extremely ugly."

"When these Biters surrounded you, why didn't you just cut them down?" Avery asked curiously. "You certainly had the firepower."

Abe eyed the boy. "Have you ever tried to maneuver in the front seat of a Volkswagen Beetle with an assault weapon half as long as yourself? Opening the door would have been like ringing the dinner bell. Sometimes to survive, you simply do nothing at all."

"Yeah, I get your point. I reckon you did the right thing."

Soon, everything that could be found was packed into boxes and lashed to the bed of the logging truck. They carried Agnes Mendlebaum to the Yukon and laid her across the back seat. She was beginning to come to, moaning and squirming, but she was only semi-conscious.

"Think you're up to driving?" Levi asked the old man.

"I believe so," he said. "The jerky that Avery provided seems to have fortified me."

"You're bound to know more about what's safe and what's not than we do," Levi said. "Maybe you can share that information with us when we get to the house."

"I certainly will." He patted the duffel that was slung over his stooped shoulder. "I have a full catalog of contaminant-free lot numbers for most manufactured food and water in the United States."

Levi walked to the logging truck and looked in at Kate. "Darling, are you up to driving?"

The young woman smiled and nodded. "I'm okay, Papa." Her cheeks flushed with embarrassment. "I'm sorry about what happened... you know, back there with Bill."

Levi's work-hardened hand lifted her chin until her eyes were level with his. "The bastard deserved everything you dished out." He thought about the last horrible accusation she had made against her abusive husband. "And I'm sorry about the..." The word stuck in his throat. He couldn't bring himself to say it.

Kate leaned over and kissed him on his bearded cheek. "I know, Papa. Sorry I couldn't tell you."

Soon, everyone was in their vehicles and ready to go. Levi lingered outside the logging truck and studied the sky. The buzzards seemed twice as thick as before. They circled furiously and erratically, as though impatient to the point of madness. Just looking at them made Levi's head swim. They had a hard-on for the carnage Levi and his family had left in the middle of the street, that was for sure.

"Should I torch 'em, Papa?" Avery asked.

"Naw. Leave 'em be." He climbed into the cab of the logging

truck. "Let's head out," he hollered loud enough for everyone to hear. "Those black devils will be down here and ready to chow as soon as we start rolling. And I don't want to be in their way when they get here."

CHAPTER 4

They were a mile up the winding logging road to Hobbs Ridge when Levi stopped the truck, climbed out, and trained the binoculars on the main street of Gatlinburg.

The sky had lightened considerably, but the little town appeared dark from where he stood, as though covered with a thick layer of soot. Buzzards had descended to clean up the mess they had left behind. Dozens of scavengers lit upon the bodies of the disabled Biters—picking, ripping, rending, and pulling at muscle, tendon, and vein with pale yellow beaks and hooked talons. They were a sociable bunch, Levi gave them that. After each had eaten their fill, they retired to the eaves of the buildings or the taut black lengths of telephone and power lines, allowing the others to partake while they digested the cold meat and tissue that lay in their bellies.

"Those birds stink as badly as the Biters," Nell said. "The stench must be horrific down there."

"You better believe it. The wind's carrying a generous helping all the way up here. It's like Hell without the flames."

"Maybe this *is* Hell."

He turned and looked at his wife, but said nothing. Nell had once been a strong, God-fearing woman, but what had happened in the world had tested her faith to the breaking point. At home, her Bible gathered dust on the nightstand and she never protested when they failed to say grace at the supper table.

Levi climbed back into the cab of the truck and they continued up the face of the mountain. They were nearly a half-mile from home, when Nell ducked her head and looked through the top of the windshield. "We've got more buzzards."

He looked toward the sky beyond the treetops and saw twelve or thirteen birds circling overhead. "Well, it's not a herd up ahead, but it's more than one. Keep your eyes peeled."

Onward the truck climbed, followed by the twins on their vehicles, the VW Beetle, and Kate's Yukon at the rear. Levi took a hairpin turn in the road and there they were... a group of Biters. Or rather a *family* of them. A man, a woman, and three children—a little girl and a boy, and a teenage girl with long, honey-blonde hair. They were pale and blood-stained, their faces sunken and their teeth as black as charcoal.

"It's the Macolmers," said Nell with a groan.

She was right. It was their closest neighbors, Ed and June Macolmer and their young'uns—Missy, Timmy, and Sarah. Levi's stomach clenched as tightly as his fingers on the steering wheel. He hadn't seen the Macolmers in months, not since the Fourth of July, when they'd had them over for supper and fireworks afterward. He still remembered the women sitting on the porch, laughing, while the little young'uns chased fireflies in the yard. He and Ed had downed a few beers and gave their two cents' worth about the handling of fireworks, which had been unnecessary, given Avery's proficiency with such things. Levi also remembered Jem and Sarah sitting beneath the big oak out front, holding hands and talking quietly. Although the boy had never said anything, Levi knew he had a crush on the girl.

He turned and looked at his wife. "What should I do?"

Her eyes were dull. "Run them down."

Levi knew that was the correct response, but it went down like a bitter pill. When he began easing on the brakes, Nell grabbed his forearm. "If you don't and you drive past 'em, they'll pull Jem and Avery right off the Honda and the Gator, and tear into them. We don't have a choice."

Levi nodded and stamped on the gas.

The big diesel truck surged forward, plowing over the Macolmers. Ed went under and the truck lurched as its tires rolled over him. The front bumper caught June and she flipped, head over heels, and landed on the hood. Her face hit the windshield, sending a thin fissure across the glass. She leered in at them, showing none of the good humor or compassion she had once been well regarded for. Her bloodshot eyes seethed angrily and her teeth, coated with swarming black motion, snapped hungrily at her two neighbors. Nell looked at her for a long moment and then turned her head.

Levi stamped on the brake. June Macolmer went spinning off the hood and slammed into the lurching bodies of Missy and Timmy, knocking them down. He sped up again and crushed the three beneath the big tires of the truck. Then he was coming up fast on young Sarah. The flawless skin of the pretty girl's face had sloughed away, leaving denuded bone with two bright, blue eyes shining feverishly from sunken sockets. Levi glanced in his side view mirror. Behind him, Jem rode the four-wheeler, standing with his fists on the handlebars, craning his neck to get a better look.

"Damn!" cussed Levi as he drove the truck forward, knocking the girl down and grinding her beneath the wheels. Although he couldn't hear it, he could sense her bones breaking and her body collapsing.

When he had driven past, he brought the truck to a stop and sat there, breathing hard for a moment. Then he and Nell climbed out and stood on the roadway. Ed was done for. A tire had gone over his skull, flattening his head into a black, gelatinous ruin. June and the kids were still moving. They were unable to get up, but still squirming and snarling and hankering to sink their teeth into those who stood around them.

Levi looked at Jem. The boy was crying as he stared at the blonde-haired girl lying in the road, her pelvis and legs shattered.

"I'm sorry, son," he told him. "It couldn't be helped."

Tears streamed down the sixteen-year-old's face. "I know."

Levi pulled the Blackhawk from its holster. "Everyone stand back. I don't want this black mess splattering all over you."

He had cocked back the hammer and was about to put a round through the top of June Macolmer's head, when a wet, phlegmy bark sounded a few yards in front of the truck. Then the bark lowered into a rattling growl and Levi heard footfalls on the road behind him.

"It's ol' Red," said Avery.

Levi turned to see the Macolmer's redbone coonhound, Red, running toward him in an uneven pace. He was shocked, for he had never seen an animal other than a human being that had turned with the awful infection—or was it *infestation*—that had damned eighty-eight percent of the earth's population. Red was emaciated and riddled with mange and weeping sores. Most of his hair was gone and his paper-thin skin clung closely to the bone. One of his eye sockets was empty and the blackness, like swarming ants, danced where a keen eye had once stalked coon in the moonlight. Canine teeth, long and equally dark, snapped like whipcracks as his pace quickened.

Lifting the Magnum, Levi fired. The .44 slug hit Red square on the tip of his nose and tunneled completely through, exiting as a flattening wad of lead out of his ass end. The dog's legs collapsed beneath him and he dropped to a long skid on the road, traveled a couple of yards farther, then flipped and lay still.

His face like stone, the patriarch of the Hobbs family did the same for June Macolmer. He paused a long moment, then ended Missy's and Timmy's misery. He was making his way to Sarah, when Jem stepped forward. His eyes were red and wet, but his jaw was firmly set.

"No, Papa," he said, his voice cracking. "Give me a moment with her, then I'll do it."

Levi nodded. "Okay, son." He motioned to the others and they returned to their vehicles. "We'll wait for you down the road a piece."

"Thanks," the boy said dully, although there seemed to be no gratitude in his tone.

They drove a hundred yards farther on and parked. Levi watched in the truck's big side view mirror. Jem knelt next to Sarah's squirming body, talked to her for a minute, then stood and swung the axe earthward. Levi looked away right before the blade struck. Then Jem climbed on the Honda and joined them.

"Get it done, son?" Levi asked him when Jem pulled up next to the cab of the logging truck.

The boy's face was rigid and pale.

"Let's head on home."

Together, they continued upward to the top of the Ridge.

CHAPTER 5

They reached the house by dusk. The sky grew vivid with brilliant hues of orange, pink, and purple, but none of them found any enjoyment in the sunset. All eyes roamed the verge of twilight for dark forms sailing and swooping in crisscross, circling patterns. Fortunately, no buzzards could be seen and, for now, they rested easy.

Quietly, they unloaded their vehicles and brought the supplies they had scavenged into the house. As they did so, Abe Mendlebaum surveyed the Hobbs property. The two-story house sat on a sloping ridge of stone interlaced sparsely with grass and tall stands of oak, long-leafed pine, and silver poplar. At the back of the old house stood a three-bay garage big enough to hold the logging truck, the Yukon, and a red Ram pickup truck that had been left behind on their excursion to the valley. On one side of the garage were two three-hundred-gallon tanks—one for diesel and one for regular gas—while on the other stood a shed holding the tools of Levi Hobbs' trade: chainsaws, cross-cut saws, log splitters, broad axes, and dynamite for blasting stumps. In a small lean-to at the rear of the house were two large gasoline generators for electricity, which the family only used for a few hours a night.

They carried Agnes Mendlebaum to an upstairs bedroom. The elderly woman seemed to be improving, although her return to consciousness was a slow and fitful one. Kate agreed to stay with her, while the others prepared supper. While they set to work, Avery remained on the porch and watched the steep slope and the darkening sky, cradling Abe's AR-15 lovingly in his arms.

After a supper of cornbread and canned vegetables—checked with Abe's catalog of safe lot numbers—the Hobbs family and their guest grew silent. Abe sat back in his chair and eyed the five, dreading the conversation that was about to take place.

"So, I suppose you would like to know what is going on," he said. He took a long sip of coffee from a china cup and sighed. "How much do you know already... concerning the outbreak?"

"Just what we learned from the TV and radio before everything went off the air," Levi said. "That folks were being infected by something unknown that killed them and then brought them back to life as these confounded flesh-eating Biters. That it was happening at an alarming rate with no sign of finding a cure for what was happening. Then everything went to static and we were left in the dark."

Abe nodded and leaned forward on the table, tenting his fingers thoughtfully. "What do *you* think the source of the outbreak is? From what you've seen with your own eyes so far?"

"Seems to us that it's those little black things that cover their teeth that might be causing it," Nell replied.

Abe's eyes sparkled behind the thick lenses of his spectacles. "Precisely! That is exactly what is causing it."

"Why don't you tell us about it, Dr. Mendlebaum," urged Kate, although she looked like she would rather not know.

"The 'little black things', as you call them, are parasites. A parasite totally unknown to biological science until June thirty-first of this year. It is tiny... about the size of *trombicula alfreddugesi*... the harvest mite, or as you Southerners call it, the common chigger. It is small, but ruthless. Its reproduction cycle is prolific and rapid, and it possesses a voracious appetite. It thrives on human tissue and once ingested or transferred by an open wound, it is only a matter of hours before the host succumbs, losing their mental capabilities. The parasites burrow through muscular and vascular tissue, as well as the linings of the esophagus, stomach, and intestines, and eventually make their way to the brain of the host. There they wreak havoc, destroying central sections of the cerebellum, but leaving others intact, including the lobes that control appetite and aggression. In fact, their activity *stimulates* these areas, which, in turn, instigates the Biter's violent behavior. The parasites turn the host's head into a hive, invading what is left of the brain, the nasal passages, and the mouth. The parasite loves to feed off mucus and plaque, which is why they are so prevalent on the Biters' teeth. Since the zombie's main motivation is to bite and eat without conscience or hesitation, the transference of the parasite to potential hosts is immediate and inevitable."

"But how do folks come back to life after they die from a bite?" asked Levi.

Abe raised a finger. "Ah, that is because they are not actually dead. The ravaging attack of the parasite emits a natural anesthetic, a very powerful enzyme that causes temporary paralysis, a slowing of circulatory and metabolism functions, and the appearance of a faux death. This gives the parasite time to invade the host and 'set up house', if you will, before the stimulation of the damaged brain returns to an altered state of existence—one devoid of previous memory, restraint, judgmental capabilities, or what some may regard as the 'soul'. This sedated coma lasts for an indeterminate period of time. Sometimes mere hours, sometimes days or as much as a week; it depends on the previous health and physical capacities of the individual host. During that time, rigor mortis and decomposition sets in, giving the outward appearance of death. When the neural restructuring is completed and the host revives, he is like a walking corpse… but with an overwhelming desire to attack and consume."

"How did this all begin?" asked Katie. "Where did these parasites come from?"

"That is what puzzled us," Abe told them. "There seemed to be four points of origin, almost simultaneously—Lima, Peru; Berlin, Germany; Beijing, China; and Provo, Utah here in the United States. The outbreak—or rather *infestation*—started at those points and spread. By the time the threat had been identified, it was too late. The parasite was transferred through food and water, mostly fresh fruits and vegetables, meat and poultry, as well as some processed foods shortly following the outbreak. High concentrations of parasite eggs were found in drinking water, both from in-ground sources and water-bottling facilities. Water filtration systems seemed to have no effect on preventing or detecting the presence of parasitic eggs or larvae. They are nearly microscopic in size and cannot be detected by the naked eye. Also extreme temperature—such as boiling or cooking—seems to have little effect, although fire has been known to destroy them, if the heat is intense enough. And in the case of freezing, they simply go into a dormant state of hibernation. They are tough little bastards."

Avery looked suspicious, "So is this a natural phenomenon... or was it a terrorist plot?"

Abe shrugged his narrow shoulders. "We have insufficient data to prove or disprove either. As far as we know, it could be an act of Jehovah. Perhaps He is raining a plague upon our heads."

Levi looked over at his wife. Nell dropped her eyes and said nothing.

"You know, there is one very puzzling absolute that we discovered," the old man told them. "The bugs will inhabit every kind of living creature, except one."

"And what is that?" Jem asked.

"Birds... particularly flesh-eating birds like carrion crows, buzzards, and vultures. There is something about their physiology that the insects find incompatible with their needs. Whatever the reason, it was a complete mystery to us."

"So is that what you were doing in Oak Ridge?" Avery asked. "Trying to locate the source and find a cure?"

"Yes," said Abe with a sigh. "Twenty think tanks and research labs were implemented internationally. Five were set up in the United States—Washington D.C.; Houston, Texas; the Center for Disease Control in Atlanta; Boulder, Colorado; and Oak Ridge. Here in Tennessee alone, we had two dozen of the greatest scientific minds known to man, but could determine very little as far as how this all came about or how to remedy it." He laughed bitterly. "Toward the end, we began to run out of food. Some of the military personnel raided the snack machines in the break room. They had no idea the food inside was contaminated... put there by the vendor before the outbreak truly became known. Within a week, everyone at the installation was dead or had turned. Agnes and I were fortunate enough to escape. We were heading east for North Carolina, when you came upon us."

"It looks like we're just a handful of survivors now," said Levi. "Eighty-eight percent of the population gone... or shambling around like the living dead."

Abe removed his eyeglasses and polished them on the front of his shirt. His gray eyes grimly surveyed those who sat at the table, moving from face to face. "I am afraid we had to modify that estimation shortly before my escape. As it stands, nearly ninety-four percent of the Earth's population has succumbed to the effects of the parasite. That was nearly five days ago. It could be an even larger percentage by now."

For several moments, everyone sat silently, attempting to digest the information they had been given. Then Avery spoke up, suggesting something that only he would have had the guts to suggest. "What about nukes? That would fry 'em, wouldn't it?"

The scientist nodded. "The parasite perishes when exposed to intense radiation. We certainly had the capabilities at Oak Ridge, but no one considered that a viable option... especially me."

Again, silence permeated the room. Everyone was immersed in their own private thoughts.

"I think I'll go check on Mrs. Agnes," Kate said quietly, excusing herself.

Nell got up and began to gather the supper dishes.

Suddenly, a hoarse shriek cut through the night air. They got up from the table and walked to the front window of the dining room. In the gloom, they could see motion beneath the big oak tree. Something lay there, thrashing, moaning, and crying out.

Levi turned to Jem, who stood a few steps behind them, his eyes on the floor. "You didn't take the axe to her, did you?"

The boy released a long, shuddering sigh. "No, sir."

"Lordy Mercy!" said Avery. "You mean that gal crawled halfway up the mountain with her legs busted up and her guts hanging out?"

"Shut up!" his brother grated between clenched teeth.

"Want me to do 'er? I will, if'n you want."

Jem's eyes blazed. "Don't you touch a damned hair on her head, Avery." He turned to his father. "Papa?"

Levi shucked the Blackhawk from its holster and pressed it into his son's hand. Then he laid his hand across the back of Jem's neck and drew him close until their foreheads met. They didn't look at one another. Both stared down at the gun in Jem's hand. "Sarah was a high-spirited girl. She wouldn't want to be like this."

Jem nodded, then turned and stepped out onto the porch, closing the door behind him.

Levi and Abe headed back to the table. Avery lagged behind, peering out the window.

"Avery, go help your mama with the dishes," his father told him.

"Aw, Papa! That's women's work!"

"Ain't no such thing, son. If a woman can take up a gun and blow a zombie's brains out, a man can help with the cooking and cleaning. Now get your ass in there."

Grumbling, the boy left the window and headed to the kitchen to help his mother.

Levi and Abe sat at the table for a couple of minutes, before the boom of a large-caliber gunshot cracked through the night. Abe jumped, then picked up his cup and took a long swig of lukewarm coffee. "For as long as I may live, I will never grow accustomed to that sound."

"Been hearing it all my life, Doctor," said Levi. "But it sure doesn't sound like it used to."

Nell appeared in the kitchen doorway. She dried a Blue Willow plate while her eyes stared at the front door.

"No need to baby him, dear," Levi told her. "He's nearly a man now. Let him deal with it in his own way."

Anger rolled off of her like a heat. "Easy enough for you to say! It ain't you out there putting a bullet betwixt the eyes of your beloved. Who knows? Maybe someday you'll be forced to do the same."

As she stomped back into the kitchen, Abe upended his

coffee cup and swallowed the rest, dregs and all. "I believe I shall go upstairs and visit my sweet Agnes." As he passed, he patted Levi on the shoulder. "Sometimes women can make you regret opening your mouth to even breathe."

Levi Hobbs simply nodded, afraid to agree, lest he find himself at the end of his wife's lashing tongue once again.

CHAPTER 6

That night, lying in bed, the distance between them narrowed. Neither apologized or said they were sorry. Her hand snaked into his and he clasped it firmly. It was as warm and small as it had been when they had dated, but with differences. Calluses thickened her fingers and palm, and the skin was looser and the veins larger across the back, between knuckles and wrist.

"What are we going to do?" she asked in the darkness.

"About what?" He knew good and well what she was referring to.

"Staying here, on the Ridge. We won't remain untouched forever. They'll make their way into the mountains sooner or later... looking for food, or just someone to take a bite out of."

"We can hold them off," he said. Levi listened to his own words and found them weak and lank upon his tongue, lacking steel or conviction.

Although he could not see her face, he felt her eyes directed toward him. "The buzzards have been plentiful lately. Moving across the sky thick and black like storm clouds. They don't move unless the dead move beneath them. They'll come, with the scent of us in their nostrils."

He swallowed dryly. "I know."

"What are we to do then? Stand our ground or turn tail and run?"

"You know my choice."

"Yes... and we'd die because of it. A house and a piece of land ain't worth dying for... or changing into one of *them*."

Levi knew that she was right. "Tomorrow, I'll hook the gas

tanks to the back of the truck and haul them to either side of the house. Have Avery wire them up in case the house gets over-run. If need be, we can head down that little road out back to the other side of the Smokies and escape."

Nell sighed in relief. "Maybe you ain't half as stupid or bull-headed as I've thought all these years."

"Maybe," he replied with a soft chuckle.

His wife shifted her weight, rolling to face him. "Another thing... no more axe and chainsaw for the boys. I want them armed like the rest of us... a handgun and longarm for each. This toe-to-toe fighting is downright foolishness."

"I'll do that tomorrow," he promised her. "Let them pick what they want from the arsenal Katie brought with her."

"Well now, you're being mighty agreeable."

Levi grinned in the darkness. "If I'm not, I won't be getting me some, now will I?"

"Oh, is that what you're aiming to do?" Her hand turned from work hard to velvet soft in an instant.

"Yes, ma'am." He felt the jounce of the mattress springs as she straddled him. Levi ran his hands under her flannel gown, searching for panties, but finding only her bare hips. "Seems to me you had the same idea."

Nell emitted that throaty giggle that never failed to turn flesh into iron. Then she leaned down and attacked him with her mouth... but in a good way.

Three days passed without incident.

Levi was true to his word. He and the boys pulled the fuel tanks—one half full of gasoline and the other three-quarters full of diesel—to the northern and southern walls of the old house. Nell left her chores and came outside long enough to watch Avery work his magic—fastening a stick of dynamite to the side of each tank with duct tape and then running the wires along the back lot to a plunger box that sat on a rock beyond a split rail fence.

When he was finished, Nell leaned up on tippy-toes and kissed her son on the jaw.

"What's that for, Ma?" he asked.

"For giving me peace of mind," she replied, before going in.

Avery had never connected such an emotion with explosives before, but he accepted her affection just the same.

On the second day, they weeded out a third of the supplies they had taken from Gatlinburg, using the information Abe had brought with him from Oak Ridge. They buried the contaminated food in a large hole that Levi and the boys dug with shovels and muscle. While they were tossing the tainted provisions into the trench, a gray squirrel leapt down from the limb of a sycamore tree. It shuddered violently for a moment and then ran toward them, squeaking and chattering loudly.

It was nearly twenty feet from them when Levi pulled the Blackhawk from its holster and plugged it with a .44 slug. The animal exploded into a tangle of torn tissue and hair. As it lay in the autumn leaves, they walked up and studied it.

"Rabid?" asked Jem.

"Worse," said their father. The squirrel stank of decomposition and was teaming with swarming black mites.

Carefully, Avery gathered it up on the spade of his shovel and chucked it in the hole. Then they quickly placed the earth back into place and tamped it down firm.

On the third day, Abe Mendlebaum and the Hobbses took up weapons and began to practice.

Jem and Avery chose their guns from the multitude that their sister had looted from her ex-husband's gun safes. Jem chose a .45 Colt semi-auto pistol, a Buck knife, and a Remington 1100 shotgun, while Avery chose a brace of .357 Smith & Wesson revolvers and a machete with a blade nearly as long as his forearm. He remained attached to the AR-15, which Abe had graciously given him as a gift.

Katie held on to the twin Glock pistols and added an Uzi 9mm with a folding stock to her arsenal. Nell brandished the Colt Python from the glove box of the logging truck, as well as a .30-30 Winchester lever-action rifle. Abe found an Olympic MFR 5.56mm assault rifle to be his best choice, along with a Bersa Thunder Combat .380 pistol. Levi kept his trusty Blackhawk and the 870 pump shotgun.

For several hours, they familiarized themselves with their weapons, learning to load and draw at satisfactory speed. They also fired at a number of targets—tin cans, soda pop bottles, and plastic milk cartons—that Avery had set up on the weathered lumber of the split rail fence at the far end of the property. At first, their accuracy was erratic, especially from the guns with considerable recoil. But, eventually, they began to find their marks and cans spun skyward, while bottles shattered into sprays of gleaming fragments.

Midway through their practice session, Agnes Mendlebaum appeared on the back porch. Agnes was short and heavyset with iron-gray hair and delicate cats-eye spectacles that hung from her neck on a silver chain. Her health had improved steadily during the past few days and she had begun to stir a bit, leaving the house and taking leisurely walks around the Hobbs property. She seemed nervous and agitated, which Abe assured them was due to her desire to leave and continue to North Carolina to locate her sister, Angela.

"Come join us, darling!" Abe called, waving.

Agnes slowly made her way to where they stood in a line beside the storage shed. Avery and Jem looked at one another. "Watch," said the wilder of the two beneath his breath. "She'll jump clean out of her skin when the first shot is fired."

The elderly woman nodded politely to the Hobbs family then spotted something leaning against the wall of the shed. She walked over and lifted a camouflaged compound bow. She lifted it in both hands and plucked at the nylon cord strung between the pulleys of the bow's fiberglass arms.

"That's called a hunting bow, ma'am," Avery said, as if speaking to a two-year-old child. "Not the kind of weapon you'd want to fool with."

Agnes eyed him, a bit amused. "You think not, huh?"

"No, ma'am," Jem replied. "That thing has alot of tension to it. It's hard for even me and Avery to handle."

The old woman fished her eyeglasses up by the chain and perched them on the bridge of her nose. "Hmmm... PSE Visions usually are," she said, studying the thing in her tiny hands. She hooked a finger against the string and pulled. "About seventy pounds, I'd say. Could get up to 306 fps, if you put enough lever-age behind it."

The twins looked at one another, puzzled.

Agnes reached down and took a 31-inch Easton Nemesis arrow with a narrow, four-blade broadhead from a quiver nearby. She cradled the feathered end of the shaft against the cord and, seemingly without effort, pulled it back until the string creaked with strain.

Silently, the Hobbses watched as she found her target—a gallon milk jug that had fallen on its side, with the open mouth pointed toward the house.

"You might just have some luck hitting that, Mrs. Mendlebaum," Avery told her. "It's big enough a target."

Agnes squinted through one eye, her cheek lying easily against the thumb that clutched the rear of the arrow. "I'm not aiming for the milk carton… just what's inside it."

Then, before anyone could utter another word, she released her hold on the arrow. The string of the compound bow pro-pelled the feathered shaft at an arching angle that rose gently and then fell at a slow and calculated trajectory. Avery and Jem watched, amazed, as the arrow entered the inch-and-a-half opening of the mouth of the milk jug, passing through without touching the rim. The broadhead speared the bottom of the car-ton, punched through, and then carried the jug fifty additional feet, pinning it to the knothole of a hickory tree.

"Needs a little fine tuning," she said with a frown. Then she leaned the bow against the wall of the shed and walked slowly back toward the house.

Abe grinned at the stunned look on the twins' faces. "Nineteen fifty-two Olympics, Helsinki, Finland," he explained. "Archery. She won a bronze medal."

"Well, I'll shit a brick," Avery said, utterly flabbergasted. His face reddened a bit. "Sorry, Ma."

"No need, son," said Nell, watching Abe's wife slowly make her way up the back steps to the kitchen. "I was about to say the same thing myself."

CHAPTER 7

On the morning of the fourth day, Nell Hobbs lurched from her sleep and sat upright in bed.

Startled, Levi turned over. The light that filtered in through bedroom curtains was sparse and gray. With a sigh, he settled back into his pillow. "Looks like rain."

"No," whispered his wife. Her face was pale in the gloom, her eyes bright with fear.

"What's going on?" After all their years together, he knew Nell's ways, how she could sense something before it even happened.

"They're coming."

Quickly, they dressed and left the room. When they stepped out onto the front porch, the sky seemed more like twilight than early morning. They stared upward, their hearts beating wildly.

The sky was dark with buzzards. Not just one swirling cloud of the predatory birds, but *three.* One loomed from the west from the direction of Knoxville, another rolled in from Chattanooga in the south, and a third moved from the northern direction of Virginia.

"Oh God!" said Levi. "They're going to box us in." He turned and yelled into the house. "Avery! Bring the binoculars... and my guns!"

Soon, everyone in the house was up and gathered on the front porch of the old house. Levi lifted the field glasses to his eyes and peered, from left to right, at the forest stretching down the slope of Hobbs Ridge. There were hundreds of Biters milling around in the trees, stumbling, staggering, slowly making their way toward them.

He turned and found that everyone was half-dressed. The Mendlebaums were still in their pajamas, Kate wore a Minnie Mouse sleep shirt, and the twins were parading around in their tighty-whities. "Y'all get dressed! Hurry!"

"We'd better take care of this first wave, husband," Nell said from the porch railing. "Before we go to doing anything else."

Levi whirled and joined her. He didn't need the binoculars this time. A dozen Biters had emerged from the woods and were heading up the embankment toward them.

The others lined the railing of the porch, guns in hand. Like a firing squad, they prepared their weapons. A metallic cacophony of working slides, cocked hammers, and jacked shells filled the air, followed by a hail of lead. The Biters spun and sank as hollow-point slugs and buckshot assaulted them, ripping through putrid muscle and brittle bone. Katie and Levi took the heads, centering well-placed shots between bloodshot eyes and in the pale domes of their exposed foreheads.

Agnes Mendlebaum stepped up and held a .22 Ruger MK III in a two-fisted hold. She aimed calmly, then squeezed off a single round. The little slug skewered a Biter's eye, ricocheted around in his brain for a second, then exited out the opposite orb. It almost looked as though she had shot out both of the zombie's eyes with a single shot.

"Don't tell me…" said Jem.

Abe nodded. "Melbourne, Australia, nineteen fifty-six. Women's target shooting. She got the silver for that one."

After the first wave fell, a second appeared, twice as many as before. The Biters seemed agitated and angry, wailing hoarsely and snapping their fuzzy, black teeth with bone-cracking intensity.

"I've got this, Papa," said Avery. He lit the fuse of a home-made grenade and lobbed it down the slope. It bounced twice and fell among the shuffling feet of the zombies. The fuse reached its end with a spitting and sputtering of sparks and the explosion went off, nearly deafening them all. Amid the fire and shrapnel, dismembered limbs and severed heads took flight, then fell with meaty thuds, rolling back down the hill or laying still in the scorched grass.

Avery looked around at the others, who stood there, addled. "Y'all go on and get the trucks loaded. I'll hold them off as long as I can."

Jem stepped forward and lifted the Remington scattergun to his shoulder. "I'll back you up, brother."

Nell looked to the left and right of the porch. Biters were advancing from those directions as well. "I'll grab your clothes on the way out. But don't stick around too long," she told her sons. "Those things are slow, but a lot of them together can get the best of you before you know it. When you hear our horns honking, come running."

"Yes, ma'am," they said in unison, then went to work. Avery flung grenade after grenade down the face of the Ridge, while Jem pressed the 1100's trigger time after time, hammering alternating loads of double-ought buck and rifled slugs into the Biters that made their way toward the front porch.

The others fled into the house. While Abe and Agnes hurriedly dressed, Levi, Nell, and Kate began to carry provisions to the vehicles parked out back. As he grabbed a couple of duffle bags of food and bottled water, Levi couldn't help but remember the tension of the night before. Nell had been in an oddly nervous mood, insisting that they pack most of their food and ammunition, as well as topping off the tanks in the logging truck, Yukon, and Ram. Levi had been more than a little peeved at Nell's wild hair, but now that irritation changed to admiration and relief. It was as though she had had a premonition of what was coming.

"We'll have to ditch the VW," Levi told the Mendlebaums. "It'll never make it down the road that we'll be taking."

Abe and Agnes looked at the Bug regretfully, then climbed into the back seat of Katie's Yukon. Nell took the Ram pickup, while Levi cranked up the logging truck. As he turned toward the open gate in the fence, he looked through the rear window of the cab. Six five-gallon jugs of gasoline and diesel sat lashed to the flatbed with bungee cords. Another one of Nell's annoying ideas that had paid off.

They were through the gate and heading down a rutted dirt road that led along the peak of Hobbs ridge, when Nell leaned on the Dodge's horn. For a minute nothing happened. Then the back door of the Hobbs house burst open and Avery and Jem piled out. Avery twisted the lock and kicked the door shut. Through the plate glass of the door's window, half-a-dozen zombies could be seen. Their faces pressed against the glass, slobbering, gnawing, and coating the pane with a nasty mixture of black saliva and blood. Soon, more faces appeared at the windows along the back of the house. Most were strangers, but a few were familiar, folks they had known and grown up with in the mountains they had once called home.

"Jump in, boys!" Nell yelled to them.

Jem did as she instructed, tossing his guns into the bed of the Ram and then jumping the tailgate himself. Avery, however, had other plans. "The house is full of Biters," he said, running to the plunger box on the rock. "There must be a hundred of the bastards inside, maybe more!"

Nell looked ahead. Levi had stopped the logging truck and was standing next to the open door of the cab, staring back toward the house. From where she was, she could see tears in the man's eyes. It was the first time she had ever seen her husband cry.

Avery clutched the bar handle of the plunger, but hesitated. He looked over his shoulder. "Papa?"

"Do it," Levi said hoarsely. "Just… do it."

Avery nodded. "Everybody plug your ears. This is gonna make one hellacious boom."

His family and the Mendlebaums took his advice. Avery grinned broadly, then slammed the plunger home.

The Hobbs house erupted into a massive cloud of fire and black smoke as the dynamite on the gas tanks detonated. Ancient boards, shingles, and nails rained through the morning air, along with the charred remains of the zombies who had invaded the structure.

Levi Hobbs stood numbly beside his truck, stunned. In a flash of gunpowder and ignited fuel, the center of his family history was gone. The house he had been born and raised in—and had hoped to grow old in—was falling in a hail of blackened boards and refuse around him.

"We've got to go," his wife said gently from the window of the pickup truck. "Levi... please." She looked through the back window of the Ram's cab and saw Biters picking their way through the thicket on either side of the burning crater that had once been their home. "They're still coming... and they're hungry and pissed off."

Levi shook his head in disgust. A charred hand landed in the grass three feet from where he stood. It thrashed on its back for a moment, then flipped over and scuttled erratically toward him like a blind spider. Cussing, he kicked it away. With a sigh, he pulled himself together and climbed back into his truck. "Okay, let's get the hell out of here. There's nothing left for us on the Ridge now."

He shifted the vehicle into gear and took point. Silently, the others followed, making their way along the rutted dirt lane that exited from the Hobbs property.

Before they made their way down the opposite face of the Smoky Mountains, however, there was one stop Levi wanted to make... one person he needed to see... before they put the state of Tennessee behind them for good.

CHAPTER 8

Three miles south, as Hobbs Ridge gradually rose to the higher elevation of Pea Ridge, wild with thick stands of tall pines and jagged outcroppings of limestone and shale, Levi parked his truck on the rutted track of a mountain road, holding his hand up from the open window. The others slowed and stopped as well.

Levi left the cab, taking the shotgun with him. "I'm going up by myself," he told Nell as she looked at him from the passenger window of the Ram pickup. Jem had taken over the driving, while Avery crouched in the back, holding the AR-15, vigilant for movement in the surrounding woods. "She's known me all my life. If anyone can talk some sense into her stubborn head, it'll be me."

His wife nodded. "Good luck. And be sure to tell her that we'd be happy to have her."

Levi nodded and then started up the steep road. He looked for signs of Biters, be they human or critter. Since encountering the Macolmers' hound and the gray squirrel, each transformed into the ravenous undead, he knew anything could turn, man or beast. But he found no recent sign, no droppings, and no distorted footprints of shuffling steps. The only tracks he discovered were tire tracks from an ATV that had traveled just so far and then had quickly turned back in the direction from which it had come. Fragments of clear glass from a headlight told him that something had reinforced that need to retreat, perhaps a well-placed gunshot.

Soon, he came within sight of an ancient log cabin—dovetailed and chinked with clay mud—and topped with rusted sheet tin. On the porch sat a solitary figure, small and slump-shouldered, head bent over a worn Bible in her dark hands. The fingertip of her right index finger ran slowly along the print of the page as she read. Levi knew that was impossible, however. The old woman had pretty much been blind for years, the corneas of both eyes shielded by cataracts as thick and opaque as his thumbnails. If the scriptures came to her, they came by memory alone.

He halted in his tracks. "Auntie!" he called up to her. "Auntie Rose!"

The elderly black woman lifted her head. Her face was heavily lined with age and her wooly head of hair was as white as virgin snow. She peered down the hillside with both curiosity and suspicion. In an instant, she traded the Good Book for an old lever-action Winchester that leaned against the cabin wall behind her. "Who goes there?" she hollered out.

"Levi Hobbs, Auntie."

"How's I know you be Levi?" she asked gruffly. "Tell me something he would only know, or I'll pierce your left ear." She worked the lever and lifted the rifle to her shoulder. "And if'n I miss it and plug you a couple o' inches to the right, well now, that would be a doggone shame, wouldn't it?"

Levi swallowed nervously. Auntie Rose was nearly blind, but she didn't need her eyes to fire that rifle and consistently place the bullet anywhere she wanted. Last summer he had been out hunting and had chased a jackrabbit across Pea Ridge, onto Auntie Rose's property. Before he could bring it down, the old woman had beaten him to the shot. She had tracked its progress by sound alone and drilled it cleanly through the temples, just below its oversized ears.

"On my fifth birthday, you whittled me a toy," he told her. "It was this little dancing man on two sticks. When you squeezed those sticks, that feller would flip and carry on something funny. Mama said you carved it from the branch of a white oak tree that'd been struck by lightning and that it was full of heavenly magic, that if I played with it enough, I'd grow up to be a special man someday. One who cherished family and hard work over hard drink and carousing, like my pa did."

"And so you have," grinned Auntie with toothless gums. She returned the rifle to its place against the wall. "Come on up to me, young Levi."

He couldn't help but grin as he trudged past the smokehouse, the ramshackle chicken coop, and the narrow structure of a single-seat outhouse. "Auntie, I'm over fifty years old now."

"Still a babe compared to ol' Rose," she told him. "Emily Hobbs' sweet little boy."

Levi thought of his mother, who had died of cancer twenty-two years past, and the lasting friendship she had shared with the old black lady in the rocking chair. They had grown up together in a time when Negroes and white folks distanced themselves from one another, afraid of what might be said or thought by others. Emily and Rose had been an exception, enjoying each other's company on the sly, even when the threat of reprisal from men with white hoods, liquor on their breath, and a wicked fondness for fire and braided leather that split air and flesh was a genuine possibility. If there were ever twin daughters born of different mothers of separate colors, they were truly that pair of young'uns.

"Not as sweet as I once was," he said as he reached the porch and sat on a riser midway up the rickety steps. "I've done some godawful things, Auntie. Sinful things that sickened me down deep in my belly."

"If'n you're talking about those confounded Biters," she told him, "rest easy in your mind, Levi. They ain't the ones you knew before summer took hold. Their souls have flown the coop long before you split their skull or put a bullet betwixt their eyes."

"I'm hoping you're right, Auntie. I truly am." He spotted a wire cage sitting next to her chair. Inside were three laying hens. "What're the chickens for?"

Auntie laughed. "Whenever a Biter wanders up here, hankering for some dark meat, I fling one of these birds out into the yard. They go after it and forget all about me. Probably for the best. I'd be a lot more gamey and harder to stomach than them there pullets."

The two were silent for a long moment. Then the elderly woman spoke again. "You didn't come all the way up here on

Pea Ridge to unburden yourself and talk about chickens, did you?"

"No, ma'am."

"You're leaving, ain't you? Leaving the Smokies behind."

"That's right." he admitted. He glanced up into the sky. The three clouds of buzzards had thinned. Some still soared over-head, but most had taken to ground, likely feasting off the bits and pieces of Biters that scattered Hobbs Ridge for the better part of a quarter mile. "We had us some trouble over our way. Got overrun... had to resort to something I'd never dreamt of doing several months ago."

Auntie Rose nodded solemnly. "I heard it rolling over the ridge like thunder. A sad thing to be forced to erase one's past in a flash of gunpowder and flame, ain't it?"

Levi felt an aching in his chest, like a fist closing in around his heart. "It surely is."

"But that ain't why you came, is it?"

"No." He gathered his nerve and came right out and said it. "We're heading down the far side of the mountain into North Carolina, Auntie... and we want you to come with us."

The elderly woman chuckled and spat tobacco juice off the porch to the side. "Now why would you want a shriveled-up, old husk like me getting in the way and slowing you down?"

"You wouldn't be," he told her. "You'd be invaluable, Auntie. You've got more knowledge about surviving in the wilderness and living off the land in your pinky finger than the whole of us put together."

Auntie Rose grinned. "You're probably right about that, Levi. But I'm still not a-going."

He had expected such a response from her, but it still pained him to hear it straight from her lips. "How come?"

"Here I was born and here I'll die," she explained. She bent down and laid a bony, black hand upon his shoulder. He reached up and squeezed it gently. "As fond as am of you and of the cherished memory of your mother, God rest her blessed soul, I love this old place of log and mud and tin even more. It's as much a part of me as the blood in my veins or the breath in my lungs. Separate us... take me away from here... and I'd be dead within a week's passing. Having my feets upon these here floorboards is what keeps me anchored to this ol' world, as ugly and twisted as it has become."

"I understand," Levi replied. "I thought the same, but after it was gone in splinters and ash, I'm still here. My heart's still pumping and alive, even though it's broken clean in half."

"Maybe you're a stronger soul than ol' Auntie is," she mused, her jaw working the chaw in her cheek like a cow chewing its cud.

Levi couldn't help but chuckle. "I doubt that very much. You're like an iron horseshoe... it'd take some doing to bend or break what you're made of."

It was Auntie Rose's turn to laugh. "I'm in my eighth decade now. My bones are brittle and my skin as thin as cobweb. Both can be torn asunder by bullet or hungry teeth." She shook her wrinkled head. "Horseshoe, my ass."

"That's why you should come with us. So we can take care of you... prevent such a thing from happening."

"You're a stubborn cuss, ain't you?"

He eyed her with both admiration and regret. "Reminds me of that old saying about the pot calling the kettle black, you know."

"Well, you've got the black part right."

They laughed together for a while, then grew silent.

"So, I reckon this is it," he said.

"I reckon so, Levi Hobbs," she replied softly.

He stood on the warped risers of the old steps, leaned forward, and embraced her. The two remained that way for a long moment before parting. He pressed something into the leathery palm of her hand—a box of ammunition. "For that ol' rifle of yours. Use it sparingly and shoot straight."

She accepted the gift graciously. "You know I will. Much obliged."

Levi took up his shotgun, canted it over his shoulder, and started back down the hill toward the dirt road. Halfway there, he turned around. "Auntie... I saw tracks in the dirt down yonder. A four-wheeler from the looks of 'em."

Auntie Rose nodded. "Lonnie Pendergast and his boys. But

they weren't looking for me. It was the Biters they were after."
Her face grew grim. "They used to torment us niggers—beat us,
lynch us... rape us." Pain, deep and bitter, shown in her cloudy
eyes. "But now they got themselves something new to hate.
And if that takes the pressure off me and my kind, then the better I'll be for it."

Levi stared at her for a long moment, knowing that it was
for the last time. "I love you, Auntie."

"Love you, too, boy. God be with you in your travels, wher-
ever it might lead."

Silently, Levi walked back down the rutted road to the line
of vehicles that sat there waiting. As he passed the red pickup
truck, Nell eyed him warily. "So she wouldn't... "

"No. I told you that she wouldn't, didn't I?"

His wife shrugged. "Never hurts to try, though, does it?"

Levi turned reddened eyes toward her. "Nowadays, everything seems to hurt... right down to the quick."

Nell could do nothing but agree. She knew by looking at
Levi that, at that moment, he was hurting to no end.

He climbed back into the Ford flatbed, cranked the engine,
and, taking the lead, headed over the crest of Pea Ridge and set
out for parts previously unknown.

CHAPTER 9

They took a steep mountain road down the eastern face of Pea Ridge, winding through dense stands of timber and natural outcroppings of wind-scrubbed stone. As they drove, they were aware of the absence of wildlife. The buzzards continued to circle tirelessly a few miles behind them, but other than that, they saw no birds or small animals, like squirrels or rabbits. The woods seemed unnaturally empty.

An hour later, they left the rutted dirt track and began to travel eastward along the park roads toward the North Carolina border. As they drove, they saw several cars abandoned by the side of the road. On most of them, the doors had been wrenched open and the upholstery of the seats was torn and dyed a nasty brownish-red with dried blood. One vehicle, a Ford Mustang, had been flipped onto its roof at the edge of the forest. The driver's side had been battered and caved in, as though rammed by something of incredible force. Levi figured it had been hit by another vehicle, but traces of thick black fur told him that the Mustang and its occupants had been attacked by a thing of flesh and blood, rather than something mechanical.

Levi found his eyes roaming from the two-lane road toward the thick stands of pine, cedar, and oak on either side. He saw nothing amid the shadows between the trees, but he felt watched. *This is a dangerous place,* he thought to himself. *Damn dangerous.*

Once they spotted half-a-dozen buzzards circling above the trees up ahead and slowed, preparing for a confrontation. But it was only a couple of Biters—a tall, thin man in a park ranger's uniform and a dark-haired woman dressed in hiking gear, still wearing a backpack across her emaciated shoulders. Levi sped around them and the others in the caravan followed. The two zombies lurched after them, but soon lost ground and stood in the center of the road, hollering hoarsely with frustration, their dark teeth gnashing.

They were ten miles from Cherokee when Levi rounded a sharp curve on a downhill slope and suddenly found a tree halfway down in the road. He steered sharply and attempted to dodge the outermost branches, but a jagged limb impaled the right front tire of the logging truck, flattening it with a bang. Levi cussed as the truck limped a few yards farther down the road. He brought it to a halt and engaged the parking brake, then hopped out of the cab.

The Dodge Ram stopped a few feet behind him. Avery and Jem got out. "You hit that stob good, Papa," Avery told him. "Tore that tire plumb to hell."

They smelled something dead, but saw no carcasses in the roadway. Perhaps something had crawled off into the woods and given up the ghost.

"Tell your mama to stay in the truck," he told them. "There's things in the woods. You saw those cars back yonder."

The twins nodded. Their eyes surveyed the close-grown trees around them, their guns unslung and unholstered. "Want us to change it for you?"

Levi took a heavy-duty jack from the tool chest behind the Ford's cab, as well as a cross-bar lug wrench. "I'll do the changing. You stand guard. Hopefully, I can get this done in a few minutes and we'll be on our way." He looked upward, hoping to see past the treetops, but the forest formed a thick canopy across the two-lane road. From the sparse light filtering from in between, he determined that it was already late in the afternoon, maybe three-thirty or four o'clock. It would be getting dark soon and he didn't cotton to the idea of spending the night out there in the wilderness. God only knew what would be on the prowl after twilight.

He dropped the spare from the cradle beneath the truck's bed and went to work jacking the front end up. When the damaged tire was off the pavement, he went to work with the lug wrench. He had all the nuts loosened except one, when he heard a deep growl coming from the woods behind him, perhaps twenty yards away.

"Hear that?" he asked his sons. Nervously, he shucked the Blackhawk from its holster and laid it on the ground next to him.

"We did," admitted Jem. "What do you think it was?"

Levi shook his head as he fumbled with the nuts and then pulled the heavy tire from the rotor of the wheel. "No earthly idea... but it was big, that's for sure."

Another growl sounded, different from the other one, on the opposite side of the road. Avery absently thumbed his AR-15 from single shot to full automatic. "We've got more than one."

Levi wrestled with the spare and aligned the rotor bolts with the wheel holes, then slid it into place. "If something comes out of the woods, shoot it. In the head."

"Sure enough." Jem lifted the 1100 shotgun and warily swept the muzzle along the tree line behind his father. A twig snapped as something shifted in the thicket. Jem's finger caressed the Remington's trigger lightly, itching to fire.

Levi was screwing on the first lug nut, when something screamed a few yards behind the Yukon. At first he thought it was a woman, but it was wilder, more feline in nature. "A bobcat," he said as he worked.

"Levi?" called Nell from the cab of the Dodge.

"It's okay," he told her, not feeling that way at all. "Stay put... and roll up your window."

A rustle and crunch of dry leaves broke the silence as they heard motion on both sides. The stench of decay grew heavier, nearly unbearable. If there were buzzards above the treetops, they couldn't be seen.

"We're surrounded," said Jem in a low voice, not wanting his mother to overhear.

"You got that right," Avery told them from the far side of the truck. "Look."

Levi and Jem turned their attention to the eastern end of the park road. A large buck with a twelve-point rack stood on the center line. Its dark eyes were moist and hollow and its hide was filthy and sunken in, with bone showing from the ribs, legs, and skull. They could not see its teeth, but its antlers were teaming with swarming, black parasites.

They watched as it snorted wetly, then lowered its head and pawed at the blacktop.

"It's going to charge," said Avery, facing the animal.

"Watch those antlers," Levi warned. "If they gore you, or even wound you, you're one of them."

The deer's decaying muscles quivered with strain and then it galloped toward them. The animal seemed shaky and off-kilter at first, but it soon stretched and sprang, as though a memory of its former life had kicked in. Its hooves drummed hollowly against the pavement, gaining speed.

Avery raised the butt of the AR-15 to his shoulder and began firing.

Levi figured it was about time to postpone changing the tire. He grabbed the .44 Blackhawk off the ground and stood up. He didn't have time to turn and face the buck at all. Without warning, the wall of thicket on the right side of the road burst open and something massive and black exploded into the open, filling his view. He stumbled backward and landed on his ass as the thing hit the passenger door of the logging truck. It struck with enough force and weight to rock the vehicle, lifting it four inches off the ground on one side before it settled once again.

It was a black bear, or had been before it had turned. Now it was a great, bloated mass of matted ebony fur, mad red eyes, and teeth and claws coated with swarming darkness. The animal staggered backward and shook its huge head after the impact of the collision. Then it rose up on its hind legs and roared loudly. Erect, it was nearly seven feet tall. From where Levi sat on the ground, it looked even taller.

There was a loud bang and a tortured squeal of metal, and the logging truck rocked backward on its brakes a few inches, knocking the jack loose beneath it. Levi glanced over his shoulder and saw the big deer's haunches around the edge of the front fender. *The son of a bitch head-butted the truck! Put his rack right through the grill!*

"Out of the way, Papa!" Jem called out.

Levi reacted, rolling to the side and nearly into the woods. Jem fired his twelve-gauge, putting a load of buckshot into the bear's back, between its shoulder blades. Levi flinched as the animal's chest exploded and most of its heart and lungs—dark and infected with parasites—littered the gravel shoulder beside the road. The bear staggered for a moment, then bellowed loudly and whirled, bringing a paw the size of a catcher's mitt swinging toward Jem. The boy dodged the blow by fractions of an inch. If the bear's claws had made contact, they would have peeled Jem's face completely off his skull or decapitated him.

I don't give a shit what Abe says, thought Levi, *the thing is dead. You can't be alive and lose your heart and keep on going!*

He struggled to his feet and aimed the .44 Magnum at the back of the bear's head. "Aim for the brain, son!" Past the bear, he saw Jem nod and lift the 1100, jamming the muzzle against the critter's forehead. "Now!"

Together, they pulled their triggers.

On the far side of the truck, Avery had his hands full.

A bee swarm of slugs from the AR-15 had failed to bring the zombie buck down. They had stitched across his broad shoulders and a few had knocked a few points off his rack, but none had found his skull. Avery lurched backward as the buck rammed the front end of the Ford, its antlers impaling the grill. *Damn!* he thought. *There goes the radiator!*

Slinging the assault rifle over his shoulder, he drew a machete from a scabbard on his hip and walked up to the front of the truck. The deer huffed and struggled to pull free from the grill, but its rack was firmly embedded. The animal's bloodshot eyes rolled wildly and its black teeth snapped like gunshots, yearning to sink into living flesh.

Avery took the haft of the machete in both hands and hacked the deer's head from its body. It took several swings, but soon the body dropped to the pavement, bucking and twitching, while the head with its magnificent parasite-covered rack remained attached to the grill of the logging truck.

Behind him, Avery heard a high-pitched squeal, like a hog that had been grabbed by the hind legs. He whirled and saw a wild boar barreling out of the thicket at the opposite side of the mountain road. It was a big one—at least two hundred and fifty pounds—oily black with crazy eyes. Its tusks were long and curved, the yellow of the ivory obscured by a dense coating of seething black parasites.

Unable to reach the AR-15 in time, he dropped the machete and drew his pistol. Gripping the gun in both hands, he fired. After three shots in the head, the animal failed to slow down. Wild boars were notorious for possessing thick skulls. It would take a heavy-caliber round, point blank, to penetrate the bony plate between its eyes. It was at that moment that Avery wished that he was holding his father's .44 Blackhawk.

"Shit!" cussed Avery. Soon, his revolver was empty and the thing kept right on coming. Only fifteen feet of pavement stretched between him and the zombie boar. Holding the smoking gun in his hand, he knew that his options were limited. The machete was beyond reach and he would be a few seconds short of grabbing the AR-15 and bringing it around into line.

Right when he was certain that the critter would gore him, a streak of narrow motion flashed from his left and the boar dropped to its knees and flipped. Avery side-stepped as the animal's hindquarters forcefully struck the door of the truck. Startled, he looked down to see that an arrow had pierced the boar's skull, entering one temple and exiting out the other.

Avery looked toward the Yukon and saw Agnes Mendlebaum standing beside it, holding the compound bow in her tiny, liver-spotted hands. He simply nodded his thanks, so out of breath that he was unable to speak.

Levi and Jem left the fallen carcass of the black bear and headed around the truck to where Avery stood. Almost immediately, the shriek of the bobcat sounded from the far end of the caravan, followed by the rattle of Kate's Uzi.

"Come on!" their father instructed and, together, they started toward the Yukon.

They were nearly past the Ram pickup, when something dropped from an overhanging tree limb and landed with a thud on the roof of the cab. Avery heard a snarl and turned to see a gray flash leaping toward them. "Look out!" he yelled as the thing launched itself at his brother's head.

It was a possum, shriveled, its gray fur missing in broad clumps. Its rodent-like head was more a skull with feverish red eyes than anything else. It landed on Jem's shoulder, wrapped its fleshy pink tail around his neck, and bit savagely into his left ear.

Jem cried out and dropped his shotgun. He grabbed a fistful of the possum's hair, but it came out in his hand. Avery stepped over and tried his best to pry it loose. The animal's sharp teeth— seething with swarming blackness—were clamped firmly shut, refusing to let go.

The pained look in Avery's eyes matched that of his twin. "Sorry, brother," he said, then reached down to Jem's belt, took the six-inch Buck knife from its sheath, and cleanly sliced his ear off at the base, next to the skull.

Jem screamed and sank to his knees, blood jetting from the wound. Avery got a firm hold on the possum, but its tail remained wrapped around his brother's throat. With a growl of anger, he cut the tail loose with the Buck knife and then tossed the animal to the roadway. It hit on its side and struggled to get up, eyes blazing, teeth still clamped around the cartilage of Jem's severed ear.

Before it could escape—or attack again—Avery leaned down and impaled the possum's skull between the eyes. The blade entered with a brittle crunch, passed through the brain, and exited through the back. Almost instantly, a surging stream of blackness erupted from the wound and began traveling up the blade toward the hilt of the knife. Avery let loose and stepped back before it could reach his hand.

A moment later, Nell and Abe were beside the wounded sixteen-year-old. "Someone bring me some gasoline!" the old man instructed. "And a bottle of water."

Jem cried mournfully as blood soaked the shoulder of his shirt and ran down his left arm. "It bit me! It bit me, Ma! Oh God!"

"Just keep calm, son," his mother said soothingly. "Your brother got to you in time... cut it off before those things could get inside you." Her voice was steady, but the fear in her eyes told a different story.

As Avery went to fetch a gas can from the bed of the logging truck, Levi stood over them expectantly. "Abe?"

The scientist looked up at him, his face grim. "I can try something, but there are no guarantees."

Levi nodded. He reached down and ran a hand gently through his son's hair. "Take care of him," he told Nell. "I'm going to check on Kate."

When he reached the Yukon, he found his daughter and Agnes at the rear of the vehicle. They stood above a large bobcat, about five feet long from nose to tail. It was riddled with 9mm bullets and was still alive, breathing raggedly, air whistling wetly from its punctured lungs.

"Stand back," Kate told them, then aimed one of the Glocks, thumbed back the hammer, and put a single round through the spotted feline's brain. When she turned toward her father, she saw the stricken look on his face. "What is it?"

"Your brother. Jem."

Kate looked past him and saw Jem on the ground, covered with blood, with her mother and Abe Mendlebaum beside him.

"He was bitten," her father told her. "By a possum."

"No!" Kate took off running. Levi and Agnes followed.

By the time they got there, Avery had returned with a five-gallon can of gasoline and a bottle of drinking water. "There you go."

"And I'll need a match."

Reluctantly, the teenager took a match from the box in his pocket and handed it to the doctor. He looked regretfully at his mother. "I'm sorry, Ma. I couldn't think of anything else to do."

"Don't worry, son," she told him. "You did the right thing."

"Hold him down," Abe instructed. "This is going to hurt like unholy hell."

Levi and Avery did as he requested. "What are you going to do?" asked the boy. Tears streamed down his cheeks as he stared at his frightened brother.

"Attempt to kill two birds with one stone. Cauterize the wound and destroy any parasites that might have infected the tissue." Tilting Jem's head—so that the inner ear canal would not suffer—Abe took the gas can and let a trickle of fuel fall over the open wound in his head, covering the area as sparingly as possible. Jem bucked and screamed at the flare of pain. Abe opened the bottle of water and handed it to Nell. "It will need to burn for ten or fifteen seconds to be effective. When I tell you, put out the flames with the water."

"Flames?" shrieked Jem. "What do you mean—?"

Abe struck the match and lit the gas-soaked wound. The side of Jem's head caught fire and began to burn.

Those fifteen seconds were the longest fifteen seconds of their lives. The others looked away as Jem thrashed and screamed. Avery held on firmly to his twin brother and cried like a baby.

"Now!" said Abe.

Nell—also in tears—dumped the entire bottle of drinking water on the flames, slowly extinguishing them. Jem continued to scream for a minute, then stiffened and passed out from the shock and pain. Abe laid two fingers against the side of his neck and checked his pulse. "He'll be unconscious for a while. We'll need to see if we can find a pharmacy when we reach Cherokee. He'll need antibiotics and something for the pain... if the place hasn't already been ransacked."

"Did any... any of those *things*...get into the wound?" asked Levi. He remembered the possum's jagged teeth, covered with black parasites.

The elderly man shrugged. "Only time will tell, I suppose," he said truthfully. "There was so much blood, it was hard to tell. If there were, hopefully the fire destroyed them."

Levi looked around, puzzled. "Where's Mrs. Agnes?"

"I believe she is over there, tightening the lug nuts on your truck."

Avery shook his head in wonder. "She's just a jack of all trades, ain't she?"

Abe smiled affectionately. "She always has been." He opened a first aid kit that Nell had brought from the pickup truck and began binding Jem's blackened wound with gauze and surgical tape.

Levi and Avery walked around to the front of the logging truck. Taking a fallen limb from the side of the road, they pried the head of the buck loose. It dropped from the grill onto the pavement. They kept their distance. Thousands of parasites still swarmed from the animal's antlers, as well as its nostrils, mouth, and the ragged stump of its neck. They popped the hood and examined the radiator. "No punctures as far as I can tell," said Levi. "A half inch more and one or two of those points would have gone right through the front."

Gently, they loaded Jem into the bed of the pickup truck and covered him with a wedding ring quilt Nell had sewn with her grandmother when she was a child. Avery sat in the back of the truck with him. He was strangely quiet, a trait that had never been a major part of his personality. It was plain to see that he was concerned for his brother and scared at the prospect of what might soon happen to him.

"I reckon we'd best be going," Levi told Nell and Kate. "It'll be getting dark soon and I'd hate be caught out here at night." He nodded to the carcasses of the permanently dead animals. "Especially with critters like those roaming about."

Nell's face looked pale and drawn. "Levi... will Jem be okay?"

Levi shook his head. "I don't know. I reckon all we can do is pray on it."

His wife frowned bitterly at the suggestion. "Done my fair share of praying, Levi. Prayed until I was blue in the face... with no relief in sight. I don't reckon another one would make a damn bit of difference."

As he watched her climb back into the cab of the big Ram, Levi felt saddened by the woman's cynical remark. Nell had always been their rock in times of trouble and hardship, and a big part of her strength and wisdom had been hewn out of her faith in God. Now that that faith was faltering, it seemed like a piece of her was dead and buried. A very important piece.

CHAPTER 10

Cherokee, North Carolina—also known as Cherokee Indian Reservation—was a wannabe Gatlinburg, but on a much smaller scale. There were a few attractions and museums—mostly dedicated to its Cherokee heritage—but it was also a gambling town. Because of its status as a Native American reservation governed unto itself, there were bingo halls among the souvenir shops (which sold Indian blankets, beaded jewelry, and feathered "dreamcatchers" … most with a Made in China tag somewhere on them) and there was even a Harrah's Casino on the side of one of the wooded foothills. Before the outbreak, tourists would be bussed across the mountain from Pigeon Forge and Gatlinburg, to play the slots or a little roulette or blackjack.

From all outward appearances, the place was utterly deserted. There was a distinct absence of Biters, too. The streets were dark and empty. If there were any buzzards around—circling the black sky or roosting in the trees of the surrounding forest—they were staying out of sight.

There were only three restaurants in town: a McDonald's, a Dairy Queen, and an IHOP, all with their doors securely locked. Toward the end of town, they found what they were looking for. The Walgreens was also locked up as tight as a drum, but from their vantage point outside looked to have been untouched. The shelves were still fully stocked, as though the end of civilization had taken place only hours ago.

It was a little unnerving to find the town in such a pristine state, with no signs of looting or vandalism. It was as though the residents had all awakened as Biters one morning and simply wandered off.

Levi busted out the glass of the front door with the butt of his shotgun and he and Abe went in. Avery stayed in the bed of the truck with his brother, while the others waited in the vehicles.

The two made their way directly to the pharmacy in the back. All the shelves were stocked. No one had taken anything, which was odd, since every drugstore in America—or even the world, for that matter—had been looted shortly after the chaos had started, mostly by junkies, drug dealers, or folks who intended to barter pharmaceuticals for other supplies.

Levi wouldn't have had any idea what he was looking for, but fortunately Abe did. Taking a mop bucket from the cleaning supplies aisle, the scientist filled it to the brim with various kinds of antibiotics and painkillers, including Oxycontin, Lortab, Percocet, Cefalexin, Zithromax, and Amoxicillin, as well as gauze and first aid supplies to change the dressing on Jem's wound.

"We'll come back in the morning and get the rest of what we need," suggested Levi. "Right now, we need to cook us up some supper and get a good night's sleep. It's been a hard day on all of us."

Abe agreed. "It has been a grueling *week*. A lot has taken place… has changed… in a short period of time."

They left the drugstore and headed down the highway to the end of town. There were several large hotels near Harrah's—a Holiday Inn Suites, Hampton Inn, and Days Inn, among others—but they chose a little place named the Tomahawk Motel with connecting rooms. If trouble came in the form of Biters— like it had earlier that day—they would have quick access to their vehicles. If they stayed in one of the big, multi-floored hotels, they would be packed in like sardines in a can. If the place was attacked or overrun, it would be nearly impossible to escape.

They took three rooms. The Mendlebaums stayed in one; Jem, Avery, and Kate in another; and Levi and Nell in a third. Nell had protested, wanting to stick with her injured boy, but her husband assured her that his sister and brother would attend to his needs. Besides, Nell needed her rest. She didn't need to sit up all night fussing and worrying over something she could really do nothing about.

After supper, Levi and Abe left the others and sat on the open tailgate of the pickup truck. They smoked—Levi from a pack of Marlboro 100s and Abe his pipe full of Borkum Riff—and quietly surveyed the empty thoroughfare of Cherokee.

"How is Jem doing?" Levi asked him.

"He's resting comfortably," the doctor told him. "I changed his dressing and gave him a generous dose of Oxycodone. He'll sleep through the night."

A tense silence stretched between them. "Do you think he'll turn?"

Abe shrugged. "I'm not sure. I saw many men make the transition back in Oak Ridge and I know the symptoms of the parasitic infestation, but so far Jem has exhibited none of them. There is normally immense swelling of the facial features, ruptured blood vessels in the eyes, and signs of parasites in the mouth and nasal passages. Also signs of lethargy and loss of mental faculties as the victim lapses into the faux death and begins to make the transition. I have seen none of that taking place with your son."

"But it could."

"There is always the possibility," the doctor admitted. "We just need to keep him under close observation." He took a long draw on his pipe and exhaled blue smoke through his nostrils. "Have you considered what you will do... if he *does* turn?"

Levi said nothing. His hand absently rested on the butt of the Blackhawk holstered at his hip, then dropped away.

After a couple of minutes, he spoke again. "What happened today... on the park road... was that normal?"

"The animal attack?"

"Yeah. The way they ambushed us. It wasn't a random attack. They were lying in wait... and they weren't acting individually."

"Yes, very disturbing... but intriguing, too," admitted the scientist. "I've been a biologist for nearly forty years and I've never seen different species band together and purposely attack in such a way. It is against their basic nature to do so, but they did it nonetheless. And it was a calculated attack, too. The deer served as a distraction, while the bear and boar took the right and left flank, and the bobcat attacked from the rear. The possum... well, that was just a fluke."

"And it did the most damage." Levi considered something for a moment. "What happened out there... do you think it was due to a collective intelligence?"

Abe was surprised that the man would use such a term. "No... it's tempting to believe so, but no, I don't think that was what motivated them. The way the parasites invade the brain—the damage implemented and the remaining areas overstimulated—are nearly identical in all the hosts. Therefore, they tend to act likewise. I've seen human Biters work in tandem to gain access to a living victim, much like ants methodically picking apart a scrap of food abandoned from a picnic lunch. It is not unthinkable that organisms of a different species would act in a similar way."

"In any case, I think it'd be better if we took to the main highway or the back roads on our way to Hendersonville," Levi told him. "And steer clear of the woods."

"I agree," the old man replied. "No need to take unnecessary risks." Abe sat there for a couple of minutes, staring into the night, then shuddered.

"What's wrong?"

"I'm not sure," he said, looking uneasy. "It's just that I..."

"Feel like you're being watched?" asked Levi.

"Yes."

"We are. We have been since we drove into town. Someone's out there, but it's not a Biter. If it was, it would've attacked us by now... or tried to."

"Perhaps they mean us no harm," mused Abe. "Or they are waiting for the right opportunity to harm us. Either way, we had best be on guard. I'll be glad to take a watch tonight. Agnes says that she will, too."

Levi smiled appreciatively. "Do you think she's up to it?"

Abe's face grew grim. "I saw her take down three Biters

back in Oak Ridge... all big, strapping Marines... from three sides with scarcely fifteen feet between them and her. Her back to a concrete wall with nowhere to go. She put a bullet between their eyes so skillfully that the measurements would have corresponded precisely. She will do what needs to be done, when the time comes. I have no doubt about that."

"Makes me thankful that she's on our side," said Levi.

Abe chuckled. "You'd better believe it."

"You and your lady take the first shift," Levi told him. "Avery and I will relieve you at two AM."

"Sounds good." Abe hopped off the tailgate, knocked the burnt tobacco from the bowl of his pipe, and went into his motel room to prepare for his watch.

Levi sat on the tailgate a while longer. He smoked and thought and did some watching of his own. *You're out there. I know you are.*

He stared intently into the night. Seeing nothing more than motionless darkness between the moonlit buildings and trees, he grew weary of his suspicions and, leaving the truck, went inside to check on Jem and the others.

CHAPTER 11

The following morning, they went scavenging.

Cherokee was beautiful that time of year. The surrounding foothills, steep and covered with tall stands of maple and oak, were ablaze with autumn color. Still it seemed strange and surreal, a picture postcard frozen in time. None of the customary crowds were present, and the souvenir shops and gambling houses that had once operated so briskly were now locked and deserted. The place was a ghost town and it felt like it.

Levi and Kate took the western end of town, while Abe and Avery took the eastern. Nell and Agnes stayed behind to tend to Jem. The two bands of scavengers broke into restaurants and stores, taking only what they needed and leaving the rest. The process was an uneasy one. The businesses had once been the Cherokee people's livelihood. Stealing from them felt like looting a graveyard.

Avery and Abe were picking through the aisles of the Walgreens, gathering various over-the-counter and prescription medicine, first aid supplies, and basic toiletry items, when the boy posed a question.

"What do you make of this town, Mr. Abe? Why was it locked up and deserted? Like no one even lived here to begin with?"

Abe considered it for a moment. "The Cherokee are a proud people," he said. "A persecuted people with a troubled past, much like the Jews were in Hitler's Germany. They are survivors, though. Perhaps they saw what was coming and decided to cut their losses. Left it all behind and took to the forest before it could arrive and strike them down."

Avery nodded as he crammed a pack of Stayfree pads into his sack, a personal request from his sister. "Yeah, sounds like a bunch of redskins."

The old man's eyes flashed. "Native Americans!" he corrected sternly. "It takes no more breath to honor a man than it does to tear him down."

Avery's ears reddened. "Yes, sir," he said respectfully. "Who said that? Abraham Lincoln... Martin Luther King?"

"No," Mendlebaum told him. "Me."

They worked in silence for a few minutes. Then Avery spoke again.

"Can I ask you another question?"

"Certainly."

"Is it just me, or does this place—this whole damn town—give you the creeps?"

Abe regarded him through the lenses of his spectacles. "More than any other place I've visited on the face of the earth, and believe me, I've been all over."

Avery turned his head sharply as a small noise echoed from the back of the store, near the pharmacy. "What was that? A mouse?"

"Hopefully," said the elderly man, looking as uneasy as the boy.

"Let's speed it up a little, okay? Grab what we came for and get back out into the sunshine."

"I'm with you, young man," Abe agreed. "This is no place to linger."

Together, they finished procuring what they had come for and hastefully left the place.

The few restaurants that the reservation boasted turned out to be a bust.

The food in the freezers, which had stopped working when the country gradually lost power, was spoiled, and so was much of the bread, fresh fruit, and vegetables. Only the canned food seemed alright and even that was chancy until they checked the manufacturing lot numbers against those that Abe had gathered at Oak Ridge.

They loaded what they found into the bed of the Ram and drove toward the outskirts of town, to the avenue of newer hotels built there about the time that Harrah's had come into the picture. As Levi drove, he pointed skyward. "Look."

Kate peered through the windshield and saw a dozen or so buzzards circling lazily at a distance. "Maybe we ought to turn around," she suggested. Her freckled hands nervously caressed the Uzi in her lap. "There might be Biters heading this way."

"If they are, they're the first ones we've seen since we got here," her father told her. "But something isn't kosher. Let's check it out."

When they reached the double row of moderately-priced hotels, they found that the buzzards were circling, not over a crowd of zombies, but over a single building. It was a five-story Best Western, tall and bricked, with tinted windows that revealed absolutely nothing from the inside. Only a small percentage of the buzzards were in mid-air. The rest roosted on the edges of the roof, the ledges, and on the hoods of abandoned cars in the parking lot surrounding the structure. Some craned their slender pink necks, eyes glittering hungrily, while others preened lazily, digging into their oily feathers with hooked beaks, scratching an itch or two.

The sight—the sheer volume of the gathering—caused Levi to shudder. It reminded him of an old Alfred Hitchcock movie, with hundreds of crows perched upon swing sets and seesaws, waiting for the schoolhouse doors to open for recess.

The hotel looked as it might have looked months before, except for the birds… and something else. The main entrance in the front and three secondary ones around the other three sides had been blocked off by vehicles. A large brown UPS truck was parked flush with the double doors in the front, while pickup trucks and panel trucks blocked the other entrances.

"What's going on here, Papa?" asked Kate.

"I'm not sure," he said, parking the truck. "Let's take a look."

The moment they stepped outside the cab, they smelled it—the putrid stench of death and decay, not overwhelming, but strangely muted.

"Oh my God," Kate said in amazement. "They're all in *there*."

She was right. They could hear the milling of a multitude of Biters beyond the windows and doors of the Best Western. Not only on the ground floor, but *all* floors. Levi and Kate stepped up to one of the first-floor windows and peered past the dark tint of the glass. Biters shuffled and roamed in the lobby and down the halls, behind the registration desk, through the dining area, and in and out of the open elevator. They moaned and hissed, ravenous, but with nothing to eat or sink their infected teeth into.

"How did they get in there?" his daughter asked.

Levi saw the scattered remains of several animals lying across the lobby carpet. He smiled and shook his head in admiration. "You mean *who* put them there." He couldn't help but laugh. "The clever son of a bitch."

Katie looked at her father. "Papa, I've had the strangest sensation…"

"That someone has been watching us? They have, since the moment we rolled into town."

"Who is it?"

"I don't know," he admitted, "but maybe we'll come across them before we hit the road."

A loud bang on the window made them jump. Several zombies had noticed them standing outside. Their presence was beginning to agitate the trapped creatures.

"Let's go, before we start a stampede," Levi suggested. "That glass looks sturdy, but not sturdy enough to hold two or three dozen if they decided to tackle it all at once."

Quickly, they climbed back into the truck and headed out, leaving the frustrated Biters to nibble and lick the panes of the hotel window, disappointed that their intended meal was swiftly driving away.

Jem was conscious, but had grown quiet and morose. He refused to speak to anyone… wouldn't look at anyone. He just lay on his bed in the gloom of the hotel room with his face turned toward the wall.

Earlier that morning, before leaving, Abe had pulled Levi and Nell aside. "I've done all that I can do," he had told them. "The rest is up to him."

Around noon, Nell knelt next to his bedside, holding a bowl of chicken noodle soup she had warmed on the camp stove. "You've got to eat something, son," she told him. Nell attempted a smile, but failed miserably. "If not for yourself, do it for me."

The left side of his face was bruised and discolored, while the cauterized area around his missing ear was covered with gauze and surgical tape. His left eye was swollen shut, but the right stared past his mother's head, focusing on some unidentifiable stain on the wall.

"Go away," he said emotionlessly. "Don't look at me."

Defeated, Nell stood up. She set the bowl of soup on the nightstand between the two beds and started for the door.

Agnes Mendlebaum stood in the doorway. With a sympathetic smile, she laid a comforting hand on Nell's shoulder. "He'll be alright," she assured her. "Just give him time."

"I don't know," said Nell. "I've never seen him so low. Like he's given up... or knows something that we don't."

"We'll have Abe check him again when he gets back."

Nell shook her head. "But what if...?"

Agnes squeezed her shoulder gently. "There has been no indication of an infestation so far. If anyone knows the signs, it's my husband. A lot of people turned at the facility at Oak Ridge. Jem has shown none of the symptoms."

Nell was about to say something in reply, when a sound came from behind them. Startled, they turned to see a Biter stumbling across the parking lot of the Tomahawk Motel toward them. It was the park ranger they had seen on their way down the mountain road the day before. The woman with the hiking boots and backpack was several yards behind him, closer to the road.

As the zombie grew nearer, Agnes stepped outside and took the .22 Ruger, which lay in the seat of a chair she had been sitting in. "I'll take care of him."

She extended the pistol at arm's length. When he was no more than twenty feet away, she squeezed the trigger. It only moved halfway and then stopped. The gun was jammed.

"Damn!" Agnes attempted to work the slide, but it wouldn't budge.

Nell looked over her friend's shoulder at the front stoop of the motel, which she had turned into a makeshift kitchen of sorts. Both her Winchester and the Magnum revolver were sitting on the concrete, next to the cook stove… twenty feet away.

The ranger was scarcely three yards from them now, his arms outstretched, his black teeth snapping and gnashing like an angry Pit Bull.

The Biter was nearly on the stoop, when a gunshot rang out. It was crisp and precise—a rifle shot—echoing through the empty streets like a crack of lightning. The left side of the zombie's head imploded, while the right side exploded. Blackened brains and fragments of skull splattered against an overhang post nearby, clinging there for a moment, then slowly dribbling toward the ground. The ranger stumbled forward a couple more steps, then fell flat on his decaying face.

Almost immediately, a second shot rang out and the hiker suffered the same fate. The entire top of her head gave away and a flood of brackish blood and blackened brain matter fell across her face like a curtain. She fell onto her back, the weight of the backpack drawing her down, and, for a moment, she laid there, kicking and struggling, like a turtle on its back. Then the damage caught up with her and she slowly grew still.

Frightened, Nell and Agnes looked up and down the street in front of the Tomahawk Motel. There was no one in sight.

A moment later, Levi and Kate pulled into the parking lot, tires squealing as they braked to a halt.

"What happened?" asked Levi, stepping out of the truck. "We heard shots."

"We had visitors," Agnes told him. "Someone took care of them for us. We didn't see who it was." Her tiny eyes scanned the trees and the hills just beyond. "A sniper, I would say."

Levi looked at his daughter. "Maybe it was our mystery man."

A mischievous grin crossed Kate's freckled face. "Or *woman*."

"Well, whoever it was, they got us out of a jam," Nell told them.

"Maybe in more ways than one," her husband said. "Let me

tell you what we found." He then proceeded to tell them about the Best Western that had been turned into a makeshift prison.

"Sounds like we have a guardian angel watching over us," said Agnes.

"Maybe so," allowed Levi. "But then I get to wondering... how would I react if strangers came into my town and began breaking into stores and stealing stuff? I might not prove to be too accommodating... would you?"

"I reckon we'll see." Nell cast her eyes on the supplies in the back of the pickup. "Now what did you bring us? It's nearly suppertime and I'd like to cook up a nice meal that will stick to our ribs, before we hit the road tomorrow."

CHAPTER 12

Levi woke in the middle of the night, startled, feeling like something was horribly wrong.

He had been keeping watch in front of the motel, alone, and had fallen asleep. Where he had once sat on the edge of the Ford's flatbed, he now lay there, with the twelve-gauge shotgun forgotten beside him. He couldn't believe he had drifted off, but then it had been a busy two days and he reckoned that it had finally caught up to him.

The nagging sense of disorientation and alarm hit him again and he hopped off the flatbed onto the pavement of the motel parking lot. He looked around, searching for something out of the ordinary. He found it a moment later. The door to Room 3 stood partially open.

Quietly, he walked to the room and, taking a flashlight from his hip pocket, directed the beam inside. There were two queen-sized beds. Katie slept on one, while Avery slept on the other. The spot where Jem should have been lying was empty.

Did he go to the bathroom? Levi wondered and then ruled it out. The door of the room wouldn't have been open. The toilet in the bathroom still functioned, so there would have been no need to have gone outside.

Silently, he shut the door and surveyed the street in front of the motel. It was dark and choked with shadow. The sky was cloudy and, if the moon was out, it was completely concealed. Levi walked to the Ram pickup, which was backed into its parking space, its nose pointed toward the road. He opened the driver's side door and turned on the headlights.

It didn't take him long to find Jem. The boy sat beneath a

maple tree across the street, between a gas station and a souvenir shop. His head hung low, nearly to his knees, and he held something in both hands.

It was that *something* that bothered Levi. He walked across the parking lot and stopped at the edge of the road. From there, he clearly saw what the object was. It was one of his brother's .357 Magnums.

"Jem," he said softly. "What are you doing?"

The boy didn't look at his father. "I'm going to do it, Papa... so you won't have to." He lifted the gun, with the muzzle pointed toward his face.

Levi tried to remain calm, but it was hard. "Why would you want to, son?"

Tears bloomed in the sixteen-year-old's eyes. "I can feel them in there, Papa. Moving around... getting ready to set up house."

"It's all in your head, Jem."

The boy laughed humorlessly. "You got that right."

Levi cussed himself for his poor choice of words. "That's not what I meant to say. You just think they're in there. Abe examined you not more than four hours ago and said you were okay."

"Abe was wrong. They're in there, alright."

Levi took a step forward. "Let's get you on back to your room and we'll talk about it. Okay?"

"No," warned Jem. "Stand back." His hands trembled as he brought the barrel of the revolver to his lips. "I ain't gonna let 'em do it, Papa. Not what they did to Sarah. I ain't gonna go after you and Ma, or the rest, crazy as a mad dog and wanting to eat the flesh off your bones."

"Please, Jem..."

The boy cocked the hammer and stuck the muzzle of the Magnum in his mouth. "Goodbye, Papa," he said, his voice garbled. His teeth clicked against the steel of the barrel as he spoke.

Oh God, thought Levi, his heart hammering in his chest. *Don't let him do this.* He opened his mouth to call out to his son, but the words hung uselessly in his throat.

Then, a second before Jem pulled the trigger, a hand snaked out of the darkness beyond the tree trunk and jammed its thumb into the gap between the hammer and the firing pin.

It was a dark-skinned hand, naturally bronze and strong. Above it, a face appeared, round and brown, the hair shiny and coal black, the eyes underneath equally so. There was a grimace of pain as Jem jerked the trigger and the hammer disengaged, digging into the meat between thumb and forefinger. But other than that, there was no expression on the stranger's face.

Levi took a faltering step or two forward, and then stopped as the Cherokee raised his other hand, motioning him to stay put.

Tenderly, the man closed his captured fist around the revolver and pulled it from the boy's grasp. The second the muzzle left his mouth, Jem began to sob uncontrollably.

"Why didn't you leave me alone?" he moaned. "Why didn't you let me die?"

"Because you have nothing to die for," explained the man. Carefully, he eased the hammer off his thumb and laid the gun safely aside. "You are as healthy as I am."

Jem wept as he sagged forward. His face nestled into the shoulder of the Indian's flannel shirt, both relieved and embarrassed.

Levi started slowly across the street, his shotgun hanging at his side. He knew nothing else to say but "Thank you."

The Cherokee nodded. "He is a good man... like you."

"How do you know?" Levi had to ask.

"Because I've watched... and I've seen."

It was Levi's turn to nod. "Yes, I know."

"Let's get him back to bed," said the stranger, lifting the boy to his feet. The man was short, but stout, perhaps in his early thirties.

Together, they led Jem back across the road to the motel.

Nell cast her eyes down the street impatiently as she lifted the lid from an iron pot and checked on the biscuits baking inside. "So, is he coming back or ain't he?"

"He said he would," Levi told her. "Seemed to be a man of his word, so I suppose he'll be here soon."

The Mendlebaums, as well as the Hobbs children, sat at a

redwood picnic table within a little grove of persimmon trees next to the motel office. Jem was there, too, looking tired and worn out, but in better spirits. With his head partially bandaged and an olive drab blanket draped across his shoulders, he resembled a wounded soldier more than a boy who hadn't yet graduated high school... and probably never would.

"Wish I had more to offer," his wife said. "Biscuits and powdered-milk gravy ain't fitting for the man who saved my boy's life."

"I'm sure he'll appreciate anything you fix, sweetheart." The rumbling of a motor sounded in the distance. "There he is now."

They stood on the motel porch and watched as a car appeared, heading into town from the west. It was a silver Mercedes-Benz S65 AMG coupe, not exactly the type of vehicle they were expecting to see.

As the car braked to a halt in front of the motel, Avery couldn't help but hop up from his seat and walk over, grinning from ear to ear. Among other things, the boy was an automotive enthusiast, especially when it involved anything expensive or fast.

They watched as the Cherokee left the driver's side. Levi noticed that he wore a Smith & Wesson .41 Magnum revolver on his hip and had a .30-06 bolt-action rifle slung across his broad back. He walked around to the passenger door and helped a dark-haired woman from the car, a woman who was at least eight months pregnant from the looks of it. Like her husband, she too was full-blooded Cherokee. The third and last occupant of the Mercedes was a small girl of about six years old. She wore a Hello Kitty sweatshirt and blue jeans, and cradled a well-worn American Girl doll in her thin arms.

"Nell, this is Billy Tauchee," Levi introduced clapping the man on the back.

The Cherokee stepped up on the concrete stoop in front of the motel and handed Nell a Blue Bonnet butter bowl with a dozen fresh chicken eggs nestled inside. "I brought a peace offering," he said humbly, "for scaring you ladies with those rifle shots yesterday."

Nell smiled at the eggs as though he had handed her a

bucket full of diamonds. "Oh, these will cook up mighty fine scrambled!" She leaned forward and hugged his neck. "Thank you… and not just for the eggs."

"Yes ma'am." He stepped over and grabbed the hands of the woman and little girl. "This is my wife, Enolia, and my daughter, Jessie."

"Nice meeting you both," welcomed Nell, embracing them as well. "Y'all head over and have a seat at the table. I'll be serving breakfast soon."

"May I help?" offered Enolia, absently sweeping her back-length black hair over her shoulders and tying it with a rubber band. "Please, I insist."

"Glad to have the help," said Nell. "And the company."

As the men and the little girl walked toward the picnic table, Avery looked over his shoulder at the Mercedes. "Is that yours?"

Billy Tauchee couldn't help but smile. "It is now. I found it in the parking lot of the casino with the keys still in the ignition. Probably some old white dude's pride and joy. He drove it a long way just to cut the deck. It has Ohio plates."

"Well, it's a silver peach, is what it is," said Avery with admiration. "Bet it has a big twelve-cylinder beneath the hood and drives like a dream."

"It certainly does," Billy assured him.

When they reached the table, Levi introduced Billy and his daughter. Noticing the little girl's shyness and suspicion, Agnes patted the bench next to her. "You can come over here and sit next to me, if you want, sweetheart."

Jessie was hesitant at first, then finally gave in and sat on the bench between Agnes and Abe, snuggling close to the elderly woman.

Billy sat at the table opposite Jem. He smiled and extended his hand. "Good morning."

Jem reached out and grasped the Indian's hand, clasping it tightly for a long moment. Tears bloomed in the boy's eyes. "Thanks," he said, his voice scarcely a whisper.

Billy simply nodded and said nothing more. No one—other than Levi and Nell—was aware of what had happened beneath the maple tree across the street the night before.

Soon, Nell and Enolia had breakfast on the table: biscuits, milk gravy, and scrambled eggs, courtesy of the Tauchees' laying hens. Before they ate, Levi said grace, feeling that it was appropriate to do so. He glanced up once during the prayer and noticed that Nell was frowning and fiddling with her plastic fork, her head unbowed.

As they ate, Levi decided that it was time to talk. "So, how long have you folks been on your own?"

Billy looked at his wife. A great sadness passed between the two before he spoke. "Since early August. Everything was pretty much business as usual—the tourists were still coming in... vacationing and gambling at the casino. Everyone was concerned about what was going on... the outbreak... but it seemed like it was a million miles away. Then one morning, someone was bitten and it escalated from that point. One after the other, like fallen dominoes."

"But you cleaned up the town... got it under control," Kate said. "Exactly how did you manage that?"

"I decided to contain them," he said. "Get them off the streets and out of harms way. No matter what they've become, they are still our people." He took a sip of bottled water, paused for a moment, then continued. "My uncle had a herd of goats, twenty-nine of them. It took me a couple of nights, but I finally got them all into the Best Western. I started with the fifth floor and worked downward, tethering the goats and nailing their ropes to the floor. I propped the stairwell doors opened and tied some of them to the stair railings. When I was finished, I blocked the exit doors with trucks and went inside to bait the trap. I cut some of their throats, but left most of them alive. Then I went outside, climbed into an abandoned UPS truck, and laid on the horn. They came out of the town and the hills like I'd rang a dinner bell. They totally ignored me... went for the smell of blood instead. They piled through the front entrance, some trampling others underfoot. I could hear them tearing into those poor goats, ripping and eating... roaming around, looking for more. When I was sure they were all inside, I locked the front doors and blocked them with the truck. There was no getting in or coming out."

"Any idea how many are in there?" asked Jem.

"Five hundred and thirty-one. I kept count."

"Where did you get the idea to use the trucks?" asked Avery.

Billy grinned. "From an old zombie movie I saw once."

"And you've kept a handle on it since then?"

"We've had a few Biters wander in, but I bring them down before they get very far. There's a landfill a mile or so out of town. I burn the remains in a pit I dug with a backhoe."

"You are aware of what causes this, don't you?" asked Abe. "What makes them turn into what they are?"

Enolia nodded. "Those black bugs... in their mouth."

"How far along are you, dear?" Agnes asked the woman.

"Thirty-two weeks."

"Is it a boy or a girl?"

"A boy," said Enolia. "Or that's what my grandmother told me a few months ago. She was an ash-reader. She rubbed charcoal ash on my belly and predicted its sex."

"And where is Grandmother now?" asked Nell.

"She died," Billy said uncomfortably. "Twice."

A stretch of silence fell over the table and they ate quietly for a few minutes. Then Levi spoke. "So what are your plans? Just hang around here and pick them off as they come? There will be more, you know... in greater numbers."

"Yes, I know," said Billy. "The buzzards... they grow thicker... from the west and the north. What they follow will overrun us sooner or later."

"It happened to us back in Tennessee," said Levi. "Our only way of surviving was to just pack up and leave."

"That is harder for me." The Cherokee grew introspective. "You know, I've had this dream lately. I back up that UPS truck, unlock the doors, and go inside. And I kill them all, one by one. Put my people out of their misery."

"You know that would be impossible," said Abe. "It would be the death of you. They would eat you alive before you got halfway through the first floor."

The man nodded. "Still, it preys upon my mind. Our reservation was a tight-knit one. Everyone was family. We lived our lives together. It seems fitting that we should die together, too."

His wife reached over and took his hand. "Please, don't talk that way... not in front of Jessie."

Billy raised her hand to his lips and kissed it. "You're right. I'm sorry."

Levi looked around the table. "We discussed it before you got here and we'd like for you to come with us when we leave this morning."

Relief seemed to flood Enolia's face, but Billy seemed wary of the proposition. "Where are you headed?"

"A town called Hendersonville," Agnes explained. "My sister, Angela, lives there. She's an invalid who lives alone and has a home-health nurse who comes in every day from nine to three to look after her. Or she *did*... before all this happened. I talked to her a couple of times when cell service was still up and running... but I haven't spoken to her since mid-August. I have to go and see about her... to see if she is still alive."

Billy looked at Levi. "Not to sound rude, but you are traveling all that way, to find a woman who may already be dead or *worse*... just because this lady asks you to?"

"Agnes and Abe are like family now," Levi told him. "Part of *our* family. Besides, it may sound silly, but we simply don't have anywhere else to go. Hendersonville is as good a place as any."

They could tell that the young Cherokee was wrestling with the idea. "Can you assure me that leaving and taking my family out *there* is any better than us staying put and surviving *here*?"

"At least you'll walk among the living," Abe told him sagely.

"And we sure as hell could use a good rifle shot," chimed in Avery, his usual tactful self.

Billy thought about it for a moment. "I'll need to discuss this with my wife and daughter. Alone."

"By all means," Abe told him.

The three left the picnic table and walked a hundred feet away, to the far end of the persimmon grove. The others watched as they talked quietly. Finally Enolia smiled and embraced her husband. Then Billy knelt and talked to Jessie, face to face. The little girl listened intently and nodded. After that, they returned, hand in hand.

"Alright… we'll go," Billy told them. "When are you heading out?"

"About ten o'clock," said Levi, shaking his hand warmly. "I'm going to leave Enolia and Jessie here with you. I'll head back to our place and load my trunk with supplies."

"I'll go with you," said Avery, grabbing his AR-15. "You never know when a crowd of Biters might show up."

Billy smiled and handed him the keys to the Mercedes. "Want to drive?"

A big coon-ass grin split Avery's face. "Hell, yeah!"

When they had left, Levi pulled Nell to the side. "I've been giving it a lot of thought, and I think we should ditch the big truck."

"How come?"

"It drinks too much diesel and the thing's nearly twenty years old and due for a breakdown. The Ram will do us better. It has an extended cab and the boys can ride in the back seat." He grinned. "Anyway, I miss having you for my riding partner."

"Always the flirt," laughed Nell. She craned up on tippy-toes and gave her husband a kiss on the jaw. "It's fine with me, if you think it's necessary."

"I do. Besides, the confounded thing is loud and smelly. It's apt to draw those zombies out looking for us, where the other vehicles could sneak on past."

"I knew you had another motive," she said, crossing her arms. "One that didn't involve me."

Levi playfully slapped her on the butt. "Let's get moving, woman. We need to get that table cleaned off and our stuff packed, before Billy and Avery get back."

An hour and half later, they were heading out of Cherokee.

"It was a nice place," said Nell, "but sad."

When they reached the western side of town, they slowly drove along the stretch of big hotels. The lofty structure of the Best Western caught their eye.

As they passed, they could hear the banging of fists on windows and the restless moans and growls of Biters yearning to break free. The commotion roused the buzzards from their roosts and they took flight. Soon, a dark cloud of blackness gathered above, circling like the turbulent funnel of a hurricane.

"Those birds won't be getting at them any time soon," Jem said.

"They will if'n they get out," his brother told him. Avery regarded his father. "I reckon we'd best move on, Papa. Those Biters have caught sight and scent of us, and they're getting mighty worked up about it."

Levi knew he was right. He turned his eyes to the road and laid his foot heavy on the gas, carrying them quickly out of range, onto the scenic—and deserted—stretch of Highway 19.

CHAPTER 13

Levi and Avery entered the abandoned house through the back door. It was an old, single-story structure... what the old-timers called a "shotgun house" because one room led directly into another, straight in a row. You could have fired a shotgun through the back door and out the front, while never hitting anything in between.

Late that afternoon, following their exodus from Cherokee, they had come upon a little town called Willow Springs. There was nothing much to it, just a few houses, a church, and a post office. It seemed deserted. There were a few cars, most of them burnt down to the axle for some reason, and the streets were empty. No sign of Biters or survivors could be found.

They had decided to check out some of the houses and take what they needed. While the others searched the other residences along a stretch called Birch Street, Levi and Avery chose the shotgun house.

The moment they stepped through the doorway, it hit them. "Shit!" said Avery. "What's that godawful smell?"

Levi had smelled it before. "Someone has been cooking methamphetamine. Remember when we went hunting a few years ago—I think you were twelve or so—and we came across that shack in the woods? It was deserted, but somebody had been cooking up some awful evil stuff in there. A few days later, the sheriff and his deputies caught the folks responsible and hauled them off to county jail."

"'The devil's pipe tobacco' is what mama calls it." Avery kicked at a contraption lying in the floor—a Pepsi bottle that had been modified into a crack pipe. "Why would folks want to put that stuff inside them?"

"People have their reasons. Sometimes bad, sometimes understandable. Never good."

The two walked across the shadowy kitchen. A 55-gallon drum sat in the middle of the floor with a grate from a charcoal grill lying across its mouth... a makeshift wood-burning stove. On the grate were several pots half full of noxious contents. Scattered on the floor were empty packages that had provided fodder for the drug: ammonia, drain cleaner, brake fluid, and sinus medicine.

"Don't breathe in too deeply," Levi warned him. "It'll mess with your head."

"Let's check the other rooms."

Avery stepped through the adjoining doorway into a bedroom. It was equally dark, the windows covered with both blinds and heavy curtains. In the gloom he could see a dresser with a mirror, a chest of drawers, and a queen-sized bed with the linens stripped off, exposing the bare mattress. There was a different kind of smell in this room—the stench of sweat, semen, and the musky odor of unwashed privates. The odor of reckless sex.

"Stinks like a whorehouse," said Avery.

Levi cocked an eye at his son. "You're probably right... although I know good and well that's a smell you've never come across before."

They were halfway through the bedroom and heading for the door that led to the living room, when Levi heard a scuffling sound behind him. Before he could turn, something struck him hard in the back of the head. With a groan, Levi dropped his revolver and hit the floor, face-first.

A shrill shriek cut through the air and something wild and lanky launched itself from a closet to Avery's left. At first, he was sure that it was a bobcat, like the one they had encountered on the park road. But as it came at him, he saw it was a woman, dirty and emaciated. Her brown hair was chaotic and uncombed, and her skin was dimpled with raw lesions that looked as though they had been picked or clawed at.

Avery was slow at reacting. He attempted to lift the AR-15 into line, but was too late. The heel of the woman's hand struck him hard just below his left eye and pinpoints of white light danced before him. He stumbled backward, feeling the assault rifle and its sling being slipped over his shoulder. The edge of the bed hit the backs of his calves and he went down on his back, the springs of the mattress jouncing beneath his weight. Then there was weight from above, as the woman jumped on top of him. Straddling his hips, she shucked the brace of revolvers from their holsters and flung them away, out of reach.

"Get off of me!" he growled. Avery tried to dislodge her, but her bony knees were in his sides, clamping, holding on. He reached for the haft of his machete, but a thin line of pain crossed the back of his hand and he drew it away quickly.

"Un-uh," warned the woman above him. She brought a straight razor into view, its blade coated with his blood. "None of that now." With a mostly-toothless grin she brought the razor to her mouth and ran a tongue along the flat, lapping up the red drops that beaded there. "Yum… might get me some more of that later on."

"Who are you?" Avery asked, struggling to get up.

"I was about to ask you the same question." The woman leaned forward and ended his fighting by laying the edge of the shaving razor against the side of his neck, just above the carotid artery. "Now what are you doing poking 'round in here?"

Avery breathed raggedly, trying to clear the stars from his vision. He said nothing in reply… just looked up at the one who straddled him.

"You answer Barbie when she speaks to you!" snapped a deep voice from across the room. Risking injury, Avery turned his head and saw a big, burly man with a bushy blond beard standing there. His right foot was planted firmly on the back of Levi's neck and a .410 shotgun was aimed at his father's head. His skin was also covered with ugly red sores and his teeth were brown and rotten.

"We… we just came a-looking," the boy finally answered.

"Looking?" sneered Barbie. "For what? A taste of what we've got in the kitchen there?" She regarded him and laughed. "Naw, you ain't ever ridden the crystal lightning before." She ran a filthy hand across his face. "You're too soft and pretty.

Ain't picked the meth outta your sores and ate it like we have, have you?"

Avery felt sick to his stomach, like he was about to puke. "No, ma'am."

"A polite boy, too." She pressed the edge of the razor against his flesh, nicking him, drawing blood. "I don't cotton to that much. I like my men piledriver rough." The woman began to work her narrow hips, rocking back and forth. "Can you be that rough, boy?"

"Don't do that," said Avery. He felt himself respond, in spite of his disgust. After all, he was a sixteen-year-old.

"Why not?" Barbie leaned down and hissed into his ear. She ran a hot tongue along his clenched lips, attempting to gain entrance. "Be a helluva way to die, wouldn't it? Come and go at the same time?" Giggling, she shucked off her tank top. Lank breasts swayed and dangled in his face, pock-marked with weeping sores, the nipples dark and shriveled like prunes.

As he felt her tug at the front of his jeans, Avery's head began to swim. *Oh God,* he thought. *I'm going to pass out.*

Then a woman's voice came from the doorway at the front of the house. "Get off of him."

Barbie looked up to see her standing there, pale and skinny, with freckles and red hair. "When I'm finished, bitch. Then you can have your turn." She jammed one of her hands into the boy's underwear. Avery shuddered at the touch of her cold fingers. It was like being molested by a corpse.

Kate lifted one of her Glocks and thumbed back the hammer. "I said, get off of my brother."

The woman frowned at her impatiently. "Mick... shoot her, will you?"

The bearded man grunted and lifted the muzzle of the .410 from the back of Levi's head, swinging it toward the door.

"Damn," said Kate. She snapped off a single shot. A hole the size of a dime appeared two inches above the bridge of Mick's nose, followed by a hole the size of a half-dollar at the rear of his skull as the bullet flattened and punched through. His foot slipped off Levi's neck and he crashed onto his back in the kitchen.

"Mick?" wailed Barbie, crawling off of Avery. "Mick!" She stood up on the mattress and turned toward Kate. With crazy eyes, she lurched across the bed unsteadily, ready to leap.

Kate tucked the Glock into her jacket pocket, lifted the Uzi, and unleashed a rattling burst of 9mm slugs. The bullets tore into Barbie's chest, ripping her limp breasts into bloody shreds. The woman fell onto the bed next to Avery, lurching and gurgling, gouts of crimson shooting from her mouth and nostrils.

The boy rolled off the mattress and hit the floor, struggling to fasten his britches.

Kate walked over and crouched beside him. "Are you okay, bubba?" she asked, placing a hand on his shoulder.

Avery flinched away. "Of course I am!" His eyes were brimming with tears, but he turned his head so she couldn't see. "Just leave me alone. I'm okay."

Suddenly, the back door burst open and Jem and Abe came in. "What's going on?" Abe asked, gun drawn. He crossed over into the bedroom as Jem helped his father to his feet.

"It was a meth-whore and her fella," Avery said, standing up. "We wandered in on their operation and they jumped us."

Jem looked at the dying woman. She still held the straight razor in her fist. "She didn't hurt you, did she?"

Avery shot a warning look at his sister—one that said *don't you dare say anything!* —and then forced a swaggering grin. "Hell no! I had her under control."

"What about you, Papa?"

Levi shook his head. "I've got a whopper of a headache, but I'm alright."

Kate walked over to the bed. The woman twitched and writhed, soaking the ticking of the mattress with blood. The bullet wounds in her lungs sucked noisily as she struggled to breath, blowing frothy bubbles. "I'm sorry," the girl told her.

"Screw you!" gurgled the woman. Venomously, she spat at Kate. The girl sidestepped and dodged a wad of bloody saliva. It struck the bedroom wall, thick and stringy, peppered with bits of lung and crawling black specks.

"Abe," Kate called out. "I believe she's infected."

The elderly man reached through the kitchen doorway,

grabbed a fork off the counter, and walked over to the bed. He wedged the tines between the woman's clenched teeth and pried her mouth open. On the roof of her mouth was a moist black sack, pulsing with life.

"What the shit is *that?*" asked Avery. He scrubbed at his lips with the back of his sleeve, remembering the slick moistness of her tongue against his closed mouth.

"It's an egg sack," explained the doctor. "It's past the larvae stage. She'll be full of the things within two or three hours."

"What should we do with her?" asked Levi. "She'll be dead in a couple of minutes."

"She will be just as dangerous dead than alive," Abe told them. He looked around. "Who's going to do it?"

"I will," volunteered Kate. She reached inside her pocket for the Glock.

"No, sis." Avery retrieved one of the .357 Magnums from the floor. "She's mine." He pressed the muzzle of the revolver against her temple. "Filthy-ass bitch."

The others turned as the boy fired. The hollow-point slug disintegrated the upper part of her head, painting the bedroom wall with bloody brains and fragments of skull.

"Damn," cussed Levi. "A shame, the hell this world has come to." He looked over at Avery, disturbed by what his son had just done, but understanding nonetheless. "Jem, go out to the truck and bring a gas can. We're going to burn this place to the ground."

"Yes, sir." The boy came back in a couple minutes later with a five-gallon container of gasoline.

Avery reached for the gas. "I'll do the honors. It is my specialty, you know."

Jem handed it to him without hesitation. "Go to it, bro."

Avery saturated the body of Barbie and the mattress beneath her, then splashed the floors of the bedroom and kitchen. As he worked, the others left the house and gathered at a safe distance on Birch Street.

He had finished with the gas and was leaving through the back door, when Avery spotted a woman's purse on the kitchen table. He took a billfold that protruded from the top and opened it. The driver's license read Barbara Ann Tucker. A beautiful woman with chestnut-brown hair and clear blue eyes smiled back at him. There were other photos in plastic windows: a wedding shot of her and a handsome man in a tuxedo, the woman happily embracing two small children, and another of her in a nurse's uniform in a hospital corridor with a co-worker making bunny-ears behind her.

Looking at the pictures, Avery began to feel badly about what he had called her before pulling the trigger.

A helluva lot can happen in three months' time, he thought as he took a match from the box in his pocket.

He laid the wallet on the table. Then he stepped through the doorway, pitched the lit match inside, and ran for the street before the meth could blow.

CHAPTER 14

The following day was Sunday.

They rose with the dawn and set off down the highway, leaving the ugliness of the past few days behind. The weather was clear and bright, and the autumn trees were glorified in rustic hues of red, yellow, orange, and gold. The rural countryside rushed past them, untarnished, even more beautiful that it had been months before. The roadway was clear, except for a few wrecked and overturned vehicles, and they came across only a few Biters. They paid them no attention, passing them by and continuing onward. The zombies would stumble after them for a few hundred feet, snapping and snarling angrily, and then eventually lose interest as the scent of gas fumes and living flesh faded from their infested nasal passages.

Once Levi and his band of travelers had looked behind them and, far in the distance, seen a swirling cloud of blackness. Not gathering storm clouds, but eager buzzards circling in flight. Such a flock would have heralded a large number of Biters. It was possible that those imprisoned in the hotel had somehow escaped, but it was unlikely, given how well Billy had kept them contained for as long as he had.

"Do you ever wonder?"

Levi glanced over at his wife. "Wonder about what?"

"What drives them? Makes them move from one direction to another? Seems like they would have some purpose for doing so. Are the buzzards herding them... or is it the other way around? Are they running toward something... or from something?"

Levi shook his head. "Can't say I've given it much thought.

Just staying one step ahead of them is enough for me to ponder on." He knew what his wife was getting at; that was the way the two of them were different. Nell's thoughts leaned toward meanings and purposes... spiritual things... while he mostly dwelt on stone-cold reality and getting by from one day to the next.

He glanced at the swirling darkness in his mirror one last time, but didn't concern himself about it any further. Eight- and twelve-cylinder engines covered more ground than decayed feet and an unbalanced gait. Levi bared on the gas and the others followed. They moved eastward and, slowly, the oppressive cloud fell behind and vanished from their sight.

It wasn't until eleven o'clock that morning that they spotted a second cloud, hovering above the rural town of Woodrow. Its mass and motion were much less severe. Not more than three dozen buzzards soared in the vast blueness overhead. Their progress was slow and lazy, not frantic and hunger-fed, as though they had been there a long time and intended to remain for a while longer.

"What do you think is going on there?" Levi asked Abe when they had stopped for a bathroom break.

"I'm not sure," he replied, polishing the lenses of his spectacles on the front of his shirt. "The buzzards don't seem to be changing position, so it seems that the object of their attention isn't either. It is as though they are simply standing in one spot. Certainly not common behavior for Biters."

They were returning to their vehicles, when they heard a noise in the distance. "What is that?" asked Jem. "A church bell?"

"A dinner bell is more like it," Levi said. "If there are Biters within a mile of that bell, they'll come running... or shuffling or whatever they do."

"Not necessarily," Abe mused. "Not if the bell ringer has no concern whatsoever about a forthcoming attack."

Nell sat in the cab of the pickup truck, staring through the windshield. She had been doing that a lot lately, as if searching for something. No one knew precisely what that was... not even her.

"Let's go see," she told them.

The church on Bailey Street in Woodrow was a traditional one—immaculately white with high-peaked, stained-glass windows and a tall steeple with a cross at its pinnacle. Its bell had stopped tolling fifteen minutes ago and now the building stood there reverent and full of praise... as respectful of the sanctity of the Sabbath as a structure of timber, nails, and shingles could possibly be. Inside, there was praying and singing, old-time hymns like "Bringing in the Sheaves" and "Go Tell It on the Mountain" sung by a gospel choir that was far from the Caucasian persuasion.

When they arrived, they discovered several things. One was that there were cars parked on either side of the street. Not abandoned cars, but working cars. Cadillac coupes and big Buicks, as well as a white church bus with Calvary Hill Baptist Church painted on the side. Secondly, the church was surrounded by a sturdy chain-link fence a good eight feet high with curled razor-wire on the top. And, third, there was a fifty-by-one-hundred-foot compound constructed of steel poles, concrete, and chain fencing located directly to the left of the church building... a compound full of Biters, perhaps two hundred or so.

When they parked on the street out front, they saw that the double gate in front of the church was guarded by a large black man, as bald as a cue ball and as big in the chest and shoulders as an NFL linebacker. He was dressed in a dark gray fedora, gray pin-striped suit, white shirt, and red tie. He also held an old-fashioned Tommy gun in his dark hands, complete with wooden stock and barrel magazine. He looked like a gangster from the 1930s... if Al Capone had been an equal-opportunity employer.

Levi ducked his head and looked out the top half of the windshield. The buzzards continued to drift slowly overhead, while a dozen more perched on the top edges of the zombie compound. They would have been inside, picking at the decayed flesh of its occupants, if there hadn't been a lid of chain-link stretched tautly across the top, providing a barrier between the two.

"Well, we know what's going on," he told his wife, "although I can't figure out why. What now?"

Nell stared at the front of the church for a long moment. "I want to go in."

"Are you sure? Who knows if King Kong there will even let you cross the street."

She laid her hand on the door handle. "He's a church-going man. He isn't going to shoot me."

"Want me to go with you? Or maybe Kate?"

"No," she simply said, her face tense. "This is something I need to do alone."

Levi reached out and touched her shoulder. "Then give me a kiss before you go." She leaned toward him and their lips joined for an instant. "Are you okay?"

"I hope to be." Then she was out of the truck and crossing the two-lane street.

Halfway there, Nell raised a friendly hand. "Howdy."

The man regarded her appraisingly, then smiled. "Good morning, ma'am."

"Mighty pretty church you've got here."

The smile broadened. "We're right proud of it. Can I help you?"

"I know I'm not exactly dressed for the occasion..." She looked down at her clothing: jeans, a flannel blouse, and a denim jacket. "...but would you mind if I come in for a few minutes?"

"The Lord's house is always open for business," the big man replied. He cocked his head slightly to the side. "Is that what you have... business to take care of?"

Nell's heart pounded in her chest. "Yes, sir. Most definitely."

He nodded toward the three vehicles. "What about them?"

"They're sitting this one out," she told him. "It's me who needs to get a few things off her chest."

He chuckled and took a ring of keys from his pants pocket. "Then come on in and make yourself to home."

As he unlocked the big padlock that held the gates together, Nell looked up at him. "What's your name?"

"Tyrone, ma'am. Tyrone Jackson. Or Big T to my friends."

As the gate swung open, giving access to the sidewalk beyond, Nell reached out and took his hand. It was like David shaking hands with Goliath. "Thank you, Big T."

She didn't think his smile could have grown any larger, but it did. "Yes, ma'am."

Nell made her way up the sidewalk and the concrete steps nestled between tall, white columns. She hesitated before the big oak doors for a moment, and then glanced back. Levi sat in the truck across the street, giving her a big thumb's up. She smiled at him, took a deep breath, and stepped inside.

She passed through a foyer and entered the sanctuary. The singing had ended and now the sermon was in progress. The church pews weren't as full as she had expected. There were maybe eighty people scattered among oaken pews that normally held four hundred. The men were decked out in suits and shiny patent-leather shoes, while the women wore pastel dresses and matching hats. The preacher was short and lanky and loud, sporting a salt-and-pepper beard and horn-rimmed glasses. His voice—which seemed like it should have belonged to Big T instead of this bantam rooster—rebounded off the walls with a combination of authority, righteous fury, and a genuine love and respect for his Maker.

Nell found an unobtrusive spot on a back pew and sat there, hoping no one would notice. No one did. The audience was captivated by the pastor. His voice was first passive, then thunderous; his fist pounded upon the pulpit, both to drive his message home and awaken anyone who might have dozed off during his recitation of the Gospel.

He preached for half an hour, gave the invitation, and then dismissed the service. As he stood at a door near the back of the sanctuary and shook hands with the congregation, Nell stood up. She took a deep breath and then slowly walked up the aisle to the altar. She stared at the wooden cross behind the pulpit, draped with purple linen in semblance of Christ's crucifixion. Then she slowly sank to her knees.

She remained there for several minutes, weeping, praying, cursing, pounding the risers of the altar with her small fists. All that had been bottled up inside her for the last few months came pouring out in a bittersweet mixture of sorrow, confusion, elation, and rage. When her tide of emotion finally subsided and she crouched, spent, before the cross, she felt strong hands cradle her shoulders firmly, yet lovingly.

"You feel better now?" asked a deep voice like thunder in a barrel.

She turned her head to find the pastor kneeling with her. He beamed a toothy smile, but there was concern in his magnified eyes. "I'm not sure," she said honestly. "I feel like I could give it another round, if I got my second wind."

The preacher threw back his head and laughed. "Well, if you feel the Spirit move you to do so, then you go right ahead. And, to tell the truth, I might just join you."

Together, they rose and sat on the front pew. The lanky black man extended his hand. "My name's Reginald P. Dandridge. But you can call me Reverend Reggie. And you are?"

"Nell Hobbs from Tennessee."

The preacher nodded, impressed. "Quite a ways from home. Are you by yourself, Ms. Hobbs?"

"No, my family is outside and some others we're traveling with." She looked at the cross behind the pulpit. "They wanted to give me some space... knew I had to come in here and try to sort things out."

"You're a woman of faith then?"

"I have been for forty-three years, since I was baptized when I was nine," she told him. "But I'm not so sure now. My faith has been mighty lacking lately."

"So, you're angry with God? About what's going on in the world?"

Nell nodded. "Yes! Why has He done this, Reverend? Set this plague upon us... these *parasites*? I've seen awful things take place in the past couple of months. Friends and neighbors turned into these walking, eating things, neither dead nor alive. And my family has changed, too, and not for the better. My children have lost their innocence. They're killing folks... both zombie and those who are still alive. My daughter... my sweet little girl who once made mud pies and played with dolls... can shoot a man betwixt the eyes without a second thought. My husband lost his family home... had to blow it up because Biters had overtaken it. There's no longer any good in the world, no hope. It's dragged my spirits—and my trust in the Lord—down to rock bottom."

The pastor scratched his wooly beard. "Maybe God has a reason for doing this. Maybe he's weeding out all the sinners... or maybe just all the stupid people. His ways are known only to Him sometimes and are beyond our comprehension. We have a tendency to blame Him whenever something goes wrong and praise him when everything is sunny skies and rainbows. And what's happening now is as wrong as it can get."

"Yes, I understand," she said, the lines on her face easing a bit. "Or I don't understand, but I accept. It's just so hard to see something as tiny as a speck of dust turn our lives inside out. And it's hard to see my family transform into something they weren't before."

"I know that feeling well," the preacher said, his bright eyes growing dim with hurt. "All too well."

Nell began to stand. "Well, I'd best be getting out to the others. I thank you for talking with me."

Reverend Reggie took her hands in both of his. "Now don't go running off just yet! We're having a big meal in the fellowship hall... a lot of good food you folks probably haven't had in a while. And it's safe food, too, not tainted by those confounded black bugs. Please, stay awhile and break bread with us."

Nell thought about it. "Well, a hot, home-cooked meal would certainly be a blessing, and some fellowship with good, God-fearing folks would be one, too. I'll go out and fetch the others."

"Good!" said the preacher with a smile. "I'll prepare a table for y'all. And I'll send someone to relieve the man at the gate. Just tell him..."

"Big T?"

Reverend Reggie laughed. "Yes! Tell Big T to come on in and join us."

Nell Hobbs walked down the center aisle of the sanctuary and through the big double doors. The autumn sunshine hit her face and she smiled. Not everything had been settled between her and her Lord that Sunday morning, but she felt on steadier ground spiritually and ready to face adversity once again.

As Levi and Abe sat at a table and ate with Reverend Reggie, they looked out the broad, plate-glass window of the fellowship hall. The fenced-in compound stood a hundred feet from the church. The area looked to have once been a picnic area, with redwood tables and benches and a metal swing set for the kids. Inside the compound, Biters, both black and white, wandered aimlessly. Some stood with their faces plastered against the chain-link fence, gnawing at the metal strands, while others sat dumbly at the picnic tables, glaring at one another. A little girl sat on one of the swings, feet dangling, black teeth grinding. Her toe bones poked through the flesh and cut furrows in the earth as she slowly swung back and forth. Several ugly bites had been taken out of her arms and legs. They wondered if a Biter had done that to her… or she had done it to herself.

"What's the deal here, Reverend?" Levi asked him. "Why are they out there?"

The pastor shook his head. "To tell the truth, I don't really know. We've been praying over them, like we used to pray over the sick and dying. Maybe we're just hoping that the Lord will place His healing hand upon them and turn them back the way they were."

"You know that isn't going to happen, don't you?" asked Abe flatly. "This has nothing to do with God. It is the parasites that are causing this hellish outbreak. God has no hand in it."

Reverend Reggie's eyes were challenging behind his glasses. "God has a hand in *everything.*"

"We could argue theology all day and it would get us nowhere," Levi told them. He looked back at the preacher. "Why don't you just do the merciful thing? Put a bullet in their head and end it for them?"

A sad look crossed the reverend's face. "That would be a difficult and sorrowful thing for us to do. We grew up with a lot of those folks out there. Loved and respected them. You see that woman out there in the purple dress?"

They picked out the one he was referring to—a small, elderly black woman with snow white hair, dressed in a bloodstained lavender dress with matching flats. A white pillbox hat deco-rated with a lavender rose sat askew on her head, held in place with bobby pins.

"That lady out there was my third-grade teacher in school,"

he explained. "Took a sassy, troubled little boy from a bad home—alcoholic mother, deadbeat father—and showed him what it was like to love and respect someone. Spent extra time with me and set my grades and my life on track. If it hadn't been for her, I'd likely have ended up in prison or homeless on the streets. Instead, she molded me into the man I am now." Tears bloomed in his eyes. "I can't just put a bullet in her brain and believe that all those tender and sweet mercies she did on my behalf never took place. She's out there and I'm in here, and that's how it'll remain… until God gives me the courage to return the favor."

"What about all those buzzards? How can you stand them hovering around all the time? Why don't you shoot or poison them?"

"They're God's creatures," he told them. "They're just doing what He programmed them to do."

They turned their eyes away from the compound and didn't look at it for the remainder of their meal.

"Are there any others here in town?" Levi asked curiously. "Other than these folks?"

"There are a few," the reverend told him. "But they aren't nearly as neighborly. They cling to the shadows and come out… creeping around, doing things no man ought to be allowed to do. Raping, murdering, and feeding off children. I suppose that's what happens when there's no law to speak of. You folks take care out on the road. There's liable to be more folks of that sort around, taking advantage of the current situation. And they may not wait until dark to sow their evil. They could look and act like you and me. You know, wolves in sheep's clothing, that sort of thing."

"Thanks for the advice," said Abe. "We'll certainly take it to heart."

Reverend Reggie picked at his food for a while, as though wrestling with something that was on his mind. "I have a favor to ask of you. I know we've only known each other for less than an hour, but I'm a good judge of character and I can tell you are decent folks. If you don't want to do it, I'll understand. No hard feelings."

"What is it?" Levi asked.

"Would you take Big T with you?"

Levi and Abe looked at one another. "I don't know..." began Levi reluctantly.

"Just hear me out and then decide. Something's been preying heavily on Big T's mind lately. His parents live outside of Asheville and he has no idea what's become of them. He has it in his head to go looking for them, but I worry about him being out there on his own. Tyrone's a good man, but he's naive. Tends to want to trust *everybody*. If someone held a knife to his throat, he's likely to think they were giving him a free shave, instead of about to slaughter him. If he's going to go, he needs folks around to look out for him... *good* folks. He's strong as a bull and good with guns. And he's as loyal and tenacious as a bulldog. He'd be an asset in a fight, that's for sure."

"Where did he get that Thompson machine gun?" asked Levi.

The preacher laughed. "Believe it or not, *I* gave it to him. It was my grandfather's. He was a moonshiner back during Prohibition. My grandmother told me once that he stole it out of the back of an FBI man's car while he was traipsing through the woods, looking for him. I don't have much from my mother's side of the family, but I did get that Tommy gun."

"I'll have to talk to Nell and the rest about it," Levi told him. "And, if he did go, it'd be a while before we made it to Asheville. I promised Abe and his wife a while back that we would be going to Hendersonville to check on Agnes' sister, so that's our main priority. Anything else comes afterward."

"I understand... and I'm sure Big T will, too." Reggie looked over at where the big man sat between Nell and Kate, laughing and digging into a plate piled six inches high with food. "I would hate for him to get a wild hair and head out on his own one morning... and we find him later on, crucified on some telephone pole a mile or so down the road."

"If I know Nell, she'll say yes," Levi told him, taking a swig of sweet tea from a red disposable cup. "Looks like she's taken a shine to him already. Kate, too. If it comes down to it, he could ride in the bed of the pickup. He'd be out in the open in case of a

Biter attack, but that machine gun ought to even the odds right nicely."

"Just lay it on the table and let them decide," the preacher told him. "You'd be doing him a huge favor and it would give this old preacher man some much-needed peace of mind."

As Levi finished his lunch, we considered Big T and what he could bring to the group. The way it was shaping up, he would end up with a small army rather than a band of travelers. And if things were as bad as Reverend Reggie suggested, they just might end up needing one.

CHAPTER 15

It was 5:30 in the evening and the shadows of dusk were gathering thickly around them when they saw headlights approaching from ahead.

Levi watched as they slowly made their way around a broad curve about a mile and a half away. There were a lot of them, perhaps fifteen or twenty vehicles.

"I don't like the looks of that," Nell told him.

"Me either," he agreed.

Someone rapped on the rear window of the Ram's cab and Jem slid it open. "Mr. Hobbs?" came Big T's voice from the bed of the truck.

"Yeah?"

"See that turn-off up ahead? Cut your lights and ease on down in there."

Levi didn't argue. He did as Big T said. When Billy and Kate saw what he was doing, they too doused their headlights and followed. Soon they were heading down a steep dirt road that lead into a backwoods hollow.

"Where does this road go?" Avery asked.

"It circles down through the woods and comes back out on the highway five miles farther on," the black man told him. "I figured it was best if we ducked down here and give those fellas the right of way. They've passed through Woodrow a time or two and they're a nasty bunch."

Carefully, they drove to the bottom of the hollow. It was dark in the thick of the woods and it was hard to see where you were going without headlights. As the steep grade leveled off, swinging parallel to the highway above, Levi stopped his truck.

The Mercedes and Yukon eased to a halt behind him. Silently, they sat and watched the caravan of vehicles pass by three hundred yards above them. They couldn't tell much, just that it was several large transport trucks, SUVs, a jeep or two, and about a dozen motorcycles, Harleys more than likely.

"I heard tell that they ambushed a National Guard unit and looted their armory," Big T said from the back window. "Escaped prisoners and such. Not the kind of men you want to tangle with... especially if you have women and children traveling with you."

Listening to Big T, Levi began to think that he wasn't nearly as naïve and blindly trusting as the good reverend believed. When the long procession of vehicles roared past and the sound of them faded toward the west, he started the truck back up and turned on his lights. "We'll come back out onto the highway and drive a little farther. According to Agnes, Hendersonville is only about thirty-five or forty miles from here."

"Not telling you what to do, Mr. Hobbs," Big T interrupted. "But I'd go down this road a mile or two farther and park for the night. These fellas, they roam up and down the highway all night long, looking for trouble, and sleep in the daytime. If we can hide out down here until dawn, I think we'll be okay."

"We've sort of been avoiding the woods lately," Avery told him. "We had a run-in with a zombie bear a few days back."

Big T laughed. "Don't worry. There ain't no bears around these parts."

"These days, a squirrel or a possum can be just as dangerous," Jem told him, pointing to the blackened, earless side of his head.

Big T swallowed dryly, turning his eyes from the ugly wound. "I still think it'd be worth taking the risk. Those men up yonder, they'll gut you like a fish or skin you alive in a heartbeat. And they'd do worse to Miss Nell, Kate, and Miss Enolia."

"Then that's what we'll do," said Levi. He put the Ram into gear and headed slowly down the rutted back road, toward the middle of the forest.

That night, Big T took his turn at keeping watch.

While the others slept in sleeping bags on the leaf-scattered ground or on the seats of the vehicles, he sat on the tailgate of the pickup truck. He held the Tommy gun loosely in his big hands, feeling like he was about to nod off at any moment. He wasn't accustomed to staying up in the middle of the night and it was getting to him. His big head would droop and then he would awaken, startled and disoriented. To tell the truth, sitting out there in the dark woods with no nocturnal light to speak of and no telling what sort of infected critters on the prowl, scared the fool out of him.

He was nodding off for the umpteenth time, when he distinctly heard a rustling noise come from the direction of the Mercedes, like the shuffling of dead leaves. Big T peered toward the expensive car and saw movement in the darkness, heading away from the camp and into the shadows of the woods just beyond.

Quietly, he hopped down off the back of the truck and made his way to the Mercedes. Enolia slept on her side, wrapped in a quilt. The blankets that her daughter had slept in were tangled up. The American Girl doll lay face down, abandoned. The place where Billy had slept was empty as well.

As Big T stepped past the Mercedes and out into the dirt roadway, he heard someone talking quietly, as well as the muffled weeping of a child. *Good Lord,* he thought. *Is that the Indian girl?*

The big man nearly jumped out of his skin when someone laid a hand gently upon his shoulder. He turned to find Levi standing directly behind him.

"What's going on?" he asked him in a whisper.

"I'm not sure. I heard a noise by the car. Checked it out and found the girl and her daddy gone."

Together they grew silent and listened. Someone was talking on the far side of a big oak across the road. It was a man… but not Billy Tauchee.

"You just be quiet and I ain't gonna hurt you," the voice said, half out of breath. "Holler out and I'll cut your throat. Feel that? Sharp ain't it?"

The little girl whimpered, scared half to death.

"Now we're gonna walk up the road a mile or so and I'm gonna flag down some guys and we're gonna make us a trade. You for enough black tar to last me a week or so. They search high and low for sweet stuff like you. It's gonna be like Christmas morning, me showing up with you out of the blue."

Big T took a step forward, but Levi's hand restrained him. The bearded man nodded toward the tree. They watched as a patch of shadow separated from the darkness of the trunk and silently slid around to the opposite side. There was a heap of dead leaves piled around the base of the tree, yet they heard nothing.

"Billy?" Big T asked quietly.

"I think so."

The man's voice came again, low and vile. "Oh, my, ain't you a piece of candy! I'd do you myself, but they like 'em fresh. If I sell 'em spoiled goods, I won't get enough skag to get me through the night."

They could hear the six-year-old thrashing in his grasp, her voice rising. "Mommy! Daddy!"

Her cry was muffled as her abductor clamped the palm of his hand firmly against her lips. "You do that again and I'll cut out your voice box and give it to you for a play-pretty. Understand me? Now come on."

They heard the rustling of leaves as the man began dragging her farther into the woods, apparently intending to put as much distance between the sleeping travelers and himself as possible before trudging up the hollow toward the highway.

Big T's heart pounded wildly in his chest. "I think we need to get her, Mr. Hobbs… right now."

Levi agreed. "Okay. But we'd best be careful, or he'll kill her, sure enough."

The two men were halfway across the road when they heard the girl gasp in surprise.

It was followed by the voice of the stranger. "Here now! Get the hell away from—"

Then came a crack as high and brittle as the report of a gunshot.

Levi and Big T ran across the road and passed the tree. They feared the worse... that perhaps the man had pulled a pistol and fired at either the girl or her father.

Instead, they were surprised to find Billy standing there, tightly embracing his weeping daughter. A few feet away, lay a man—undoubtedly the girl's abductor—as dead as one could possibly be. His lean, filthy body was draped over a fallen log, a kitchen knife still clutched in his right hand. His head was twisted at an awkward and unnatural angle. His face was aimed at the ground behind him, rather than directly ahead.

"What happened?" asked Big T.

"I... I went... to pee... behind the car," sobbed Jessie. Her face was buried tightly against her father's chest. "He came out of the night... and grabbed me."

"Shhhh," whispered Billy softly. "It's over now. You're safe."

Levi walked over and prodded the man's head with the toe of his boot. It swung loosely with no resistance whatsoever. "His neck is broken." He turned and looked at Billy. "Now how did that happen?"

Billy stared back at him, his eyes dark and impassive. "I startled him when I stepped from behind the tree. He tripped and fell... fell hard. Busted his neck on that log." A hint of a grin creased his dark face, but only for an instant. "Damnedest thing I ever saw."

"Yeah," said Levi. "I suppose so."

Big T and Levi watched as Billy led his daughter gently back to camp.

The black man crouched and lifted the dead man's head a few inches with the muzzle of the Tommy gun. The addict's bloodshot eyes were wide and glassy with shock.

"So... do you believe it, Mr. Hobbs? That he just fell down and broke his neck in half like that?"

Levi studied the way the man was laying for a moment. The column of the log was positioned just beneath his shoulder blades... a good ten inches from his neck. "If Billy says it happened that way, then we'd best believe him. We weren't there to see it ourselves, now were we?"

Big T stood up and let the man's head hit the ground with a thud. "No, sir. We weren't." The big man hesitated, a troubled look on his face. "But should we just leave him there? Out in the open like that?"

"Think of what he had in mind for Jessie," Levi said. "I say leave him for the critters to fight over... or the Biters to gnaw on."

Big T nodded grimly. "Amen to that."

Then, together, they walked back across the road, leaving the dead man where he lay.

CHAPTER 16

They reached the city of Hendersonville around ten-thirty in the morning. The place was seemingly deserted—the same as Cherokee—but there were more signs of carnage along the main stretch, from the highway to the middle of town. The blackened hulls of burnt-out cars, as well as vehicles that had suffered devastating crashes and been abandoned, littered the two-lane thoroughfare. Several restaurants and businesses had been set on fire as well. The empty buildings had collapsed on their fire-weakened supports weeks ago and lay in piles of charred wood and steel. A few bodies lay here and there, some burnt to the bone, some simply shot in the head and left there to be picked apart by birds and animals.

Clouds of buzzards were more prevalent in some areas of the city than others, so they deliberately avoided those zones. Kate took the lead in the Yukon as Agnes provided directions to her sister Angela's house in a suburb near Highway 25. When they arrived at North Edenburg Street, they found it deserted, too. The houses looked average, like any other residence in a small, Southern community. A gray house with blue trim sat on the corner where Dundee Street converged with North Edenburg. There was a low, waist-high wall of recent construction around the property, made of mortared concrete blocks with sharp iron spikes set along the top, angled forward. It was a clever idea. Biters weren't good climbers and even if they managed it, the spikes would have impaled them and kept them at bay. The only entrances through the wall were a heavy wooden gate directly in front of the house and a larger one around the side, where the driveway connected with Dundee. It was obvious that someone occupied the gray house—either an individual or a family—but they were wise enough not to show themselves when strangers came around.

On the opposite side of North Edenburg were a modest split-level house, a double-wide trailer, and a small white house with a picket fence and a wilted flower garden out front. It was this house that the Yukon pulled up to. The name on the mailbox read A. TRESSLER.

Levi climbed out of the pickup truck and appraised the sky. It was overcast that day with dark storm clouds rolling in from the southeast. A few buzzards swooped and soared overhead and he saw a dozen or so perched on the limbs of trees up and down the street.

He reached into the truck and took the pump shotgun with him. "Stay put and keep an eye out for Biters," he told Nell, Jem, and Big T. Avery had joined his father on the sidewalk, holding the AR-15. "There are a few buzzards hanging around, so there must be at least one or two Biters in the neighborhood. We'll try to keep as quiet as possible in there, so as not to rile any up within earshot."

Nell held the .357 in her lap. "We'll be okay."

Levi joined Abe and Agnes in front of the house. "Are you folks ready to go in?"

Agnes looked at the house apprehensively. "I suppose so."

"Don't get your hopes up," he told her. "The place looks deserted. She might not even be in there."

The elderly woman looked irritated. "I'm a realist, Levi. I know this is a long shot. This is just something I needed to do, whether it was a wasted effort or not."

"I understand," he said. "No offense meant."

She smiled. "None taken. I'm just a little nervous, I guess… of what I might find."

Kate stood near the front grill of the Yukon. "Papa, do you want me to come with you?"

"Stick around out here, will you?" he suggested. "If you see Biters, give the horn a toot and we'll come out."

His daughter nodded. She laid the Uzi on the hood and took a Glock in each hand. "I'll keep my eyes open."

Together, Levi, Avery, and the Mendlebaums walked past the white picket fence and up the sidewalk to the front porch of Angela Tressler's house. Several of the front windows were broken, showing darkness just beyond the shattered panes, and obscene graffiti had been sprayed upon the outside walls. The door was partially open. Dead leaves had blown across the porch and into the foyer inside. A wheelchair ramp ran along the house's front wall on the right side. It, too, was covered with fallen leaves.

"It doesn't look very promising, dear," Abe told her quietly.

Agnes simply nodded and held the .22 Ruger in both of her liver-spotted hands. Even from outside, they could smell the offensive stench of decay. "Let's go inside."

They found the first few rooms of the house to be empty. The parlor was untouched, still decorated with antiques, comfortable furniture, and copies of *Newsweek* and *Women's Day* on the oval coffee table. A copy of *People* lay among them. The bold headline on the cover read THE WALKING DEAD... FOR REAL! Below it was an out-of-focus photograph of a dozen or so Biters walking down the center of a New York City street.

The odor of rotting flesh grew steadily stronger, nearly overpowering. "Angie's bedroom is at the back of the house," said Agnes. Her voice was small in the gloom.

Together, they started down a narrow hallway. The door to the rear bedroom was partially open.

Abe slid his hand through the crook of his wife's arm. "Agnes..."

She looked at him and nodded. Her eyes were already moist with tears. "I know. I'm ready for it, dear."

The four were halfway down the hallway, when Levi, who took the point, heard a shuffling noise come from the open doorway of a small bathroom. He turned abruptly and found himself face to face with a Biter. It was horribly decomposed and, at first, he couldn't determine whether it was male or female. Then he saw the stained material of a set of designer scrubs—Mickey and Minnie Mouse dressed up like doctor and nurse on the short-sleeved top—as well as a pair of sagging, bloated breasts tenting the material from underneath, and he knew it had once been a rather large and matronly woman.

She came lurching out of the doorway and barreled into Levi with the force of a linebacker. With a yelp of surprise, he hit the opposite wall hard, and slid down the drywall, landing on his ass. The twelve-gauge slipped through his fingers and clattered loudly on the hardwood floor. He looked up and saw her looming above him. Most of her face had rotted off and the lower jaw was missing. The open sockets of her eyes and the dark, blood-ingested crater of her exposed nasal passages and mouth were swarming with black parasites. Her skeletal hands—interlaced with equally-infested muscle and sinew—clawed blindly at the wall, searching for the rich scent of living flesh that emanated from the man beneath her. Her legs—grotesquely swollen, the ankles split open with dark, glistening wounds—straddled him on both sides, preventing him from escaping. Levi attempted to draw his Blackhawk from its holster, but it was nearly impossible from a sitting position.

Avery was at the rear of the procession, so the Mendlebaums were between him and the zombie. "Get out of the way!" he yelled. He lifted the assault rifle to his shoulder, but knew that he couldn't get off a shot without hitting Abe or Agnes.

"Calm down, boy," the old woman told him. Agnes placed the muzzle of the Ruger an inch from the Biter's temple and squeezed off four shots. Gummy, black wads of brain exploded from the opposite side of her weakened skull, splattering the walls and the door at the end of the hall. A glob the size of a dog turd hit Levi in the chest and dribbled down the front of his shirt. He could feel the clot of tissue pulsing and moving through the material, a mini-hive of parasites searching for a new host.

"Get this shit off of me!" Levi cried out, his voice more of a frightened shriek than its usual deep baritone.

Avery struggled past the Mendlebaums in the narrow corridor and kicked the body of the Biter to the side. The toe of his boot punched through the dead woman's side, unleashing a dark gorge of nasty, black fluid. The Biter went down hard, jittered sluggishly for a moment, and then grew still. Almost immediately, Avery and Abe were on their knees, carefully unbuttoning Levi's shirt, attempting to remove it without touching his skin with the creeping clod of infested brain matter. When it was undone, Levi quickly shucked his arms out of the sleeves and cast the shirt on top of the fallen Biter.

Avery looked as pale as a ghost. "Mrs. Agnes, that wasn't your...?"

"No," she told him flatly. "I'd say it was her caregiver, Mrs. Thompson." She turned to the partially-open door at the end of the hallway and stared at it for a long moment.

"Do you want me to check it for you?" Abe asked her, wiping his hands on his pants.

She shook her head. "She's my sister. I'll do it myself."

The men stood and watched as she stepped over the decaying carcass of Mrs. Thompson and walked to the bedroom door. She hesitated, took a deep breath, and opened it.

"Dear?" Abe asked with concern.

Agnes turned. Her face was a mixture of confusion and relief. "It's empty. She isn't here."

They joined her at the doorway and looked in. The bed was a mess. The bedclothes were twisted and half-lying in the floor. Objects from a cherrywood nightstand—a lamp, an alarm clock, several prescription bottles, and a pair of reading glasses—lay scattered across the floor. On the far side of the room, lying against a wall below a window was a flannel nightgown, turned inside out. Between it and the bed was a pair of women's panties, also wadded up and discarded. All four walls were covered with spray-painted graffiti of the vilest kind.

Agnes moaned softly, her eyes troubled. "Oh, dear Lord, what's happened to her?"

"She could've left, couldn't she?" asked Avery. "Just got up and walked out?"

"No. She was an invalid... confined to a wheelchair for years." She entered the room and looked around, even checked the closet. "I don't see her chair anywhere, though."

Abe walked over and put his arm around his wife's stooped shoulders. "Well, at least there's still hope. Someone could have helped her... maybe took her out of here."

Agnes smiled half-heartedly, but her eyes were grim. "Or

she could be crawling down some street, in the same shape that Mrs. Thompson was."

Levi was about to reply, when the sound of a horn blaring— not tooting—came to their ears.

Immediately afterward, there was the crack and boom of gunfire.

Nell sat in the cab of the Dodge Ram with the window rolled down, staring at the front of the little white house.

They had only been inside for a few minutes, but it seemed like an eternity. She was concerned about Agnes and what she might discover inside. It would be devastating to have traveled so far simply to find her sister dead… or worse.

Jem's hand slid across the back of the seat and patted her on the shoulder. "Don't fret none. They'll be out in a second."

She nodded silently, but never took her eyes off the front door. The Colt Python felt heavy in her lap.

Suddenly, a clatter echoed from inside the house. Someone cried out… a man's voice. "Lordy Mercy!" she rasped. "That sounded like Levi!" Nell grappled with the door handle and stepped out. Frightened, she crossed the sidewalk and stood at the picket fence.

Jem was out of the truck and behind her in a flash. "What is it, Mama?"

"I thought I heard your daddy's voice," she said. Her heart pounded in her chest. "Didn't you hear it?"

The boy looked frustrated. He brought his fingertips to the burnt side of his head, but refrained from touching it. "To tell the truth, I can't hear much of anything out of this side anymore."

"I thought I heard something," admitted Big T as he joined them. "Not sure exactly what it was, though."

Then, abruptly, Avery's voice sounded like a bullhorn. *"Get out of the way!"* It was followed by four gunshots in rapid succession.

"I sure heard that!" said Jem. He jumped the fence with no trouble at all. "You stay here."

"The hell I will!" snapped his mother. She stepped through the open gate and, together, the three started up the sidewalk toward the front porch.

They were halfway to the house, when five buzzards perched on the eaves of the roof spread their wings and took flight. The sound of fluttering from several different points drew their attention. They looked around to see more buzzards leaving their vantage points and taking to the sky.

"I think trouble's coming," said Jem.

He was right. Biters began to show up out of nowhere. From behind trees, hedges, and outbuildings they appeared. At first, they seemed confused. They stumbled around, looking for the source of the gunshots. Then Levi's voice shouted from inside the house— *"Get this shit off of me!"*—and they suddenly knew which way to go. Dozens of zombies in various degrees of decay began to make their way to the little white house of Angela Tressler.

Someone began laying heavy on a horn and Nell realized it was Kate reaching through the open window of the Yukon. Her daughter then turned and began firing the two Glocks at approaching Biters with the accuracy and stone nerves of a modern-day Annie Oakley.

Jem and Big T began to fire as well. The quiet autumn air was split wide open by the thunderous boom of her son's Remington shotgun and the rattling roar of the black man's Tommy gun. Biters went down, but when one dropped, two or three seemed to take its place. Soon the entire stretch of North Edenburg Street was swarming with zombies.

A woman in a pink terrycloth housecoat and large curlers in her oily brown hair shambled past the picket fence and started up the sidewalk toward Nell. Half of her face was beautiful, the other half a collage of naked bone and raw meat. Nell lifted the Python in both hands and snapped off a shot. The recoil pulled the barrel sharply to the right and the jacketed hollow-point ripped off the woman's left check and ear. Nell's second shot found its mark, however. The bullet entered an inch above the zombie's right eye and exited in a fist-sized clump of brains and shattered skull.

"Look out, Mama!" yelled Jem.

Nell quickly turned to her right and found herself standing, face to face, with a Biter. It was a good-sized one, too—a tall, heavyset man in a brown UPS uniform. Before she could bring her revolver up, he reached out and grabbed her by the throat. Nell strangled as he lifted her bodily off her feet and regarded her with a skeletal grin that swarmed with tiny black motion. Then he reared his head back, mouth open, preparing to bite her across the face.

Suddenly, Nell heard a brittle *crack* and saw a hole the size of a dime appear in the Biter's temple. A bigger hole appeared in the opposite temple as the projectile tunneled through and exited. As the Biter dropped to his knees and released her throat, Nell stumbled backward, nearly losing her balance. She turned her head and looked across the street. Behind the low wall of concrete blocks, peering between two of the slanted iron spikes, was a boy with shaggy blond hair. He looked to be no more than eight or nine years old. He held a slingshot—one with a black metal frame with yellow rubber tubing—in one hand.

"Good shot, Jake!" someone said. Nell turned her eyes and found that more folks were behind the wall. One was a tall man with long dark hair, eyeglasses, and a mustache and beard. A woman with brown hair stood next to him, while a young man in his early-twenties—the spitting image of his dad, without the facial hair—took position on the other side of his little brother.

Levi, Avery, and the Mendlebaums were out of the house now and making their way down the sidewalk, firing at the tightening knot of zombies, which still seemed to be appearing out of nowhere. In the street, Kate and Billy Tauchee were taking down as many as they could, but it appeared to be a losing battle. There were just too many of them.

"Everybody over here!" called the bearded man. He let loose with a modified AK-47, ripping a trio of Biters into bloody ribbons. "Quick… before those bastards bite a chunk out of your asses!"

Levi, Nell, and the others did as he said. With their heads ducked, they made their way across the crowded stretch of North Edenburg Street. As they dodged the hands and teeth of a dozen hungry zombies, the bearded man and his family picked them off, one at a time. The woman brought the butt of a twelve-gauge shotgun to her shoulder and fired repeatedly, pumping the slide as she swept the barrel from right to left. The boy continued to fell zombies like David dropped the mighty Goliath, while his older brother held a MAC-10 machine pistol in both hands, spraying the advancing Biters and mowing them down like weeds beneath the whirling blade of a lawn mower.

Finally, they made it to the wall and ducked through the open gate. As Nell passed the mailbox, she saw that J. NEWMAN was painted on the side. The last ones in were Billy and his family. The Cherokee ushered Enolia and Jessie through the gate, then whirled on his heels and fired the .30-06. The heavy grain slug took the top of a Biter's head off above the eyebrows, then struck another directly behind it, bringing it down as well.

Levi clapped the bearded man on the shoulder as he passed. "Thanks! We really appreciate it, Mister...?"

"The name's James," he said. The man reached over, traded a handshake and then released another bee swarm of 7.62 mm slugs from the AK-47, mowing down four Biters in one burst. "This is my wife, Glenda, and my two boys, Jamie and Jake."

"Well, we're much obliged to you," Nell told him.

"Y'all go on in the house and make yourselves at home," James suggested. He slung the assault rifle to his side and slammed the gate closed, securing it from the inside with a heavy, iron bolt and a Yale padlock. Glenda and the boys continued firing at the dwindling crowd of Biters, taking down as many as possible. Several of the zombies attempted to scale the short wall and were skewered by the angled spikes. They wiggled and squirmed on the jagged lengths of iron, snapping and snarling angrily. James took a .44 Magnum Auto-Mag from a belt holster and walked from one to the next, delivering shots to their heads. As they slumped, their skulls disintegrated, he took a long painter's extension pole and dislodged them from the spikes. "Like to keep my property neat and tidy," he said with a half-assed grin.

As Avery made his way to the front door, Glenda stopped him. "You'll have to go around to the back door. That one has a couch blocking it."

"Good idea, to barricade the door like that," said the boy.

"No, it was already like that," said little Jake. "Before the zombie apocalypse."

"Is *that* what we have here?" asked Big T.

"Duh!" said the boy, rolling his eyes. "Isn't that what it looks like?"

"Jake!" his mother scolded disapprovingly.

The boy hung his head and pooched his lip. "Sorry, mister."

Big T laughed and tousled his blond hair with a giant hand. "Anyone who can handle a slingshot like that is okay in my book, little buddy."

Soon, they were all heading around the side of the house, past a trampoline and a combination swing set and clubhouse, talking and trading introductions as they went.

In the sky, the cloud of buzzards continued to swoop and soar, growing increasingly heavier and darker as scavengers from adjoining neighborhoods joined them, drawn by the heady stench of raw and lasting death. They watched and waited until the last person entered the Newman residence. Then they slowly descended upon the smorgasbord on North Edenburg Street and, picking and pulling, feasted until their bellies were full.

CHAPTER 17

A very stood at the front window of the Newman house and watched the massive flock of buzzards tear into the bodies that littered the stretch of North Edenburg Street. "Filthy things. Won't hunt for themselves. Always relying on others to do their dirty work... then they swoop in and chow down. Disgusting!"

"You'd better thank your lucky stars for those buzzards," James told him as he thumbed 7.62 mm rounds into a banana clip. "They're like a big red flag. If they show up, you know the Biters are on their way."

Avery nodded. "You're right about that, hoss. But when this storm blows over and the sun comes out, that street's gonna reek after they've filled their bellies and flown off."

"Yeah, it's going to stink like a Texas whorehouse in August."

"James!" snapped Glenda. "We've got company here." She looked around apologetically. "You'll have to excuse my husband. He has a way with words."

The bearded man grinned. "Yeah. Old habits die hard."

Jem stood at a bookcase, perusing the titles. "Did you write these books?" he asked. "*Midnight Rain, The Wicked, Animosity, Ugly as Sin?*"

James nodded. "Yep. I used to write the stuff. Now I live it. Ironic, huh?"

Levi and the others sat around the living room, eating a lunch of tuna fish on saltine crackers that the Newman's had provided. They washed it down with flat Dr Pepper. Levi wore a black t-shirt that James had loaned him. The caption on the front of it read WOLFMAN'S GOT NARDS! with an image of the werewolf from *Monster Squad* just beneath it.

A thunderclap roared overhead and the clouds opened up. Avery watched as the buzzards fed until the downpour grew too heavy. Then they fled to the shelter of nearby trees. There were a dozen or so Biters still roaming around the street. They seemed oblivious to the bad weather. "It's raining, sis," he told Kate, "and I think your window's down."

Kate looked up from where she was busy cleaning everyone's guns. She seemed extremely proficient at it. "Okay... so are you going to run out and roll it up for me?"

"No, ma'am! Not me."

"I guess I'll just have soggy upholstery then," she replied, running a lubed patch through the barrel of Jem's shotgun.

James glanced into the adjoining room. Big T, Jamie, Jake, and Jessie sat on the floor, flipping through old issues of *Fangoria* and *Famous Monsters of Filmland*. He couldn't help but smile. "The boys needed some company. I think they were getting sick and tired of hanging out with mom and dad."

"So, you've been holed up here since the outbreak began?" Abe asked him.

"Yes, sir. When I saw that the shit was about to hit the fan, me and Jamie built that wall around the yard and we gathered up as many supplies around the neighborhood as we could. That's where we found this firepower." He slapped the banana clip into the AR-47. "You'd be surprised what you can find in someone's garage."

A stretch of silence occupied the living room for a long moment. Only the sound of the children's, and Big T's, laughter could be heard. Then Agnes asked a question. "James, Glenda... do you know what happened to my sister?"

Husband and wife looked at one another uncomfortably. "We think Nathan took her."

"Nathan? Who is that?"

"A little pimply-faced prick who lives a couple of blocks over," James told her. "Back when times were normal, he was a first-class geekazoid before this whole zombie thing started. He was harmless, introverted, and more comfortable with his computers and video games than real people. I even signed a couple of books for him. Then his parents and his little sister turned and he changed. Got downright mean and joined up with some guys from his high school who were assholes to begin with. You know, jocks and rednecks. They used to bully him and push him around, but now he's their freaking king. I reckon Neanderthals are drawn to someone with superior brain power when things get tough. They roam around Hendersonville like they're a bunch of gangstas, looting, raping, killing folks, raising all kinds of hell."

Agnes remembered the ugly graffiti and her sister's discarded clothing. "What would they want with Angela?"

James looked at the kids in the next room, then back at the elderly woman, his face grim. "There aren't many women and children around anymore. Miss Angela and Glenda were the last in the neighborhood... and Mrs. Thompson, before she turned. You know how teenaged boys are... how desperate they can be. That's why I keep a close eye on Glenda and the boys." He dropped his eyes, no longer able to look Agnes in the eyes. "I heard them across the street the night before she disappeared. I heard her crying... screaming. I wanted to go to her, but I couldn't risk leaving my family here alone. I couldn't take the chance of Nathan's goons breaking in and taking Glenda and the boys with them. They think I'm a bad-ass, armed to the teeth. But I'm not. I'm just a scared man doing his best to keep his family safe."

Agnes reached over and took his hand. "It's okay. I understand. No need to blame yourself."

Glenda reached over the armchair her husband was sitting in, wrapping her arms around him and kissing him on top of the head. "My fellow is a good man. He's all heart... sometimes to a fault. That's why I love him so much. Every now and then I think he needs a little sense knocked into his head, though. A tree limb almost did that once..."

"...which we won't be going into right now." He smiled and flexed his left hand absently. A network of scars crisscrossed his forearm.

They sat in the living room, listening to the rumble of the storm overhead. Then Agnes spoke. "James... do you think my sister is still alive?"

A pained expression crossed his face. "Knowing Nathan and how cruel he has become… I almost hope that she isn't."

The elderly woman looked toward the couch and the man in the werewolf t-shirt. "Levi, I know I have no right to ask…"

"Yes," he said flatly.

"Yes, *what?*" Nell wanted to know.

"Yes, we'll go and get her." He looked over at James. "How many are there?"

"Besides Nathan, maybe eight… ten at the most."

"Any idea how they're armed?" asked Avery.

"Shotguns and handguns," James said. "Maybe a rifle or two. They looted a gun store in town and Nathan's father was a big hunter."

"Any major artillery?"

"No, if you mean a Tommy gun or an AR-15." He looked at the assault rifle in his hand. "Or an AK-47."

Glenda's face tightened. "James…"

"I have to, baby. Besides, someone has to take them there."

The woman simply nodded and said nothing more.

Levi sighed. "Avery, could you ask Tyrone to join us, please?"

His son left and returned a moment later with the big man. When he saw the grim expressions on their faces, Big T's smile faded. "What's going on?"

"We're going to get Agnes' sister," Levi told him. "I want you with us."

"I'm in," he said without hesitation.

"It won't be Biters. It'll be regular folks… if you can call them that."

"I said I'm in." Big T's expression was as serious as a heart attack.

"James and Avery will go with us," Levi said. "The rest of you will stay here."

"Un-uh," protested Jem. "I'm going with you."

"Me, too," added Abe.

"I need y'all to stay here and protect the womenfolk," Levi explained. "If something should happen and we don't make it back, this Nathan fella and his crew might be coming here."

Enolia, who had sat on the couch quietly, hands folded over

her belly, suddenly spoke up. "I really think Billy should go with you."

"No," her husband said flatly. "I'm staying here."

"But, Billy..." The young woman's tone was insistent.

He silenced her with a warning look. "I'm staying here with you and Jessie."

Avery smirked. "Yeah, just sit this one out and be the baby-sitter. Let us men get the job done."

"That's enough, Avery!" Levi scolded. "Everyone here has a part to play... none more important than the other." He turned to the Cherokee. "Billy, if we don't make it back, I want you to take that rifle and pick that bunch off, one by one, before they even get here. Then take the vehicles and head out. Where to, I don't care. Just find someplace safe."

"I always thought the Biltmore House would make an excellent place to hole up," James said.

"Biltmore?"

"Yeah, you know... the Vanderbilt estate in Asheville. It's a damned fortress. You could hold off zombies forever in that place."

Levi picked up his shotgun and motioned to the men he had picked for their mission. "I reckon we'd best go on and get it over with."

Everyone grew silent as Agnes began to laugh. "Excuse me, but us poor, defenseless womenfolk are going with you," she said sharply. "At least Kate and I are."

"No, ma'am," declared Levi in protest. "That ain't gonna happen."

"Yes, sir, it *will*... and I'll tell you why. We can shoot better than the rest of you put together and that's a fact. So get used to the idea." She turned to her husband and kissed him on the cheek. "Abe, I know you want to play John Wayne, sweetheart, but you already have one cataract and another one on the way. You can't see the sunny side of a barn, let alone hit one with a gunshot. Besides, you need to be with them if they have to make a run for it. You may very well be the most brilliant mind on the face of the earth right now—the last surviving scientist—and you may be able to do something to slow down this outbreak or stop it all together. I know that's a tall order, but I have faith in you."

"But you should stay here with me," he said weakly.

Agnes' mind was set however. "She's my sister. I want to be there when we find her... no matter what condition she is in."

Levi opened his mouth to say something, but Kate intervened. "You know she's right, Papa. We can hold our own if a gunfight breaks out... and then some." She didn't look like she was about to back down either.

Agnes smiled. "Then it's settled."

"I reckon so," replied Levi, although he seemed none too happy about it.

CHAPTER 18

They decided to make their move at five o'clock, as the afternoon faded into evening. The storm had passed and the rain had ended, leaving a crisp coolness in the October air. The buzzards had left the dripping branches of trees and were eating hearty once again, stripping the flesh from the Biters who lay scattered along the stretch of North Edenburg. They were hungry, but not stupid. They concentrated on the arms and legs of the bodies and left the heads and upper torsos with their infestation of parasites alone.

Levi and the others said their good-byes, but tried to keep it light and not like a final farewell, like soldiers heading into a no-win battle. From what James had told them, they would be going up against a gang of high school students armed with handguns and hunting rifles. They were bound to be dangerous, but they had grown up in the suburbs all their lives and would be lacking in experience. Also, Levi's group had the advantage of full-automatic firepower.

As the evening shadows grew long, they headed out. They took the Dodge Ram. Levi, Agnes, and Kate rode in the cab, while Avery, James, and Big T rode in the bed, brandishing their assault rifles.

It didn't take them two minutes to get there. Levi pulled up in front of a large, two-story brick home with a high porch and painted white columns. It looked like the home of someone with money, a doctor or lawyer perhaps.

There were only two in sight—a big, beefy boy about the size of Big T wearing a blue and white letterman jacket and a smaller, lankier one manning a charcoal grill. They were barbequing long strips of meat. Levi wondered where they had gotten it.

When they left the truck and stood in a line along the street, the big boy picked up a twenty-gauge shotgun and walked down the slope of the yard until he was halfway between the house and the road. "What the hell do you want?" he asked, licking his lips nervously. He spotted the Thompson, AR-15, and AK-47, then looked down at the shotgun in his big fists, feeling more than a little inadequate.

"We want to talk to Nathan," Levi told him.

The big boy—Taylor, if the name on his jacket was correct—turned and yelled at the house. "Hey, Nathan! Some folks are out here wanting to see you!"

For a minute or two, nothing happened. Then the front door of the big house opened and six boys filed out, one after another. They were a mixed bag—some clean-cut jock types, while others were of the four-wheel-riding, red Solo cup-toting redneck breed. All were armed, some with revolvers or semi-auto pistols, and some with shotguns and rifles. They descended the steep porch steps, strutting and swaggering with the faux immortality of youth, acting like they were the Wild Bunch or something. The skinny kid at the grill flipped a couple of slabs of meat with a long fork, then closed the lid, picked up a Marlin repeater, and joined them.

The last one to appear in the front door of the house was the one they had come to see. To say that he was unimpressive would have been an understatement. He was small—scarcely five-foot-four and maybe a hundred and twenty pounds soaking wet. He had curly dark hair, horn-rimmed glasses of the expensive variety, and his face was covered with acne. He wore a holstered Smith & Wesson Model 29 on one hip. The big .44 Magnum seemed to weigh him down on one side, causing his right shoulder to slump slightly.

"I'm Nathan," he said arrogantly. "Who the shit are you?"

Agnes stepped forward boldly. "I want my sister back."

Nathan peered through the thick lenses of his glasses and, seeing the family resemblance, smirked. "Well, maybe I will and maybe I won't. Maybe I haven't finished having my fun with the old bitch yet."

"Let us have her, Nathan," James told him flatly.

The boy glared. "Stay out of this, Stephen King. It isn't your fight. This is between me and the lady with the granny glasses."

"We're all together on this," said Levi. "So you're dealing with the six of us."

Nathan laughed. "But I've got nine to your six. You're a little outnumbered."

Big T lifted the barrel of the Tommy gun an inch or so, pointing it at the nerd's chest. "This here evens up the odds just fine."

Nathan's face reddened until his blackheads and blemishes blended in and nearly vanished. His hand began to ease up the side of his leg a bit, aiming for the black neoprene grip of the Magnum revolver.

"I wouldn't do that if I were you," Kate warned him. She held both Glocks in her slender hands, her thumbs resting on the hammers.

"Fine!" Nathan ducked back through the front door and disappeared for a long moment. The boys who stood in the front yard shifted uncomfortably from one foot to the other. Apparently, the amount of firepower—as well as the hardened faces of those who wielded it—scared the teenagers half to death. More than likely, most of them had never fired a weapon before things went south. The situation had them sweating, that was for sure.

Maybe we can do this without anyone getting hurt, Levi thought hopefully. But the bundle of nerves in his stomach told him that things could go either way.

Then Nathan was back. They watched in alarm and disgust as he pushed something through the door and onto the concrete platform of the high porch.

It was Angela Tressler. She was naked and lashed tightly to her wheelchair with copper wire. Her pale, wrinkled body was bruised and beaten, and her white hair was a wiry tangle that nearly obscured her small face. Someone had taken a can of black spray paint and drawn eyes upon her sagging breasts and a pentagram had been carved into the flaccid skin of her belly with a dull knife. Her crotch was raw and inflamed. Dried blood coated the hollow columns of her inner thighs.

"Oh my God," whispered Agnes. She wavered on her feet a bit and then straightened herself. "Angie."

Nathan laughed, his teeth flashing with silver braces. "Here! You can have the ugly, old bitch. She's outlasted her usefulness anyway. Dry as a bone. Gotta use half a tube of KY just to get it in!" And, with that, he gave the wheelchair a shove.

It rolled down the steep steps, bouncing and bucking, until it got halfway. Then one of its wheels caught on a chipped edge of concrete and it flipped. There was a sickening *crunch* as the top of Angie's head struck one of the steps. Then the chair and its occupant tumbled until it landed on its side on the sidewalk below. The elderly woman moaned hoarsely and passed out.

Levi looked over at Agnes. She had bitten her lower lip so deeply that blood welled up and dribbled down her chin. Her eyes, brimming with tears, shifted from her fallen sister to the boy at the top of the steps. Levi watched her hand tightened on the center grip of the compound bow. Calmly, she reached over her shoulder and plucked an arrow from the quiver across her back. She hooked the notched end of the feathered shaft in the bow's nylon cord.

Don't do it, Agnes, he thought, but couldn't bring himself to say it out loud.

Nathan began to laugh uproariously. "What are you gonna do, lady? Shoot me with an *arrow*? You want me to set an apple on my head? Go on! Give it your best shot, you dried-up old cu—"

Agnes cut Nathan's final word in half, releasing the arrow and sending it upward in a well-calculated arch. The four-bladed head split his tongue in half, then sank forcefully through the cartilage of his palate and skewered the rear portion of his brain.

The boy jerked spasmodically, got his hand around the grip of the Smith & Wesson, and managed to yank it from its holster. His twitching fingers pulled the trigger and the gun went off, taking off half of his right foot. Then he pitched forward and tumbled, head over heels, down the steps.

Before Levi could stop her, Agnes discarded her bow, drew her Ruger, and began to run up the sidewalk toward her sister.

"Wait!" he shouted, but she refused to listen. Then, he too, was moving up the sloped yard. The others were right behind him.

Agnes was nearly to her sibling when the football player fired his twenty-gauge. A rifled slug hit the old woman in the abdomen, directly beneath her ribcage. It tore through her stomach, shattered her spinal column, and exited like a bloody tennis ball from the small of her back. She dropped the .22 pistol and folded over as though she were hinged in the middle. She took a couple of faltering steps, then fell protectively across her sister.

The boys in the yard began to fire, but their aim was erratic. Bullets and buckshot either went over their heads or kicked up clods of dirt and grass at their feet. Two of them lost their nerve, tossed down their weapons, and escaped around the side of the house.

Levi and the others returned fire with better accuracy than their opponents. One by one, Nathan's army fell, brought down by single shots or bursts of automatic fire. A .45 slug ripped through the meat of Big T's thigh, but it failed to show him down. With an angry yell, he powered up the grassy slope, firing his Tommy gun in a sweeping arch. By the time they reached the house, six of the nine were dead.

The big jock in the blue and white jacket looked around at his fallen comrades, his eyes wide with fear. "Keep away!" he shouted, waving his shotgun. "Keep the hell away!"

Although the boy had gut-shot Agnes, Levi couldn't bring himself to shoot him. "Just calm down, son. Let's talk about…"

Whether by accident or on purpose, the twenty-gauge went off in the jock's hand. A slug hit Levi in the side, spinning him around and causing him to fall into a blanket of autumn leaves. A burning pain lanced through him from front to back. Stunned, he placed his hand against his side. The palm came away coated with blood.

"Papa!" screamed Kate. She raised her Glocks and fired. Three holes stitched across the jock's forehead, causing him to look dazed and stagger backward. A burst from Avery's AR-15 lifted the teenager off his feet, from groin to throat. He fell on his back, sputtered and lurched for a long moment, then grew motionless.

When his son and daughter approached him, Levi waved them off. "I'm okay. It went right through. See to Agnes and her sister."

James and Big T were already there. "They're both in bad shape," James told them. "Miss Angie has a skull fracture or worse and Miss Agnes... well, the guy nearly cut her in half. Glenda's a nurse. We need to get back and let her take a look at them."

"Then let's get them in the truck and head out." Levi looked at the bodies of the boys strewn on the grass around them. "Damn! This shouldn't have happened."

"They were a bunch of shitheads and assholes," James said. "Anybody who would use someone like they did Miss Angie deserves what they got."

As they helped their father to his feet, Kate's eyes widened with horror and concern. "Papa, you're bleeding badly!"

"It just went through a love handle, darling," he assured her. "Your mama just won't be able to hang on when we do the bedroom boogie for a while."

His daughter looked even more horrified. "Ewwww! That's gross, Papa!"

As they helped him to the cab of the pickup truck, Big T tenderly carried Agnes and placed her in the bed of the vehicle. The old woman moaned, her eyes bright with agony. She reached up and touched his face. "Tell Abe... that I love him."

"You can be doing that yourself, Miss Agnes," he told her, his voice cracking. "I gotta get your sister and we'll be going."

When Big T got back, James was trying to release the elderly woman from her wheelchair. "This wire is so tight, it's cut into her wrists, right down to the bone. I have a pair of cutters, but they're at home."

With little effort at all, Big T picked up Agnes Tressler, wheelchair and all. As they started for the truck, James was shocked to see that the big man's pants leg was drenched in blood. "Brother! You've got a hole in your leg!"

"It ain't nothing," he told him. "We gotta get these folks some help."

"And a little for yourself, too." James looked overhead and found a cloud of buzzards circling eagerly overhead. "Looks like the clean-up crew is here."

They climbed into the bed of the truck with the two injured women, then James knocked on the back window of the cab. "Let's go!"

With Avery at the wheel, they swiftly left the house of Nathan Childress and headed back to North Edenburg Street.

A few minutes later, Jamie was opening the big gate at the back of the Newman property. Avery floored the gas and brought the truck in. He stopped, then slammed it in reverse and backed up to the rear door of the house.

"What happened?' asked Jake. "It sounded like a war over there."

"It was," his father told him as he hopped out of the back. "A short one."

"Are they...?"

"Yes, son. They won't be bothering us anymore." James looked toward the door and saw Glenda standing there. "We've got some hurt people, baby."

"I've already set up triage in the kitchen," she told him. "In case, it turned bad."

"It did," he told her, as he dropped the tailgate. "We've got a couple who probably won't make it."

Glenda turned to her oldest son. "Jamie, take Jake and Jessie to your room and keep them there for a while. I don't want them to see this."

Jamie nodded solemnly. "Okay, Mom."

Billy and Jem came out and helped them bring the wounded inside. After James found the wire cutters, they liberated Angela from the wheelchair she was secured to. When they laid Agnes and her sister across the kitchen table, Abe watched from the far side of the room. His face was pale and his eyes brimmed with tears. "Oh God... what happened?"

Levi grimaced with pain as he sat stiffly in a kitchen chair. Nell crouched beside him, holding a dish towel to the hole in his side. "She found her sister," he told him. "That kid, Nathan, dumped Angie down the steps and all hell broke loose. Agnes brought him down with an arrow and then some stupid jock put a shotgun slug through her belly."

Abe walked across the room as though he was in a daze. He stood beside his wife and gently stroked her forehead. It was cool to the touch. "Stubborn old woman," he said and began to cry.

She reached out and felt around until she located her sister's hand, limp and unresponsive. "I did what I came to do, Abe."

"Yes, you always do. But this time you've gotten yourself killed."

She shrugged her slumped shoulders. Even that small movement seemed to be an agonizing one. "I got her back. That's all that matters."

Abe looked up at James. "Will she survive?"

James looked at his wife. Glenda's eyes were grim as she shook her head. Then she moved across the kitchen to examine Levi and Big T.

Both men's injuries would have been potentially life-threatening if the projectiles hadn't gone completely through muscle and tissue and out the back. "No internal organ's hit," she told Levi after examining the hole in his side. "Pretty much just skewered your love handle and nothing else."

Levi winked at his daughter. "See, I told you."

"I'll clean and stitch it up with a needle and thread, and put you on some antibiotics and you ought to be fine." She then moved to Big T. He had already taken his hunting knife and sliced his britches leg open from ankle to crotch. Glenda examined the wound and whistled. "You're lucky. An inch to the right or left and it would've either hit your femoral artery or shattered your femur. We'll fix you up, but it's going to hurt like hell. We have a pair of crutches out in the garage that you can use. James hobbled around on them after he got hit by that..."

"Freaking tree limb!" the writer exclaimed, throwing up his hands. "I can't get rid of the thing. It follows me around like a love-sick puppy!"

A low moan drew their attention and Glenda hurried back to the kitchen table. Angie Tressler was coming around. She stared blindly through her cataracts. "Hello?" she gasped. "Who's there?"

Agnes slowly squeezed her hand.

The elderly woman smiled slightly. "Agnes?"

"I'm here, sis," she replied. Her voice was low, scarcely a whisper.

"You came looking for me?"

Agnes nodded. "I did. And I found you."

A violent spasm of coughing shook Angie's frail body. "I'm going, sister. I'm sorry we didn't have more time to visit."

"Oh, we will." Agnes smiled, "Because I'm going with you."

Angie squeezed her sister's hand so tightly it made her bones creak. Then a rattling breath escaped her lips and she was gone.

Agnes stared up at her husband with weak eyes. "Abe?"

"I'm here, dear," he said. Tears coursed down his face and settled in the whiskers of his beard like dew.

She reached up with her free hand and drew his head toward her. "Give me a kiss, will you?"

"You're... not... going... *anywhere!*" he cried, sounding like a petulant child. His tears changed their trajectory and dripped across her pale face.

"I hope to hell it's raining," she said, "because if you're crying, I'll get up off this table and thrash your wrinkled ass." She drew his head down until their lips met for a long moment. When he pulled away, she patted his cheek. "I hindered you back in Oak Ridge. You were so worried about protecting me, that you couldn't get any work done. Now you can go back to doing what you do best... finding solutions. Make me proud. Save the world."

"That's a tall order, woman," he told her quietly.

"You've been filling them for me for forty-eight years." She coughed raggedly. A frothy gorge of blood and torn tissue passed her lips. It slid down her cheeks, pooling on the tabletop around her head. Glenda mopped it away with a wad of paper towels. "At least try. It'll give you something to do until you see me again."

Then Agnes' fingers loosened and her eyes grew glassy and unseeing.

Abe's head dropped until his forehead rested on the edge of the table top and he expelled grief in great, heaving sobs. Kate embraced him from behind and laid her head on his shoulder, crying along with him.

"Honey, could you get my sewing box out of the bedroom?" Glenda asked her husband. "I have work to do."

With a nod, James left to get the "sewing box" that Glenda had liberated from her job at the hospital the last day she had punched the clock. The multi-compartment EM case was filled with surgical instruments, nylon sutures, curved needles, antiseptic solutions, painkillers, and every type of antibiotic imaginable.

The others grew silent and sullenly looked away. Tears were shed and hearts broke.

Death had claimed family that evening.

CHAPTER 19

A cool breeze swept across the expanse of Oakdale Cemetery, sending autumn leaves skittering across the grass and plastering them against the granite and marble stones that stood, like solemn sentinels, across its tranquil acreage. On the far side of the graveyard, Henderson Elementary and Henderson Middle School stood, while, strangely enough, Highway 64 cut directly through the middle of the burial ground. Needless to say, what was once a busy stretch of road occupied by cars and school buses was now utterly deserted.

Avery, Jem, James, and Billy took turns digging two holes, side by side, in a plot of earth beneath a shady oak tree—Agnes and Angela's final resting place. The twin sisters would have wanted it no other way—together in death, as well as in birth.

Levi and Big T sat nearby, aching to get hold of a shovel and pitch in, but the severity of their wounds prevented them from taking part in the ritual. Nell, Kate, and Glenda stood several yards away, quietly and respectfully watching. Standing with them was Abe Mendlebaum. The elderly man looked small and ancient in a black suit they had found in one of the abandoned houses along North Edenburg Street. He held a bouquet of plastic flowers they had taken from a Dollar General store before their ten-minute trip to the graveyard. Enolia sat cross-legged on the ground with her daughter beside her, chanting a "song of passage"—as Billy described it—in their native tongue of the Cherokee language.

Only a few Biters roamed among the stones of the cemetery, looking like the opening scene of *Night of the Living Dead*. Jamie and Jake took turns with the slingshot, bringing the zombies down with well-placed headshots if they wandered too close or got a whiff of fresh meat. The sound of ball bearings penetrating their skulls was no louder than someone popping the top on a Coke can—effective, but quiet enough not to draw the attention of other Biters.

After the excavation was finished, the bodies of the two women, wrapped in patchwork quilts, were laid in their individual graves. Words and prayers were said over them. Then their remains were covered over in earth, their bodies hidden, but their memories painfully present among the fourteen mourners.

Abe crouched and stuck the wire ends of the plastic bouquet in the fresh soil of his wife's grave. He spoke quietly—too quietly for the others to hear—then got up wearily, as though all the strength and spirit had drained from him. Abe walked over to Levi, who shook his hand.

"You sure you won't come with us?" he asked the elderly scientist.

"I can't leave her," Abe told him. "Not yet. I love you and your family, but Agnes *was* my family. The only family I had left."

"I know it's hard. But remember what she told you... what she wanted you to do."

Abe nodded. "I will. It's the only thing that will make me want to get out of bed in the morning."

The two looked over at Agnes' grave. Avery stood there, head lowered, staring at the rectangular patch of earth as though trying to read something there. He held the compound bow in one hand and wore the arrow quiver slung over one shoulder. "My boy is taking it hard. He thought a lot of her."

Abe smiled sadly. "Agnes was teaching him how to shoot the bow. He was a damn good pupil, too. He could pretty much hit the target as well as she could."

Guilt creased Levi's face. "I'm sorry that I couldn't have done something... you know, to have prevented..."

The old man clamped a reassuring hand on his shoulder. "It was her doing and hers alone. She was determined to get her sister back and she accomplished her objective... even though the outcome turned tragic."

Abe went from one to the other, saying his goodbyes. Then he joined Glenda and, together, they walked toward her Kia Spectra.

Levi walked over to James and shook his hand. "Thanks for everything, hoss." He motioned toward his side. "Sorry I ruined your t-shirt."

James smiled. "It wasn't a silver bullet, so the Wolfman survived. Besides, if the ill-fated jock had shot him in the nards, you'd have been a goner." He poked him playfully in the center of his abdomen.

Levi laughed. He looked to where Glenda was helping Abe into her car. "Take good care of him, will you?"

"Definitely," the writer assured him. "He just needs time to grieve. After that, we may just take a little road trip up to Durham. Duke University has some of the best research facilities in the country. Lots of sterile white labs and expensive toys and… we'll have zombified test subjects coming out the wazoo. Abe will be like a geek at a comic book convention."

"Are you willing to leave Casa de Newman?"

James shrugged. "I think Glenda and the boys need a change of scenery. They're developing a bad case of cabin fever. That and having to read my books over and over and over again for lack of anything better. It'll do us all some good. Who knows? Maybe we'll start our own mad scientist fraternity."

"If you do go, be careful," Levi advised. "There's a lot of crazy shit going on out there on the road."

"You take care, too. Avoid the interstate. The last time Jamie and I scouted it, I-26 was wall-to-wall cars, even the shoulders and median. Looked like a fifty-mile parking lot. I'd take Highway 25 north to be on the safe side." He watched as Big T hobbled toward the clutter of vehicles, the crutches seeming diminutive and inadequate for his massive frame. "I hope he finds his parents. If you get up there to Asheville and find out that all those high-browed bohemians and hipsters have turned into bug-powered cannibals, and you get yourself in a bind, remember what I said before. When in Rome, do as the Vanderbilts do… or *did*."

"I'll keep it in mind."

"Come on, boys," James called to his sons. "To the Batcave!" A moment later, they were in the Spectra, waving from the windows, heading home to North Edenburg.

Levi turned to the others. "Are we ready to go?"

"I reckon so," said Nell. She nodded toward a quartet of Biters, who were making their way awkwardly through the grave markers toward them. "We'd better go before they get here. Don't want to draw a crowd like we did back at Angela's house."

"No, ma'am." He walked over to Avery, who still stood at the foot of Agnes Mendlebaum's grave. "Are you alright, son?"

The sixteen-year-old turned and smiled, although his eyes failed to share the sentiment. "Right as rain, Daddy-O." Avery regarded the grave again, then plucked an arrow from the quiver. The head had traces of blood on the edges of the blade and Levi recognized it immediately. When they had returned to the Childress house the following morning to loot for supplies and ammunition, Avery had placed the heel of his boot between Nathan's dead eyes and, with some effort, pried the arrow from the roof of his mouth. Now the boy turned the arrow thoughtfully between his fingers and then plunged it, point-down, at the head of the grave, forming a makeshift marker. It was an odd gesture in Levi's way of thinking, but then, that was just Avery for you.

As the boy joined his twin brother and headed for the truck. Levi paused at the rear of the Ram and appraised its new addition. While prowling the Newmans' neighborhood they had found an on-bed camper in someone's back yard, sitting on concrete blocks. It didn't fit the Dodge perfectly, but it would do. He opened the back door. Boxes of canned and dried food, as well as cases of bottled water and soft drinks filled the interior. On the front seat of the truck were thirty pages of uncontaminated lot numbers that Abe had written down by hand, to help them on their journey. They had also found three crates of shotgun shells, as well as handgun and rifle cartridges at the Childress house. That cache had joined the supply of ammunition in the Yukon's cargo hold.

As the thought crossed his mind, he looked over at the big

SUV. With the absence of the Mendlebaums, Big T had vacated the bed of the Dodge and chose to ride in comfort with Kate. From the smiles on their faces and the easy way they related to one another, Levi could tell that they enjoyed one another's company. That suited Levi just fine. Tyrone was a good-hearted man, ten times more suitable for his daughter than that asshole she had been married to before.

He gave them a thumb's up. Big T did the same, while Kate grinned and blushed a bit. Levi waved to Billy, who was helping Enolia into the passenger seat of the Mercedes, while Jessie buckled up in the back. The Cherokee simply nodded in acknowledgement. Billy Tauchee was still something of a mystery to him. Quiet and reserved, almost overly polite at times, always appraising the people or situation around him with a mixture of vigilance and suspicion. While dependable, the man was difficult to read. Levi wasn't a hundred percent sure about Billy. He wasn't anything like those he had grown up with, that was for certain.

He climbed into the cab of the Dodge. Nell was flipping through a Rand-McNally atlas, determining the best route to Highway 25. "Ready to go, darling?" he asked, sticking the key in the ignition.

"Yeah," she replied. "You'll need to take Route 64 northeastward to 25." She returned her attention to the atlas and Levi noticed that she had it turned to a map of Florida. He couldn't help but smile. Although they had never been, Nell had always wanted to visit the Sunshine State. *It's a possibility*, he thought, *after we get through with our business in Asheville.*

"We're ready back here," Avery said. The boy had a whetstone in his hand, sharpening the blade of a Rambo-sized Bowie knife. Jem sat silently beside him, reading a copy of *Midnight Rain*, signed by the author himself. Jem had traded with Big T—a Rolex watch he had found in a pawn shop in Gatlinburg for the grey fedora. The teenager had taken to wearing it canted sharply to the side, not out of a sense of over-exaggerated style, but to hide most of the burnt side of his head and the ugly hole where his left ear had once been.

Starting the truck, Levi pulled out of the shade of a thick-leafed magnolia tree and headed down a paved lane toward the main road. Soon, they were away from the shadows and the cold slabs of gray stone, the bright October sunshine warming the interior of the truck and lightening their hearts, if only for a while.

CHAPTER 20

They headed north along Highway 25. The heavily-developed area of Henderson gave way to rural farmland and stretches of dense forest. The highway itself was clear, with only a few wrecked and abandoned cars along its two-lane thoroughfare, but none in a position to hinder or stop them. The highway cut through several small towns, all densely inhabited by Biters. As they drove through, the zombies would lurch toward their vehicles, but they ignored them and continued on, leaving the hoards frustrated and snapping at the autumn air with their bug-infested teeth.

In the Yukon, Kate and Big T's conversation gradually drew to tense silence. Kate could tell that Tyrone's thoughts were occupied with whether or not he would find his parents alive. He stared through the windshield pensively, as though trying to see ahead to what they would discover when they reached the city of Asheville. She understood his concern. Her mother and father meant the world to her. If something should happen to them—or, heaven forbid, they should become infested by those nasty, black parasites—she didn't know how she would handle it or what she would be forced to do. She didn't even want to dwell on the possibility. She knew Tyrone didn't want to either, but he had no choice.

Keeping one hand on the steering wheel, Kate reached out with the other and took his hand. The freckled paleness of her skin stood in stark contrast to the deep brownness of his. "You okay?' she asked.

"Yeah, I'm okay," he said, still staring straight ahead. "It doesn't hurt near as bad as yesterday."

"I'm not talking about your leg. I'm talking about your folks."

Big T swallowed dryly. "I can't seem to get them out of my mind."

"Tell me about them," she urged.

He smiled. "My dad is a forklift driver in a tool and die shop. Been with the same company for going on thirty years. He's a big guy... even bigger than me. Mama calls him her 'gentle giant'."

It was Kate's turn to smile. "Like you."

Big T snorted. "Oh, I've got my faults. Got a hellacious temper when I'm riled. You should've seen me on the football field. They called me the Mangler."

Kate laughed. "No... I can't see that at all." She squeezed his huge fingers and he squeezed back. "Tell me about your mom."

A pained expression shown in his eyes. "Now, Mama... Mama's my world. Always has been. I reckon I'm what you'd call a genuine 'mama's boy'." He sighed deeply. "She's had problems, though. Suffered from depression on and off since I was born. Tried to commit suicide once, when I was thirteen. Took a bunch of pills. We got her to the hospital in time to pump her stomach. She was never right after that... emotionally crippled, I reckon you would call it. Sometimes she would just zone out and sit like that all day long, not talking or responding to anybody. It was hard to watch her go downhill like that and not be able to do anything about it. I reckon that's why I left after graduation. Just couldn't stand seeing her sink lower and lower."

"That's understandable," she offered.

"Well, it ain't to me," he said angrily. "I shouldn't have turned coward. I should have stayed to help Daddy with her." He suddenly looked frightened. "What if we get there and they're dead? Or, worse, what if they've *turned*?"

"We'll deal with that when the time comes."

Big T shook his head. "I don't know if I could do it... you know, do away with my folks. Even if they had turned into one of *them*."

Don't promise what you can't deliver, she thought to herself, but she did it anyway. "If you can't, I'll do it for you."

He turned and looked at her, a little puzzled. "I'm not sure what to think of that... a sweet thing like you offering to do such a thing."

A blush bloomed in her freckled cheeks. "Is that what I am? A sweet thing?"

"You are to me." Their fingers entwined and they smiled at one another in a different way than they had before.

"If it comes down to it, we'll take care of it together," she told him. "Deal?"

He still looked troubled, but nodded. "Deal." The big man turned his gaze back through the windshield. "Could you do me another favor, too?"

"You name it."

"Call me Tyrone from now on. What kinda dumb-ass name is Big T for a grown man to carry around?"

"Just what I've been asking myself all along," she said with a smile.

They continued down the road, their conversation fading. But this time the silence was a comfortable one.

They approached the wide channel of the French Broad River around three in the afternoon. The bridge loomed in the distance—concrete and gray steel, stretching three hundred yards across, from end to end. Its framework rose a good fifty feet toward the sky, twelve feet higher at the very center.

Levi eyed the structure uncomfortably. The bad thing about bridges was the confinement they brought once you began crossing them. Nowhere to escape to, except the muddy water of the river forty feet to either side, if something was to go wrong.

Nell sensed his concern. "No other way to go but straight across," she said. As they grew nearer, she studied the paved stretch that ran through the bridge's center. "Looks clear enough. There are a few cars. And there's a gas tanker parked smack dab in the middle, but it's only in one lane. We ought to be able to get around it just fine."

"I still don't like it," he said. "But I reckon we don't have much of a choice."

He slowed the truck, stuck his hand out the side window,

and motioned forward. The Yukon and Mercedes behind him flashed their headlights in acknowledgement. As he began moving forward, he noticed a couple of Biters at the entrance of the bridge.

"Want I should pop 'em as we drive by?" asked Avery eagerly.

"No point in it," his father told him. "No need to waste bullets unless we absolutely have to."

They drew steadily nearer. The two spotted them and started stumbling toward the truck. Levi intended to knock them down or run them over, if they got in the way. Then, suddenly, as they reached the point where the earth sloped away to the banks of the river below, the sunken and decayed heads of three dozen Biters appeared. The crowd struggled and scrambled to make it up the steep embankments on either side of the bridge. Their eyes were angry and bloodshot, their teeth swarming black with tiny, black parasites.

There was a thud at the passenger door. Levi and Nell looked to see a Biter there, jogging alongside the truck, tugging at the door handle with an emaciated hand. His other hand struck the side window, which, fortunately, was up instead of down. The blow didn't crack the glass, but left a nasty reddish-brown smear swarming with frantic black motion.

"These bastards have it bad," Avery said. "They're full up with those filthy black boogers!" He unshucked his .357 from its holster. "Mama, roll that window down a crack for me, will you?"

Nell did as he asked and leaned toward Levi, covering her ears. Avery leaned forward over the seat, placed the muzzle of the revolver an inch from the Biter's forehead, and fired. The zombie dropped in his tracks, but his hand still clutched the door handle. They dragged him another fifteen feet before his fingers finally relaxed and let go.

"We'll get across the bridge and put some distance between them and us," Levi suggested. "Then we'll be on our way."

He pressed on the gas and increased his speed. A chubby teenaged boy in an Aéropostale t-shirt and jean shorts tottered toward them. Beside him was a small redheaded girl about five or six years old, dressed in a stained pair of Disney Princess pajamas. Whether the child was the boy's little sister or not couldn't be determined. They were both in such an advanced stage of decomposition that any family resemblance was lost in patches of putrid gray flesh and denuded bone.

Levi gunned the engine and struck the boy. He flipped end over end and hit the left-hand support of the bridge entrance. His bloated body deflated a bit and a noxious explosion of methane exited every orifice of his body, as well as some that abruptly appeared when the skin of his abdomen and chest burst open. The little girl stepped clumsily upon the bumper of the Dodge and began to scramble up the grill. Levi stamped on the brake, dislodging her. Then he traded the brake for the accelerator and ran her over. He grimaced as the tires went over her, snapping youthful bones and flattening flesh and organs.

As he started across the southern end of the bridge, he looked in his rear-view mirror. The Yukon kept up the pace, barreling through the lurching Biters, knocking them on their asses or grinding them underneath its oversized tires. Once a frail, old woman—naked, her baggy flesh tinted an ugly bluish-gray—climbed onto the hood of the SUV and crawled toward the windshield like a lizard on its belly. As she licked and gnawed on the glass, Kate braked hard. The sudden deceleration caused the woman to slide back down the hood and fall in the path of the Yukon. Kate shifted her foot back to the gas pedal, sending the vehicle lurching forward.

Billy seemed to be having a harder time. For some reason, the Biters had attacked the Mercedes en masse. There were at least twelve running alongside the vehicle or hanging on to its fenders, roof, and trunk. An overweight Biter who must have been nearly three hundred and fifty pounds, lurched from the side, his bloated arms tucked to his hips, like a whale breaking the crest of an ocean. He hit the hood of the Mercedes hard, snapping off the circular ornament and put a large indention in the metal. The weight of the zombies seemed to have dragged the car down to a creep. Levi could see the concerned faces of Billy and his wife through the windshield, unsure of what to do. He could also see the frustrated face of Tyrone in the Yukon, wanting to jump out and spray the crowd with his Thompson, but aware that he might kill the Tauchee family in the process.

Then Billy leaned on the horn. The blaring confused some of the Biters, causing them to let go and stumble backward. However, some hung on as stubborn as ticks. Minus the weight of six or so zombies, Billy stamped on the gas, shot forward, and bumped into the rear of the Yukon with enough force to dislodge the rest of them. Then both Kate and Billy sped up and joined Levi on the bridge.

"Looks like we're gonna make it," Levi told his wife when they were halfway across. The Biters—nearly fifty of them in all—were rushing across the southern end of the bridge, but not nearly as fast as the three vehicles. Before long, they seemed small and insignificant in the Ram's side view mirror.

"I wouldn't count on it, Papa," Jem said from behind him. The boy reached across the seat and pointed directly through the windshield.

At the far end of the bridge, crowding through the northern entranceway was a multitude of Biters. It was impossible to tell how many, but it could have been as many as seventy or eighty.

"What are we gonna do, Levi?" Nell asked. "We can't go through them. It'll be like hitting a brick wall."

He knew she was right. He lowered his window and looked behind him. Others had joined the Biters at the rear of the bridge. Now there were as many behind them as in front. Within a matter minutes, the two groups of undead would meet at the center of the bridge and they would be hopelessly surrounded.

Levi parked the truck and grabbed his shotgun. He left the vehicle, followed by Nell and the boys. Soon, the others were also out of their vehicles, holding their weapons at the ready. They looked overhead. Beyond the steel girders of the bridge, the sky was obscured by a swirling black cloud of buzzards.

"What's the plan, Papa?" Avery hollered. The moans and growls of the advancing Biters grew louder and louder, until it was hard to hear each other speak.

"I'm not sure!" replied Levi in frustration and uncertainty. "We've got three automatic weapons and two scatterguns, but we'd have to make every shot count as a headshot. It would be simple if we could mow them down with body shots, but we don't have that option."

The zombies to the north were gaining ground, as there was scarcely a hundred feet between them and the front of the Dodge. The ones behind them were farther away, but also closing the gap.

"Should we jump over the side?" Nell wanted to know.

He looked his wife in the eyes. "We grew up in the mountains. You know very well that neither of us can swim worth a lick, and neither can the kids. We'd all drown."

Kate stood holding the Uzi in both hands, looking pale and frightened. "Compared to the alternative, maybe that's not such a bad idea."

Tyrone jacked the bolt on his Tommy gun. "I say we take down as many as we can. Maybe one or two of us can slip through without getting bit."

Levi knew he was right. But what good would that do the survivors? On foot with little ammunition and no food... and Biters all over the place? They would be dead before nightfall. Still, there was nothing else to be done. He jacked a shell into the breach of his twelve-gauge. "Okay... half on this side, half on the other."

The nine split ranks, facing to the north and south. They lifted their guns, aiming toward the bobbing heads of the advancing Biters, praying that their shots would hit more than they missed.

But, before they could begin firing, something happened. On the northern side, halfway between the Biters and Levi and his family, something dropped from the top of the bridge.

The first thing that popped into Levi's mind was *someone's done gone and hanged themselves!* Then as the object reached the end of its nylon rope, jerked to a halt, and dangled there, swaying back and forth, he saw it for what it was. It was the headless carcass of a white-tailed deer, a buck from the size of it. It hung from its back legs and the hide had been slit and sliced, leaving broad patches of glistening meat exposed.

Ten seconds after the first deer fell, a second one dropped behind them, falling between them and the Biters at the southern end of the bridge. The bait was immediately seen and taken. Both groups converged on the sides of fresh, raw meat. They grasped at the venison with bony fingers, grabbing hold and sinking their black teeth into the meat, grunting and slurping as they devoured what they could. For a long instant, the nine trapped in the center of the bridge were completely forgotten.

Then another form dropped from the top of the bridge, directly above their heads. It was a man, rappelling down a length of black nylon rope. He landed atop the cab of the Dodge and stood there in a crouch, surveying the carnage around him.

He looked like something out of an adventure movie, tall and muscular, with short blond hair and military tattoos decorating both arms. He was dressed in an olive drab vest with a dozen flapped pockets down the front, camouflage pants, and black combat boots. He had two automatic weapons slung across his back—an Armalite AR-18 and a SIG SG 516—and had a holstered Heckler & Koch HK45C combat pistol on his right hip.

"Everyone take cover!" he ordered.

At first everyone simply stood and stared at him.

He took a grenade that was clipped to his vest and pulled the ring. "I said *move your asses!*"

His urgency and the sight of the explosive device in his hand broke the spell. They all ducked behind their vehicles as he tossed the grenade toward the northern end of the bridge. He followed suit, dropping and flattening himself against the roof of the camper. The grenade hit the pavement, bounced twice, and landed directly under the ravaged carcass of the deer. It went off seven seconds later. The explosion ripped through the tight knot of Biters. Shrapnel tunneled into their bodies and heads, sending arms and legs spiraling into the air. Out of the eighty from the north, only twenty remained standing, staggering from the brunt of the impact. The man in the military garb stood and, taking the Armalite from behind his back, mowed them down with a volley of well-placed headshots.

"G.I. Joe to the rescue," Avery uttered in amazement.

He sent a burst of 5.56 mm slugs over their heads, taking down several zombies from the south, who had abandoned their deer in favor of the ruckus before them. The man centered his attention on Levi. "Jump in and let's get to the far end of the bridge."

Levi looked at the pile of motionless Biters, four deep in some places. "We won't be able to go around them. There's not enough room."

"Then we'll go *over* them!" As they began climbing into their vehicles, the soldier pointed at Billy. "Hey, Geronimo! Grab your squaw and the kid and jump in the Yukon. That Benz won't be able to make it over."

Billy simply stood and looked at him, stunned at his choice of words.

"Do what I say before I jump down there and put the toe of my boot up your red ass!"

With a glare, the Cherokee did as he was told. He and Enolia grabbed a few bags of clothing from the back seat of the Mercedes and, taking Jessie by the hand, climbed into the back of Kate's SUV.

"What about you?" called Levi as he jumped behind the wheel of his truck.

"I'll ride up top," he told him. "Lay down suppressing fire until we get off this bridge."

"Thinks a lot of himself, don't he?" said Jem.

Levi shrugged and put the truck into gear. "He pulled our butts out of a sling. I'll give him that much."

He drove the big pickup forward. When they reached the heap of mangled Biters, he gunned the engine and sent the truck climbing upward, the tread of the tires gripping and taking hold. As the Ram advanced, Levi thought of that old commercial—the one where the pickup truck climbs a mountain of boulders with ease. The Dodge did just as well on flesh and bone. Above him, the continuous report of automatic fire rattled as the soldier exchanged the Armalite for the SIG and shot over the roof of the SUV at the zombies that advanced from the south.

A moment later, the truck had made it over and was on solid asphalt again. The Yukon did much better. Kate switched to four-wheel drive and sent her vehicle bounding over the mound of bodies as though she were going over a speed bump.

They made it to the opposite end of the bridge and parked their vehicles. As everyone got out, they saw that twenty or thirty Biters from the south side had crawled over the mound of fallen zombies and were beginning to make their way toward them. The blond man in the military garb hopped down from the top of the camper and quickly made his way to the very edge of the bridge. He opened a pocket on his vest and brought out a black object that resembled a beefed-up TV remote. He withdrew an antenna from the end and directed it across the bridge. "I'd turn around, if I were you," he told them. "This might fry your eyes."

They did as he said. Only Avery chanced a glance as the man placed his finger over a large red button and pressed it.

The gas tanker exploded in a fireball that engulfed the middle of the bridge. Concrete and steel were torn asunder and the center section was completely obliterated, along with the Biters who occupied it. Slowly, the remaining ends of the bridge collapsed and dropped with a great crash and splash of muddy water into the French Broad River. A few moments later after the debris had settled, they turned and studied the devastation. All that was left was the two entrances of the destroyed bridge hanging off each end of the riverbank.

"Shitfire!" declared Avery with a big grin. "He's got all the big-boy toys!"

Levi walked over and stood next to the soldier. "A little drastic, don't you think? Now there's no access way across the river." He thought of the Newman family and Abe, and their planned trip to Durham. If they were going, they would have to find a different route.

The man grinned. "I believe in burning my bridges behind me." He extended a strong hand. "Captain Frank Gentry. I'm from Special Forces out of Fort Bragg."

Levi shook his hand. "Levi Hobbs from Tennessee. This is my wife, Nell, my sons, Avery and Jem, and my daughter, Kate."

Avery stepped forward eagerly and shook the man's hand. "Freaking Green Beret! Now we're talking."

"And this is Tyrone Jackson and the Tauchee family—Billy,

Enolia, and their little girl, Jessie," Levi continued.

Frank glanced in the direction of the black man and the three Cherokees, but neglected to acknowledge them. It was then that they began to see what sort of man the soldier really was.

"My camp is a quarter mile down the road," he said. "Let's rendezvous there and have us some grub. Fragging zombies gives me a hell of an appetite."

As everyone returned to their vehicles, Frank stepped off the highway and pulled cut brush and tree limbs away from a military Humvee. It was painted olive drab with U.S. ARMY stenciled across the hood, and had a .50-caliber Browning M2 machine gun mounted on a swivel rig on top of the roof. He threw his automatic weapons in the back, climbed in, and headed down the road, leaving them to catch up.

Levi put the Ram into gear and followed. "Cocky fella, ain't he?"

Nell shook her head. "I can't say I like him much. Did you see how he looked at Tyrone and Billy and his family? Like he'd stepped on a dog turd. You know I don't cotton to that kind of person."

"Aw, he's just a dyed-in-the-wool bad-ass, Ma," said Avery, still grinning from ear to ear. "I don't think he means no harm."

"I reckon we'll see about that," said Jem, picking up his horror novel from off the seat. "Seems like a first-class asshole to me."

"He did pull us out of a sticky situation," Levi reminded them. "So we need to give him the benefit of the doubt... at least for the time being." He stared ahead at the Humvee and its armaments. "Besides, he'd be a handy one to have along on the way to Asheville."

"I'd just soon go alone," his wife told him. "He's trouble, through and through. I can feel it in my bones."

Levi said nothing else as he drove, but couldn't deny that he felt the same way.

CHAPTER 21

Evening slowly settled into night as Levi and the others set up camp in a leaf-strewn clearing a hundred yards off the main highway. Frank Gentry had been there for several days and it showed. A makeshift shelter of canvas tarp secured between two trees faced the road and the soldier's Humvee, which was parked a short distance from the clearing, seemed to watch sentry over the surrounding woods. Empty food packets and crumpled beer cans littered the place. Apparently, the man wasn't the tidiest person on the face of the earth, or he just didn't care anymore. Common courtesies and a regard for simple laws had gone the way of the Earth's rapidly-dwindling population.

There was tension after they reached the camp. Some of it had to do with the Biter attack earlier that afternoon, but a fair share was due to their host. Apparently, Nell wasn't the only one who felt reservations concerning Frank Gentry. The Hobbs family, Tyrone, and Billy Tauchee and his wife and daughter sat at one side of the fire-lit clearing, while the Green Beret occupied the other side. They stared across the dancing flames of the campfire as Frank downed one can of beer after the other and told his story.

"Fort Bragg was secure for a while," he told them. "Nearly a month and half. We spent our days playing pool, watching porn, and taking potshots at zombies from the sentry towers. It was like a freaking, non-stop R & R. Then a couple of our guys turned. Don't know how they got infected. It could have been something they ate or drank. Maybe they got it from a skank we had around the barracks." He winked at Nell and Kate, who sat side by side. "You know, to service our needs. Whatever the cause, they turned and turned *quick*. None of that lying in a corner and hibernating shit. We woke up in the middle of the night to screaming and gunfire. By daybreak, most of the camp was bitten or half-eaten. I made it out alive... just me and a dozen grunts. We stuck like glue for a week or two, then half of them went AWOL and headed out on their own. I came across a couple of them a few days ago, zombified, not knowing me from Adam but wanting to eat me anyway. I popped a cap in their skulls and left them where they dropped. I would have given them an honorable burial, but they didn't deserve it. They'd turned traitor on me and they deserved what they got."

"What about other bases?" asked Avery. "Lejeune, Mackall, Cherry Point?"

"Deserted from what I heard. Or overrun with Biters. It's a dead man's world. We're just interlopers in their territory now."

"A scientist friend told us that they aren't actually dead," Levi said. "He claimed that the parasites devour certain portions of folks' brains, turning them into mindless eating machines. Decomposing shells of their former selves, but still alive."

Frank laughed. He took a long swig from a can of Pabst Blue Ribbon and shook his head. "That scientist fella was full of shit. There ain't no life in those sick-ass sons of bitches. You can tell by looking in their eyes. There's no soul left in them, just a burning need to eat and kill... and breed more of their kind."

The others said nothing in rebuke. Levi looked over at his daughter. Kate sat cuddled next to Tyrone. Her eyes met her father's and she shook her head slightly. Levi understood what she meant. The man's mind was set and there was no changing it.

The soldier crumpled his beer can, tossed it away, and then popped the tab on another. "So, where are you folks headed?"

"Asheville," Levi told him and instantly felt Nell's fingernails bite into the meat of his arm. He looked over at her and saw a warning expression in her eyes. It was clear that she didn't trust or like this wandering soldier of fortune.

"And what business do you have up there?"

"We're going to find my mama and daddy," Tyrone spoke up. "Haven't seen them since this whole sorry thing started."

Frank turned hard eyes toward the black man. "Now was I talking to you? When I do, you'll know it. Right now this conversation is between me and the man here."

Tyrone tensed as he glared at the man in the camouflage fatigues. Kate tightened her grip on Tyrone's massive arm. "Just ignore him," she whispered.

The soldier took another pull from his Pabst can. "And what are you folks planning on doing after Asheville?"

Levi shrugged. "Truthfully, we haven't really thought that far ahead."

A little smile crossed Nell's face. "Florida would be nice. I've never been to the beach before."

Frank snickered harshly. "Lady, have you ever read *The Road* by Cormac McCarthy?"

"No, can't say that I have."

"The beach isn't the paradise you might imagine. In fact, it's probably a freaking dead end. If those Biters come shuffling down the shore, there's only two ways to go: back inland or out to sea. If you ask me, the ocean is probably swimming with those damn parasites by now."

Nell lowered her eyes. "Well, it was just a thought."

Levi patted her on the knee. "Florida sounds good to me."

"Well, if you decide to take that route, I'll be taking my leave," Frank told them flatly. "The best place to go is the mountains. The Rockies... Colorado or even Canada. Isolated and not nearly as populated as the lowlands."

Levi stared at him. "Mister, we've just come from the mountains. These Biters are all over. Doesn't matter where you go, you're going to have to deal with them."

"Well, I know how to deal with them just fine, thank you."

Levi regarded him across the dancing flames of the campfire. "Can I ask you a question, Captain?"

Gentry shrugged the thick shoulders. "Sure, go ahead."

"What happened to the five men who stuck with you after the other six went their own way?"

Frank grinned. A hard edge of cruelty laced his smirk. "Let's just say we had a bit of a misunderstanding about who was in command. They thought I was leading them down a wrong path, putting them into dangerous situations, as they put it."

"And they just up and left?"

The soldier's grin widened. "No, I left them. Lying in their blankets with their throats slashed."

Kate gasped. "You're joking, aren't you?"

"No, ma'am. I never joke. The good Lord failed to bless me with a sense of humor. That's why I take things to heart so much. Anyone who travels with me better understand that."

Nell turned and looked at Levi. *Did he just threaten us?* her eyes asked.

Her husband shrugged slightly, but said nothing. That was one thing that irked Nell about Levi. Sometimes he was like a book with the pages glued shut—hard to read.

"I reckon we'd better get to sleep if we're heading for Asheville tomorrow," the grunt told them. He tossed his last crumpled can into the darkness. "I'll take the watch until one o'clock. Are you up to taking the second one, Avery?"

The boy grinned like a possum in a landfill. "Yes, sir. Locked and loaded!"

As the others prepared their blankets and sleeping bags, Nell started toward the edge of the clearing toward the woods.

"Where are you going, babe?" Levi asked her.

"My before-bed bathroom break," she told him. "This old bladder ain't what it used to be."

"Want me to come along?"

"I'll be okay." She took the .357 Magnum from where it lay on top of her bedroll. "I'll tote this, just in case I come across a zombie squirrel or something."

"Just holler if you need me," he said as he prepared their beds for the night.

Nell made her way carefully into the dark thicket, her feet swishing through the brittle autumn leaves. She stopped about fifty feet from the glow of the campsite, dropped her drawers, and did her business. As she was getting up, she suddenly spotted a tiny, red glow from no less than twelve feet away. Startled, she cocked the big revolver and leveled it at the bud of smoldering ash.

"Little mama with a big gun," came a familiar voice.

Nell relaxed her aim a bit, but didn't uncock her gun. "What are you? A dad-blamed peeping tom?"

Frank Gentry inhaled, causing the end of his cigarette to flair and illuminate his broad face. "If I wanted to lay eyes on female ass, I wouldn't pick one with stretch marks and wrinkles."

"A real charmer, ain't you?" Nell stood her ground, although she couldn't help but shudder. She told herself that it was the chill of the evening, but she knew she was just lying to herself. "What do you want?"

"Just wanted to ask a question."

"Then ask it."

The soldier exhaled and Nell caught the strong scent of tobacco. Unfiltered Camels, like her late father used to chain-smoke. "Why do you allow it?"

"Allow what?"

"Allow that nigger to lay hose to your daughter, that's what."

Nell bristled. "As far as I know, he hasn't. Besides, whatever they have together, they have my blessing. Tyrone is a good man."

"But he's a black man," Frank told her flatly. "And that ain't acceptable."

Nell attempted to control her anger, but the emotion edged her words like a razor. "Mister, there are only two kinds of folks walking the earth today... the living and the dead. And as long as they're living, they're good enough for my little girl. Except maybe the likes of you."

The grunt chuckled and took a step forward. "A little hell-cat, ain't you? Maybe it's you who needs the hose laid to her."

Nell's heart pounded in her chest, but the barrel of the Magnum was unwavering. "Unless you want a hole in your belly big enough to drive that Humvee through, I suggest you step on back. You don't want that, do you? I'm capable of obliging you. Maybe even a little eager."

Frank laughed, but there was little humor to the sound. "I see you are. Didn't mean any harm, Mrs. Hobbs. Just wanted to make my opinion known about who should and shouldn't be laying hands upon your daughter."

"I reckon that's her business... and not mine or yours." Nell motioned with the muzzle of her gun. "You go on ahead. I'll follow."

Frank stubbed his cigarette on the trunk of a tree and tossed the butt away. "Yes, ma'am."

A moment later, the two stepped back into the clearing. The soldier returned to his makeshift shelter and Nell joined her husband at the far edge of the camp.

Levi's eyes hardened. "What was he doing out there?"

"Being an asshole," his wife told him. "We need to be shed of him, Levi. As soon as possible. He's a dangerous man."

"He did save our skins back yonder at that bridge," he reminded her.

Nell nestled into the patchwork quilt Levi had laid out for them. "Yeah and a shark might save a dolphin from barracudas... until it gets mean-ass hungry."

"Okay, this is how it works," Frank said, talking to Billy Tauchee as though he was a four-year-old rather than a grown man. "We're going in here and taking whatever we can find. There's precious little left to loot these days, but anything is better than nothing. If we come across any zombies—and I know they're around, because there's half-a-dozen buzzards perched on the edge of the roof—we'll try to sneak past them. No need to get them all riled up and risk the chance of getting bitten."

The Cherokee regarded him impassively. "I know the drill. I've done it plenty of times before."

The soldier smirked and spat on the sidewalk. "Oh, have you? Well, then, we won't be having any problems, now will we?"

Billy looked down and checked the loads in his .41 Magnum. "Just open the door and let's get this over with."

The Winn-Dixie was located in a little strip mall in the rural town of Fletcher, twenty-five miles south of Asheville. There was a Subway, a beauty salon called A Cut Above, and a combination vintage vinyl & comic book shop called The Great Escape. The grocery store was smack dab in the middle. The others were scouting various places along the main stretch for supplies—a Rite Aid drugstore, a Dairy Queen, and a True Value hardware store.

Billy and Frank moved cautiously through the open entrance of the store, dodging abandoned shopping carts in the outer foyer. Past a roll of gumball machines and a community bulletin board, the building opened up into the sprawling expanse of the store itself. The soldier lifted the butt of his Armalite to one shoulder, sighting down the barrel, and waved for his looting partner to follow. They made their way down a narrow checkout lane, past wire racks that had once held impulse-buy items like candy bars, gum, and women's magazines. Billy found a Kit Kat and a Snickers bar that had been overlooked by previous marauders and stuck them in his jacket pocket to take back to Jessie. Frank spotted a Slim Jim lying on the linoleum floor and scooped it up, placing it in a hip pocket for later.

Both carried flashlights, but neither put them to use. They let their eyes adjust to the gloom and made their way from left to right, checking the aisles as they went. It soon became apparent that their visit might end up being fruitless. The shelves of each aisle had been stripped of product, leaving only a few empty boxes scattered here and there.

Billy motioned toward the floor. The linoleum was covered with a thin layer of dust. The impressions of haphazard footprints showed clearly. "Fresh," he whispered. "Someone's in here. Biters from the way their prints shuffle and slide."

Frank grunted softly and nodded. He cocked his head and listened. "I hear them. A couple of aisles down. Let's try to get past them without drawing their attention."

Together, they made their way quietly toward the left side of the store. The soft noises of shuffling feet came from Aisle 10, which had once boasted breakfast cereal, pancake mix, and Pop-Tarts. They approached the open end of the aisle and paused. They could hear the ragged, phlegmy breathing of more than a few Biters who congregated in the narrow passageway of empty metal shelving.

Frank motioned for Billy to cross first. The Indian nodded and, gripping the Smith & Wesson in a two-fisted hold, stepped across. He turned for a moment and looked down the aisle way. The soft sounds of milling feet had been deceiving. He had expected five or six Biters to occupy the aisle. Instead, there were twelve to fifteen. Their backs were to them as some shuffled down the aisle and others stood in place, wavering unsteadily back and forth.

Billy was nearly to the empty endcap of the next aisle, when the sole of a combat boot forcefully landed in the small of his back, sending him stumbling into the cereal aisle and landing on his knees on the floor. So jolting was the unexpected blow that his revolver slipped from his grasp. It bounced on the floor once and slid amid the Biters' milling feet.

Frank Gentry laughed behind him. "Bon Appétit, hive-heads. I brought you some red meat to chew on."

At the clatter of the fallen gun and the sound of the soldier's voice, the Biters turned sluggishly and regarded the kneeling man before them. At the sight of Billy, their dull, lusterless eyes flared into a rapid mixture of conflicting emotion—hunger, animosity, and the desire to attack and consume. As one, they shuffled toward him.

"Oh shit!" muttered the Cherokee. As the distance between him and the Biters diminished—fifteen feet, then ten, then eight—he resisted the urge to rise to his feet. Instead, he chose to do just the opposite. With a lurch, he pushed to the rear and fell flat on his back.

Billy had noticed for quite some time that Biters weren't the most stable creatures when it came to equilibrium. Apparently, the tiny black parasites that brought them to such a horrid and sorry state also ravaged the canals of the inner ear system and totally trashed their sense of balance. If a Biter tried to stoop or bend down, they would lose their footing and fall nine times out of ten. And when they fell, they had a hell of a time getting back up. Some of the heavier ones were like turtles on their backs, legs and arms flailing, unable to regain a standing position.

He waited until the crowd of Biters reached him, then lashed out with his feet. Billy struck some in their brittle, cal-cium-deprived kneecaps, bringing them down, while others he hooked by the ankles with the crook of his insteps and swept them off their feet. One kick nailed a Biter in a county deputy's uniform squarely in the nuts. What had once served as his testi-cles ruptured upon impact, darkening the crotch of his britches and running in dark rivulets down the legs of his pants.

As the zombies dropped to the floor, one at a time, Billy reached to the snap pouch on his belt and retrieved a folding knife—a six-inch Buck blade with a black rubberized handle. It had a small silver arrowhead set in the grip. He flipped onto his stomach and went to work. The blade was thick and the point wickedly sharp. It slid easily into the gelatinous pits of eye sockets and through the thin walls of temple bone as Billy worked the knife in a circular motion, scrambling the infected brains within until they grew permanently still. As he withdrew the blade, a thick gorge of dark blood and tissue teaming with tiny black parasites spurted from the wounds. Billy dodged the infected fluid the best he could and wiped the refuse from the blade on the Biter's clothing before turning to another one.

A Biter wearing a red Winn-Dixie manager's vest with a tag that read STAN stepped over Billy and stumbled toward Frank. His black teeth gnashed and his bloodshot eyes burnt with hunger and hatred.

"You're going the wrong way, Stan," the soldier said. He flipped his AR-18 and slammed the butt of the rifle into the zombie's forehead. The Biter's head folded inward like an over-ripened cantaloupe. "The chow line is over there."

Billy scrambled over convulsing bodies as five Biters reached down toward him, blackened fingernails pulling at the material of his jacket. The Cherokee found his revolver and brought it up, firing until the cylinder was depleted. The interior of the store echoed with the roar of the .41 Magnum and the last five dropped in their tracks, Billy rose to his feet, stumbling backward, as a flood of ruptured brains, dark blood, and thousands of tiny black bugs burst from their ruined heads.

"You son of a bitch!" he said, turning toward Frank. His grip tightened on the handle of his folding knife.

"It was just a joke, Tonto," the soldier said, still laughing. "But I gotta give it to you... you took care of the situation pretty damn good."

Billy's dark eyes narrowed. He took a step toward Frank... then stopped when Levi, Avery, and Jem rushed into the store.

"What happened?" asked Levi. "We heard gunfire."

Frank winked at the Indian, then his face instantly transformed into a mask of indignation. "This little piece of shit nearly got us killed!" the captain exclaimed. "Lead us straight into an aisle of freaking zombies. Then he froze up and pissed his pants, leaving me to do all the dirty work. Nearly got us both killed—or worse—the little red-skinned bastard!" Then he shouldered his rifle and left the store.

Levi and his sons stared at Billy Tauchee for a long moment. "Is he right?" asked Levi. "Is that what happened?"

The Cherokee folded his knife and slipped it back into the pouch on his belt. "I reckon you're going to believe whatever you have a mind to," Billy said. Then he walked past the three and left the shadowy interior of the Winn-Dixie.

Avery snorted in disgust and shook his head. "That little Indian's sort of a pussy, ain't he?"

Levi turned and watched through the plate-glass window as Billy walked slowly across the abandoned parking lot. "Don't sell him short, boys. There's something about that man we don't know about... something he doesn't want us to know. And we won't know the truth until he's good and ready to tell us."

CHAPTER 22

Enolia swished the creek water around in the white Styrofoam cup five times before she was satisfied that the stream wasn't contaminated. The tell-tale sign of tiny black specks swimming in erratic patterns was absent. Just clear, cool spring water and nothing more.

Looking back up the wooded hillside and, seeing no one is sight, she relaxed and disrobed. It had been three days since she had bathed. It was difficult to find the time and opportunity to simply keep clean when you were constantly on the move. Besides, seventy-five percent of most creeks, rivers, and wells they had come across since leaving Cherokee had proven to be contaminated by the tiny, black parasites. She was lucky that this creek, at least, hadn't yet been infested.

She laid her clothes across a mossy log and crouched on a smooth, flat slab of stone that jutted over the trickling water. The sound of the current over the creek stones was melodic, almost musical. She closed her eyes and remembered how she and her grandmother had spent their afternoons when she was a small girl, fishing on the banks of the Oconaluftee River back home. She drove the memory quickly away though when the final image of her beloved *elisi* flashed through her mind, how she had died badly... then returned to life as one of *them*.

Enolia took a wash cloth and a bottle of body wash from a backpack. She dipped the cloth into the stream and wrung away the excess, then applied a small drop of the soap. Where such things had once been necessities, they were now luxuries. She was careful to use only enough to do the job; there was little chance of finding any more in the near future. Their last few raids of drugstores and supermarkets had produced bottles of shampoo, body wash, and other toiletry items that been full of the nasty parasites. Apparently, they had become contaminated during the manufacturing process shortly before the worldwide infestation had taken place.

She began to wash, starting with her face and throat, and then making her way toward her shoulders and chest. When the cool cloth reached her engorged breasts, her dark nipples hardened. Her skin stippled with goosebumps and a sexual thrill shot through her, curling her toes in the cold creek. *Naughty girl,* she scolded herself. *None of that until after the baby is born.*

The cloth continued to the swell of her belly. When it touched the taut brown skin, the baby jumped. Enolia smiled. "You're going to be a big boy, aren't you?" she whispered. "You'll be strong and brave, like your daddy." Then her smile lost its gentle cheer. *Let's just hope that you don't follow the same paths as your father once did,* she thought grimly.

She was about to finish her bath, when a hand, hot and coarse, squeezed the nape of her neck, bearing her forcefully to her hands and knees on the stone slab. Lenora's heart thundered in her chest. She knew who it was before he even spoke.

"We're gonna do this fast and very quietly," Frank Gentry's voice rasped harshly in her right ear. "So put your nose to that stone, give me what I want, and you won't get hurt."

"Please... don't," she protested, trying not to whimper, but failing miserably. "I... I'm pregnant."

The soldier laughed. "Frankly, I can't get enough of squaws with papooses in their tepee. Makes it nice and tight in there."

Enolia closed her eyes and shuddered as she heard the sound of a zipper disengaging. Something firm and blunt rubbed against her left buttock and she felt the fingers of his free hand probe along her opening, as though testing the waters. The man grunted with satisfaction. "Doesn't look like I'll have any trouble here."

The woman recalled the sensual thoughts that had overcome her earlier and felt ashamed, as though her wetness was an invitation for what was to come.

Her grandmother's voice came again, from an intimate talk

they had when she was twelve. *If a man tries to lie with you and you not wanting him to, you clench up tighter than a mussel shell. Bar the door and refuse to let him in.* Enolia didn't think that was going to work with Gentry. He was going to do what he intended to do.

Before he could act any further, she knew she had to at least try and do something to stop him. "I'll... I'll scream."

His hand left her vagina and returned a second later, beneath her belly. The cold steel of his combat knife pressed against the curve, just beneath her navel. "You make one little peep, gal, and that baby is gonna spill out and float down the creek. Then I'll leave you here bleeding from one nasty C-section and go up the hill there and kill every last one of those people, including your dip-shit husband and your daughter."

Enolia swallowed dryly and grew still... and waited for her violation.

Then she heard a man's voice behind her assailant and her grimace of degradation changed into a grin of satisfaction.

"Let go of her," Billy said coldly.

You're dead, you son of a bitch, she thought. *He's going to make you pay for what you did back at that grocery store... and what you're trying to do right now.*

But, surprisingly enough, that wasn't what happened at all. Instead, Enolia lifted her face and turned to see her husband with his back planted firmly against the trunk of a birch tree. Gentry's thick forearm was against his chest and the point of his knife was angled beneath Billy's chin.

Dazed, Enolia turned and sat on the rock, naked, looking up at what was taking place. Her pretty face flushed with indignation. Her eyes locked with her husband's. *What are you waiting for?* she demanded wordlessly. *Do something!*

Instead, the Cherokee spoke softly. "We won't allow your behavior any longer, Gentry."

Frank laughed. "*We?* Who the hell is *we?* Those hillbillies? That dumb, blue-gum nigger up there, sniffing around that skinny red-headed gal? *You?*" The soldier spat to the side and grinned viciously. "Nobody's doing nothing. Nothing but taking orders from *me*. Starting tomorrow, all of you jump when I say jump and shit when I say shit. If you don't, I'll consider you traitors and do you like I did those ungrateful grunts that followed me from Bragg. You'll either be dinner for the Biters or those little black bugs... it's your choice."

Enolia watched as Billy stared emotionlessly over Benson's shoulder at her. *End this now!* her eyes implored. *Please!*

What might have happened then never did. Instead, someone called out from the top of the wooded hollow. "Hey... what's going on down there?"

Frank pulled the blade away from Billy's throat and stepped away from the tree, releasing him. "Listen up... both of you. One word of what happened down here and you're going to wake up one morning to find that little girl of yours gone. You'll look and look, but you'll never find her. Not *all* of her. Understand?"

Enolia nodded.

The soldier turned back to Billy. "How about you, little chief?"

The Cherokee's eyes narrowed. "Yes."

"Is everything alright?" called Levi again. They could see the man and his two sons at the top of the ridge, although they could not see them clearly through the foliage of the trees.

Frank tucked himself in and zipped his pants. He returned his knife to its sheath, then strolled past the birch and started up the hill. "No problem down here. I was just having a friendly pow-wow with the Tauchee family, that's all."

A moment later, when Frank had returned to camp, Enolia hurriedly pulled on her clothes. She glared at Billy, who still stood beneath the tree. "That bastard nearly got you killed this morning. Then he comes down here and tries to... to... *rape* me... and you just stand there?"

Her husband shook his head. "Not right now. Not in front of Levi and the others. You know that I can't. I have my—"

"Yes, I know. You have your *orders!* Well, the people you made that commitment to are all dead and gone now. It's time to move on. You shouldn't have stepped back when Levi and the others went to that boy's house back in Hendersonville. If you'd gone with them, maybe Agnes and her sister would still be alive."

Billy's expression darkened. "Don't you think I know that?"

Enolia immediately regretted what she had said. The anger in her eyes softened. "Baby, I'm scared. He's a mean and vindictive man. If we don't do exactly what he wants, he'll end up killing us all. And he's sneaky. I didn't even hear him come up on me, even with all these dead leaves around. He's nearly as good as you are."

Her husband grinned. It wasn't a gesture that included his eyes. "Oh, you really think so?"

"Please... just take care of it. Before we find ourselves in a situation that we can't get out of."

"I will," he promised. "Later." He nodded toward the camp at the crest of the backwoods hollow. "But not in front of *them*."

It was nearly eleven-thirty. Everyone in the camp was asleep, except for two.

Billy Tauchee sat on one side of the fire, his wife and daughter nestled in sleeping bags behind him. Frank Gentry sat across from him, finishing off his second six-pack of the night. The soldier sat against the base of a tree, half drunk, staring at the Cherokee, trying to figure out what he was up to. Billy had cut a maple branch into eight six-inch lengths and was shaving the ends into sharp points.

"What the hell are you doing?" he asked.

"Whittling," Billy told him. "It's my hobby."

The soldier nodded toward the sticks. "What are they?"

Billy smiled. "My daughter wants a tent for her doll. These are the stakes."

Gentry's eyes centered on the folding knife with the black handle. "Where did you get that?"

"It was a gift. From my Uncle Sam."

Frank smiled contemptuously. "Maybe I'll slit your throat with it after I take it away from you. You do know I'm gonna kill you, don't you?"

Billy said nothing. He simply kept his eyes on his work and continued to whittle.

"Yeah, it's gonna happen... sooner or later. Something about you gets under my skin like a burr." The soldier shivered and pulled on a camo field jacket. "It's chilly out tonight. I think I'll turn in. You take first watch and wake me up at two for mine. And you better keep your damn eyes sharp. If you let a Biter or two get within a hundred feet of this camp, I'll take your stupid pegs and shove them cross-ways up your ass. You understand me, Geronimo?"

Billy nodded, but refused to lift his eyes. "Loud and clear."

Frank lay flat on his back on the ground. "You know something? I usually have one big-ass hard-on when I wake up. It'd be a damn shame to waste it. I may just slam it to your whore of a wife... or that red-haired gal or her mama."

The Cherokee said nothing... just continued whittling.

Soon, the soldier was asleep and snoring heavily, oblivious to all that went on around him.

And Billy grinned and whittled. Whittled and grinned.

Frank Gentry awoke in the middle of the night with a suffocating sensation of weight bearing down on the center of his chest. His eyes opened to find Billy Tauchee sitting there, staring down at him.

"What the shit?" he blurted. Frank tried to sit up, but found that he couldn't. He twisted his head from side to side and saw that he had been secured to the ground with the six-inch pegs. They had been pushed through the edges of his jacket and trousers, anchoring him to where he lay.

"Shhhhh," Billy whispered, pressing the blade of the folding knife against Gentry's lips. "Let's not wake the others. Time for a little powwow, as you call it. Just you and me."

Frank stared up at him, but said nothing.

"You know what?" Billy said. "I don't believe you are Special Forces. I don't think you're even regular Army. I think you're some dumb-ass redneck weekend-warrior who looted an armory and gave himself a promotion. You have a few skills and know enough technique and jargon to fool a layman, but you can't fool me." A thin grin crossed Billy's face like a night-crawler slithering across clay earth. "Tell me something. Have you ever heard of Black Arrow?"

Frank stiffened beneath him.

"Yeah, I thought so. An elite unit of Native Americans. Cherokee, Apache, Seminole, Blackfoot, Comanche... trained in stealth and shadow... extraction, reconnaissance, search and destroy, assassination. We did it all. Three tours in Iraq, four in Afghanistan... and other places, too."

Frank suddenly found his voice. "Let... let me up."

"Not just yet." Billy turned the blade of his knife in the firelight. "Not so high and mighty now, are you? I think the reason you're so damn mean is because you look mean. Maybe we can do something about that. Those eyebrows, for example. They make you look so damn intimidating." He brought the edge of the blade down and cleanly shaved the blond hairs over Frank's right eye away. "There. Much better. As smooth as a baby's ass."

Gentry didn't move a muscle. He laid perfectly still, his face as pale as a bed sheet.

"Okay... now the other one." Billy laid the curved blade against the soldier's skin and began to shave away his left eyebrow. Halfway there, the razor edge hit a bump, nicking the skin. "Oops. Didn't mean to cut you. Why, look at that. Your blood is red... just like me."

Frank's eyes rolled wildly from side to side, searching for help, but finding none. He looked as though he was on the point of passing out.

Billy continued to work with the knife until the other eyebrow was gone. "Ah, not so judgmental now. Face so soft and pretty... like a woman's." The Cherokee's face grew sinister in the dancing glow of the fire. "Speaking of women, if you ever touch my wife again, I'll do a number with this knife and make you eat your pride. I believe you know what I mean by that... don't you?"

Frank nodded almost imperceptibly, afraid that sudden motion might cause him to lose more than his eyebrows.

Slowly, Billy rose, departing from his place on Frank's chest. He spotted a single drop of blood on the knife's blade and wiped it on the material of the big man's jacket.

"Let me up," croaked Gentry, his voice quavering. "Please."

"Yes, I'll let you up," Billy agreed. "But one wrong move on your part and I'll slit you open from breastbone to groin. Do you understand me?"

"Yes."

Billy crouched and yanked the pegs from the man's clothing. "Stand up with your back facing me," he instructed.

Shakily, Frank did as he said. Billy reached around him and shucked the Heckler & Koch .45 from its holster. "I'll take this." He rummaged through the storage pockets of Benson's flak vest until he found the keys to the Humvee. "And these."

Frank stood there for a long moment. "Now what?"

"Now we go our separate ways. We head north and you head south... as far south as your feet can carry you. And that will be the last we ever see of one another."

"You're... you're sending me out *there*? Without a gun?"

"You can keep that big-ass Rambo knife of yours," Billy told him. "If you're as good as you make out, you should be able to fend off the Biters with it. Unless you come upon five or six of them, that is. Then my advice would be to toss it in the bushes and run like hell."

Frank Gentry stood there for a moment, hesitant.

Billy put his boot in the small of the soldier's back, sending him stumbling forward. "Go."

The man started forward, toward the darkness beyond the reach of the campfire light. He stopped one more time.

"Walk," the Cherokee told him softly. "And if you get halfway through those woods and feel like you need to come back, don't. I'll be watching and I'll put a .30-06 slug between your seventh and eighth vertebrae and leave you crippled for the zombies to gnaw on. It doesn't bother me to shoot a man in the back. I've done it before."

As the man moved forward and stepped out of the perimeter of the camp, Bill Tauchee closed the blade of his knife and returned it to the pouch on his belt. Then he retrieved his rifle from where it leaned against a tree nearby. He stood for a long time, eye to the scope, watching as the pale form of Frank Gentry slowly disappeared from sight. Then he breathed easy and sat beside the fire, to take the second watch of the night.

The following morning, Levi Hobbs awoke to find Billy crouched beside the fire, heating a pot of coffee over the crackling flames.

The Tennessean stood up and stretched. Then he looked over at the base of the tree where the soldier had made his billet the night before. "Where's Gentry?" he asked.

"Gone," the Cherokee simply said.

"Gone? What do you mean *gone*?"

"He said he was sick and tired of hanging around us losers and he took off into the woods."

Levi looked over at the tree and saw Gentry's Armalite and SG516 propped against the trunk. Then he looked toward the highway and saw the Humvee where Frank had parked it the evening before. "Just up and walked off? Without his guns or his vehicle?"

"Yeah," said Billy, pouring Levi a cup of coffee. "Strange, isn't it?" He took a set of keys from the pocket of his denim jacket. "Looks like I've got a new ride. Not as comfy as the BMW, but it does have more firepower."

Levi took the brew and downed a couple of swallows. "You know something, Billy?" he said, after a moment.

"What's that?"

"I'm a light sleeper. Doesn't take very much at all to wake me up."

"Oh, is that so?"

"Yeah." A little smile crossed Levi's bearded face. "And sometimes I have the craziest dreams. Matter of fact, I had me one last night." He looked down and, seeing a wooden peg, kicked it across the clearing. It bounced once, before ending up in the fire.

"Oh, yeah?" Billy didn't look up as he poured a cup for himself. "And what was this dream about?"

"That's the funny thing about my dreams," Levi told him. "Once I wake up, I can't, for the life of me, remember what they were about."

The Cherokee nodded, smiling. "Fair enough."

The two drank their coffee and enjoyed the solitude of the wooded clearing for a while, saying nothing, but understanding each other completely.

"We'll have a bite of breakfast, then head on to Asheville," Levi suggested. "Tyrone's parents live about twenty-five miles away. We'll go there first, then head onward."

"Sounds like a plan," Billy agreed.

The two had another cup of coffee in the gray dawn of a new day before waking the others.

CHAPTER 23

"This ain't right," Tyrone said grimly.

He stared through the passenger side window of the Yukon at the front yard of the little farm he had once called home. There were several vehicles parked in the gravel driveway and in the withered grass in front of the two-story house. One belonged to a neighbor, Luke Tatum, who lived down the road a piece—a Ford pickup with more rust than red paint and a pump shotgun still cradled in a rack in the back window of the cab. The other two were Buncombe County police cars. All sat silently with their doors open, seemingly abandoned. From the road, he could see the body of a deputy sheriff, lying face down on the front porch.

Tyrone climbed out of the SUV and stood there for a long moment, hesitant. Kate left the vehicle and joined him. "It's awful quiet. I don't think anyone's here."

"Oh, she's here, alright," he said. "I can feel her nearby. I always could."

Levi and his boys stood beside their truck, guns in hand. "Want us to come along?"

"No. I'll go alone."

"Best hurry it up," said Avery. He nodded toward the west. A swirling cloud of buzzards swooped and darted in the autumn sky. "The Zone's coming upon us... and it looks like a bunch of them."

"I'll make it quick." Tyrone stepped off the blacktop of the rural road and into the yard. He walked carefully, as though navigating a mine field.

Kate glanced into the Yukon and saw the Thompson

propped against the passenger seat, its barrel angled toward the floorboard. "Aren't you taking your gun?"

Tyrone turned and frowned at her. "That's my mama in there."

"But there could be Biters in there," she told him. "Or your mother... she could have..."

"Turned?" Tyrone's expression darkened. "If she has, I'll handle it."

Kate stepped forward. She laid a freckled hand gently in the crook of his arm. "I'm going with you."

The big man paused and then nodded. "Okay. But keep those pistols in your pockets, will you?"

She said nothing, made no promises. Together, they started toward the house.

It had taken them longer to reach the Jackson farmstead than they had first expected. A fourth of the way there, a burnt-out tanker truck and a dozen blackened vehicles blocked the highway, causing them to double-back several miles to find an alternate route. Instead of arriving around ten o'clock in the morning, they had finally reached the farm at a quarter 'til four in the afternoon. Long evening shadows were already forming and the sun was sinking toward the tree line to the west. Soon, gloom would darken the countryside and a chilly autumn night would descend upon them.

Tyrone and Kate were nearly to the rear bumper of the first patrol car, when a sound caught their attention. A thumping noise echoed from inside a small, weathered outbuilding. The door was closed and a length of heavy chain had been wrapped several times around the shed and secured with a large Yale padlock.

"Something's in there," said Kate.

"Later," Tyrone replied. "Let's take care of this first."

As they passed the police car, they looked through the driver's window. A deputy, emaciated and decayed, sat upright in the seat, his hands still clutching the steering wheel. The windshield ahead of him sported a single bullet hole laced with spider-web cracks. They followed the trajectory and found a hole about the size of a dime square in the middle of the officer's forehead. The hollow-point slug had exited the back of his skull, leaving a hole the size of a golf ball. Dried blood and brain matter coated the headrest of the seat. Looking past him, they saw another deputy lying halfway out of the open doorway of the passenger side. A bullet wound of the same size had entered one temple and exited the other. The man still hand his hand on his holstered service revolver.

"Your mom?"

Tyrone nodded. "She's a crack shot. Even better than you."

Although he failed to notice, Kate slipped her left hand into the pocket of her jacket. She gripped the butt of the Glock and snaked her finger through the guard. She caressed the curve of the trigger lightly, nervously.

They passed another patrol car—the first responder—and quietly mounted the steps of the porch. The lawman lying face down on the boards was the sheriff himself, from the looks of his uniform. Tyrone considered wedging the toe of this boot beneath the body and flipping it over but knew that it was probably stuck to the porch, due to decomposition. More than likely he had been lying there for a couple of months. There was no doubt in his mind, though, that the poor guy had a .38-caliber hole in the middle of his forehead, or somewhere in that general area.

"Look."

Tyrone lifted his eyes to where Kate pointed. Rusty red-brown letters, scrawled in blood, graced the white clapboard walls on each side of the front door. The ones on the left read STAY AWAY, while the ones on the right warned ZOMBIES NOT WELCOME!

"Lord have mercy," the black man muttered beneath his breath. He recognized the handwriting. The flawless penmanship of his mother had deteriorated into the frantic markings of a savage. "She's gotten worse... lost it completely."

They looked through the screen door and saw another body... a man in his fifties. He was surrounded by canned food and bottled water that had once been toted in a cardboard box, which lay a foot or two away. Tyrone answered the woman's questioning eyes. "Our next-door neighbor, Luke. He must have brought Mama some supplies… and she shot him down."

Kate's grip tightened on his arm. "Ty… we've gotta be careful. She's not in her right mind."

"I'm her baby boy," he assured her. "She's not going to hurt me."

Kate was doubtful, but didn't say so. "Let's go in."

Tyrone pushed the door open and they stepped into a narrow corridor. "Mama? Mama, it's Tyrone."

At first, they heard nothing. Then they heard a hoarse voice echoing from a room at the back of the house.

"The Lord is my shepherd… I shall not want…"

Tyrone stepped over Luke Tatum's body and started down the hallway, toward the kitchen. "Mama?"

"He maketh me to lie down in green pastures… He leadeth me beside the still waters."

"Mama, it's Tyrone," he called. "We're coming on back, okay?" There were three bodies sprawled in the doorway of the kitchen. All were Biters from the looks of them. All had taken headshots and perished instantly. Tyrone nudged them with the toe of his shoe, just to make sure they weren't playing possum. They weren't. Then he stepped over them into the kitchen.

Kate followed. She slipped the pistol from her jacket pocket and held it down, behind her right thigh, where Tyrone wouldn't see it.

The narrow kitchen looked like a war zone. There were decaying bodies strewn everywhere. Most looked to be Biters who had gotten into the house one way or another. There were a couple, though, who had come into the house as healthy as Tyrone or Kate. They were big, strapping men, and scavengers, more than likely. Both had suffered multiple bullet wounds and sported well-placed shots in the center of their foreheads. There were flies everywhere… on the bodies, on the table, on the walls. Maggots pulsated in the decayed remnants of empty food cans and dirty dishes.

"Sweet Jesus in heaven!" Tyrone moaned softly. "Mama?"

The woman sitting in the chair at the end of the kitchen table was barely recognizable to him. She rocked back and forth, her eyes glazed and focused on some unknown point on the cluttered tabletop. Her hair was frizzy and unbrushed, and was streaked with premature gray. Roaches and lice moved freely throughout the tangled mess. The woman was skin and bones. Her flesh—once dark and robust—had an ashen hue, and Tyrone could see the sunken relief of her breastbone and ribs past her ratty and stained terrycloth bathrobe. The flesh around her eye sockets and beneath her cheekbones looked bruised and caved in, more skull than face. The odor of urine and feces mingled with the stench of decomposition and death.

Tyrone's heart ached. *She looks like she's lost a hundred pounds. Maybe more.*

Kate was more focused on the object she clutched in her right hand, a nickel-plated Smith & Wesson .38 revolver. There was an open box of cartridges next to a plate of moldy pork and beans.

"Mama?" he said softly.

The woman's head bobbed aimlessly as she mumbled. "He restoreth my soul... He leadeth me in the paths of righteousness for His name's sake."

"Mama... it's me. I've come home."

She seemed oblivious to their presence. "Yea, though I walk through the valley of the shadow of walking, shambling, stinking death... I will fear no evil... no bug-infested, flesh-devouring, hell-spawn evil..."

"Mama... it's me... Tyrone."

The name, uttered in the stillness of the kitchen, gave her pause. She frowned, the muscles of her face working like worms beneath a shallow layer of soft earth. Then her eyes—and gun-filled hand—lifted from the table at the same time.

Her lips were cracked and dry, and her teeth yellow, as she spoke. "Get the hell out of here, zombie."

Tyrone wavered a little on his feet. Kate reached out with her left hand to steady him. The muscles of his broad back were tensed, as hard as iron.

"I ain't no zombie, Mama. It's your boy... Tyrone."

Again, her face worked, as though trying to digest the name that was given her. "Tyrone is dead."

"No, I ain't."

"Yes, he is," she insisted. Her eyes were feverish and angry. "He was killed. Eaten up by a damned Biter."

"That ain't true, Mama," Tyrone told her. "Who went and told you a thing like that?"

Kate watched breathlessly as she directed the muzzle of the gun at her son's face. "His daddy. That's who told me."

It was Tyrone's turn to frown. Had his father really told her that? Or was it some delusion of her already off-kilter mind.

"Are you the one who did it, zombie?" she demanded. Hot tears blossomed in her bloodshot eyes. "Are you the one who ate my baby boy and took his skin to walk around in?"

Kate licked her lips. Her mouth was bone dry. No spit whatsoever. Silently, she thumbed back the hammer of the hidden Glock.

Tyrone took a desperate step forward. "Come on now, Mama. You know me. Please... put that thing down..."

The woman's body and face trembled, but her right arm—and the gun at the end of it—were unwavering. Kate's abandoned nursing training from months ago came back to her. She knew which muscles and tendons of the human arm and hand did what, which ones were used to pick up a ball, clutch a fork to eat... or pull the trigger of a gun. It was those latter muscles that she watched carefully. It was no surprise when they thrummed and tensed beneath the skin, and her upper knuckle bulged almost indiscernibly.

Without warning, Kate lifted her arm and fired. The explosion of the gunshot was deafening in the close confines of the kitchen. Tyrone's mother rocked back in her chair as a single slug punched a quarter inch above the brow of her left eye. As the woman fell backwards—chair and all—the gun in her hand discharged. Instead of hitting Tyrone, as intended, the bullet cut air six inches above his head. Bits of plaster and white dust rained down on them as the hollow-point slammed forcefully into the kitchen ceiling.

Tyrone stood there for a long moment, as if attempting to comprehend what had just happened. Then his eyes widened and his jaw grew slack with shock. He turned and stared Kate in the face. "What...?"

"Tyrone," she said, reaching out for him.

The big man recoiled, as though her touch was poison. "What did you do?" He looked back at his mother, who lay on her back on the floor, still sitting in the kitchen chair. *"What the hell did you do?"*

Kate flinched. Deep brown eyes that had recently regarded her with affection—and perhaps something even more—now flared with a growing malice. "Tyrone...baby... please. I... I had to."

Tyrone took a couple of faltering steps, then sank to his knees beside the body of his mother. "Had to do *what*? Blow my mama's brains out?"

Gunshots rang from outside. The measured reports of hand-gun fire, as well as the staccato of her brother's AR-15. But there was not time to consider them. Their portion of time and cir-cumstance was the only thing that matter at that moment.

Kate watched as Tyrone began to sob uncontrollably. He lifted his mother's head and cradled it in his lap. The man's grief was palatable, like the electrified air before the coming of a vio-lent storm.

"Tyrone... honey... she was going to kill you. She was going to kill *both* of us. I had to."

"Had to?" he screamed angrily. "You didn't have to! You just...you just... *did* it. Put a damn bullet in my mama's head!"

"Ty, baby... please..."

"Get out of here!" The hatred in his eyes cut deep into her heart. "Get the hell out of here, you lying, murdering *bitch!*"

Tears blurred the girl's vision. Regret and sorrow were swal-lowed up by hurt. "Ty... no... please."

"GET OUT OF HERE!!"

Feeling as though there was nothing else to be said or done, she turned to leave... and ran smack-dab into her father. Crying, she buried her face in her father's broad chest.

"What's wrong?" he asked. "What happened here?"

"She... she was going to *shoot* us." Kate's voice was muffled and mournful against his shirtfront. "I had to shoot first. I had no choice."

Levi looked over his daughter's shoulder at the big man. Tyrone was embracing his mother, kissing her staring face, oblivious to the blood and brains that were soaking into the fabric of his trousers. "Lord have mercy," he muttered beneath his breath.

Gunfire from outside jolted Levi back into the urgency of a moment ago. "Kate... I know this will sound mean and uncaring... but I need you to get outside and help your mama and the others. We've got company. A lot of unwanted company... coming at us from all sides."

His daughter pulled away from him and stared at the Glock in her hand. She shuddered and tossed it to the floor. "No... I don't want it... I... I can't!"

Levi sighed, bent down, and picked up the gun. It was still warm around the ejection port. He pressed it gently into her hand. "Not trying to be ugly or anything, don't want you to think I don't give a damn... but get your ass out there, young'un, and help your mother and brothers before they get overrun. Now ain't the time to go pacifist on us."

Kate's freckled hand closed tightly around the butt of the 9mm. She pulled the Glock's mate from her other pocket. "Okay, Papa. I'm sorry."

"Just go out and keep those bastards at bay, and me and Ty will be out directly," he told her. "Gonna have a little talk with him now."

Kate wiped her eyes with the sleeve of her jacket. "Yes, sir." She disappeared down the hallway. A moment later, he heard the steady report of his daughter's twin pistols and knew that dead meat was hitting the ground.

Levi laid his shotgun on the kitchen table and crouched next to Tyrone. He had brought the Thompson along and he set it beside the big man. "Son, I know this is a bad time... a hard time... but we gotta go. Now."

"Go?" Tyrone seemed confused. "Why do we need to go?"

Levi laid a comforting hand on his shoulder. "Because the sky is black with buzzards. There's about three dozen Biters around us, closing in, and more on the way. They're coming across the fields, down the road, out of the woods. Listen... the others are out there trying to drive them back. Waiting for me and you… so's we can get away from here."

"But… my mama," Tyrone said dully. "What about her?"

"It's a hurtful thing, I know," Levi said, "but you're going to have to leave her. Say your goodbyes and go. She wouldn't want you here right now, don't you think?"

Tyrone closed his eyes and sighed. "No. She worried about me all the time in life. Sure wouldn't want her doing the same in death." Heavily, he got to his feet and laid his mother gently on the floor. Then he walked over to a china cabinet in the corner and opened one of the glass-paned doors. He took an antique coal oil lamp and a box of matches that sat beside it. Tyrone tossed the glass chimney to the side, unscrewed the wick assembly, and doused the woman's frail body with kerosene.

"What are you doing?" asked Levi.

"Ain't nobody gonna eat my mama," he told him flatly. Then he lit a match and tossed it onto her fuel-drenched body.

Outside, the big .50-caliber on top of the Humvee was going full-force. "We've got to go now. Sounds like the shit is hitting the fan out yonder."

Tyrone watched his mother burn for a long moment, then picked up the Tommy gun in one hand and the half-full container of kerosene in the other.

"What are you taking that for?" Levi asked him.

"I got a use for it," he replied grimly. Tyrone stepped out onto the front porch, set the kerosene on the rail, and began spraying a wall of Biters on the west side of the property with a steady stream of .45-caliber slugs. He fought the machine gun's recoil and kept the muzzle aimed low enough to obliterate everything above their necks.

After taking care of sixteen or seventeen, he took the kerosene and walked over to the shed with the chain wrapped around it. When he stood before the door, the grunting began again, belying the frustration and hunger of the creature trapped inside. Several massive fingers, dark and riddled with decay, forced their way through a crack between the door and the wall that bordered it. On one of them was a gold wedding band big enough to drop a half dollar through.

Tyrone laid his hand across the fingers. They were cold...
the skin coarse and cracked. They felt both alien and hauntingly
familiar to him.

"I'm sorry I left you holding the bag," he said softly. "If I'd
stayed, maybe things would have turned out different. Maybe
Mama would be alive and you... maybe you wouldn't be the
way you are now."

Tyrone stepped back and saturated the front of the shed door
with the remainder of the kerosene. Then he lit it with a match.
The wood of the building was as dry as tinder. The fire spread
swiftly and soon the structure had changed from a simple tool
shed into a flaming funeral pyre.

"Come on, Ty!" hollered Avery, standing in the bed of the
pickup truck, firing his assault rifle from the hip. "You're the
only one who knows what's what around these parts."

Tyrone made it to the road and regarded the head of the
Hobbs clan. "So, where are we headed?"

Levi remembered James Newman's suggestion. "How far is
it to the Biltmore?"

"Four miles." The black man looked down the country road,
in the direction of the main highway. The lane was choked with
Biters. To get through would take a bulldozer. "We'll have to
take a short cut down the east end of the road. There's a logging
road that cuts off to the left, It will take us a little longer, but
there's less chance of getting swarmed the way we are now."

"Let's head out everybody!" called Levi. He glanced back
toward the Jackson household. The back of the house where
the kitchen was located was beginning to burn. The tool shed
was totally engulfed. He looked back at Tyrone. The big man
stared at the place where he had spent his childhood. There was
a weary, pained expression on his face. He seemed to have aged
twenty years in the past thirty minutes.

"Do you mind I ride in the back of your truck," Tyrone asked
him. "I think it's best if I steer clear of your murdering bitch of a
daughter for a while."

Levi felt his temper flare, but said nothing. Given the circum-
stances, he supposed Tyrone's feelings were understandable. He
nodded toward the open bed of the Dodge. "Help yourself."

Kate snapped another couple of shots, reloaded with fresh clips, and headed toward the driver's side of the Yukon. Levi caught her before she climbed in. "You okay, hon?"

"Yeah," she said dully. She looked like she was shell-shocked... as though she'd lost an important piece of herself back in the kitchen of that house. "I'm just dandy."

"Jem!" Levi called out. "You drive and let your sister ride shotgun."

"I said I was okay, Papa." A spark of the girl's red-headed temper flared for a moment and then was swallowed by pathos once again.

"Just do as I say!" He steered her toward the passenger side. By the time Levi reached his truck, brother and sister were inside the Yukon and ready to roll.

The big pickup took point and they headed out. Jem followed. He glanced over at his sister and frowned. She sat silently in the passenger seat. Her green eyes stared through the windshield, but she seemed to be looking inward more than outward.

"Are you okay, Sis?"

"He hates me," she mumbled.

"Who hates you?" he asked.

"Tyrone."

Jem shook his head. "No way, Kate. That man is flat-out in—"

She turned tearful, burning eyes toward him, causing his tongue to freeze in mid-sentence. "He HATES me. Now just shut the hell up and drive."

Her brother said nothing else. Jem focused on the shadowy road ahead and kept pace with the others. He wasn't sure exactly what had taken place inside the Jackson farmhouse, but whatever it was, it had altered some things mighty fast. And weakened, perhaps even destroyed, a bond he had seen strengthen, day by day, since they had left the little church in the town of Woodrow.

CHAPTER 24

In 1889, George Washington Vanderbilt II, grandson of railroad and shipping magnate Cornelius Vanderbilt, envisioned an ambitious project—a project that only vast wealth and a propensity for luxury could have brought about.

Purchasing nearly 700 parcels of land—including 50 farms—he set out to construct a summer estate in the rural countryside near Asheville, North Carolina. Enlisting the expertise of New York architect, Richard Morris Hunt, Vanderbilt began construction on his "little mountain escape" as he referred to it. As the project expanded in stature and excess, he named his estate "Biltmore" after his family's place of origin in distant Holland.

Seven years in the making, Biltmore became the largest privately-owned manor house in the United States. A three-mile stretch of railroad track was laid to transport tons of materials to the construction site. While over a thousand workers and sixty stone masons labored on his elaborate Chateuseque-style home, Vanderbilt went on extensive buying sprees in Europe, purchasing lavish furnishings, paintings, statuary, and tapestries for the estate. By its completion in 1896, Biltmore resembled a vast castle more than a simple summer home. The rich and famous of that time period, as well as men of great power and influence, visited Vanderbilt's country estate, enjoying its extensive grounds—near 125,000 acres worth—and its four-story, 250-room mansion. The grounds featured lavish gardens and a conservatory at the southern end of the house and stables for Vanderbilt's prized horses and twenty private carriages on the northern end. Biltmore itself was equipped with such nineteenth-century innovations as electric elevators, forced-air heating, centrally controlled clocks, fire alarms, and a call-bell system for summoning the estate's legion of servants.

For years, Biltmore was a paradise of luxury and excess. But by the turn of the century, driven by the impact of newly imposed income taxes and the fact that the estate was getting harder to manage economically, George Vanderbilt initiated the sale of 87,000 acres to the federal government. Following Vanderbilt's untimely death in 1914, his widow found it increasingly difficult to maintain the vast manor house and its property, and sold additional land, whittling the estate to 7,000 acres. Financial difficulties plagued the estate though the Great Depression in the mid-1930s. It was then that Vanderbilt's daughter, Cornelia, opened Biltmore to the public as an upper-scale tourist attraction.

When conjuring and constructing his dream project in the latter half of the nineteenth century, George Washington Vanderbilt could have never foreseen or dared fathomed that his palatial summer estate would someday become a fortress against the unimaginable.

By the time Levi and the others reached the main road entrance to the Biltmore Estate, evening had begun to set in. The November sun had dropped below the dense forest to the west and the long-cast shadows between the ancient oaks and maples of the vast property deepened and broadened into the darkening gloom of dusk. The narrow one-lane access road wound sharply through the trees. Among them, shuffling, disjointed motion and the pale forms of Biters could be seen, working their way, en masse, through the woods on each side of the roadway.

"There's sure a lot of 'em," Nell said grimly. Every now and then one would lurch out of the forest and collide with the fender of the truck, either careening back in the direction it had come, or falling beneath the tires to be run over and crushed underneath.

Levi said nothing in reply. His attention was fully on his driving and the treacherous curves of the roadway ahead. He glanced at his wife once and saw that her face was tense and her eyes alert and bright with fear. The knuckles of her right hand were pale with strain as she clutched the nickel-plated Magnum revolver tightly in her grasp.

Every now and then, Tyrone would make his presence known with short bursts from the Thompson. The collective roaring of the three vehicles were drawing the Biters out of the forest. Bold and hungry, they began stumbling into the open, teeth gnashing and pale fingers working feverishly for a handhold on anything that sped toward or past them. Sometimes three or four would lurch toward them in unison. That is when Ty would unleash a burst of a dozen rounds or so, obliterating their heads and dropping them in their tracks.

"Damn!" said Avery. "This is getting downright intense."

The boy's simple remark seemed to irritate his mother's already-frazzled nerves. "Oh yeah?" she snapped. "You really think so?"

"Yes, ma'am," replied Avery, ducking his head a little, as if he'd been swatted at. "Sorry."

"We're all a little on edge," Levi said aloud. "But we'll get through this. We'll get to that big ol' house and we'll be just fine."

His wife and son nodded silently, looking more doubtful than hopeful. To tell the truth, his own words came across flat and unconvincing in his own ears. Levi glanced in the rearview mirror. He could see the Yukon and the Humvee following closely behind him. As the sky darkened and daylight faded, the vehicles' frames were swallowed up by the glow of their headlights. But that in itself was comforting. At least he knew they were still with him and hadn't been overpowered by a disabling wave of the bug-ridden corpses.

Avery slid open the back window of the truck's cab. "Hey, Ty! Where is this place? How much farther do we have to go?"

Tyrone's dark face filled the opening of the little window. His face was bathed with sweat, despite the chill of the evening. "It's kind of hard to tell, it getting dark and all. To tell the truth, I've only been here once before… on a field trip when I was ten or eleven. I remember there's a visitor center up ahead and, past that, a parking lot and the iron gateway that leads onto the main property where the house is."

Levi nodded. "I see it up ahead."

Fifteen seconds later, he was speeding past the low, brick structure of the visitor center. Most of the glass in its tall windows was gone and he could see Biters wandering aimlessly inside. Levi recalled what Frank Gentry had said about how the dead tended to gather where they had once congregated in life. He figured tourist attractions around the country were probably full of Biters... the rims of the Grand Canyon, Yellowstone, maybe even Disney World.

Suddenly, the truck's headlights shown on the slender, black rails of a tall, wrought-iron gate. It was a pretty piece of work and had probably cost a fortune back when it was installed in the late 1800s. But, then, "fortune" was what the Vanderbilt family had been all about in that day and time.

Levi didn't slow down. He stamped on the gas and headed straight for the gate. As he neared it, he could see a heavy chain snaking through the openings between the bars and wrapped around the huge stone pillar to the right, secured in place with a large padlock as big as Levi's fist.

"Y'all hold on!" he yelled. "This is gonna be a bitch to get through!" He hoped that Tyrone was braced in the back of the truck. If he hit the iron gate and it held fast, the big man was liable to flip over the roof of the cab upon impact and be thrown forcefully against the unyielding metal bars like a rag doll flung by an angry child.

A moment later, the grill of the truck collided with the gate. It felt like they had hit a brick wall, but their momentum did the trick and carried them through. The chain snapped and unfurled. Its heavy links struck the passenger side of the windshield, in front of Nell. The safety glass fissured, but didn't shatter.

"Lord have mercy, Levi! You're gonna give me a heart attack before we set a toenail inside the place!"

Her husband couldn't help but grin. "Stop your bellyaching, old woman. I got you here, didn't I?"

He took a sharp right turn onto a paved lane and there it was.

The Biltmore House was massive, towering, standing in

dark relief against the evening sky. It was constructed of lime-stone, timber, Pennsylvania steel, and bricks fired in a kiln Vanderbilt had built on the property. Levi had seen the place before in magazines and on television, but neither could do justice to the sheer magnitude of the structure. It was truly an American castle.

Levi had half expected the grounds around the mansion to be empty, but instead there were at least two or three dozen Biters on the vast rectangular lawn directly in front of the house's main hall. Apparently, there were places other than the main gate that led onto the property and the zombies had taken full advantage of those access points.

The three vehicles made their way down the right-hand lane and pulled to a halt in front of the tall oaken doors of the main entrance. They noticed that the windows had been boarded up from outside. Sheets of plywood and particleboard had been screwed securely in place with masonry screws, stretching to a height of seven feet. The remainder of the eight-foot windows was uncovered, but completely out of reach from the destruc-tive reach of any Biter that might attack the front of the house.

As they left their vehicles and started for the archway of the main doors, they saw the Biters coming for them. They sham-bled across the leaf-strewn grass of the lawn, black teeth snap-ping hungrily. Steep steps, guarded by two stone lions, led to the doors of the entrance hall. The heavy slabs of timber were scuffed and splintered, as well as decorated with dried blood, clots of flesh, and dislodged fingernails and teeth. It appeared to have withstood zombie attacks many times before.

Levi bounded up the steps to the door and pulled on the ornate handles. Considering the boarded windows, he really wasn't surprised to find the barrier securely locked. It didn't budge an inch.

"Somebody must be here, or it wouldn't be shut up, tighter than a drum," he told the others. "Or else they left and locked the door behind them."

The brittle crack of a rifle shot told them that his former the-ory was the case. It echoed high from a parapet directly above them. They ducked their heads, figuring maybe the shot was intended for them. It wasn't, though. A biter that was stumbling across the lawn from the direction of the rose garden suddenly dropped in its tracks, the uppermost portion of its skull obliterated by a .375 Magnum round.

"Shitfire!" exclaimed Avery. "What was that? An elephant gun?"

"Holland & Holland Magnum," called a female voice from overhead. "Good for elephant, rhino, water buffalo... and the occasional zombie. Which isn't quite as 'occasional' as it used to be."

Levi and Avery stepped back into the courtyard and peered up into the gloom. They were surprised to see a dark-haired teenage girl wearing glasses and sporting a huge bolt-action rifle with a scope mounted on top. As they watched, she worked the bolt smoothly, jacked another cartridge into the breech, and centered the scope's crosshairs once again. This time a matronly woman Biter bit the dust. She dropped to the ground, twitching, nothing much left above her splintered neckbone but the rise and fall of jetting blood and tiny black bugs.

"It's an antique," she said, matter-of-factly. "George Vanderbilt took it to Africa with him a month before he died of a ruptured appendix. It's old, but works like a charm."

"Miss, we don't have time for a gun review or a history lesson," Levi called up to her. "We just need to get inside as soon as you can unlock that door."

At that moment there was a series of metallic clicks and clacks, and the big door swung inward a foot or so. "What makes you think we'll let you in? Do you know how many assholes have showed up on our doorstep, asking for the same thing?"

The girl at the door was identical to the one above, with the exception of wearing no glasses and an elaborate tattoo of several knights on horseback and a king on his throne that graced her left arm from elbow to wrist. She had a holstered .50 semi-auto Desert Eagle pistol across her chest and held a pump shotgun—a ten-gauge from the looks of it—with a bore big enough to stick three fingers and a thumb in, with room to spare. The cannon-sized muzzle of the scattergun was aimed from her hip and both men knew that, if she fired, it would likely cut both of them in half above the navel.

"Damn! There's two of 'em!" declared Avery. "Are you twins?"

The girl smirked sarcastically. "No, we're clones. Of course we're twins, doofus." She shifted her eyes to Jem. "Looks like you have one, too... but better looking and sporting a higher IQ, I'd say."

Avery glared. "You're a brutal one, ain't you? I'm not sure I'd want to step in there now. It'd be like sticking my pecker in a meat grinder."

She couldn't help but smile. "Damn straight! Anyway, who says that you're coming in? I don't recall sending out invitations."

"Please," said Nell, "we have a little girl out here and a woman who's expecting. You wouldn't want them to get hurt, would you?"

The H&H boomed loudly overhead, dropping another Biter twenty yards away. It was followed by the clatter of Tyrone's Tommy gun and the heavy-caliber rattle of Billy's M2 mounted on the roof of the Humvee. "For heaven's sake, Chelle!" hollered the girl with the rifle. "You know my night vision isn't worth spit and it's getting darker—and more crowded—by the minute!"

The girl with the shotgun peered past the gathering of people. There were perhaps fifty or sixty zombies on the lawn with more coming down out of the woods. "You're such a party-pooper, sis! Well just don't stand there like a bunch of mouth-breathing, inbred hillbillies... even if you are. Get your asses inside before they get gnawed down to the tailbone!"

A moment later, they were all inside. The last one through the door was Katie, blazing away with a Glock in each freckled hand. A biter lunged at her from the far side of a stone lion, but their host stepped in, drawing the .50 Magnum. The pistol went off with the roar of a cannon, punching a softball-sized crater through the zombie's chest, clear past its spine. As it toppled off the steps, a second shot destroyed its skull, leaving only its lower jaw and thick black tongue behind.

Holstering the Desert Eagle, she locked four heavy deadbolts.

"Well that was too damn close! We haven't had a zombie within a hundred yards of this place in two weeks and then you show up and they're all over the place! And what's with ruining our gate? I loved that freaking gate!"

Levi and the others looked around the spacious entry hall. To the right was a small atrium with a marble fountain in the center, a winter garden as it was called in the Victorian era. Beyond that was a wing leading to the pool room and grand dining hall. To the left was a great, winding staircase. Ornate candelabras of gilded gold had been lit and cast a muted glow upon the stone walls and marble floors. They heard rapid footsteps on the stairs and turned to find the first girl making her way to the ground floor. The rifle was canted easily across her narrow shoulder. In addition to the bolt-action, she sported a long-bladed MTech survival knife on one hip and a holstered Ruger GP100 .44 Magnum revolver on the other.

"Hi!" she said, almost cheerfully. "Sorry we were so cautious. We don't get many visitors showing up out of nowhere. I'm Melissa Webb and this is my sister, Michelle."

"Much obliged for your help, Melissa," Levi said. He then introduced himself, his wife and kids, as well as Tyrone and the Tauchee family.

Outside they could hear the shuffling of feet on the flagstones of the outer court and the grating of fingernails scrabbling desperately against the vast oaken doors of the manor house. "Do you think they'll go away?" asked Jessie, clutching her doll to her chest.

"Sure, honey," Michelle told her, dropping her defensiveness a couple of notches. "If we're quiet for a while, they'll forget we're even here and wander off. If there's one trait these zombies have in common, it's their short-term memories."

Her sister looked doubtful. "Maybe... except for the ones who come back here time after time. And it's not like they're looking for food, either. It's like they know the place."

Despite his initial irritation at Michelle, Avery couldn't help but be impressed by the twins' firepower. The Holland & Holland and the ten-gauge looked like a Howitzer and a bazooka in their small hands.

"So, how many do you think you've killed?" he asked them. He figured fifteen or twenty at the most.

The one with the glasses frowned and shrugged her shoulders. "Now how in the world would we know—?"

"Two hundred and fifty-seven," replied the other. "Two hundred and fifty-seven and three-quarters, if you count a baby and a chipmunk."

Avery smiled and laughed. "We got us some hardcore, sharp-shooting gals here! The Sisters of Slaughter!"

Melissa rolled her eyes. "Come on. Give me a break!"

"I don't know," said Michelle with a sly grin. "I kinda like it."

They all stood in the big vestibule for a long moment. Awkward silence threatened to take over. Then Melissa stepped in and offered an olive branch, as usual. "I'd love to invite you to a wonderful supper, but truth is, neither one of us can cook worth a darn. Our idea of a gourmet meal is PB&J sandwiches and Ramen noodles."

Michelle nodded grudgingly. "She's right. We've got a pantry to beat all pantries, stocked with a two or three years' worth of food, but we would burn water if we tried to boil it."

Nell glanced over at Enolia and Kate. "Well, now I believe your hospitality deserves something in return. Just lead the way and leave the cooking to us."

"I'm afraid our kitchen is sort of old-fashioned," Melissa told them apologetically. "It's huge, but it's primitive."

"Honey," said Nell with a smile. "I grew up on primitive."

As the twins showed Nell, Kate, and Enolia to the kitchen, Levi and the others remained in the entrance hall.

"Well, I'd say we got damn lucky," he said. "If those gals hadn't let us in, we'd be holed up in our vehicles out there right now, with Biters slobbering on the windshield and beating their skulls against the windows. Either that or on foot, running through the woods with a zombie at every twist and turn."

"I don't know, Papa," said Avery shaking his head. "That Michelle... she's like two hell-cats cinched up in a tow sack, doused with kerosene. If she breaks out the voodoo doll and needles again, I'm liable to take my chances with those bug-headed bastards outside."

CHAPTER 25

They ate in the massive dining hall in the west wing.
Their voices echoed off the high walls and the cavernous ceiling of the elegant chamber as they talked and laughed. The ten sat at one end of the long mahogany table, warmed by a crackling fire in the huge fireplace. Nell, Kate, and Enolia had prepared a meal that the Vanderbilts themselves would have approved of: canned summer squash, tomatoes, and green beans, as well as large slabs of country ham cut from one of the dozen that hung from the ceiling of the huge pantry. Stone-milled flour and cornmeal had provided the ingredients for buttery yeast rolls and cornbread muffins. For dessert they had hot cobbler made with canned blackberries and peaches.

"So," asked Levi, "have you two been living here by yourselves since this whole thing began?"

Michelle and Melissa looked at each other and laughed. "Yes. To tell the truth, you could say we practically grew up here," said Melissa. "Our father was the head curator at the Biltmore. He was a history professor at the University of Arizona in Tucson until we were seven years old. After our mother died of breast cancer, he left the college and we moved to Asheville, where he took the curator position here. He was one of the most knowledgeable men in the country on the Vanderbilt family, the estate, and its history. But away from here he was different. He was something of a survivalist, you might say. He felt that someday something would happen that would put an end to normal existence as we knew it—a nuclear war, viral epidemic, or something like that. As it turned out, he was right. But I don't think even Dad would have thought one tiny bug as big as a grain of sand would be the catalyst that brought civilization to the brink of extinction."

"When we were nine, he started making preparations," Michelle said, continuing the story. "He instructed us in the use of various kinds of assault weapons, and had us trained in hand-to-hand combat and martial arts. He also began to stockpile previsions—weapons, ammunition, food, water, medical supplies—and secretly stashed them here in the main house."

"How did he manage that without making the staff suspicious?" asked Jem.

Melissa smiled at the boy across the table and, blushing, adjusted her glasses self-consciously on the bridge of her nose. "Being the head curator, he would pack the supplies in wooden crates marked as antiquities and ship them here. There are rooms on every floor of this house that are unfurnished and pretty much serve as storage areas. He would have the crates moved there by the maintenance crew, where they would sit, completely forgotten... until we needed them, years later."

Nell regarded the twins sympathetically. "And what happened to your father? You don't have to tell us, if it's too personal."

A mutual sadness shown in the girls' faces at the thought of what had happened. "Dad passed away of a massive stroke two weeks before the shit hit the fan," said Michelle. She looked toward Nell apologetically. "Pardon the language, Mrs. Hobbs."

"That's quite alright, dear. Go on."

"We were getting ready to move back out west, to live with an aunt in Mesa, Arizona, when the infestation hit full force," she continued. "People started to turn and those who didn't took to the road or had to stay and fight the Biters. We knew what we had to do; stick to our father's plan. We armed ourselves, took Dad's keys, and came here. We were surprised to find the property abandoned. You would have thought someone would have seen the potential in using it as a haven against all this madness, but apparently no one did... not even the ones who owned the estate or those who worked here. Since then, it's pretty much just been me and Lissa holed up in here."

"Oh, people show up every now and then," Melissa told them. "But we don't let just anyone in. We can pretty much tell when someone is on the level or bad medicine. Well, most of the time we can." She dropped her eyes for a long moment, staring at her plate as she picked at her food. When she looked up, her face was grim, devoid of her usual cheerfulness. Her eyes studied the dark wood and elaborate stonework of the dining room. The glow of the hearth extended only so far, leaving the rest of the room in deep shadow. "No one ever stays very long. This place is dark and depressing... oppressive. After a while it starts feeling like a prison instead of a refuge. Then they pack up and leave, and it's just me and Chelle again."

Conversation turned to other things as dessert and coffee was served. Afterward, they left the table and headed toward the winding staircase in the great stone foyer.

"You can take your pick of where you want to sleep," Melissa told them, leading the way with a candelabra. "There are two hundred and fifty rooms in this house and thirty-five are bedrooms. The guest bedrooms are on the second and third floors, while the servants' quarters were on the fourth."

As they started toward the stairs, Michelle spoke up. "Mr. Hobbs... can I talk to you for a sec?"

Levi nodded. He turned to his wife. "You go on. I'll catch up in a minute."

When the others had gone, Levi regarded the teenager curiously. "What can I do for you, young lady?"

"Since you seem to be the leader of the pack, I figured it's you I should deal with," she said. Her eyes grew somber and unwavering. "My sister is a sweet person... got a heart of gold and is smarter than I'll ever hope to be. It seems like she was blessed with cotton candy, unicorns, and rainbows, while I ended up all barbed-wire, piss, and vinegar. It's the way we're different. She's trusting of folks and a little naïve, while I'm coarse as a cob and naturally suspicious as hell."

"I'm certainly not going to fault you for being suspicious," Levi told her. "You and your sister have a right to be... us just showing up out of nowhere, barging in and upsetting what you've got here. If I were in your shoes, I'd likely do the same."

"I want to trust you," said Michelle. "I really do… more than you know. But we've gone through this before. And it ended badly." The girl hesitated and then continued. "We had visitors a month and a half ago. Two men and a woman. They seemed nice and normal at first. Then I sensed how things really were. The woman was scared shitless of those men, hardly said a word and had bruises and burns on her arms and neck. Claimed the bruises came from fending off a Biter attack. Maybe… but zombies don't smoke unfiltered Camels, so that didn't explain the burns.

"They were with us for nearly a week. Lissa was happy for the company, but I knew things were turning sour. The men were watching us too much. They started making lewd comments and talking among themselves out of earshot. I could see in their eyes that they wanted us… badly. And after they were done, they'd want us out of the picture for good. I tried warning my sister, but she said I was being paranoid. I thought maybe I was. I tried to see it her way. I really did."

Levi could see the hurt in the girl's face, hear it in her voice. "What happened?"

"One night, after supper, Lissa went to the library for a book. The men followed her, while the woman distracted me, acting like she'd tripped and twisted her ankle on the stairs." Michelle grew silent and closed her eyes, shuddering. Levi could see a hint of tears seep beneath her dark lashes. "They cornered Lissa and tried to rape her. By the time I got there… they already had her… panties… off." When she opened her eyes, the tears flowed freely. "Mr. Hobbs, my sister is the only good thing I have in this shitty, messed-up world, and I will do anything in my power to protect her. *Anything.*"

Levi didn't want to, but knew he had to ask. "And where are those men now?"

"Buried in the woods out back of the stables," she said, wiping her cheeks with the palm of her hand. "We asked the woman to stick around. I couldn't really blame her. What she'd done, she'd done out of fear. She stayed for a couple of days. Then we woke up one morning and she was gone. I have no idea where she went… or if she's even alive."

"Michelle, we're not like that," Levi assured her. "I swear to God we're not."

"I know. I'm a pretty fair judge of character. I can tell that you are decent folks. But on the slimmest chance that you're not... that you're something other than you claim to be... well, I just wanted to let you know where I stand. And what I'm capable of."

"I appreciate your honesty," he told her. "And, to tell the truth, if it came down to protecting me and mine, I'd do the same."

Michelle smiled. The gesture was sincere, as though a load had fallen off her shoulders. "Thanks for hearing me out, Mr. Hobbs."

"Levi," he corrected.

Her smile broadened. "Levi, then." As an afterthought, she extended her hand. "Good night... and welcome."

"Much obliged." He reached out and took what was offered him. Her hand was small in his grasp, but firm and strong. It reminded him of Nell's, capable of tenderness, but sturdy, not afraid of hard work and adversity.

And not afraid to do the unthinkable if absolutely necessary.

CHAPTER 26

L evi and the others adjusted well to their new home. Although they were unaccustomed to the elegant surroundings that the Biltmore provided, most were mountain people in one way or another. The Hobbs had lived in the lofty foothills of the Smokies, while the Tauchees had dwelt amid the peaks of the Carolina Appalachians. The Blue Ridge Mountains provided a familiarity that put them at ease and one that would provide the sustenance and materials that they had enjoyed—and relied on—back in the regions they had been born and bred in.

They also took on individual responsibilities to do their part in keeping up the estate, a job that Michelle and Melissa had done alone for three and a half months. Nell and Enolia did the cooking and cleaning, while the elder Hobbs also tended to the rose garden and the surviving plants around the huge glass and brick conservatory. Tyrone drew upon his knowledge of farming to assist Nell in raising produce like tomatoes and other vegetables in the glass-paned greenhouse, using kerosene heaters to provide warmth on the frigid November nights. He also helped with security for the main house and the surrounding grounds, along with Melissa, Kate, and Jem.

Levi, Avery, and Billy took advantage of the dense forests that surrounded the estate. Using the tools of their trade, found in some of the outbuildings of the property, they harvested the timberland for firewood—the Biltmore did possess sixty-five fireplaces—and for fortifying the barriers that the twins had already put in place at the massive windows and French doors that graced the mansion from one end to the other. They also hunted and fished, finding healthy, uninfected wildlife, such as deer, rabbit, turkey, and pheasant in the woods and pastures, and trout, crappie, bluegill, and catfish in the mountain streams—waterways that had escaped contamination from the tiny black insects that had poisoned most of the earth's freshwater and saltwater sources.

Michelle acted as the unofficial head of the estate, scheduling chores and security shifts, and did a little bit of everything, including working timber and hunting alongside the men. Part of her interest in such things was to genuinely help out, but Levi suspected a large amount was to provide some good-natured competition to Avery and knock his rambunctious son down a few notches. More than once the boy had stomped, red-faced, back to the main house, outdone by the pretty brunette in cross-cut sawing, deer hunting, frog-gigging, and a dozen other activities he prided himself on being an expert at.

The two girls seemed to be genuinely grateful for their new company and the contributions they made. In turn, the Hobbs, Tauchees, and Tyrone Jackson were glad to finally be off the road and able to settle in one place for a while.

One week led into another. Gradually, suspicions faded and emotional bonds were built and solidified among those who lived and worked together. More and more, what they had formed within the remote confines of the estate began to resemble what had once been known, before the death and devastation of the Infestation, as community.

Jem opened the door leading to the main hall's outer balcony. It was four o'clock in the afternoon, but the sun was already on the verge of setting.

His watch wouldn't end until eight that night, but he didn't mind. He enjoyed the solitude of being by himself. He always had—hiking, reading, whatever. He was more at ease with himself than anyone else. In that way he was totally unlike his twin brother, who always seemed to require an audience for his grandstanding and bullshitting.

When he saw Melissa standing at the balcony railing, a lump formed in his throat and his pulse quickened. He swallowed dryly. "Hey."

Startled, the girl turned at his voice. He couldn't tell for sure, but she seemed to react in the same, fumbling awkward way as he. They always did when they crossed paths.

"Hey yourself," she said, leaning her rifle against the balcony railing. She pushed her glasses up the bridge of her nose nervously, a habit she only seemed to display when he was around. "Here for your shift?"

"Yep." He looked around the balcony, which stretched the width of the central building's third floor. If trouble came, they were loaded for bear. Various hunting rifles and assault weapons stood at intervals along the railing and the corners of the platform. Billy and Avery had even removed the .50-caliber M2 machine gun from the roof of the Humvee and mounted it on a grounded tripod on the stone parapet that overlooked the rectangular lawn below. The next time a pack of Biters showed up, they would be able to mow them down in a matter of minutes, instead of picking them off one at a time.

The two stood there silently for a minute, before Jem spoke. "Ma's fixing a good supper tonight. Chicken and dumplings."

Melissa seemed surprised. "Now where in the world did your mom find a chicken?"

"Over at the farm at Antler Village," he said. "She found two or three of them. Kinda scrawny, but healthy enough, and not full of those dadblamed bugs." He shuffled his feet and looked down at the Armalite in his hands. The AR-18 had been his personal weapon since Frank Gentry had up and disappeared on them. "Well, you can go now, if you want."

The girl gave him a false pout. "Trying to get rid of me?"

"Uh... no!" Jim stammered. "Of course not." His mouth was as dry as cotton. "I... I like you being here."

Melissa hesitated and then walked across the balcony toward him. "I don't mean to be rude... but does that hurt?"

Jem blushed. She was talking about the left side of his head. The missing ear and the burn tissue from Abe's torching of the parasites. "It's still a little tender... but it doesn't hurt. Most of the nerves are dead, I reckon."

She lifted her hand toward his face, but stopped in mid-reach. "Sorry."

He couldn't believe that he actually did it, but he took her hand and guided it toward the ugly mass of scar tissue. It was soft and warm between his fingers. His heart pounded like a jackhammer. "No. It's alright. Go ahead."

Gently, she touched the side of his head, running her fingertips from his temple to the nape of his neck. There was nothing sexual about her attention, only heartfelt curiosity and concern. Just having her standing there, scarcely a foot away, made him a little lightheaded.

"What happened?" she finally asked.

Jim told her about the wildlife ambush on the park road to Cherokee, of the zombie possum attack and his brother's only course of action to prevent him from infestation. He also told her how Abe had set his head on fire to kill any lingering parasites that might have been transferred through the bite. The only thing he didn't tell her about was the despair he suffered afterward and his misguided brush with suicide, before Billy Tauchee had relieved him of the Magnum pistol and saved his life.

"That's frightening," she said, pulling her fingers away from the scarred flesh. "I bet you were scared half to death."

Not one bit! I can handle that kind of thing. That was what his brother would have said in his swaggering, boastful way. Instead, he said "I was absolutely horrified."

As she lowered her hand toward her side, he caught it and held it. She didn't pull away. "Can I ask another question, Jem?"

"Sure."

"Did you, uh… have a girlfriend… back in Tennessee?"

He felt sick to his stomach. *She just had to ask that, didn't she?* "Yeah. Sort of."

"What was her name?"

"Sarah." The thought of her was as fresh and raw as an open wound.

"Is Sarah… is she still…?"

"No," he said flatly. He left it at that. He certainly wasn't going to tell her what he had done to her with his father's gun on that awful night beneath the oak tree. "How about you? Any boyfriends?"

"Me?" she said, as if in shock. "Chelle has always been the boy-crazy one. She's had two or three. Actually, I thought her and Avery would have hooked up by now."

"Really? I doubt that very much. They hate each other's guts!"

Melissa grinned. "No, I don't believe so. I think they're so much alike that they can't help but rub each other the wrong way. Both are bound and determined to prove themselves and get the upper hand. They're both perpetual show-offs with a dash of asshole thrown in for good measure. Sort of the polar opposite of you and me."

"But I wasn't asking about Michelle, was I?" he said. "So, tell me? Boyfriends?"

She ducked her eyes shyly. "No, not me. I guess I never found the nerve. To be honest, I'm a terminal nerd if there ever was one."

Jem clasped her hand tighter. "Well, hello, Miss Nerd. Allow me to introduce myself. I'm Mister Dweeb."

They both laughed at the lame joke, then grew silent.

"Well, I guess I better get to work," he told her. He tried to release her hand, but she refused to give it up that easily.

"I tell you what," she said, "why don't I bring you up a plate after supper and keep you company for a while. That is… if you want me to." Her hazel eyes looked up at him, questioning.

Before he could even think about it, Jem bent down and kissed her. He half expected her to pull away and slap the fire out of him. Instead, she leaned closer. Although it couldn't have lasted but a few seconds, it felt like it lasted forever… in a wonderful way.

When they pulled away, reluctantly, he studied her face. Melissa's face positively glowed, but still couldn't outshine her smile. "Well, I guess that answered my question."

Jem couldn't help but smile himself. "Yeah, I reckon so."

Following supper, Enolia stood on the rear veranda that adjoined the mansion's main entrance hall. She breathed in the crisp November air and ran her hands over her belly. She waited and smiled when the baby kicked.

The woman closed her eyes. Her smile broadened. "Even

with all that training, you can't sneak up on me, Billy Tauchee."

She felt her husband's arms encircle her and a low chuckle as he kissed her on the back of the neck. "If I'd had to reckon with you on all those missions, I would've never made it home."

Enolia's good humor faded. "Please don't joke about a thing like that."

"Sorry." He laid his head on her shoulder and caressed the swell of her abdomen. "He's going to be a big *atsutsa*."

"*If* he ever comes. It seems like I've been pregnant forever."

"He will come soon. Your grandmother said early December, did she not?"

Sadness weighed heavily upon her heart. "Yes... and she was always right about such things."

They stood there for a while, enjoying each other without the presence of the others.

"We should go over it again," he whispered.

"Billy," she sighed, "there's no need. I know it by heart. So does Jessie. The names, the addresses, the map coordinates, the code words. God forbid something should happen to you... but if it does, we will know what to do."

"Even so," he insisted, "let's do it one more time."

You said that the last time, she thought to herself, but didn't say so.

"Please...from the beginning of the list."

She nodded. "Kuruk Shanta, Mescalero Apache. Desert Route 12, Ruidoso, New Mexico. 33 degrees 19'54.2964" North... 105 degrees 40'22.9512" West. Code name: Stalking Bear."

"Next," he urged softly.

"Janice Biauswah, Chippewa. East Cedar Parkway, Red Lake, Minnesota..."

Tension hung heavily in the darkness of their bedroom.

Levi reached out for Nell's shoulder. She shuddered beneath his touch.

"What's wrong, hon?" he asked softly.

It took her a moment to reply. When she did, his stomach sank.

"The dread is upon me, Levi."

He knew what that meant. It was something they had shared for a long time, since even before they were married. Nell's intuitions, if the term could be put that lightly, were a part of her as much as flesh or blood or bone. When the moods hit her, they were one of two kinds. Joy or dread. When the joy was upon her it meant babies born and lovers wed, a financial wellspring or a good report from the doctor. But dread... dread carried a dark and cumbersome weight. Sickness, cancer, stillbirth, mountain wakes, and the planting of loved ones, six feet under.

Levi recalled the last few episodes she had suffered. Nervously preparing for departure before the zombie attack on Hobbs Ridge, seeing Frank Gentry for the dangerous and unstable man that he was, as well as other instances.

He lay behind her and held her tight. The trembling continued, unable to subside. "Why would you feel that way?" he asked. "We're in a good place with good folks. We've got a dry roof over our heads, plenty to eat, and we haven't seen a Biter in the two weeks we've been here. Seems like there would be a joy to such blessings."

Nell stiffened in his embrace. "You know I can't control this. Can't turn it on and off like water from a spigot."

"I'm sorry," he said and felt her relax again.

Silence filled the room for a while, then she spoke when she was ready. "Something's gonna happen, Levi. I don't know what or to whom, but it will. I want you and the boys to be extra careful when you're out timbering or hunting for game."

"We always are. More so now than before the world went to hell."

She turned and nestled in his arms. He felt her head nod against his chest. "I know that, but things happen. A tree could fall upon you or you could cut yourself with a saw. You could get sick staying out in the cold all day. Get pneumonia or some such ailment. Even if there are no Biters within shouting distance, other dangers can befall a man. Things that can't be predicted."

"Nell." He held her tighter, attempting to quell her fears. "Sweetheart, you can't be thinking of such. It'll gnaw you down to the raw nerve with worry."

"It can't be helped," she said in resignation. "The dread will have its way."

"I promise we'll be careful," he whispered in her ear. "We're safe here. The Lord led us here for a reason, now didn't He?"

Nell laughed. It was a flat, humorless, contemptuous sound. "The Lord is full of surprises these days. His way was once straight and narrow... undeniable. But now... now there's no certain way about it. His punishments seem to outweigh His blessings tenfold."

Again, Levi felt hurt by her flagging faith. He had thought she had made amends with the Almighty after her time at the church in Woodrow, but now he wasn't so sure. "You mustn't think that way, Nell. Please... for the children. For me."

The woman shuddered again, as if deathly cold.

"The dread will have its way," was all she would say and said nothing more the remainder of that night.

CHAPTER 27

"The last rose of the year."

The words held a finality in her ears that disturbed her. She had seen too much finality in the world since the height of summer. Now that fall was in full swing and winter approached, death—both natural and unnatural—manifested itself daily. She supposed it was wearing her down spiritually, seeing mortality revealed and realized so plentifully.

Nell knelt in the vast rose garden in front of the conservatory, clippers in hand. She gripped the stem and snipped it cleanly, eighteen inches from the bloom. She had always loved flowers, particularly fresh-cut ones. She had enjoyed displaying them… in a vase on the kitchen table, on the pillows of her husband and children, on the graves of those she had cherished and loved.

It was a sobering thought, that these would be the last blooms of the season. She placed the hybrid rose, peach-colored with hints of pink along the rims of the petals, into a basket with the other surviving beauties. Nell looked around her. Some greenery remained, but there was mostly the shriveled brown of death, as well as the stark gray and muted red brick of the walls and arbors that surrounded it. She hoped that the following spring would bring renewal, an abundance of color as rampant and vibrant as the photos she had seen magazines and on television. But she could only hope. Things of years and decades past were no longer etched in stone as they once had been. If the destructive black bugs could inhabit human beings and animals, what was there to say that they wouldn't conquer nature next? The trees, the grass, even the flowers that she loved so much… all could lose their beauty and luster as the parasites infested their leaves, stems, and pedals, turning them into dark things of contempt and avoidance.

The sound of hammering echoed from the direction of the main house. Levi had chosen to do repairs around the place that morning, instead of venturing into the woods to cut timber or hunt. She supposed that he had done so to appease her fears. It did, knowing that they were near, within sight and earshot.

Nell felt ashamed of the way she had acted the night before. She knew it had upset her husband, carrying on that way. In broad daylight, in the garden, she felt foolish. The sun was out, burning away the chill of dawn and she experienced none of the awful dread that had gripped her hours before. Working with the flowers, harvesting their beauty, always lifted her spirits.

She closed her eyes and raised her face toward the sun. She felt its warmth upon her cheeks and its brightness bathed her eyelids. "Lord, I do trust in you," she whispered. "I weary of cursing you, so I'll praise you and your blessings instead." She stood up and retrieved her basket, brimming with the last remaining roses of the past summer. "Just find a little patience and grace for a sinner like ol' Nell."

She was turning back toward the main house, when she heard a shuffling sound behind her. Nell glanced over her shoulder. She was startled to see a Biter—a shaggy teenaged boy wearing a black Anthrax t-shirt and plaid pajama pants— stumbling along the walkway in front of the conservatory. He must have wandered through one of the arched doorways in the western garden wall.

The dread threatened to overcome her again, but she managed to stifle it. *You're faster than he is. Just head up to the house and have Levi and the boys come back down here to take care of the poor thing, bless his heart.*

She quickened her pace and headed toward an archway at the northern wall. Beyond, she could see the cobbled pathway that lead past a columned palisade and curved up the hillside to the manor house. As she reached the doorway, she looked back toward the conservatory. The boy had spotted her. He limped in her direction, dragging his useless right foot behind him. His hands stretched outward, showing ragged tissue and partially denuded bone. His face was black with activity. Parasites swarmed from every orifice in his head—mouth, nostrils, the channels of his ears.

The dread was upon her full-force now. *Leave me alone,* she thought. *I can see the thing.* She reached inside the pocket of her denim jacket and drew the Colt Python. Stepping backward through the entranceway, she lifted the revolver and cocked the hammer. She centered the sights just above the bridge of the Biter's nose.

And was totally unaware of the two that were on either side of her.

Nell gasped as teeth bit into the back of her neck. They sank deep, tearing away a mouthful of flesh and grating against the bone of the vertebrae underneath as they pulled away. She screamed shrilly as she dropped to her knees. Blood jetted hotly down her back, soaking her jacket and the flannel shirt underneath.

"Oh God!" she groaned as the second Biter attacked, grabbing her left arm and tearing away most of her tricep muscle... clothing, meat, and all. "Have mercy, Lord!"

She attempted to regain her feet to flee, but the two refused to let go. With all her strength, she turned back toward the rose garden. Nell moaned in despair as the teenager finally reached her. His weight, along with that of the others, bore her to the ground. The boy in the heavy-metal shirt burrowed into her chest like a bore hog rooting in mud. The material of her shirt and bra gave away. His teeth latched onto her left breast. With a triumphant lunge backward, he tore the sack from its moorings. For a moment, the appendage stared back at her like some pale, blood-streaked eye. Then it was devoured before her eyes.

She screamed again, but this time her lungs couldn't seem to muster the wind to accomplish much. A low, rasping wail lifted into the autumn air, brimming with frustration and defeat. Her thoughts flashed to more pleasant things—Levi, her children, the safety of the big house a hundred yards away. She thought of the notion of working the garden that morning and how it had been a good thing... and not the nightmare that it had ended up to be.

Nell looked down at her right hand and realized that she still held the .357 in her grasp. She lifted it and pulled the trigger. The hollow-point slug punched through the teenager's upper forehead. A dark explosion of blood, brains, and bugs fanned against the North Carolina sky, then settled on the walkway behind him. The Biter dropped the mammary in his hands and folded into a motionless heap on the flagstones.

The biggest Biter of the bunch—a good six-foot-two and nearly three hundred pounds in weight—took her extended arm as an invitation. He bit down on her lean wrist, shattering the fragile bones beneath the skin. Her hand dangled by a ligament for a moment, then tore away and landed on the pathway beneath her. The tendons jerked spasmodically, firing the Magnum a couple of times before growing still.

Abruptly, motion erupted around her. She turned her head stiffly and saw Avery loping down the hillside, screaming wildly. He swung a broad axe at the overweight zombie. The edge cleaved cleanly through his fat neck, sending his bald head spinning away. It struck the garden wall and bounced off the mortared stones with a sickening crunch.

"Mind your temper," she muttered and fell to her back. Her thoughts seemed fuzzy and disjointed.

Levi followed directly behind his son. With a yell that was both primal and grievous, he gripped a hammer in both hands and brought it down upon the crown of the last zombie's head. The decay-weakened state of the Biter's skull caused the clawed head to sink in deeply. Levi let go as a gorge of gore and insects surged up the hardwood handle. He stepped back and Michelle stepped in. She jacked the pump of her ten-gauge in rapid succession, firing blast after blast of double-aught buckshot at the zombie, driving it backward. The momentum of the shotgun blasts plastered what was left of the thing against the garden wall. It clung there for a long moment and then slid, piece by piece, to a jumbled heap in the grass.

As they tossed their weapons aside and approached her, Nell lifted her only good hand and spoke in the loudest voice she could muster. "Don't you dare come near me!" she croaked. "I'm full of that nasty vermin! Stay away from me!"

"She's right," Avery declared. Tears streamed down the young man's face. "They're all over her!"

Levi looked around and spotted a garden shed. "Avery, check and see if there's a tarp in there. If there is, fetch it."

As the boy headed for the outbuilding, Kate and Jim arrived. Kate carried a large tackle box, a makeshift medical case that she and Glenda Newman had put together before they had left Henderson. "Oh, God!" Kate moaned. "She's... she's..."

"Don't carry on so, Katydid," Nell told her, calling her by a name she hadn't used since the girl was three years old. "I'm just dying, is all."

"No, you ain't!" Levi said loudly. He took a deep breath and knelt next to his wife. "You just hush up, old woman, and relax. Kate'll fix you up." He looked up at his daughter. "Won't you?"

Kate could do nothing but shake her head. "I... I can't, Papa. They did too much damage. She's..."

"All in pieces." Blood teeming with parasites spurted from her nose and mouth as she giggled. "You can't put Humpty Dumpty back together again when she falls off the garden wall, you know."

"She's delirious!" Avery sobbed, dragging a large black tarpaulin behind him.

"I'm as sound of mind as you, Avery Hobbs!" his mother reprimanded. "And stop that sniveling! All of you! Do you think I want to go to my reward with your squalling faces the last thing I see?"

As Levi and Avery started toward her with the tarp, she shook her head. "I told you not to come near me."

"Ma, we've got to do this to get you up to the house," Avery told her.

"I ain't going in the house."

"Of all the stubborn...!" Levi muttered beneath his breath. "And why not?"

"Cause all I'll do is bleed all over the floor," she explained, as if to a small child. "It'll soak into those fine Persian carpets, seep into the cracks between the floorboards, and a generous helping of those bugs will go with it. The entire ground floor will be contaminated and, as those things breed and multiply, the whole house will follow."

Kate looked at her father. "She's right, Papa. We can't take her inside."

Frustration blazed in Levi's eyes. "Where then?"

"Beneath that big ol' spreading chestnut tree down behind the house," Nell told him.

"How come?"

"Because that's where I want to be buried."

A sad silence engulfed the group. Any hope of saving her, of setting things right, was settled now. "We've still got to wrap you to take you down there," Jem told her.

Nell considered it for a moment and nodded. Levi and his sons moved in carefully and went to work. They positioned the tarp over her body and began to gently roll her in the weatherproof canvas, careful not to get any parasite-infested blood on their skin or clothes. Soon she was wrapped up, as if in a cocoon.

Silently, Levi and the boys lifted her and began to carry her back up the walkway toward the veranda outside the mansion's south wing. There they would be able to take concrete stairs to the expanse of the back lawn.

"Hold up for a second," Nell told them. Her face was as pale as baking flour and her eyes were slightly glazed, as if having difficulty focusing. "Michelle?"

The girl stepped up to her. She wanted to reach out and touch the woman, offer her comfort, but knew that was impossible. "Yes, ma'am?"

"I want to ask a favor of you. Something I think you can do for me, being that you're not kin and all." She looked up dully at her family. "Something that would be too hard for them."

"Anything, Mrs. Hobbs. Just ask."

"My right hand is lying over yonder on the path. Could you fetch my wedding band and bring it to Levi when you're done? I've never had it off my finger once in the thirty-five years we were married, so it's liable to hang on tight."

Michelle glanced over and saw the woman's hand, pale and

motionless, still holding the Python Magnum. She felt bile rise into her throat, but choked it back down just as quickly. "Yes, ma'am, I will." She looked over at Avery, half expecting to see a snickering grin on his face. Instead, he looked horrified.

"We better hurry, Papa," Kate said grimly. Her eyes were red from crying and her freckles stood out starkly against her pale skin. "There's not much time."

Michelle watched as they carried the tarp-wrapped body of Nell up the hillside. Before they reached the top, Avery looked back at her and mouthed *Thank you!*

You betcha, she thought. Most of the time, the boy from Tennessee was as irritating as turpentine on a bare-assed cat, but at the moment her heart ached for him.

She walked over and eyed the severed hand for a long moment. Her stomach rolled. *The things you get yourself into, Chelle.* Kneeling, she careful pried the revolver from the hand's stiffening fingers. As she stuck the gun in her coat pocket, the hand flexed and jerked, causing her to cry out. *Did you just squeal like a sissy-ass little girl?* She was thankful that Avery hadn't been there to witness it.

She took a deep breath and reached for the hand again. It was still warm to the touch. She pulled on the golden band on Nell's ring finger, but as she suspected, it failed to budge. The bile in her belly threatened to rise again. *Stay put! I'm gonna do this!*

Michelle drew a Gerber LMF from a sheath on her belt and laid the five-inch blade between the finger's second and third knuckle. Gritting her teeth, she began to saw. There was a moist ripping as the blade sliced through flesh and then a coarse grating when it hit bone.

This time more than bile came up. She turned away and heaved. *Oh God! Don't let anybody see me puke!* When she was finished, she grimaced. *Gross! I got it in my hair!*

She went back to work. Soon the finger was off and she had the wedding ring in the pocket of her jeans. As she turned to go, Michelle heard a damp croaking noise. She spotted the severed head of the fat Biter lying a few feet away. Its bloodshot eyes rolled and its black, bug-covered teeth chomped at empty air.

CLACK-CLACK-CLACK

"What are you laughing at, numb-nuts?" Michelle gave the head a good swift kick. It rolled across the grass and ended up beneath a hydrangea bush.

Quickly, she climbed the hillside to join the others.

"So... here we are."

Nell's voice was no more than a whisper. Even sitting on the ground beside her, Levi could scarcely hear her. A breeze whistled through the branches of the chestnut tree, dislodging a few dead leaves, sending them drifting downward. One landed on his wife's face. Gently, he swept it away. Her skin seemed nearly transparent, as pale as a garden slug. Her lips and eyelids had turned blue from loss of blood and waning oxygen.

"Yeah," he told her softly. "Here we are." His heart thudded in his chest, forcefully, almost painfully. *If I'm to have a heart attack, Lord, let it come now. So I can go with her.* But he knew that wasn't to be.

Levi turned and looked back toward the main house. Everyone stood on the rear terrace that ran along the back of the structure: the Tauchee family, Tyrone Jackson, the Webb twins, and their own young'uns. All waited expectantly, respectfully, giving him his time with her. Avery, Jem, and Kate clung to one another. He knew the grief they shared was a hurtful thing. Losing one's mother always was.

"Do you have the ring?" she asked.

He nodded and opened his hand. The wedding band, which had been warm with her closeness for over three decades was ice cold now. "Michelle brought it to me."

"She's a good girl. Feisty and headstrong. Just the kind to hold reign over an ornery, headstrong man. I'm hoping her and Avery stop their cockeyed bickering and take on the yoke. Same with Jem and Melissa, and Kate and Tyrone."

Levi was optimistic about Jem and Melissa, but unsure about the other two couples.

"We never made it to the beach, did we?" she muttered. "Never saw the to and fro of the waves, or listened to the sea in a shell, or smelled the salt air."

"No, we didn't."

"Go there for me," she told him. "Go there and wiggle your toes in the sand and watch those little crabs dance sideways in the sunshine. And when you're there, you'll take me with you." Feebly, she nodded toward the ring in his palm. "Promise?"

It pained him to think of such things, but he knew that he would. "I promise."

Nell sighed, half from failing lungs, half in satisfaction. "That's the first promise. Now for the second." She paused for a second and then continued. "Do you have your gun?"

Lord, help me! "Nell... babe... I..."

"Do you *have* it?"

The Ruger hung heavily at his hip, ever present, both on body and in mind. "Yes."

"You remember how Jem was after that possum latched onto him? How he was certain that those godawful parasites were inside him?"

"I remember."

"His was imaginary... all in his mind. Mine is not. They're running through me like an army of ants in that ant farm we bought for Avery on his eighth Christmas. And it burns like unholy hellfire. Feels like someone lit a fuse that's running through every vein in my body. They're in my brain, too. Chomping away, making tunnels, heading for the places they love the most. It's getting harder to think. I feel like I'm losing myself... like they're taking control. My mouth is watering, like I'm hungry. My temper's itching, aching, like I want to hurt somebody... or bite the living fool out of them."

Hearing her talk like that frightened him. His right hand dipped to the butt of the Blackhawk. It was far from a comfort to him.

"I'll be gone soon," she declared. "I scarcely have the strength to keep my eyes open. But I won't be gone for long. It won't be a day or even hours. Those little bastards are working overtime to build their zombie and it's gonna bust loose, fierce and strong."

"I know what you want, Nell. Truth be told, I'm not sure that I can."

"Of course you can," she said smiling. "Because you love me."

"That I do." His words felt hot and scorching inside his mouth, like pig iron out of a furnace.

"I know you always carry a bandana in your back pocket. After you're done, you can tie it around my head, so the young'uns won't be upset when they come down to pay their respects."

Levi frowned at her. "You know, for a dying woman, you sure are mighty long-winded."

Nell stared at him for a moment, then burst out laughing. It was a sound he cherished and hadn't heard in a good long while. "You always could tickle my funny bone, old man. This'll be the last laugh we share in this life. We'll have an eternity to cut up and fool around in the next."

His eyes grew hot and moist as her breathing grew more and more shallow. *Nell... sweetheart...*

"You know something else that's funny?" she asked. Her voice was barely audible. "Back at the garden? Three Biters roaming together... rotten and ripe and stinking to the high heavens... and not one buzzard in the sky."

The thought struck Levi not as peculiar, but disturbing. Matter of fact, none of them had seen a single buzzard since the evening they had arrived at the Biltmore. The question was... *where had they all gone?*

He was about to answer, when her eyes sharpened and her breath hitched violently in her chest. The tendons in her neck tightened like cables pulled taut and her head lifted a couple of inches.

"Nell? What...?"

"Praise Jesus!" she declared in a voice as clear as he had ever heard it. "Lord of Lords and King of Kings!"

Then her head fell backwards and she was gone. Or had lapsed into what Abe Mendlebaum had called the "hibernation period".

Levi Hobbs sat there motionlessly, for how long he had no idea. He stared at her as though she was the only thing in the world... the only thing that mattered or ever had. He had felt that way as a seventeen-year-old boy when he had laid eyes on her for the first time and he felt that way now.

He knew that he could wait for the first twitch of an eyelid or the involuntary flexing of a muscle. But he would be damned if he'd allow it to go that far. He reached into his back pocket and withdrew the red bandana. Then he unsnapped the holster's retaining strap with the ball of his thumb and shucked the .44 free.

Nell's words came back to him, from an eternity ago. *Easy enough for you to say! It ain't you out there putting a bullet betwixt the eyes of your beloved. Who knows? Maybe someday you'll be forced to do the same!"*

The tears broke free then, hot and plentiful. "To hell with it!" he groaned. The big gun was heavy as lead in his fist as he pressed the muzzle to his beloved's forehead and cocked the hammer.

Kate, Jem, and Avery jumped when the shot came. Hearts leaped into throats, then fell just as quickly. The cannon boom of the Blackhawk resounded off the tall, somber walls of the ancient house and then faded. It was immediately followed by a high-pitched, grievous wail unlike anything they had ever heard before. It took some convincing on their part to realize that the source of that terrible and lonesome sound was truly their father.

They waited a while longer. Then Kate took each of her brothers by the hand and, together, they went down to be with their parents.

CHAPTER 28

"So, how is your dad doing?"

They were walking through the estate's northern woods—Levi and Billy up ahead, Avery, Jem, and Michelle a few yards behind—when the girl's question came up.

The brothers looked at one another. It was a valid question, but an uncomfortable one for them to even think about. It had been a week since the Biter attack had taken Nell from them. Since that time, nothing about their father had been the same or predictable. Like his sudden impulse to cut down half a forest to build a wall completely around the Biltmore house. It was a plan that was foolish and ill-thought-out, but something to keep him occupied nonetheless.

"I reckon he's doing okay," Avery told her.

"That's not the way I see it," she said. "How's he *really* doing?"

Jem shook his head. "It's hard to tell with Papa. He never was much of a talker or one to show his feelings. It's been, what, a week or so since that Biter took Ma? It's hitting him hard, that's for sure."

"I understand that," Michelle agreed. "But lately he's all over the place. One minute he's off to himself, quiet, not saying a word to anybody. The next he's come up with some crazy project or another, barking orders, criticizing folks for what they are or aren't doing. I know he's had a rough time, but he's starting to get on my ever-loving nerves. And that goes for Melissa, too."

The boys knew where she was coming from. The twins weren't the only ones that Levi's behavior was alienating. Everyone was growing weary of the man's emotional instability.

Before he definitely seemed like a man in control and everyone had respected his judgment and sought his advice. But now everyone seemed intent on avoiding him rather than see him in his depressed, incommunicative state or be put down or berated when he was in one of his more volatile moods.

"There's not much we can do about it," Avery told her flatly.

His attitude ruffled Michelle's feathers, as usual. "I'm not asking you to do anything about it, Bozo. I'm just letting you know how I feel. Or is that not important to you?"

Jem could see where the conversation was headed, so he attempted to stop it before it started. "I think it's the way Ma went that's bothering him. He was always the provider and protector of the family. When those zombies took her down and he wasn't able to get there in time to stop it, it sort of threw his sense of identity out the window. I think he doubts himself... who he really is and what his role is now. He still has us young'uns, but Ma was his pride and joy... who he stood for and who stood for him. Now that's gone and he's, well, lost. He's trying to cope, but he doesn't know how. Half the time he's depressed and doesn't have the will to do anything, while the other half he's angrier than a red wasp and fights to find something constructive to fill his time. Plus, I think he's carrying some guilt around. For having to... you know... take care of Ma the way he did at the end."

Michelle was impressed by Jem's insight. "I think you've hit the nail square on the head. I can sort of see it his way now." She looked over at Avery. "What do you think? Is Jem right?"

The boy grimaced, as though suffering a headache. "Well, to tell the truth, I couldn't follow half of what he was talking about."

Michelle and Jem looked at one another. Jem shrugged his shoulders in resignation, while the girl rolled her eyes.

"And another thing," Jem said. "He's got those buzzards on his mind."

"What about the buzzards?" she asked.

"How they just upped and vanished. It wasn't normal... wasn't *right*."

The girl shrugged. "Maybe they migrated or something.

That's what other birds do. Winter is almost here, you know."

"Buzzards don't migrate," Avery told her flatly. "Summer or winter, they hang around the same spot... biding their time, waiting for something to die. Jem's right. It's not the natural order of things."

Michelle laughed. "Oh? And what is these days?"

They walked onward for a few minutes, following the two men ahead of them. Then the brunette spoke again. "Jem... you like my sister, don't you?"

The boy's face reddened a bit. "Well... yeah."

"A little more than 'like', I'd say."

He kept walking, staring straight ahead. "I reckon so."

"If things went from bad to worse, would you do for Lissa what your dad did for your mom?"

Jem thought about Sarah, back home in the Smokies, and felt sick to his stomach. *Now why did she have to ask me that?*

"Well... would you?" she insisted.

Jem thought about it for a second. "I suppose I would, if it came down to it."

"How about you, Avery? Would you do it for me? Bust a cap in my noggin if one those stinking Biters took a chunk out of me?"

The question seemed to annoy the boy. "Even if I feel like I'd *like* to shoot you sometimes, I don't think that I could."

His answer seemed to anger her. "You mean, you'd rather let my brain be eaten by bugs and watch me wandering around trying to take a bite of everyone's ass? Rather than do the decent..." her voice cracked. "...*caring* thing and putting me out of my misery?"

"Well..." stammered Avery, "if you put it that way..."

"Oh no," she said, throwing up her hands, "never mind. If you wouldn't do that for me, then just forget it!"

"Chelle, what're you—?"

"Forget it!" Then she stomped off, head thrown back and shoulders squared in defiance.

Avery looked bewildered. "Now what the shit is the matter with her?"

His twin brother stared at him. "You don't know?"

"Hell no!"

"Haven't got a clue, do you?"

"Should I?"

Jem just shook his head. "Forget it then. Just forget it."

"*What?*" Frustrated, he threw up his hands as Jem quickened his pace to catch up with the others. "Whose side are you on anyway?"

It was two days until the last Thursday of November and Enolia had Thanksgiving on her mind.

She knew that, had Nell still been alive, she would have, too. That was something that both women had had in common—cooking. Both had used food and preparation of such to both nourish and please their families. She recalled their times in the kitchen, talking and laughing, neither offering advice or criticism, knowing that they were both more than capable at their particular task. It had been a joy having such companionship; it had been something akin to torment losing it.

Enolia vowed to make up for the loss by preparing Thanksgiving dinner. But, of course, no Thanksgiving meal was complete without a turkey.

She knew that they were around. Enolia had seen their tracks, found their droppings, heard a distant gobbling that was eventually answered by another. The men promised to provide one, but Enolia wasn't as trusting as they were confident, not even of her husband, who was an excellent hunter.

The week before she had disassembled a couple of lavish wicker chairs in the winter garden and formed them into six turkey traps, like the ones her grandmother had taught her to make back in Cherokee. She had set them up in intervals around the estate the day before, hoping to catch something healthy and eatable. And, if she was lucky, she would bag two or three.

That afternoon, she, Jessie, and Tyrone entered the thick forest that stretched between the stables and the Antler Village complex, with its winery, shops, and hotel. The trees were nearly bare of foliage and dead leaves lay in thick blankets around the bases of the ancient trees. Some drifts were nearly knee-high in places.

The first two basket traps they came to had failed to be sprung and were empty. The third, however, in a deep hollow a half mile from the house, had caught something. They could see it from the upper rim of the wooded basin.

"Looks like you got yourself a big Tom," Tyrone said with a grin. He slung the Thompson across his back and started down the slope. "Let's go get it."

Enolia took Jessie's hand and, together, they descended the slope. Halfway there, mother and daughter lost their footing and slid the rest of the way, landing in a deep pile of maple leaves at the bottom. Jessie giggled and held tightly to her American Girl doll. She was afraid if she dropped it, it would get lost in the leaves and she would never find it.

The three waded through the leaves until they reached the base of a sycamore tree. Enolia had cleared the spot six feet around the day before, to give the intended bird plenty of room to reach the dried corn beneath the basket. The limb that had served as a trip bar lay in the leaves and the rim of the big wicker trap rested flat against the ground. A heavy stone she had lashed to the top of the basket held the trap firmly in place.

As Enolia approached the base of the tree, she slowed to a stop. She cupped her hands and issued a turkey call that Tyrone and Jessie wouldn't have been able to tell from a real one. When there was no response, she reached to a holster clipped to the belt of her jeans and withdrew a Taurus 9mm pistol.

"What's wrong, Mama?" Jessie asked. She knew her mother well enough to realize that something about the basket trap wasn't quite right.

"Nothing is moving inside," she told her. "And there's blood on that rock beside the basket... and on those leaves."

"Want me to lift it up for you?" Tyrone offered. "If it turns out to be a zombified turkey, you can shoot it when it comes out."

I don't believe that's our problem, she thought. She held the 9mm in both hands and surveyed the hollow. It appeared to be deserted, except for the three of them. She took a step toward the trap. "Okay. Go ahead."

Carefully, Tyrone placed his huge hands on both sides

of the basket and raised it to reveal what was inside. It was, indeed, a turkey—a large male from the size of it. But it lay there motionlessly on the ground... and there was a very good reason why.

"Its head is gone, Mama!" Jessie gasped, her eyes widening.

Enolia nodded grimly. "Someone cut it off."

"But where is it?"

Tyrone stiffened and let the basket slip through his fingers. "I found it," he said, nodding to the far side of the clearing. "On that tree."

Enolia turned, her fingers tightening around the butt of the Taurus. The turkey's head was nailed to the trunk of an oak tree, six feet from the ground. It was what pinned it there that sent a thrill of alarm through her. It was a combat knife with a serrated black blade and neoprene grip.

"Gobble," came the voice of a man nearby.

They whirled, trying to locate its source. All they saw were bare trees and mounds of dead orange and gold leaves.

"Gobble, gobble," came another. Then another came in the opposite direction. And another from an even different spot.

Suddenly, Enolia knew. *Oh my God! They're beneath the...!*

Before she could react, a pair of arms burst from a deep drift of leaves behind her, grabbing her around the knees and bringing her down hard. She attempted to hold onto the 9mm, but her chin came down hard on one of the sycamore's exposed roots, causing her to bite her tongue and stunning her nearly senseless. The gun spun from her hands and landing a couple of yards away, swallowed up by dead vegetation.

Enolia heard a scream and saw someone stand up directly behind her daughter. He grabbed the girl by the arms, causing her to thrash and lose her hold on the doll. The Cherokee struggled to stand, but her head spun dizzily from the blow she had received from the fall. The man who held Jesse was young; he couldn't have been any older than Avery or Jem, maybe even younger. He didn't look to have a gun on him, but he did have something sticking out of his jacket pocket that puzzled her. A can of Krylon spray paint with a cap that was candy-apple red.

She struggled to her knees and looked in the direction of

Tyrone. She was just in time to see someone appear from the far side of the sycamore and strike him in the back of the head with the butt of an M416 assault rifle. The blow took the big man down. He spun with the impact, dropping the Tommy gun, and falling face down in the leaves. She hoped that he would get up, but he simply lay there, motionlessly, either unconscious or dead.

As Jesse continued to scream, Enolia managed to make it to her feet. Her jaw throbbed and her head continued to swim. She took a couple of faltering steps, before someone grabbed her from behind and shoved her back down to the ground again. She landed on her stomach forcefully and dread filled her as pain seized her from navel to backbone. *The baby!*

Stunned, she rolled over and gasped, attempting to regain her breath. The tall, broad silhouette of a man stood over her, blocking out the sun that shone through the naked branches of the surrounding trees.

It was a familiar silhouette with an equally familiar voice.

Oh God! she thought. Her heart hammered in her chest. *No!*

"No meddlesome shithead of a husband to interrupt us now," said Frank Gentry. "Time to finish what we started, squaw."

CHAPTER 29

"Hold still, Ty," said Kate. Her face was intent and her eyes focused as she worked. "I'm almost done."

"It hurts like hell!" grumbled the big man. He was stretched out in a leather armchair in the pool room of the main house, looking as though he didn't have an ounce of strength left in his body.

"It usually does when someone is putting seventeen stitches in your head with no local anesthetic," she told him. "There… the last one."

Tyrone flinched as the woman applied antibiotic ointment to the long gash that ran from the crown of his head, all the way to just behind his left ear. The black man stared across the room at Billy, who stood leaning next to the big billiard table. His voice was as regretful as the expression in his eyes. "I'm sorry, man," he said softly, as he had a dozen times before. "So sorry."

"It was an ambush," Billy told him, his voice flat. "It couldn't be helped."

"But if I'd been on my game, maybe…"

"They would have killed you," stated the Cherokee. "Better that they jumped you from behind and left you for dead."

"Come on and let's get you to one of the ground-floor bedrooms," Kate said, helping him up. "I'm sure not going to try to get you upstairs in your condition."

Tyrone glared at her and pulled his arm away angrily. "I ain't going nowhere with *you!*"

Kate could tell that he was tempted to add the word *bitch* to the protest, but given the variety of moods her father displayed lately, he was more than likely afraid to. "I don't care what you think of me, Tyrone Jackson. You can hate my guts if you want. But, at this point in time, I'm your nurse and I'm putting your contrary ass in bed!"

Tyrone grew quiet and said nothing more as they left the room and headed across the entrance hall to the bedrooms that faced the rear veranda.

Everyone in room was silent for a while—Levi, Jem, Avery, and Michelle watching Billy, wondering what sort of turmoil raged behind those dark, expressionless eyes. His demeanor was as black as his outfit—long-sleeved turtleneck, trousers, and boots... all as ebony as a starless night.

Finally, Billy looked toward a corner of the room. The impassive expression wavered, but only for an instant. "Jessie... baby, come here."

She stood next to Melissa, wrapped in a burgundy and emerald-green afghan. "No, Daddy," she whispered. She backed up a step. "I don't want you to... look at me."

"Please, sweetheart. Come here."

"Go on, dear," Melissa urged.

The girl stood there a moment more and then walked across the floor to her father. As she approached, he crouched and looked at her, face to face. "Jessie... I'm going to remove the blanket."

Tears bloomed in the child's eyes. "Don't... please. I don't want..."

"You did nothing wrong," he assured her calmly. "Now let's take a look."

Billy reached out took the folds of the afghan from around her narrow shoulders and pulled it away. Melissa was there to take it from him.

"Oh dear Lord," Michelle said and looked away.

Jessie Tauchee had been stripped of her clothing and spray-painted candy-apple red from head to toe. Before the paint had dried, someone had taken their finger and written something across her shallow chest.

WINERY
BILLY COME ALONE
FRANK

Billy stared at the words, then lifted his eyes and looked at the thing that encircled his daughter's head. It was a nylon pull tie with a single buzzard feather stuck in the back—someone's sick idea of an Indian headband. He gently took the band from her head and flung it to the far side of the room.

"You've got to tell me what happened, Jessie."

"No!" she sobbed. "I... I can't!"

"Listen," he said, tenderly cupping her face in his hands. "You need to tell me... so I can get your mother back. And the baby."

Jessie nodded and took a deep breath. "Well... after they jumped up out of the leaves and grabbed me... they hit Mister Tyrone hard and knocked him out. Then the men... there were six of them, including that mean man named Frank... they threw Mama down in the leaves and they... they... oh, Daddy, they made me *watch!*"

Billy gave her a moment to compose herself before continuing. "Go on, baby."

"They hurt Mama again and again, all of them except the boy... the teenager. He didn't want to. They pushed him down on top of her, kicked him... said they were going to do the same to him when they got back to the camp if he didn't have his turn. But he wouldn't do it... he refused to."

"These men who were with Frank... what were they like?"

"Frank told me to tell you that they were... regular Army," she said, as if reciting something that she had been forced to memorize. "And that one was Harley Jenkins of Fort Bragg... a Green Beret. He said to tell you that he had done three tours of duty in Iraq. He said the others had fought there, too. And other places... Afghanistan for one."

"Okay," he said. Billy took the afghan back from the teenage girl and wrapped it comfortingly around his daughter again. "Everything will fine, baby. Time for Daddy to get to work."

Jessie nodded as if she understood. With a sob, she launched herself at her father. "Be careful, Daddy! Please come back. I don't think I could lose you, too."

He embraced her for a long moment. "We will all come back... me, your mother, and little *agido*." When he pulled away from the child, Billy looked up at Melissa. "Please... take care of my little girl."

"I will," she promised. Then she ushered his daughter out of the room.

The five stood silently in the pool room, immersed in their own thoughts. Then Levi spoke. "We need to figure out what we're going to do... how we're going to deal with this."

Billy walked to the pool table. Resting in the center was a black duffel bag, one he had brought down from his and Enolia's bedroom. "There is no *we* to it," he told them. "Gentry wants me alone and that is what he'll get."

"Are you crazy?" Avery said, laughing. *"You're* going up against Gentry and those soldiers? By yourself?" He shook his head incredulously. "You got a freaking death wish or something?"

"Avery," warned his father, "cut it out."

"No!" declared the boy. "Here this little pussy sits out most every battle we've been in and now he wants to fight. If he'd been there when we went up against Nathan and his boys, Mrs. Agnes and her sister might still be alive right now!'

"Don't, Avery," Michelle said, grabbing at his arm.

Angrily, he pulled from her grasp. "No, I ain't afraid of this little turd! I wanna know why he's such a damn coward... why he didn't show some balls and stand up like a man and join in when we needed him."

Billy said nothing in defense. He unzipped the duffel and pulled a black stocking cap over his dark hair. Then he took a can from the bag and, opening it, began to apply black greasepaint to the bronze skin of his face and neck.

"You got an answer for me, dipshit?" the teenager taunted. He took a step forward. "Do you?"

"Son... he couldn't," Levi told him sternly. "He had his orders."

"Orders?" The boy scowled, half out of confusion, half out of disgust. "What the hell do you mean...?"

"For God's sake, Avery... he's Black Arrow."

Avery looked as though someone had clouted him between the eyes with a sledgehammer. His eyes widened and his face paled a couple of shades. "Holy shit! You mean to tell me... damn! Black Arrow? Bad-ass ninja injuns on the warpath?"

"Avery!" scolded Michelle.

The boy swallowed nervously. "Uh, sorry... no offense meant."

Billy pulled on a pair of sheer leather gloves, black like the rest of his outfit. "None taken." He looked around at the others. "What I do, I do with those of my own kind... or I do alone." A thin smile crossed his face. "No offense."

"None taken," Levi told him. "But are you certain? Maybe we could be of some help to you..."

"If these men are who Gentry claims them to be, one or more of you would die at their hands," he told them bluntly. "Alone, I can infiltrate their camp, do what needs to be done, and bring my woman home."

"If that's how you want it," Levi told him, "we can respect that."

Billy fastened a black nylon pack around his waist and placed a roll of black duct tape inside, along with other items. The last thing he took from the duffel was a sheathed knife with an eight-inch blade. It was as black as coal, the neoprene handle bearing the same arrowhead symbol that graced the folding knife he had carried since Cherokee. He clipped the sheath to his belt and tied it securely to his thigh.

"Not necessarily how I want it," Billy said. "But how they chose it to be."

Then, without warning, he stepped backward through the doorway, merged with the shadows beyond, and was gone.

Harley Jenkins took the last draw of his cigarette. Irritated, he tossed it to the floor of the winery lobby and ground it beneath the sole of his combat boot. His eyes were focused forward as they had been for two hours—on the dark parking lot that lay beyond the glass of the front doors. He had three men on sentry throughout the complex known as Antler Village. One was at the main road leading from the direction of the Biltmore House and one was at the entrance of the winery parking area. The third had taken a sniper position on the roof of the main winery building, ready to aim his M24 rifle and take out anything that moved. The sound of crying echoed from a room near the facility's main office. The noise grated on his nerves. It had always been that way with him and members of the opposite sex. Talking, giggling, complaining... he would rather haul off and bust them in the mouth and shut them up, than take five minutes of their bitching and moaning. In the soldier's way of thinking, women and submissive silence should go hand in hand.

"Shut the hell up, you red whore!" he snapped, loud enough for her to hear. "You wake up the boss and you'll be damned sorry. You know how ol' Frank is. Grouchier than a grizzly and hornier than a jackrabbit on a first date. I would have thought you'd had enough for today. If not, I can oblige you after my shift."

The woman's crying stopped, but she could not suppress the moans of pain and discomfort that overcame her.

"That's it!" he growled beneath his breath. "Maybe a couple of kicks in that knocked-up belly of yours will stop your whining."

The Green Beret was about to turn, when he sensed someone behind him.

"Harley Jenkins," a voice said quietly. The man's lips couldn't have been more than ten inches from his left ear.

The soldier stiffened. His hands tightened around the blued frame of the M416 assault rifle and he felt that familiar whiskey-shot of adrenalin that came before a firefight or a particularly brutal bout of hand-to-hand. Jenkins knew who it was at once. *How the shit did he get in here?* The thought caused his nutsack to draw up tightly into his abdomen.

"Billy Tauchee." The name left a taste in his mouth like hot copper... or the letting of fresh blood. He thought about the three who stood sentry outside. "My men?"

"Dead."

Jenkins' heart began to pound in his chest. His initial alarm had changed to fear and, in turn, fear had changed to terror. He hated himself for his weakness. He had not felt that way since the first week of his first tour of duty, twenty-three years ago.

"My woman," the man's voice came again. "Did you disrespect her?"

The soldier shifted his weight, planting his feet, tensing his muscles for a swift turn. A cruel grin crossed his unshaven face; he just couldn't help himself. "Yes, sir. In every hole she had."

Jenkins could feel rage radiating off the man behind him like a palatable heat. "Face me." The words sounded the way the low growl of a Pit Bull might sound in pitch-black darkness.

Oh, I will, you son of a bitch! The grunt knew what he had to do. Turn smoothly on his heels and bring the butt of the assault up into the man's throat as forcefully as he could. Then, as Tauchee stumbled backwards, he would empty the M416's clip into the Cherokee's abdomen, cutting him nearly in half. No problem. He had used that particular maneuver before.

However, a man's intentions, even those seasoned by experience and battle-hardened nerve, could sometimes fail to meet his expectations. As Jenkins prepared to turn, Billy slid the blade of his knife, the flat of it upward, beneath the man's ribcage on the left side. The soldier whirled swiftly and unintentionally gutted himself with his own momentum. By the time he had reached his planned position, the flesh and muscle of his abdomen had parted and his insides spilled out. Jenkins doubled over in mounting agony and watched, amazed, as his small and large intestines unraveled, falling in a wet, sloppy heap on top of his boots.

As the man sagged, dropping to his knees, Billy withdrew and inverted the knife. The tender underside of Harley Jenkins' jaw fell heavily onto the point. The blade tunneled upward through the man's tongue, the palate of his mouth, and into the soft tissues of his nasal cavity. It stopped in the center of the soldier's frontal lobe, just behind his dying eyes. Motionlessly, he continued to the floor. His fall was cushioned by a bed of warm entrails.

With some effort, Billy dislodged the blade from the man's skull and cleaned it on the back of the dead man's shirt. He neglected to return it to its sheath, gripping it tightly as he followed the sound of his wife's painful cries.

He found her in a room behind the winery's reception desk. She was lying on the bare floor, naked and cold. Her face and body were covered with bruises, cuts, and cigarette burns. Her hands and feet had been bound tightly with the same sort of zip tie that had formed the band around Jessie's head. Carefully, he slipped the edge of the blade beneath the nylon and released her. Almost immediately, she rolled onto her back and painfully opened her legs. The folds of her vagina were swollen and bloody, both from abuse and premature labor.

"My water broke," she said. Her voice was hoarse and wracked with pain. "The baby is coming."

Billy crouched beside her and laid a gentle hand upon her distended belly. "It's almost here. I can see the crown of its head."

Enolia reached out for him. He took her hand and pressed it to his lips. His wife sobbed violently. A mixture of tears and blood seeped from the slits of her blackened eyes. "They... they *raped* me, Billy. Over and over again. It hurt so bad... I felt like I was going to die. Like I *wanted* to die."

The Cherokee closed his eyes and breathed deeply. He couldn't believe that a man could experience such anger without being consumed alive, but he didn't reveal that to his wife. His face remained impassive, unreadable. "Two more objectives and I'll return. And we will deliver our child."

"Don't kill the boy," she said, tightening her grip on his hand. "He didn't hurt me. What they did to me... it sickened him. They tried to force him on me... but he *couldn't*. From what I heard afterward, they made him pay for it."

"He's one of them."

"Out of necessity," claimed Enolia. "To keep from starving or getting eaten by Biters. I'm sure of it, *asgahah aninela*. He's not like them. He would have stopped them... if it had been possible."

"He was the one who stripped your daughter naked and painted her red," he told her. "He made her watch your violation."

"Forced to, I'm sure."

"Breathe deeply and try not to push, no matter how much you feel like you need to," he told. "This will only take a minute."

As he walked toward the door, she called out to him softly. "Billy? The boy... please."

His ebony face was an unreadable mask. "I will be back soon."

Then, before she could say another word, he was gone.

Frank Gentry was stirred from his sleep by a velvet hand.

The man sighed and smiled. He stretched lazily on the army cot in the manager's office, feeling a thrill of pleasure as it traveled from his groin and ran up the length of his back. He was nude, having had another go at Enolia after they had brought her back to the winery. Frank remembered his last thrust, a particularly violent one that ruptured the sack within her. "Let's see if the little bastard lives through that," he had whispered cruelly in the weeping woman's ear.

Frank felt himself begin to harden and wondered if he was dreaming. He had once known a whore in New Orleans capable of delivering such pleasure with a palm full of warm oil and the right rhythm. *A little faster,* he thought. *Yes, that's right. Just like that.*

As the pleasure mounted and he neared the point of release, it all went south. A thin, burning sensation ran like a hot thread at the base of his testicles and grew in intensity as it traveled swiftly upward. Frank jolted away and was aware of several things at once: a moist ripping noise; his lower abdomen and thighs bathed in jetting, hot liquid; and a pain like none he had ever known before.

He tried to sit up, but found that he was confined to where he lay. Last time it had been the whittled pegs that held him down. This time it was a sturdy band of duct tape that secured him to his bed.

Frank Gentry's mouth yawned wide for a scream, so wide that his jaw nearly came unhinged. The shriek was abruptly silenced as something large and bloody was forced past his teeth and crammed firmly down his throat. It lodged in his esophagus, blocking his windpipe. He attempted to breathe, but his lungs deflated and stayed that way, completely deprived of air. He strained and struggled, blood spurting out his nostrils, as he panicked and struggled to find oxygen.

Then, out of the darkness, a familiar face emerged. Its eyes were as dark and devoid of warmth and mercy as the autumn night around them. "I always keep my promises," rasped Billy Tauchee.

The Cherokee wound several strands of black duct tape tightly around Frank's head, sealing his mouth and nostrils, then left him alone to deal with his atonement.

Marty Bryant lay in his bunk in the darkness and waited to die.

He had heard the sounds—the struggles, the dank noises of bodily devastation, the muffled grunts and groans of suffocation. He had also smelled the stench of blood, piss, and shit. The boy knew the rank odor of death well, from traveling with Frank Gentry and his band of soldiers for the past few weeks.

Marty lay perfectly still, trying to be as silent and invisible as humanly possible. His body ached and bled from the beating he had received at the hands of Frank and the others. His nose was broken and so were two of his ribs, maybe more. And what they had done to him with the broom handle...

Suddenly, Death stood over him, soundlessly, appraising him for a long and endless moment. *Just do it!* his mind screamed. *For God's sake, get it over with!*

Then the assassin crouched beside him. Although the room was dark, faint light shown from the outer corridor. The shine of dark eyes hovered inches from his battered face. "Frank and his men are dead," the black form told him. "You have been granted a reprieve."

"You're... you're not going to..."

"Kill you?" Marty heard a humorless chuckle that chilled him to the bone. "No. You have my wife to thank for that. If it were up to me, you would die for what you did to my daughter and that alone."

Tears ran freely as shame overtook him. "I'm sorry, mister. Really sorry."

The man in black said nothing, offered no comfort or forgiveness. He only stared at the boy, long and hard, devoid of pity.

"Can you drive?" he finally asked.

"Uh... yeah," replied Marty, surprised. "I can."

In the darkness, a set of keys were pressed into the palm of his hand. "Take their weapons and the transport truck outside. There's enough food and water in the back to last you for months. Leave this place and head west. And never let me see your face here again."

Relief replaced terror and dread. "Yes, sir. I will." Then he thought of something. "What about Frank and the others? You know when those bugs set up house, they'll..."

In the sparse light of the outer hallway, Marty saw the flash of a knife. "I'll take care of them," he assured him. "Believe me, I wouldn't want Frank Gentry to show up for a third time in my life."

He sensed rather than heard as the man crossed the room. In the pale glow of the doorway, his silhouette stood outlined for a moment. Marty was surprised to see that he wasn't nearly as big as he had imagined. "Stay put. You will know when to leave."

Thank you, Marty Bryant almost said, but didn't. The man in black was already gone.

He lay there for a while, alone in the dark, and listened. He heard the agonized wails of a woman in the throes of labor, followed by the cry of a newborn baby.

"Your grandmother was right," he heard a voice say, a voice much different than the one that had spoken to him out of the black of night. "It is a boy."

Shortly afterward, he heard the sound of an engine starting. He knew it was Harley Jenkins' jeep outside. As the vehicle departed and roared into the distance, Marty rose from his bed, dressed with difficulty, and took advantage of the second chance he had been given.

CHAPTER 30

It was the week before Christmas when Levi Hobbs said, "We need a tree."

They were eating breakfast around the long table in the dining hall when he made his revelation known. The others were surprised, to say the least... especially his children. "Are you serious, Papa?" Kate asked him.

Levi pushed his chair back, stood up, and looked around. He surveyed the big fireplace at the far end of the chamber as well the massive organ at the other. Through the vast, open doorways he could see the winter garden, the pool room, and the lofty entrance hall.

"Hell... we need a bunch of trees!"

Avery and Jem looked at one another and grinned. "That's our specialty, ain't it?" asked the more rambunctious of the two. "And we got two or three forests full of pine, fir, and blue spruce to choose from."

"I say let's gather up the axes and saws and get to work!" said Jem, unable to contain his excitement.

"Maybe," mused their father. "But what would we do for decorations?"

"Are you kidding?" Michelle jumped out of her chair as though scalded. "Have you ever seen this place around Christmastime? It's like a hundred Christmas movies rolled into one! I know of at least six rooms in the attic stacked to the ceiling with ornaments, wreathes, garland, and all the fixings!"

"I'll help you bring it down," offered Melissa.

"Me, too!" squealed Jessie, jumping up and down. She held an antique china doll cradled in the crook of her arm, a replacement for the doll that had been defaced a month ago.

"It would be nice," agreed Enolia. "Very nice." She sat in an armchair before the hearth, breastfeeding her baby. The horrifying incident in the wooded hollow and the winery had left its scars, physically and emotionally, but the woman was strong and resilient. She had survived the violation and humiliation, and had actually come out thriving. So had her son. He was healthy an infant as any, despite the fact that Frank Gentry's actions had nearly cost him his life. Enolia and Billy had named him Usdi Austenaco or "Little Chief", but they called him Austen for short.

"We can take the truck down that maintenance road in the south forest behind the garden," Tyrone suggested. "There are a lot of fine trees out that way, trees big enough to fill this place up."

Kate left the table and joined her father. She hugged his arm and put her head on his shoulder, something she hadn't done since she was twelve.

"Why the sudden change of heart?"

"Maybe because I'm sick and tired of being a contrary asshole with a stack of chips on his shoulder," he told her. "And because your mama loved her Christmas tree in the month of December. Didn't matter whether she had lights and store-bought ornaments or popcorn garland, corn husk angels, and paper snowflakes... she said it was the only time of year when we used a tree not for burning or building, but just to dress up and look pretty."

"Thanks, Papa," she said, stretching on tippy-toes and planting a kiss on his whiskered jaw. "We needed this. All of us."

Levi kissed her on the forehead. "I'm sorry I've been such a burden, daughter. Your mama's death... it broke something inside me. It's mending... slowly, but it's getting there."

"Let's get our coats on and get going!" Avery urged, wiping his mouth with a napkin. "We can get the trees—a dozen at least—and the others can tote the decorations down from the attic. I know there's a keg of cider in the basement and plenty of stuff in the pantry to snack on. We'll have us one helluva

Christmas-tree-decorating party!"

"Austen will have a good first Christmas," Billy said, flashing a rare smile. "One that we will cherish and always remember."

"Amen," said Enolia. The woman smiled as he leaned down to kiss her. "Now move your *hawini* and join the others, before I kick it out the door myself."

Billy laughed and headed through the doorway, where the men shrugged on their winter coats and gloves in the entrance hall.

"Come on, Chelle!" called Melissa. "Let's get up there and start bringing down those decorations!"

"I'm right behind you, sis!"

"Wait for me!" piped Jessie, setting her doll next to the hearth. The girl paused to give her mother a hug and her baby brother a kiss on the crown of the head. "Isn't this wonderful, Mama?"

Yes, it is, the woman thought. She laughed as Jessie ran through the dining room doorway to join the Webb sisters. Sitting there alone, with her son cradled in her arms, Enolia thought of Nell and the awful void she had left. A shadow threatened to fall across the happiness she was feeling, but she fought past it. *Nell would have loved this… loved it with all of her heart.*

The Cherokee woman knew that this celebration was not only for them, but for *her* as well. *We will honor you with this,* Enolia promised. *Our strength and perseverance… our love for one another… it will be our memorial… our final gift to you, precious Nell.*

For several days they decorated the Biltmore. It was a time of celebration, as well as a much-needed reprieve from the monotony of their daily routine.

A dozen trees were cut and erected in various rooms on the ground floor. The largest—an eighteen-foot blue spruce—stood beside the massive hearth. The fireplace was adorned with lush garlands of holly, pine cones, and red velvet bows, along with a row of stockings hanging from ornate brass hooks, one for each person present, as well as one for the Hobbs' absent matriarch.

The curving banister of the grand staircase was also decorated with garland and, although the greenhouse of the conservatory had produced no live poinsettias that year, they found a roomful of dried arrangements.

The smells of the holiday season were plentiful as well. The heady scent of pine, cloves, spiced orange, cinnamon, and peppermint filled the rooms, as well as the delicious fragrance of freshly-baked cookies and pies from the kitchen's wood-burning cook stove. As Christmas Eve grew near, hunting and foraging supplied such holiday delicacies as smoked trout, glazed ham, candied sweet potatoes, cornbread dressing, and cranberry relish.

In the evenings, following supper, they would sit around the great hearth, enjoying a crackling fire that drove away the chill of December. As they sipped coffee, cider, or a cabernet from the winery, they shared ghost stories, read Christmas tales from ancient books found in the library, and sang Christmas carols. Spirited conversation and laughter echoed through the cold, stone halls of the old mansion, turning what once felt like a prison into a home.

If there was one out of the eleven who was not completely immersed in the Christmas spirit, it was Melissa. The girl did her best to join in and enjoy herself, but sat quietly most of the time, unsmiling and preoccupied. She tried to shake off the dark mood, but couldn't seem to.

"Cheer up," Jem told her, sensing her reluctance. "It's Christmas. Time for us to count our blessings and be happy."

"I am happy," she would reply, smiling and snuggling up to him on the big sofa before the fireplace. But, deep down, she knew that she was lying through her teeth.

Nell had been on her mind lately. Melissa had no idea, but the woman seemed to be a link to her gloomy disposition. If she had truly known of Nell's feelings and intuitions, and the way she had expressed them during times of impending misfortune, she would have said that the dread was upon her.

"So… what the hell is going on?"

Melissa turned to see her sister standing in the doorway

that led onto the upper balcony.

"What do you mean?" she asked absently. Her eyes stared across the long front lawn, toward the treetops of the forest beyond.

"I mean you've been out here an awful lot lately, while the rest of us have been inside, taking it easy and enjoying ourselves," Michelle said. She walked over and stood next to her sister. "Why is that?"

"Someone has to stand guard."

"Sure, but not you... not all the time. You've been acting downright spooky the past few days. Like you're just waiting for something to happen."

"Maybe I am," Melissa told her. "Maybe we all should."

Michelle couldn't believe her ears. "What's gotten into you, Lissa? You used to be the positive one... Pollyanna on a freaking unicorn farting pixie dust and sunshine. Now you're more of a pessimist and fatalist than I ever was. It's not right, you being like this. You're totally screwing up our yin and yang... the natural order of us."

Melissa understood what she was getting at. "Why does it bother you so much that I'm being a little overly cautious? It seems that you used to promote that pretty heavily... and criticized me for being so naïve and trusting."

"Things have gotten better, sis. You've seen it. Everybody's getting along great and we don't have to be on our guard twenty-four seven, like before. We haven't seen one Biter since Nell's death and not one actual person since Frank Gentry and his bunch showed up a month ago. It's like the world has reached the ninety-nine point nine percent minus-population point... and that includes buzzards and Biters, too. Maybe the cold weather did a number on those little black bugs and killed their tiny asses. It's like we have a chance to start over again, without having to worry about that old survival shit, like we did before."

"Yes, things have been rainbows and candy hearts before," Melissa admitted. "We let our guard down and where did it get us? Nell got eaten by zombies and Enolia got brutalized. When we grow lax, when we get too comfortable, something happens. Something bad."

Michelle didn't know how to answer. Maybe her sister was right. Maybe they had grown too complacent. But it had felt good, hadn't it?

"Take a look over there," Melissa said, nodding toward the tree line. "What do you see?"

Michelle looked to the west. A long line of thick black clouds reached from north to south for as far as she could see. "Looks like a storm is brewing."

Melissa shook her head and smiled softly. "Where is Levi?"

"He and Billy headed out this morning," she said. "There's tons of mistletoe at the top of some trees in the east forest. They took rifles, said they were going to shoot it down. Levi said Christmas wasn't Christmas without mistletoe." Michelle winked at her sister. "I'm sure Jem will take advantage of it."

Melissa simply stared toward the far side of the estate. "When Levi gets back, tell him I need to see him. Okay?"

"You got it, sis," said Michelle. She sent one more worried glance toward her twin, then left the balcony and headed downstairs.

An hour later, a deeper voice drew her attention from her vigil.

"You wanted to see me?"

Melissa turned to see Levi. She wasn't surprised to Jem standing next to him.

"Come here," she said. "Got something I want you to see."

When Levi joined her at the balcony railing, she pointed westward. "See those clouds?"

"Yes."

She handed him a pair of binoculars. "Look a little closer."

He took the binoculars and studied the darkness in the sky. "What *is* that?"

"Not clouds," she told him. "Wind currents and circulation patterns aren't that synchronized. They don't swoop and rise like that."

"It's buzzards, isn't it?" Levi lowered the binoculars and shook his head. "Lord have mercy."

"I saw one the other day, you know," she said. "A buzzard. Just one. It flew in from the west, over those treetops and landed on the lawn, near the fountain there. It stared at me for a moment... stared at this place... then took flight and flew back the way it came."

"Almost like a scout," said Jem.

"*Exactly* like a scout." She stared at the far-reaching mass of swirling blackness. "I saw this yesterday, thought it was a storm coming, like my sister did. And it is... in a horrible unimaginable way. There must be thousands of buzzards on the wing, and for each buzzard maybe fifteen or twenty Biters. That's not a herd... not a horde... that's an exodus. They may not be here today or even tomorrow, as slow as they stumble and stagger. But they'll be here before the twenty-fifth. We're in for a helluva Christmas Eve... literally."

Levi looked again at the western horizon. "It's a theory."

"It's more than that. And you know it."

"We'll see," he said. "We'll see."

And they did.

CHAPTER 31

Confirmation of Melissa's theory came the following morning, halfway through the breakfast hour.

Avery looked up from his plate and listened. "I hear something."

His brother heard it, too. A low roar that gradually grew in volume. "What *is* that?"

"It's a car," Billy said. "And it sounds like it's heading this way."

They left the table at a run, picking up their weapons from a rack that stood in the entrance hall. Michelle tripped the four deadbolts and opened the front door.

It was bitter cold that morning and spitting snow. They stood on the concrete porch at the top of the front steps and watched the lane that led from the direction of the main entrance road. The wrought-iron gate had never been repaired following the ramming it had received from Levi's truck; it would have taken a blacksmith and welder to have done the job. The entranceway between the two stone pillars was open, giving access to anyone who had an inclination to show up.

A moment later, they did just that. It was a white Toyota Camry... except that it was no longer white. Blood and gory clots of tissue covered the frame of the car, which was battered and dented from the front bumper to the rear. Spider-web cracks fissured the windshield and side windows to the point where it would have been almost impossible to clearly see where you were going.

The car was going fast, probably seventy or eight miles per hour. As it roared up the road toward the mansion, they realized that it didn't intend to stop, either intentionally or due to some mechanical problem.

Billy lifted the M24 sniper rifle he had taken from one of Gentry's men during his attack on the winery and brought the sight of the scope to his right eye. He centered the crosshairs on the driver's side of the windshield. Through the shattered glass he saw the face of a woman. She was in her mid-thirties, blonde, and scared clean out of her wits. The Cherokee lowered his weapon and motioned for the others to retreat. "She's coming straight for us! Get back!"

They stepped through the doorway just as the car hydroplaned on the slick roadway. She fought for control and, rather than run up the steps of the front stoop, the car rammed forcefully into one of the massive stone lions that stood sentry at the side. The impact caused the statue to crack at its base and tumble forward. If it had landed across the right side of the car, it would have killed the driver instantly. Instead, it hit the passenger side, crushing most of the hood and caving in the front portion of the roof in an explosion of glass and buckling metal.

"Let's go!" ordered Levi. They headed down the steps to the Toyota. The car's engine was still running, its rear wheels spinning in one spot, throwing a cloud of black smoke in the air as its tires burned rubber. "Be careful! There are Biter guts and bugs all over this thing!"

Avery shucked off his flannel shirt and his brother did the same. They wadded the garments up and attempted to open the doors without coming in contact with the contaminated handles. "It's locked tighter than a drum, Papa!" said Jem.

Avery looked through the driver's side window. The air bags had deployed and the woman was lying unconscious, her face buried in the white nylon material. He looked in the back seat and saw a boy of about seven staring at him, utterly terrified. "Hey, boy! Unlock the door, will you?"

The boy said something, but his voice was muffled.

"What'd you say?" Avery asked, trying to hear him over the whining roar of the car's tortured engine.

"I SAID, IS SHE DEAD?" the boy screamed. "IS MY MOTHER DEAD?"

Avery's stomach sank. He studied the woman through the cloudy, cracked glass of her window again and saw her stir a little. "She's going to be okay!" he yelled. Inside the car, he could hear a child crying, younger than the boy who sat behind the driver's seat. "Can you climb up front and unlock the door for me?"

The boy fought off his panic and fear long enough to lean over the seat and pop the door lock. Avery opened the door and, with some difficulty, reached past the woman and the folds of the air bag, and turned the key in the ignition. Instantly, the engine died and the tires stopped spinning.

After Avery and his brother had opened the doors, they tossed their shirts away. The fabric of the flannel was covered with black parasites. Avery and Levi carefully pulled the woman from the driver's side. "Be careful," the man told his son. "I think her arm's broken."

Jem helped the seven-year-old out of the back, while Kate entered the car and found a four-year-old girl, every bit as blonde and pretty as her mother, secured in a car seat, screaming her head off. "Mommy! I want Mommy!"

"Mommy's going to be just fine, honey," she assured her. Kate was stunned to see that the buckled roof of the car was no more than two inches from the little girl's head. As she worked to unfasten the straps of the seat, she saw that, like the boy and his mother, the little girl was dirty and disheveled. Junk food bags and cartons littered the seat and floorboards, and a milk jug looked to be nearly full of urine. It was clear to see that they had been stuck in the car for quite a while.

Kate lifted the girl into her arms. The child clung to her, weeping uncontrollably into her shoulder. "Shhhh… it's going to be alright, baby."

"What's your name, son?" Levi asked the boy as he and Avery carried the woman up the steps and through the front door.

"Brandon," he said. Unlike his mother, he had dark brown hair. "Brandon Stapleton. My sister is Becky and my mommy's name is Diane."

"Let's get y'all inside, Brandon," the man told him, "and we'll see to your mom."

"Is she going to be okay?" he asked anxiously. "Is she going to live?"

"She'll be okay, buddy," Jem told him, placing reassuring hands on his narrow shoulders. "Now let's get in out of the cold and see what we can do for her, okay?"

"Okay," agreed Brandon. "But we better hurry. They're coming, you know."

Michelle frowned at the boy. "Who are *they*?"

Her sister nodded skyward. "You know who he's talking about. Look."

She lifted her eyes and was shocked. The black clouds that had seemed so far away the day before were much closer now... so close that the swooping patterns of the buzzards could be seen for what they were, instead of only guessed at.

"Shit fire and fly my freaking ass to the moon!" said Michelle.

"You've got a foul mouth, lady," Brandon told her bluntly. "My mommy would give me such a spanking for talking like that."

"Yeah, I know, kid," she said. "Sorry. It's a bad habit of mine. Now let's get inside, before *they* get here... okay?"

"Okay," he said, "but it isn't going to help."

"What do you mean?"

"You'll see," Brandon told her. "When they get here, you'll see just what I mean."

"He's right," said Diane Stapleton, taking a long sip of hot coffee and settling against the pillows of the big sofa. She grimaced in pain as Kate worked to set her fractured left arm. "When they get here, there will be no stopping them."

"Why don't you start from the beginning, Mrs. Stapleton," Levi said. "So we know what we're up against."

The woman nodded and took another sip of coffee. She looked around, making sure her children were nearby. Brandon was sitting in front of the hearth playing Chinese checkers with Jessie, while Becky sat in Melissa's lap in the big armchair, flipping through a picture book about Santa Claus and his reindeer. The four-year-old sucked her thumb and stared at the illustrations, on the verge of drifting to sleep from sheer exhaustion.

Satisfied that they were safe and with good folks, she began to speak. "We're from Lynchburg, Virginia. I was a real estate agent and..." she paused, a pained look crossing her face. "... my husband, Chuck, was a car salesman at a Toyota dealership there. For a while, after all this began, we were okay. There was an empty house about fifteen miles out of town that I was trying to sell for the owner, who had retired to New Mexico. It was on a farm, out in the middle of nowhere. We holed up there the first few months and laid low. If Biters came along, we acted like we weren't there and they passed on. If looters and troublemakers came, we hid in the cellar until they'd taken what they wanted and left."

"So why did you leave?" Melissa asked her.

"Daddy was out chopping wood one day and he got bit," Brandon said absently as he played his game. "A Biter was on top of him before he could turn around. Tore a hunk right out of his right shoulder before he could split its head with the axe."

Levi looked back to the woman to see tears in her eyes. "What happened to your husband? After he was bit?"

"He got sick," she said, wiping her eyes. She drained the last of her coffee and set the cup aside. "I tried to treat him, but I knew it wasn't going to get any better. I could see the bugs in the wound, burrowing into the muscle, and then the bruised color of his throat and neck as they began traveling up to his head. He told me to lock him in the cellar and we did. I could hear him down there moaning and crying; it hurt so badly. Then he stopped. I got up the nerve to go down and check on him. He was curled up on a blanket in the corner. I thought for sure he was dead. I checked his pulse, but couldn't find a heartbeat. I was heading back up the stairs when I heard something. I turned around and there he was, standing at the bottom, staring up at me. Chuck smiled at me and... God... I could see that his mouth was full of those nasty things. He started coming up after me and... and I kicked him in the chest. He fell down the steps and broke his neck. But we wouldn't... stop... coming! His head was twisted halfway around, but he was bound and determined to get to me. So I shot him. Took the 9mm pistol I carried with me and put a bullet in his head. And that was the end of it. He fell back down the stairs and didn't get up again."

"We're sorry," Kate told her. She thought of her own husband and how she had ended up taking him down. A bullet in the forehead would have been much easier... but in Bill's case, less satisfying.

"Thank you," the woman said dully. "Could I have more coffee? I can't seem to get rid of this chill."

Enolia took her cup. "Of course. I'll be right back."

"And after your husband's death?" Levi asked.

"We stayed there for a week or two," she said. "Lord, how it stank in that house... him rotting down there in the cellar. But we ignored it and stayed... because it was safe. Then one afternoon it got dark, just all of a sudden. At first, I thought it was a solar eclipse or something. When I went outside, I saw it for what it was."

"Buzzards," said Melissa grimly.

"Yes. The sky was full of them for as far as the eye could see. There was a row of hills west of the farmhouse and those things... the zombies... just poured down into the valley... and didn't stop. There were thousands of them... maybe *millions*... I don't know, it was hard to tell. They were shoulder to shoulder, one behind the other, and they weren't stopping for anything. I watched as they took down trees and fences with the sheer weight of their bodies, tore down a church like it was made of nothing.

"By the time we grabbed some supplies from the kitchen and got to the car, about a hundred of them were crossing the pasture and coming toward us. We had to drive through them to get to the main road. They clawed and bit at the car, trying to get inside to us. Some of them butted the glass, flailed at the windshield with their fists, leaving bloody smears and flesh all over the car. I thought for sure they would bust the windows out and get us, but we got through them and headed south. We left Virginia and made it to North Carolina. But we kept running into herds of the things... it was like they would never end! Chuck had filled up several gas cans and put them in the trunk before he got bit. I stopped only long enough to add some gas to the tank a couple of times. Once I nearly didn't make it back inside… they were upon the car so fast. There were so many of them, they almost pushed it onto its side. If they had, we would be dead right now… or worse. Luckily, I made it past them and hit the road again. I thought of this place…" Diane began to cry again, "… because Chuck and I spent our honeymoon here. So I hit the road and didn't stop until I got here. My tank was nearly on empty when I wrecked in front of the house. I tried to stop, I really did, but I hit that slick spot and… well, that's all I remember until I woke up on this couch."

Jem and Billy came into the room, bundled up in heavy coats and stocking caps. There was snow on their heads and shoulders. "It's starting to come down pretty heavy out there," the Cherokee told them. "I'd say we'll have a foot or so by this afternoon."

"And the buzzards?" asked Levi.

Jem shook his head. "The snow's not slowing them down… or what they're circling over either, I'd say. They're even thicker than before. And they're close enough that you can see with binoculars what they are. Sometimes they swoop down and come back up with something in their claws… maybe pieces of Biters. I reckon they get tired of flying all the time… need meat to keep their strength up."

"Gross," muttered Becky from the armchair, half asleep.

"Mrs. Stapleton…"

"Diane," she insisted.

"Diane," continued Levi, "do you think we can make a stand here? Do you think we'll be able to hold them off?"

"No," she said truthfully. "I'm sorry, but there are too many. I don't know where they all came from or why their migrating to the east, but they are moving as one and they aren't stopping. I saw them take down an old railroad bridge at the state line… wooden timbers that had stood for a hundred years, just torn down like it was nothing at all. These walls might withstand the weight of them, but the doors and windows won't, no matter how much you've fortified them. If they sweep through here, they'll be in the house before you know it."

"So staying here is pointless," said Levi solemnly. "I thought as much."

"Oh no," moaned Michelle. She looked on the verge of tears. "Not this place."

"I'm afraid so," he told her. "Our best bet would be to prepare to head out of here as soon as possible. Pack whatever we can and head east. From the way that that cloud of buzzards stretches north to south, I'd say they are two hundred miles strong. If we wait to fight them and get stuck in the middle, there will be no hope for us."

"I hate the thought of them taking this house," said Melissa. "Our father cherished this place. For those... those *things*... to get inside here, to walk through its halls... the thought of it is *unbearable*." She shook her head and sighed. "I'd rather see it fall to the ground, than to see them overtake it."

A thought suddenly came to Avery, a memory that surfaced from a couple of months ago... one that he had hoped to forget, but now was glad he did. "Papa," he said, "there's fifty pounds of C-4 out there in that Humvee, along with the wiring and blasting caps to go with it. And there are two signal receivers like the one Gentry used at the bridge."

Levi knew exactly what he was driving at. "How would you manage it? A house this big... this sturdy?"

"I could rig the supports of the foundation," his son suggested. "If I could figure out exactly where they were."

"Richard Hunt's original blueprints are in the library," said Michelle. The very thought of what they were planning to do made her sick to her stomach. "I can show you where they are."

Melissa was horrified. "You mean you're going to..."

"Turn the tide on those Biters, if they make it into the house," said Avery. "Blow the supports and bring the whole place falling down around their nasty, bug-ridden heads. We did it before, back on Hobbs Ridge. We can do it here, too. It won't take out but a fraction of them, but it'll be that many that we won't have to worry about any longer."

Levi could tell that the idea devastated the twin girls. "In my way of thinking, you two hold ownership of this place. Your pa left it to you, to use as a sanctuary and do with as you please. It's not our decision. It's yours."

Michelle and Melissa looked at one another. They knew

what each other was thinking, knew the decision that that had been mutually made. "Let's squash the bastards and the things inside them," said Michelle.

"And if it takes destroying the Biltmore to do it," agreed Melissa, "so be it."

CHAPTER 32

As late morning passed into early afternoon, time moved quickly.

Levi knew that they had a very narrow window of opportunity if the darkening of the sky and the growing stench of putrid, decomposing flesh was any indication. Their plan was to pack a few necessities—food, water, and clothing—then depart in the four drivable vehicles. They would take an access road southeast away from the estate and head toward the state border and South Carolina beyond. If they could outrun the tsunami of Biters and continue south, perhaps they would have a chance of surviving.

He thought of Nell and wished that she was there with them. Not only for the obvious reasons, but for her sense of "joy and dread", as she put it. He couldn't help but think they could have prepared for their escape if his wife had shared a feeling of impending disaster, like she had many times before. Levi suspected that Melissa Webb possessed a bit of an intuitive nature similar to Nell's, but not as strong and developed. True, she had sensed that something was potentially wrong, but the realization of what it was had come too late to motivate them into action.

They parked the pickup truck, SUV, Jenkins' jeep, and the Humvee in front of the mansion's front entrance. Diane Stapleton's mangled Toyota sat where it had crashed earlier that morning. The two-ton lion still lay embedded in the passenger side of the car and would remain that way from then on.

Billy and Jem removed the metal chest of C-4 plastic explosives and separate crate containing spools of wire, tubular blasting caps, and the signal-triggered detonators up the steps to where Avery and Michelle were waiting. "Time to get to work," the boy said. With the brunette's help they began to fasten the first of the two detonators above the doorway of the grand entrance and then link the current wires to the connectors. Avery intended to install the signal detonators in two key positions—at the front entrance and at the basement exit that led onto the back lawn. That way they could detonate the charges from either direction, in case bad went to worse. The two disappeared into the house. Avery fed the wire from the spool, while Michelle followed, toting the yellowed floor plans from the library stuck under her arm.

Levi carried a box of canned and dried goods to the Dodge and secured it in the bed. The snow continued to fall, but not as heavily as before. He believed it was partly due to the number of buzzards circling directly ahead. The birds that left the airborne flocks and descended to the limbs of leafless trees and the eaves of the big house were crusted with wintery precipitation, having taken the brunt of the snowfall.

"Lord have mercy, it stinks out here!" Jem said. The boy was right. The ripe odor of rot and decay hung heavily in the air and grew stronger by the minute.

"They're almost here," said Billy. "Listen."

In the distance they heard the sound of shuffling feet en masse, as well as brittle cracks and crashes as the ancient trees of the forests surrounding the Biltmore were uprooted and sent toppling by the sheer force of the zombie migration.

Jem noticed the Cherokee rooting around in the back of the Humvee. "What are you looking for?"

Billy opened an ammo box and stuffed a fragmentation grenade in each pocket of his coat. "These," he said. "They could slow them down if they get here before we have a chance to leave."

Levi and Jem took a few grenades as well. "You think we should take the fifty-caliber?" asked Levi.

"Unfortunately, I don't believe we'll have the chance," said Billy. "Look!"

Levi and Jem looked toward the forest that faced the far

end of the rectangular lawn. Several dozen Biters were already emerging from the woods, followed by seemingly endless wave behind them. The towering maples and cedars that stood to the west began to splinter and drop, one after another. A massive oak tree, twice as old as the estate itself, was pushed over by a wall of zombies. It fell with a crash across the road, blocking the stone entranceway and their sole way out.

"Damn!" cussed Levi. A mixture of anger and panic threatened to overcome him, but he fought it down. "Back inside! As much I hate it, we're going to have to take to foot and hope we can outdistance them." He took inventory of where the others were. Enolia, Kate, and Tyrone were upstairs on the third floor gathering clothes and possessions, while Diane and Melissa were watching over the children in the dining hall.

"Jem, check with Avery and Melissa in the basement and see how they're doing," Levi told him. "If they have a ways to go setting the charges, tell them to abandon it and meet us at the chestnut tree in the meadow."

"Yes, sir," said Jem. Soon he had disappeared through a doorway that led downstairs.

"Billy, you head upstairs and get Tyrone and the girls. I'm going to fetch Diane and Melissa and the young'uns and get them to safety."

"Right!" agreed the Cherokee.

Billy bounded up the curving staircase, while Levi shouldered his shotgun and ran for the dining hall. Outside, the uneven marching of thousands of unbalanced footsteps could be heard, crunching in the snow, scraping upon the cobbled roadway, as well the brittle toppling of timber and splintering of the stables being flattened and torn to the ground.

And above it all, stirred to a frenzy by the stench of rampant death and decay, flew the buzzards, dark and ravenous, anxious to partake of the restless carrion, but seeing no opportunity to do so.

"Where's the next one?" Avery asked. According to the blueprints, there were eight major support structures within the foundation of the Biltmore. So far, they had found five and affixed six-pound blocks of C-4 to each one. After each charge had been secured to the ancient columns of stone and mortar, blasting caps inserted, and the caps wired for detonation, they moved on to the next.

Michelle held a flashlight over the folds of the blueprints. "There should be another one sixty feet behind you," she said, squinting in the sparse glow, trying to decipher the floor plan. "After that, we have two more at the north end of the basement, beneath the dining hall."

Suddenly, they heard Jem's voice from the head of the stairs. "Avery?"

"Down here, brother!"

"Hurry it up, will you?" his twin hollered. "We're switching to Plan B. The Biters are already here... crossing the lawn and nearly at the house!"

"Aw hell!" growled Avery. "Of all the blasted luck! Where are the wheels?"

"Out front with the zombies," his brother told him. "No chance of getting to them and, if we did, we'd be half eaten and full of black bugs before we could get inside."

"Dammit!" Michelle had grown up in the desert outside Tucson and absolutely hated the cold. And now it looked like they would be traipsing through ankle-deep snow for no telling how long.

"Papa said if you've still got a ways to go, forget the explosives and get your butt up here."

"We've got three more to go!" Avery called. "We'll be up as soon as they're done!"

"Well, you'd better make it fast!" Somewhere upstairs they heard a splintering crash, then another, as the fortified windows at the front of the house began to give away beneath the weight of the hungry dead. "Sounds like they're already in the house!"

"We're a-coming!" his brother promised. Avery hefted the bag of remaining C-4 over one shoulder and his AR-15 over the other, then looked at the girl next to him. Michelle's face was pale and drawn in the glow of the flashlight. "How are you holding up?"

"I'm okay," she said.

"Scared?"

He could feel her bristle at the question, rather than actually see it. "Hell no!"

"Me neither!" he proclaimed in his customary swagger. "Let's get those other three columns and head on up. Lead the way!"

As Michelle used the old blueprints to navigate, neither one of them said another word as they made their way through the gloomy cellar. Truth be told, both were more afraid that they had ever been in their lives, although neither would have ever admitted it.

Becky Stapleton began to cry as Levi knelt to fasten her coat. "It's okay, sweetheart," he told the four-year-old soothingly. "We're just gonna bundle up and go out and play in the snow for a while."

The four-year-old's face screwed up into a frightened mask as she stared the lanky Tennessean in the face. She began to bawl uncontrollably as he slipped her pink mittens over her tiny hands. "Please... if they hear you crying, they'll want to come inside." Worried, he looked over at the child's mother, who was working on her son's winter clothing.

She shrugged apologetically. "Becky is... well, she's frightened of men with beards. Sorry."

"I'd sure have shaved this morning, clean as a whistle," he told her, "but there was no predicting that I'd need to."

Diane was about to answer, when a crash sounded from the boarded windows of the adjoining pool room. They could hear the splintering of wood, the shattering of glass panes, and the guttural growls and groans of Biters, where they had only heard faint echoes a moment before. "Oh dear God! They're inside!"

"Melissa?" he asked. The dark-haired teenager nodded. "Jessie, you got your little brother?"

"Yes, sir," she replied, holding the blanketed baby tightly to her chest. "I'm ready, too."

"Then let's go."

Together, the seven left the dining hall and made their way past the winter garden to the entrance hall. Several Biters were already inside. They caught sight of Levi and the others and started toward them, their black teeth snapping savagely. Levi pumped his shotgun and drove them back with three blasts of double-aught buckshot. Melissa and Diane fired as well; the girl cut loose with the Uzi that Kate had left with her and the mother with her 9mm Beretta M9.

"Go!" Levi told them. They herded the children ahead of them and headed for the French doors that led onto the rear veranda. Before they got there, the doors opened and Jem was there. Melissa rushed into his arms. "Thank goodness! I didn't know where you were."

He hugged her back, then ushered the others outside. "Be careful going down those back steps. They're a mite icy!" He gave Melissa a quick peck on the lips and pushed her toward the others. "Get them under that chestnut tree. We'll be down directly."

As he turned to join his father, a tremendous crash sounded and the vast oaken doors at the front of the hall caved in. With it came the Humvee. The military vehicle was smashed and battered and had been flipped onto its roof. A wall of Biters was behind it, pushing it through the barrier and into the circular foyer. A steady stream of zombies climbed over the Humvee and pushed past it, filling the entrance hall.

"Get back!" Levi yelled. He took a grenade from his coat pocket, pulled the pin, and tossed it beneath the stumbling feet of the invaders. He and Jem ran and made the veranda as the grenade went off. The explosion took down a dozen or so zombies, throwing dismembered limbs and scorched flesh and bone in all directions. But it did little to show the flow of Biters as they moved onward, seemingly unstoppable.

"Where's your brother and Michelle?" Levi asked him, sending another blast or two of buckshot toward the approaching zombies. The shots were as ineffective as battling a herd of rhinos with a fly swatter.

"They're finishing up," he told him. "They should be wiring the detonator above the basement door right about now." At least he hoped what he was saying was true. To be honest, he had no idea where the two were at that moment. "Where's Tyrone and Kate and Enolia?"

"Upstairs," Levi said, his voice heavy with despair. "God help them... they're still up there." He looked toward the winding staircase and saw a steady stream of Biters climbing toward the second-floor landing.

"Papa! We gotta help them!"

"We can't, son," he told him. "We've got children out there in the cold...plus Melissa and Diane. We can't leave them to fend for themselves. I'm afraid we're going to have to go, whether we like it or not."

The zombies were halfway across the entrance hall. Fifteen seconds more and the two would be completely overrun by the bug-ridden hoard.

Jem and Levi turned, closing the French doors behind them. They knew the barrier would give away in a matter of seconds, but perhaps it would be the seconds they needed to make it to the snowy stretch of lawn below.

Billy Tauchee found his wife and the others in a corridor on the third floor, toting backpacks and bags of clothing and other belongings. "We've got to get to the first floor!" he told them. "They're already in the house!"

"Do you think we can get past them?" Enolia asked him. "Oh dear God... Jessie and Austen!"

"They're fine," her husband assured her. "They're with Levi... probably down at the tree by now. Is there another way down from the third floor? A service staircase?"

"Yes," said Kate. "But we've already tried it. There's a door between the corridor and the back stairs, and could hear them coming up. There's no getting out that way."

"Then we'll have to take our chances down the main staircase."

"We'll get down there," Tyrone declared. "Because I got this here mutha!" He lifted the M2 Browning his huge hands. A long band of .50 ammunition hung from the loading port of the machine gun and dangled over his left shoulder, while the Thompson machine gun was slung across the right. "I ran upstairs and fetched it while Kate and Enolia packed their stuff."

"I could kiss you, Tyrone," Billy said with a grin. "Since you've got the heavy artillery, you can take point." The Cherokee jacked a round into the breach of the M416 he had taken from Harley Jenkins during his raid at the winery. "I'm second and you ladies take up the rear."

Enolia looked at Kate. Given what they had been through together, the two were more like sisters than friends. "We're ready," said Kate. She pulled the two Glocks from her coat pocket and held them loosely beside her lanky legs. Enolia pulled a Magnum revolver from her own coat—Nell's nickel-plated Colt Python, the one she had attempted to fight her attackers off with. She raised the .357 and held it aloft, muzzle aimed toward the plaster ceiling.

As one, they descended the staircase that led from the third floor to the second.

Halfway down the steps, a dozen zombies crowded into the narrow channel between the railing and wall. As their bloodshot eyes spotted the four coming down, they surged forward, arms outstretched, bug-blacked teeth snapping and yearning for warm, living flesh.

Tyrone braced himself and sent a burst of 50-caliber rounds into the knot of Biters. The slugs ripped through their decayed bodies, obliterating bug-infested skulls and cutting bloated abdomens in half. The four hung back, attempting to avoid the spray of infested blood and mangled tissue.

When the first wave had fallen, Tyrone looked over his shoulder. "Step over them... just try not to step *into* them!" They did as he said, stepping gingerly over the heaps of torn, decomposing muscle and bullet-shattered bone.

They reached the second-floor landing. As they turned the corner and approached the stairs that led to the ground floor, a flood of zombies surged up the steps and filled the landing. Tyrone stepped to the side, allowing the other three room to fire. Full and semi-auto weapons filled the air with a deafening staccato as bullets drove the Biters back. They dropped limply to the landing floor and fell backwards down the staircase.

We're going to make it, thought Enolia. She looked over at her husband, but didn't see the same confidence in his face. His features were stern, but she saw concern and apprehension in his dark eyes. It was as though he was staring into the future and seeing something that he didn't like at all.

Midway through a burst, the Browning jammed. "Damn!" Tyrone cussed and flung the M2 to the floor, grabbing over his shoulder for the Thompson.

"My turn for point," Billy said, raising the M416 to his shoulder and sighting down the barrel. He stepped forward and headed for the staircase.

"Billy!" Enolia called out. Fear seized her heart as he started down the steps, firing in short, concentrated bursts. A bee swarm of 5.56 mm rounds drove the zombies backward at first, then the sheer number of Biters prevailed, surging over their comrades and continuing upstairs.

"Get back up here, man!" Tyrone told him. He raised the Tommy gun and fired over the Cherokee's head, taking six or seven down... which was immediately replaced by two dozen more. "It's getting too thick!"

"I can route them," Billy said as he fired his weapon. "I can clear the stairs and we'll be in the clear... across the lobby and out the back doors."

As they paused at the top of the curving staircase, they saw the zombies closing in on Billy, despite the amount of ammo he expended on them. A couple of them reached past the M416 and sank their fingers into his jacket.

"Billy!" screamed Enolia. "Come back, baby!" Then his own jargon came to mind. "Retreat! Retreat!"

But it was too late. The Biters were already on him. Billy refused to scream as teeth slashed at him, tearing away shreds of clothing and tatters of flesh and muscle. He dropped the assault rifle. It clattered beneath churning feet. The Cherokee attempted to take a couple of steps back up the stairs, but death-stiffened fingers punched through the flesh of his chest and abdomen, refusing to let go.

"BILLY!" Enolia shrieked and stepped forward, but was restrained by Tyrone and Kate.

Painfully, Billy Tauchee turned his head and looked at them. The right side of his head been stripped of its flesh, leaving only raw muscle and tendons, and stark patches of naked bone. "Back across the landing!" he yelled. "Take cover behind the corner! Now!"

As the three retreated, Enolia saw her husband bring his arms up out of the milling sea of angry, ravenous zombies. In each bloody hand he held a grenade.

"Billy... *no!*" she screamed. She fought against the hands that held her and, for a second, slipped free. She was nearly to the staircase, when the black man's massive arms entwined her, making escape impossible. "No, Billy.... no."

Before she was pulled away from her final glimpse of Billy, he stared at her. Their eyes locked and his torn lips mouthed two things, two parting gifts from her husband. One was *I love you.* The other was *remember.*

She saw him pull the pin from each grenade with his teeth and then pull both hands down to crowd level.

Enolia and the other two were around the corner, sheltered by sturdy timber and plaster, when the grenades detonated. The scent of burning flesh and gun powder filled their nostrils. The awful sound of rampant hunger and feeding grew silent.

"Come on," said Tyrone.

"No!" shrieked Enolia. "No, I can't... I can't... see..."

Kate took the woman's tear-streaked face in her freckled hands. "Just take hold of my waist. Just hold on and close your eyes. We'll get you down. Okay?"

The woman nodded dully and did as Kate said. "He did it," she heard Tyrone say softly. "He cleared the path."

Slowly they made their way down the steps, stepping on and over torn and shrapnel-shredded bodies. When they reached the spot where Billy had last stood, Tyrone stopped. "We've gotta be careful here... cause the stairs are gone. About six feet worth of them."

Enolia opened her eyes. Blood and dark refuse hung everywhere—on the walls, the staircase railing, from the huge chandelier suspended over the expanse of the entrance hall. She also saw the black-rimmed crater that the dual explosions had caused.

"How are we going to get across?" she asked. Her voice

sounded like it came from a thousand miles away.

Tyrone stepped back, then leapt and barely landed on the opposite side of the chasm. He nearly lost his balance, but steadied himself before he could fall. "Now you, Enolia."

Without protest, the woman reached out for him. He hooked his big hands beneath her arms and lifted her over the crater with no trouble at all. Then he reached out for Kate.

"I... I can't..." she said. She lifted her gaze from the jagged hole and looked him in the face. Her lips trembled and tears filled her eyes. "You... you don't want..."

"Kate," said Tyrone. "Look at me, baby."

She focused on his broad, dark features through the prism of her tears. She was surprised to find no contempt, no hatred.

"Give me your hand," he said. "I'm not going to let you fall." His features softened and his own eyes grew moist. "I love you, baby... and I'm sorry. I know you did what you had to do. Now give me your hand. We don't have much time."

Kate slipped a Glock in her pocket and extended her right hand. He took it gently in his giant's grasp and, with the other arm, scooped her up and lifted her bodily over the dark crater of burnt and splintered wood and marble. Soon, she was safely on the other side.

Below, a sea of milling, flesh-starved Biters filled the entrance hall with more pushing their way through the open doorway by the minute.

"There are too many of them," Enolia said. "We're never going to make it." Her voice had lost its shell-shocked quality. Her eyes were sharpening, returning to the reality of what they were up against.

"We have to," Kate told her as zombies began to climb the risers of the stairs, coming for them. "For Jessie and Austen... for my daddy and my brothers..." She looked at Tyrone. "For *us.*"

A flash of a smile crossed his face, if only for an instant, as if saying *amen!*

"Stay close," Tyrone told them. Then he started forward, firing the Tommy gun and mowing down the first wave of Biters. "Let's go!"

"Hold it still, will you?" Avery complained. "You're gonna make me fall!"

"If you weren't such a runt, you wouldn't have to stand on a damn trash can!" Michelle told him as she attempted to hold the galvanized container steady.

"If they hadn't made such tall doors way back in the old days, I'd be able to reach it!" He stretched and wound the shaved end of the wire around the connector bolt of the second signal junction box. On the other side of the sturdy double doors, he could hear the stirring of Biters, dozens of them, and see a slight bulging of the wood as their weight bore heavily against the barrier. He knew it wouldn't last very long before giving way and releasing a gorge of the ravenous undead.

He was tightening the wire for a good connection when he lost his balance and tumbled off the garbage can. He grunted loudly as he landed on his backside.

"We'd better check you for a concussion," the girl suggested, helping him to his feet.

"Very funny," he said. He eyed the detonator box and nodded. "Looks good enough to me. Let's get the hell outta here."

The two ran down the slope to where Levi and the others waited beneath the chestnut tree. When they got there, Avery sensed that something was wrong. "Where's Kate?" Billy and Enolia Tauchee and Tyrone Jackson weren't present either.

Levi's face was grim and lined with worry. "They were upstairs when the Biters overran the house and forced me and Jem out the back," he told his son. "I heard an explosion a couple of minutes ago. It sounded like it came from an upper floor."

"We heard it, too," said Michelle. "I wonder what happened."

Levi figured that it was one or more of the grenades that Billy had carried with him. Whatever his motivation for detonating them, it couldn't have been a good one. He thought of his daughter and felt sick to his stomach. *Lord, please don't take my little girl. It was hard enough losing Nell... but Kate too...*

Then his heart lightened as Melissa smiled and pointed toward the concrete stairs at the far end of the veranda. "There they are!"

Levi turned and was relieved to see Kate trudging through the snow with Tyrone and Enolia behind her. The Cherokee woman looked as though she was in a state of shock. It was then that he realized that someone was missing.

"Billy?" he asked.

Tyrone simply shook his head sadly and said nothing.

Jessie looked at her mother, her face growing frightened and confused. "Mama?"

"He's... he's gone, baby," she said. She embraced her daughter and newborn son, deriving strength from their warmth and closeness. "You know your father. He was a soldier... and he did what soldiers do. He did what he thought necessary... to give us a fighting chance."

Levi looked to the north and south of the Biltmore Estate. Waves of zombies, shoulder to shoulder, marched on both sides, continuing eastward. They seemed oblivious to their presence beneath the chestnut tree. He looked back at the house and saw Biters milling restless on the rear veranda. Some toppled over the railing and fell twenty feet onto the paved walkway below, shattering bones and rupturing bloated organs and rot-weakened muscle. Others were making their way down the rear staircase. He knew it would only be a matter of time before they noticed them and attacked.

"We've got to head out," he told them. "A bunch have already gone past us and we'll have a hard time making it around them if we stay here much longer." He looked over at his son. "Are you ready?"

Avery took the signal remote from his pocket, extended its antenna, and aimed it toward the back entrance of the basement level. "Y'all better cover your ears. This is gonna make one hellacious bang!"

He hesitated, savoring the moment, then pushed the red detonation button. Nothing happened. "What the hell?"

"What's wrong with the thing?" asked Jem. "Is the battery dead?"

"It's fine. Something's wrong." Avery looked over at Melissa. "Let me borrow those binoculars, will you?" When she had handed them to him, he focused on the junction box above the door. A green light on its side was lit up, signifying that it was armed and ready. Then he noticed that the connector bolt on the side was bare. The wire had slipped loose.

"Shit!" he cussed. Avery tossed Melissa the binoculars and, without hesitation, headed back toward the house.

"Get back here, son!" Levi ordered. "Just forget about the house. Let's get to the woods and be on our way!"

"Hell no!" Avery said defiantly. "Their rotten asses have got to pay! For driving us out here in the cold and snow... for what they did to Ma!"

As he turned to go, Michelle ran after him. "Hey, hold up! I'm going with you!"

Avery turned on her, his eyes blazing. "The hell you are! Get your ass back there with the others." When he saw her expression harden, his softened. "Chelle... I'll be okay. It'll only take me thirty seconds at the most. Then I'll be back." He handed her the remote unit. "Here... if something happens... if you see me go down... you know what to do."

"Are you crazy?" she snapped, "I couldn't..."

"You *have* to." Then, without another word, he turned and trudged back up the snowy hill toward the basement.

When he got to the door he was shocked to see that the wood was cracked and splintered, and the hinges were bent and bulging against the pressure of those on the other side. Quickly, he retrieved the fallen end of the wire and carefully mounted the trash can. He almost lost his footing several times, but finally steadied himself enough to thread the copper filaments around the connector bolt tightly. *There,* he thought. His heart pounded as the heavy wooden panels of the basement doors bulged and cracked. *That'll do the job.*

Avery Hobbs crouched, preparing to climb down off the trash can, when the doors exploded in a hail of splintered wood... and all hell broke loose.

"*No!*" Michelle screamed as a flood of Biters burst from the ruins of the weakened doors and attacked the first warm-blooded thing they saw.

She stuffed the detonator in her coat pocket, picked up her shotgun, and began to run.

"*Chelle!*" her sister wailed. "You can't... get back here... *please!*"

Michelle turned and looked at Melissa. "I'm sorry, sis!" she called out. "But I have to." Tears bloomed in her hazel eyes. "I *have* to!"

She pumped the foregrip of the ten-gauge, jacking a shell into the breech. Soon she was up the rise and at the rear entrance of the basement. She fired, pumped, fired, and pumped again. Zombies flailed backwards, their heads disintegrating in explosions of decaying brains, blood, and tiny black bugs. But she knew there was no saving him. They had dragged Avery to the ground and were tearing him apart. She had never seen so much blood in all her life. She saw a Biter pulling at something, dragging it away, and realized that it was a stringy length of intestine. The sight both horrified and enraged her. She fired the shotgun until it was empty, then fought her way past the emerging hoard. Unsure of what else to do, she flung herself bodily upon the teenage boy.

Why? she thought as the weight of the zombies descended upon her and she was engulfed in searing agony as teeth tore at her scalp and back, stealing shreds of clothing, then fragile skin, then the throbbing tissue of exposed muscle underneath. *Why am I doing this? I can't save him.*

But she didn't have to ask. She knew. Deep down in her heart, she knew.

"Hey," she said as she stared Avery in the face. It was splattered with his own blood and covered with crawling black mites, searching for entrance. Some of it was gone, torn away by hungry teeth and covetous fingers to be taken and devoured.

"Hey," he said back. His eyes stared at her sorrowfully, as though saying *why the hell didn't you stay down there with the others?*

Michelle screamed as the flesh of her back was stolen and bug-blackened teeth grated against her shoulder blades and the column of her spine. "You dumb-ass!" she cried. "You stupid, stubborn dumb-ass!"

For a moment, all they could do was look at each other, being torn apart, reduced to something much less than they had been a minute before.

"Chelle?"

She felt them bear upon her, driving her down toward him. "Yeah?"

Avery sobbed. Tears mingled freely with blood, running down his cheeks in crimson streams. "Chelle... girl... I love you."

Michelle cried too and shook her head angrily. "I hate it... when you get the... upper hand." The pain had grown so unbearable that it was difficult to speak. She leaned forward and pressed her lips against his. Their first—and last—kiss was thick with blood and regret. "I should have... said it... *first.*"

"Have you... have you got the... detonator... with you?" he asked haltingly. He heard, and felt, a wet ripping at his left shoulder as the tendons were stretched beyond capacity and his arm was torn savagely away.

She fought against the weight of their awful hunger, reached into the pocket of her tattered winter coat, and pulled the remote free. "I have it."

Then Avery flashed that half-assed, redneck grin of his, despite the fact that a good portion of his face was gone. "What do you say we blow this joint?"

Michelle matched his grin, wicked and mischievous, even as she felt frantic hands invading her, plunging past her ruined kidneys into the depths of her abdominal cavity...searching, grabbing, tearing away. "Damn straight!" she said.

Pulling the detonator between the two of them, Michelle's right hand found Avery's only remaining one. And, together, they brought their collective agony to a swift and merciful end.

The others watched, stunned, as a chain of explosions shot through the foundation of the Biltmore House. Melissa and Kate screamed mournfully as the supports beneath the mansion buckled and crumbled. The massive structure imploded in an inward rush of dislodged stone, spinning steel, and dust. They watched as the stone walls of the basement level collapsed,

covering Avery and Michelle with tons of refuse, along with the Biters that engulfed them.

Levi heard Kate and Jem cry out. He heard Melissa scream her sister's name, again and again. The sounds echoed distantly in his mind as shock and despair seized his entire being and he felt himself falter. Levi's legs gave away and he fell forcefully to his knees. All of his strength seemed to drain away as a spinning, disorienting darkness closed in upon him. Grief like nothing he had ever felt in his lifetime threatened to overtake him... to drive him to the earth, never to rise again.

Then he felt slender arms around his shoulders, attempting to comfort that which seemed beyond comforting. "Levi," a voice urged softly. "Levi...we have to go. *Now.*"

He shook his head violently, words unable to form through the awful aching in the back of his throat. He sagged forward once again, but the hands held firm, fighting to lift him up.

"I know you are hurting," Enolia told him. "So am I. More than I have ever known. I feel like I want to give up... like I want to die... with *them.*"

"Yes," his voice croaked hoarsely.

"But we can't. We've got to go now... got to get the others to safety."

"No... I can't..."

"*Yes!*" she said sharply. "We can't do it without you, Levi... if you give up, we might as well give up, too."

It was at that moment, when he had nearly abandoned all hope, that *she* came to him. He couldn't tell if what he felt was merely his imagination... or something beyond mortal comprehension. All he knew was that her voice rang in his ears, just as clearly as if she had been standing there before him.

Get your ass up, Levi Hobbs! You're embarrassing me.

The bearded man breathed deeply, feeling as though he was ascending from some black and depthless place in his soul. Soon, he was on his feet. He turned and embraced his remaining son and daughter. Jem and Kate clung to him, their hearts broken, their tears freezing on their cheeks in the frigid chill of the winter afternoon. When they parted, Jem held Melissa tightly as she mourned for the part of her that was lost… the part that had been her strength and comfort, her constant companion, since the day of her birth. Levi knew Jem's loss was just as hurtful and real as hers, for he and Avery had not only been brothers, but the closest of friends.

He leaned down and picked up his shotgun, then shifted the holstered .44 Blackhawk on his hip. "Let's go, people," he said, surprised at the steel in his voice. "Into the woods… and don't stop until I tell you."

Together, they moved past the gnarled trunk of the big tree and headed for the cover of the forest. Levi lingered a moment longer. He stared at the slab of wood he had fashioned into a makeshift marker. On it was carved a single word and nothing more.

He recalled the promise he had made, one made under grief and duress, but one that was rock solid and undeniable nevertheless.

Levi lifted his eyes and saw that the others were nearly to the woods. He leaned down and kissed the name of his beloved.

Nell…

Then he shouldered the shotgun and ran to join the others.

CHAPTER 33

He smelled the salt air.

He watched the waves, flow to and fro.

He listened to the sea in a shell.

He wiggled his toes in the sand.

He would have watched tiny crabs dance sideways in the sunshine... if there had been any left alive to watch.

Levi pulled on his woolen socks and laced up his hiking boots. He stood and allowed the ocean wind to fully engulf him. In the summer it would have been warm and pleasant. In mid-January, it was frigid and chilling to the bone.

He sighed and reached into his shirt pocket. Nell's wedding band gleamed in the winter sun. Crouching, he dug a hole in the sand.

Before he could act, a slender brown hand closed gently over his. "Not here. She would want a warmer climate."

Levi nodded. He placed the ring back in his pocket and stood up. He regarded Enolia gratefully. She stood beside him, as she had since they had left the ruins of the Biltmore, bundled in a heavy hooded coat, toting her baby in a padded pack across her back like a papoose in the old western movies. Enolia reminded him of Nell a lot—strong, compassionate, spiritual. She possessed wisdom beyond her years as well, and he respected her opinion.

"I reckon Myrtle Beach isn't far enough south to be considered tropical, is it?"

She smiled. "Not in the dead of winter, no."

"Nell, always talked about Florida," he said. "Like it was some magical place."

"I'm not sure magical places exist anymore," Enolia said. "But if it was for her, maybe we should go. We've traveled over three hundred miles. We can walk three hundred more... or farther."

"And what would we do then?"

Enolia closed her dark eyes. Her face grew grim and sad for a moment, then she smiled ... remembering. "Abiaka Treadaway, Seminole... Long Pine Key, Everglades, Florida... 25 degrees 17' 11,8140" North, 80 degrees 53' 55,143" West... Code name: Gatorback."

Levi frowned. "And what does all that mean?"

"Billy gave me a dozen names," she explained. "Men and women he served with in Black Arrow. They considered each other to be of one tribe... family. And their families—wives, husbands, and children—were considered to be kin, like their own. Who knows.... they may all be dead. But if they are not... like Treadaway... it could be a new start for us. A chance to settle down and stop roaming like nomads."

"I thought we had that back in North Carolina," Levi told her. "I was wrong."

"Yes, but I could be right. I'm willing to take that chance. What do we have to lose?"

Levi looked off down the beach at those who walked before them. Jem and Melissa, Jesse Tauchee, Diane Stapleton and her children. And Kate and Tyrone, walking hand and hand.

He also thought of those who had been left behind, either alive or dead. The Mendlebaums, Auntie Rose, the Newman family, Michelle and Avery, Billy Tauchee... and Nell.

"Chances are hard to come by these days," he told her. "I reckon we'd best grab one when we can."

Enolia smiled at him. Just seeing it warmed Levi's heart and gave him hope.

Together, they followed the others.

The collective cry of seagulls shrilled from overhead.... growing from several to many.

"We're in the Zone, folks," he called out. "Look sharp."

"We see 'em, Papa," Jem called back. On the beach ahead were Biters... twenty or thirty, maybe more.

Together, they fanned out, drew their weapons, and walked southward.

The salty ocean sky churned with frenetic shades of blue, gray, and white; surging, flowing like the crashing waves below. It was not an ill turn of the weather promising rain or storm or hurricane. It was keenly alive. Ever moving, ever watching.

Ever vigilant for what was commonplace in those dark and dangerous days.

Always with its scavenging eye upon death.

ABOUT THE AUTHOR

Ronald Kelly was born November 20, 1959 in Nashville, Tennessee. He attended Pegram Elementary School and Cheatham County Central High School before starting his writing career.

Ronald Kelly began his writing career in 1986 and quickly sold his first short story, "Breakfast Serial," to *Terror Time Again* magazine. His first novel, *Hindsight* was released by Zebra Books in 1990. His audiobook collection, *Dark Dixie: Tales of Southern Horror*, was on the nominating ballot of the 1992 Grammy Awards for Best Spoken Word or Non-Musical Album. Zebra published seven of Ronald Kelly's novels from 1990 to 1996. Ronald's short fiction work has been published by *Cemetery Dance, Borderlands 3, Deathrealm, Dark at Heart, Hot Blood: Seeds of Fear,* and many more. After selling hundreds of thousands of books, the bottom dropped out of the horror market in 1996. So, when Zebra dropped their horror line in October 1996, Ronald Kelly stopped writing for almost ten years and worked various jobs including welder, factory worker, production manager, drugstore manager, and custodian.

In 2006, Ronald Kelly started writing again. In early 2008, Croatoan Publishing released his work *Flesh Welder* as a standalone chapbook, and it quickly sold out. In early 2009 Cemetery Dance Publications released a limited edition hardcover of his fist short story collection, *Midnight Grinding & Other Twilight Terrors*. Also in 2010, Cemetery Dance is planning on releasing his first novel in over ten years called, *Hell Hollow* as a limited edition hardcover. Ronald's Zebra/Pinnacle horror novels are being released by Thunderstorm Books as The Essential Ronald Kelly series. Each book contains a new novella related to the novel's original storyline.

Ronald Kelly currently lives in a backwoods hollow in Brush Creek, Tennessee, with his wife, Joyce, and their three children.

Curious about other Crossroad Press books?
Stop by our site:
http://store.crossroadpress.com
We offer quality writing
in digital, audio, and print formats.

Enter the code FIRSTBOOK
to get 20% off your first order from our store!
Stop by today!

www.ingramcontent.com/pod-product-compliance
Lightning Source LLC
Chambersburg PA
CBHW060406180626
46817CB00007B/2529